ELWYN

ELWYN

HEIR OF THE EUDAIMONIANS
BOOK ONE

CHRISTINE SHARP

THYGATER PUBLISHING

ISBN: 979-8-9907052-1-0
Library of Congress Control Number: 2024913027

Published by Thygater Publishing: Buena Park, California

Cover Illustration by Cliff Cramp, www.cliffcramp.com

Visit the author's website at www.christinesharpbooks.com

For Tyler, the one on whom I lean.

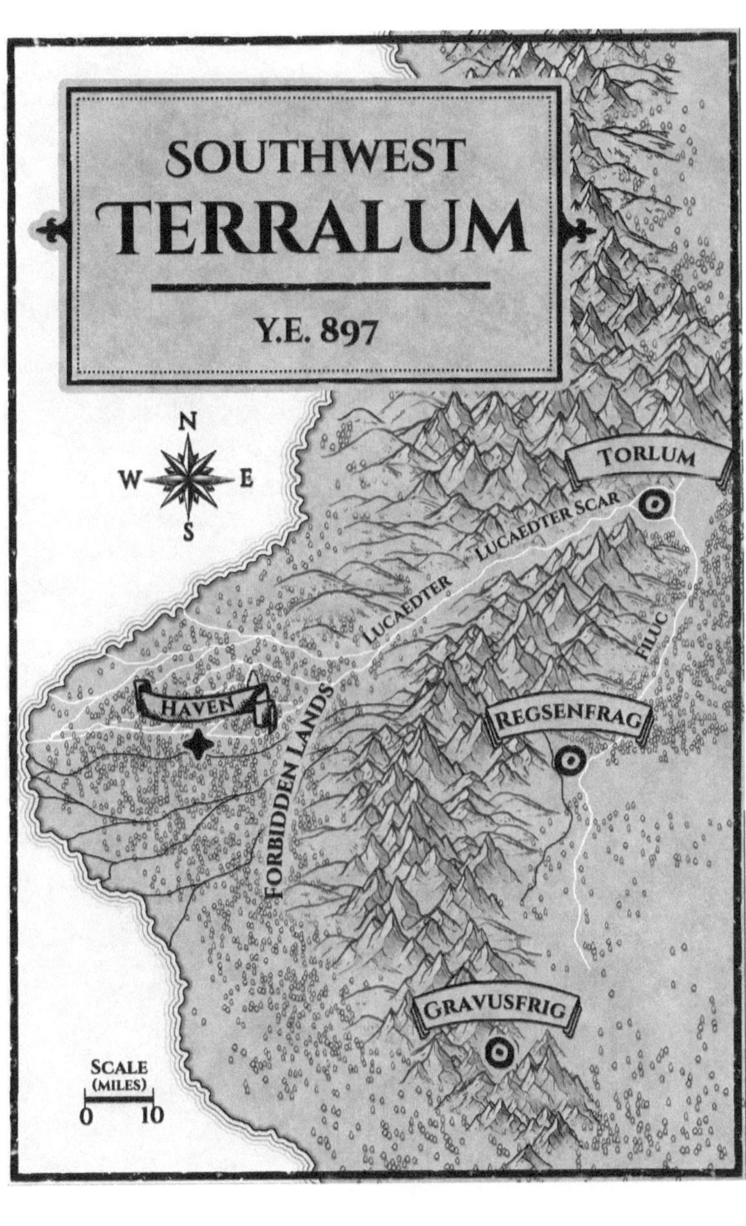

SOUTHWEST
TERRALUM
Y.E. 897
N
W E
S
TORLUM
LUCAEDTER SCAR
LUCAEDTER
FILUC
HAVEN
FORBIDDEN LANDS
REGSENFRAG
GRAVUSFRIG
SCALE
(MILES)
0 10

1

Elwyn Hakon had been stuck underground for three months straight. Today, she'd get to smell fresh air again. Better than that, she'd get to be free, if only for a few hours.

Her hand bumped a vial, tipping it over. No!

She caught it as the first bit of ginger extract spilled. She righted the vial, wiped the spill with her rag, then took a calming breath. Focus! Stop thinking about the surface.

She scanned the medic-training room's glass tables, where her classmates stood at cauldrons working on their own healing drafts. Most of them had their vials of ginger extract in their hands, ready to pour. Good, she was still on track.

She checked her vial. There was enough left—she hoped. She tipped the vial over the cauldron on her work table, which was held above the flames by an adjustable, iron stand, and she carefully let three drops fall. It emptied her vial, and the last drop was smaller than the first two.

She peered into her cauldron, holding her breath. Please work, please work.

Her healing draft swirled yellow. Yes! She let out her breath.

Elwyn watched it until the rich color permeated the whole draft. It was almost time for the next step.

She searched her table, and she had to squint against the light radiating from the floor. Under the glass floor, the lucten river flowed slowly, like glowing, liquid crystal. Its silver light, varied with blues and purples, shone up from the floor and filled the room. The lucten's warmth radiated into her boots and up her legs.

She found the hexagonal glass bottle that held a silver, pointed petal from the sacred therapeian flower. She carefully uncorked it, and the petal lifted from her bottle into the air.

She caught it delicately, then she turned to the table to her right and rolled her eyes. Her best friend Neilan Eudynam grinned, his dimples standing out. He waved his hand toward her, and again her petal flew up into the air.

She tried to glare at him, but a smirk pulled at the edges of her lips. He moved his fingers, and the petal settled back into the open bottle. He winked at her then turned to his own healing draft.

Her chest warmed. She turned back to her cauldron, the smile still pulling at her lips.

At the table on her left, a draft caught fire. Chief Keeper Wuervik waved a hand toward it, and the burning draft condensed into a rock glowing with heat at the bottom of the cauldron. "Did you lower the stand too far, Jathdi?" Wuervik asked.

Jathdi's eyes shadowed, and he leaned forward, grumbling. A lock of brown hair fell in front of his eyes.

Elwyn took a deep breath and checked her draft. Yellow, not boiling, okay. Still good.

On her right, Neilan's eyes were closed, and his hands were under his flameless cauldron, an inch from the metal, raising the temperature with Magic. He didn't need fire like the rest of the Keepers-in-training who didn't have Magic yet. The silver glow of lucten light shone on his dark-brown forehead, accentuating the concentration-crease between his eyebrows.

She smiled. It was fascinating to watch him work.

She checked her draft again. There, the first rising bubble. She tipped the hexagonal bottle over her cauldron and the therapeian petal slipped into it. The silver petal floated momentarily, then sank.

The draft swirled, streaked with blue, then faded to cloudy periwinkle. It was working! She was going to do it this time.

Now for the lucten powder. She grabbed the glowing, crystalline nugget of hardened lucten and her pestle. She crushed the nugget into powder then scooped it into the measuring bowl. She ran her knife across the top of the bowl, making sure the measurement was perfect. She had to do this right.

She'd never have Magic, though all her classmates eventually would. She had to learn to do it for herself, to be self-sufficient. If she learned to survive on her own, she'd be halfway toward escaping this place. To being free. Then she wouldn't be able to hurt anyone.

The periwinkle liquid thickened. Almost time. She picked up her wooden spoon as the draft's swirling slowed. Almost, almost.

It stopped swirling. Now!

She dumped the lucten powder into the cauldron then stirred three times. The color deepened to shining indigo.

Time to lower the cauldron, to help the draft reach just the right temperature. She grabbed the handle of the iron stand.

"Ow!" she cried out and let go. Where was that rag? Her hand pulsed with heat and pain, but she couldn't worry about that yet. She only had seconds before the draft would be ruined.

She scanned her work table. There! She grabbed it, wrapped it around her hand, and reached for the hot, iron handle again.

Before she touched it, the handle moved on its own. The stand responded, and the cauldron lowered just the right amount. Her heart dropped.

Bubbles rose in the draft, growing to a boil. Just like it was supposed to. The indigo liquid turned translucent and brightened. Her throat tightened, and her eyes burned. She turned to Neilan.

He grinned at her, dark brown eyes sparkling in the lucten light.

She forced a smile onto her face. "Thanks."

"Couldn't let you burn yourself again," he said with a laugh, and he looked down at his own cauldron. His draft was boiling away, perfectly silver.

He'd been trying to help. But her draft turned silver, and her insides knotted. Her flawless draft was a lie. She had to do it on her own, to prove she could. To prove to herself she could stand on her own.

Her hand radiated hot pain. She inspected it, an excuse to avert her eyes from Neilan. Angry red stretched across her palm and fingers, blisters just starting to form. She'd have to ask Wuervik for help. He'd been a Medic-Keeper before he became Chief Keeper of the Haven—the underground safehouse they lived in. Elwyn looked across the room at him.

Wuervik noticed her gaze and walked toward her, his boots clunking on the glass floor. Before she could mention her hand, he looked into her cauldron. "Well done, Elwyn."

Her face grew hot. Wuervik walked away, glancing into each person's cauldron as he passed.

From the next table, Jathdi whispered quietly enough for only Elwyn to hear, "Maybe one day you'll actually do your own work."

Her chest constricted, but she kept her face ahead, staring at her cauldron while heat rose up her neck and face. Jathdi snickered. Elwyn's exceptionally pale skin must've betrayed her blush. She shook her long, blonde hair into a curtain around her face.

She'd get a break soon. Two more hours then she'd get to go to the surface, alone. Well, alone except for Wuervik, but he wasn't much in the way of company. Usually, she and Neilan went up together, but Wuervik was still punishing them for sneaking into the Certified Keepers' Wing. Twice.

It wasn't so bad, though. Alone, she wouldn't have to worry about anyone else. She wouldn't have to hold anything in, to pretend—even for Neilan.

"Time to pack up," Wuervik said. The room filled with movement.

"Your usual instructor will be back from her surface mission by Dawnday for your next lesson," Wuervik said. "You have three hours until sparring practice. As Elwyn will miss sparring today," he scanned the room, "Jathdi will partner with Neilan."

"What? Chief Wuervik!" Jathdi yelled.

Wuervik glared down at him.

Jathdi shrunk from him, but still protested. "Why me?"

"Neilan will not use Magic against you, he knows the rules," Wuervik said.

"I know, but—"

"Then there can be no objection. Report to the sparring room in three hours." Wuervik turned to the rest of the room. "You're dismissed."

Jathdi opened his mouth again, but Wuervik bore down on him. Jathdi looked down and finished cleaning up, working his jaw muscles.

Elwyn peeked at Neilan out of the corner of her eye. He stood entirely still, glaring at his table. She took a hesitant step toward him, but he turned away and started cleaning up.

Throughout the room, the rest of the Keepers-in-training cleaned up and hustled out. Wuervik strolled from cauldron to cauldron, waving a hand over each of them. The drafts inside condensed into rocks, which he placed into a sack.

At one cauldron, rather than get rid of the contents, Wuervik picked up the empty hexagonal bottle from the table and pressed a hand against it. The glass thinned as the bottle expanded, as though he was glass-blowing it. He tipped the cauldron and filled the now large, hexagonal bottle with translucent, silver liquid.

Wuervik reached Elwyn's table and glanced into her cauldron. He nodded to her approvingly, enlarged the empty bottle from her table, and filled it with her perfectly silver, disappointment of a draft.

As he turned away, the painful pulsing in her hand forced itself into her consciousness. In a tiny voice, she said, "Wuervik?"

He glanced over his shoulder and raised his eyebrows.

She held up her hand. "I burned myself."

He came closer and slowly waved a hand over hers. As he did so, the hot pain drained out of it. The redness faded, and the blisters shrank and flattened.

If only Elwyn could be an Heir of Magic, her life would be so much simpler. She could heal people, instead of being a danger to everyone around her. And she wouldn't be hunted, at least as much.

Wuervik strolled on, emptying the cauldrons. Once he'd bottled up Neilan's draft, he turned back to Elwyn. "Meet me in the Concourse by noon."

She nodded. Most kids' parents chaperoned their monthly trips to the surface, but Elwyn and Neilan didn't have parents, so Wuervik was in charge of them. Wuervik paused and glanced at Neilan. He looked like he might speak, but instead he turned back to Elwyn and said, "Happy birthday."

Elwyn's shoulders tightened. She didn't want to think about her birthday. She looked down and said, "Thanks."

Wuervik nodded and strolled out of the room.

Elwyn walked up to Neilan, but before she could speak, he turned to her with a big, forced smile. "Two hours till you go up. What now?"

Elwyn paused, wanting to make him feel better about Jathdi's mean-heartedness and about having to pair with him for sparring, but she couldn't think of anything to say. She forced a smile and said, "The library, where else?"

Neilan gave an exaggerated sigh. "We're *always* there. It's your sixteenth birthday! Let's do something else."

"My birthday only tells me I've spent sixteen years in this place without figuring out how to leave."

"Well, technically you're leaving in two hours." He smirked.

She glared at him. "You know what I mean. I can't leave for good until I can figure out somewhere to go where I won't be found by *him*."

"Yeah, yeah. But come on, can't we do something else for once?" He clasped his hands, begging.

"You can. I'm going to the library."

Neilan's eyes shadowed. "You know, it isn't such a big deal. All the things you think are so important. Anyone being here is dangerous. It's a risk. You being here is no different." He paused. "You don't have to leave."

Elwyn glared at the floor. "You know I'm different. Everyone does. And even if everyone's in danger either way, I don't want to be the problem."

He shrugged. "Yeah, I know. I just think you could ease up a bit."

Elwyn's insides twisted. She met Neilan's eyes, but she couldn't form words. She didn't know how to explain how desperate she felt, how much she needed to do it. She wouldn't be the reason people were hurt. She couldn't. She didn't know how she'd survive if she was. So she had to leave before anything happened to them. Then she wouldn't have to worry about anyone else, and the pressure inside her could finally let go.

Neilan sighed. "Fine." He took a step toward the door, then he stopped and looked at her with a mischievous gleam in his eyes.

2

"What?" Elwyn asked.

"Nothing," he said. "I'm gonna get something to eat." But his eyes still sparkled with whatever idea he'd just hatched.

"Of course you are," she said, laughing. He was always eating. She sometimes wondered if he used Magic to assist that uncanny digestive system.

But what was he really up to? Knowing him, it could be anything. They strolled to the door of the medic-training room, Neilan pretending to be casual. Through the open door, the round tunnel glowed from the natural lucten-vein that ran under the glass floor of the whole Haven. Silver light danced on every surface, moving with the slowly flowing lucten river.

A little kid walked by, holding his mother's hand, and he looked at Elwyn curiously. She smiled at him, but his mother pulled him closer and passed by with eyes straight ahead.

Elwyn's stomach tightened, and she dropped her gaze to the floor. She slipped into the hallway, walking as close to the wall as she could.

Averting her eyes from the flow of people, she stared at the wall.

One of the few comforts of the Haven for her, along with the ever-flowing lucten, was the roots from live trees that paneled its walls and ceilings. They were cleaned and tightly packed, sealing out every speck of the dirt that lay behind them. The roots' natural unevenness, their slightly variant color, and their gentle sturdiness soothed her soul. She felt connected to them, grateful for their commitment to seal out the damp soil.

Magic was probably involved, but Elwyn preferred to think that the roots chose to protect the Haveners. She ran her hand along the root-lined wall, reveling in the feel of the uneven cylinders under her fingers. Neilan strolled next to her, head high and gait loping. He practically screamed confidence. How did he do it? If only she could feel as serene as he looked.

They neared the open door of the library and Neilan said, a little too eagerly, "In you go!"

"I need to grab my notebook from my room," she said, continuing toward the Concourse.

He paused a moment, obviously torn between keeping his plot a secret and wanting to stay with her as long as possible. After a second, he caught up to her. Her chest warmed, and she smiled to herself.

Through the archway ahead glowed a cascade of liquid lucten, falling from the ceiling in the center of the Concourse, giving the impression of a glowing pillar. At its base was a shallow basin, decorated with the Eudaimonian crest: a single therapeian flower with five mature petals and five new petals budding from the center. In the middle of the basin, a wide hole opened through the glass floor and lucten flowed from the pillar under the glass in every direction.

The luctenfall's light moved on the walls, like the time Elwyn swam in a surface pond and watched the sunlight dance across the pond's bottom. Haveners flooded the massive Concourse, flowing in and out of the round hall's six archways, which led to the five branches of the Haven and the exit: the Enex Staircase.

A pair of Certified Keepers headed toward the Enex Staircase with leather bags full of what was probably medical aid. A few Qualified Keepers, those who'd finished training and received their Gift but hadn't been approved for sensitive assignments yet, followed the Certified Keepers up the Enex Staircase with sacks of grain. The Haven, which kept Heirs of the Eudaimonians safe and trained them to use their Gifts, aided surface-dwellers in the mountains and small towns who couldn't get adequate care.

Leaving the archway of the Training and Recreation Wing, Elwyn took a breath and waded into the crowd. Neilan joined her, cutting through the throng with his tall, broad frame.

"Why'd they put the K.D. Wing so far from the T.R. Wing?" Neilan complained, a fact he'd grumbled about countless times before. He squinted at the archway directly across the Concourse, the Kitchen and Dining Wing.

Elwyn laughed. "They probably weren't thinking about hungry teenagers when they designed the place."

"They were thinking about hungry adults, though," Neilan said resentfully. Elwyn laughed again. It certainly was suspicious that the K.D. Wing was right next to the Certified Keepers' Wing.

Across the Concourse, two people stood out from the crowd, heading to the C.K. Wing: Wuervik and a man with long, black braids, silver eyes, and harshly upright posture.

"Astur's back?" Neilan asked in a low voice.

Elwyn's skin prickled. Why was the Protector of the Haven here? Was something wrong? She asked aloud, "It's been what, two years, since the last time he came back?"

"At least," Neilan said, unconsciously moving closer to Elwyn and putting himself between her and Astur. Despite her own apprehension, Elwyn sighed to herself. Neilan's protective instincts were intense.

They didn't know exactly what Astur did on the surface, but they thought it was something to do with preserving the secrecy and security of their safehouse. All they really knew was that he was important, and he was unsettling.

Seeing Astur and Wuervik together made the gray in Wuervik's hair stand out. There was much more of it since the last time Astur was here. But Astur looked exactly the same, as always. As long as Elwyn could remember, Astur hadn't aged. When she was a kid, she would've sworn Astur was years older than Wuervik, but if she met them now, she'd be sure Astur was the younger of the two.

"How does he do it?" Neilan asked, apparently to himself.

"Hmm?" Elwyn raised her eyebrows at him.

"The Magic. It's gotta be Magic that keeps him from aging. He must be crazy powerful."

Elwyn shrugged, uneasy talking about it out loud. "Must be."

"I wonder if I'll be able to do that," Neilan said, his eyes bright with the idea.

Neilan certainly was powerful, exceptionally so, but she wasn't sure if she liked the idea of him being able to do that. "So you'd be the next Astur and only come around every couple of years?" she asked.

"Nah. I'd stay with you."

"But what if everybody needed you to do whatever it is that Astur does?"

Neilan shrugged. "Nobody but you matters."

A shiver ran down Elwyn's arms. She forced a smile and tried to laugh, but pressure settled in her chest. That was a lot of responsibility. Too much. Being the only thing that mattered to him meant she held all of his happiness in her hands.

What if she hurt him? She would. It was inevitable, no matter how hard she tried to protect his happiness.

He was the most important to her, too, but he wasn't the only thing that mattered. She had her own needs, was her own being. She cared for him, and she also wanted to be her own self. Couldn't both of those happen at the same time?

They neared the Residential Wing archway, which pulled Elwyn from her spiraling thoughts. "See you in a few," she said.

Neilan started, then his mischievous grin returned in full-force. "Until then, my queen." He bent into a mock bow, his dimples deepening.

She rolled her eyes and turned into the Res. Wing, picking her way through the flow of Haveners. The long residential tunnel, full of people coming and going, was lined with shut doors. It curved left and right until it disappeared around a bend forty paces ahead.

Beyond the bend were the couples' and families' apartments, which held whole homes with several sleeping rooms branching from a main room. At least, that's what Elwyn had heard. She'd never seen past that first bend. The rooms for lone inhabitants were right here, just inside the archway. The lone inhabitants each had a sleeping room that opened straight off the main tunnel, at the outskirts of the Res. Wing.

Elwyn's room was the third door on the right, directly across the tunnel from Neilan's, which was right next to Wuervik's. She lifted the latch and slipped into her room, quickly shutting the door behind her, which muffled the ceaseless sound from the tunnel outside. As soon as it closed, tension flowed out of her body. She was alone.

Her little, round room was unlit. The Hospitality-Keepers hadn't come in yet, so the darkening mat still covered the floor. She bent and rolled up the woolen mat that covered the small patch of lucten-lit floor between her narrow sleeping pallet and her washstand. Silver lucten-light flooded the room, which was barely three paces across. She'd heard that the common rooms in family apartments could be up to fifteen paces across, but she loved her little room. It was cozy. But more than that, it was hers: the one place she could be entirely alone.

She sat down on the edge of her pallet and reached under it for her small, spiralbound notebook, where she'd catalogued all the scattered information she'd gleaned about the surface world, especially anything that showed potentially safe routes and destinations.

She pocketed her notebook, but she didn't get up. She sat there, taking long, slow breaths. The muffled sounds drifting to her from the tunnel outside somehow made the peace of being in here more poignant.

She was alone, what a luxury. No one knew or cared where she was at this exact moment.

A gentle tingle arose deep inside her chest, the familiar reverberation of the High King's Magic. It was a reminder that she was never entirely alone. The High King always knew where she was, and his presence was always with her. But that didn't detract from the peace. His presence was as much a part of her as her own heart—it was what made aloneness not loneliness.

She laid back on her pallet, her ankle-length white dress wrapping around her legs like a blanket, and she watched the lucten light play on her root-lined ceiling. It moved so slowly it wasn't trackable unless she stayed perfectly still.

She should get going. She didn't have much time to research before her surface trip, but it was so peaceful here. The tension in her chest was almost unnoticeable. What a life it would be to have it completely gone.

That thought was the motivation she needed. The only way for her tension to be gone for good was if she wasn't here risking everyone's safety. The only way to be gone from here was to figure out where to go, and how to travel there, without being caught. She pushed herself up from her pallet and headed for the library.

3

Balancing a pile of scrolls and books in her arms, Elwyn scanned the T.R. Wing library. Rows of shelves reaching to the ceiling covered the root-lined walls, which were packed with scrolls, spiralbound books, lucten lenses, and leatherbound books.

Lucten-light from the floor glinted off the packed shelves, most of which were in a state of disorder from the negligence of the Keepers-in-training. The top shelf was orderly, since few of the Haveners were tall enough to get anything down from it.

The open space between the shelves was scattered with glass study tables. Elwyn's usual table, the one in the corner, was open. But at the table just in front of it, Vacca held court. Her silky, auburn hair fell down her back like a shiny waterfall, and her followers fawned and giggled. Just what Elwyn needed.

She skirted the shelves closest to her usual spot, staying out of Vacca's line of sight. She set her materials down quietly to avoid catching Vacca's attention and slipped sideways into the chair. Shelves blocked her right side, and the root-lined wall blocked her back. She was only exposed from two directions, and she could watch both of those at the same time.

She pushed her small pile of materials to one side of her table and unrolled a topographical map. Terralum expanded onto the table, backlit through the glass from the lucten light below. The map's ink lines stood out sharply against the glow.

She leaned over the map. It was the crowndom she was born in, the crowndom she technically still lived under. But it felt separate from her, like she didn't belong there, even though she was descended from its ancient rulers.

Elwyn pushed those thoughts away and studied the map's topography lines. She fingered the stretch of uninhabited forest on the western coast between the mountains and the sea. Right now, she was somewhere beneath that forest, but the Haven wasn't marked, even on its own maps.

She looked closer and found the spot she'd left off yesterday, a point just inland from the narrow mountain range that divided the coast from the valley.

She reached for the travel log she'd been studying. The Keeper who wrote it decades ago had tried traveling without using any of the homes or inns known to be safe, which Keepers usually stayed in. She'd wanted to see if she could travel without staying in any human dwellings at all—to travel Terralum without putting anyone's home or business at risk.

There weren't any records in the library of the dwellings regularly used by Keepers as temporary safehouses. Unqualified Keepers-in-training weren't trusted with that sensitive of information, yet. This log didn't reveal any of them, which was probably why it was kept where trainees could find it.

The log was a starting point at least. Elwyn was mapping the route the Keeper took exactly as she had taken it, then she'd make adjustments.

Many of the places the Keeper stayed in wouldn't be safe enough for her. Plus, Elwyn could only travel on Darkday, when Fainor eclipsed the sun, for extra cover. She'd need places she could stay hidden for the three light days of the week: Dawnday, Brightday, and Twilitday, in between Darkdays. Sometimes she could maybe push it and travel from full-dark on Twilitnight to first light on Dawnday morning, but that could be more dangerous, as well as tough to travel straight through for a night, a day, and a night.

She'd also have to be careful of the types of people who tended to be out during Darkday. From what she'd read, most people stayed home or at least inside on the day of rest, but some used it like she intended to, for cover. Then, of course, she still didn't have a final destination. She'd yet to discover a place to stay long-term where she wouldn't be found.

Her heart ached with the futility, but she kept going. She had to keep going, had to do something.

She pulled her spiralbound notebook from her dress pocket and opened it to the next available page. She folded the rest back along the spiral and laid the open page on the glass table. She made a note of the spot she'd left off yesterday, then turned back to the travel log.

It was a leatherbound book, crafted with beautiful precision. All those words, handwritten with such care. The letters were consistent, the edges crisp, the margins straight. Elwyn had only made one attempt to craft a leatherbound book so far in her training, but the final product hadn't come close to the ones in the library. Keepers probably used Magic for such precision.

The precision steadied her. However, being leatherbound, it was more difficult to read than the spiralbound ones that could be backlit. She opened the page and held it above her head, to reflect the light from below.

A giggle rang through the room. Vacca glanced over her shoulder at Elwyn, her eyes glinting. Then she leaned toward the girl next to her and whispered. Her followers burst out laughing, then Vacca looked back at Elwyn and smirked.

Elwyn's face grew hot, and she put the book down. The giggling dragged on.

Once again, her traitorously pale skin advertised her blush. She shook her hair around her face, and she reached into her dress's left-hand pocket. She found the wooden sancan that Neilan had whittled for her so long ago and rubbed the smooth head with her thumb. She felt the outstretched wings, the feathery back, the clawed forelegs, and the webbed hindlegs. She remembered the live sancan he'd based it on, the one they'd seen flying overhead during a surface trip when she was eight and he was nine. It was the only three-domain animal she'd seen in real life. It had looked so free and peaceful.

She took a long, slow breath. She could take it. At least, she'd have to take it. She refused to become the danger that everyone told her she was, that her Gifts made her.

Her worthless Gifts. What she wouldn't give to abandon them, but there was nothing she could do about her ancestry.

She was descended from two of the ancestral Gifts: Logic and Linguistic. There were five ancestral lines: Logic, Linguistic, Magic, Music, and Aesthetic. Everyone else in the Haven was born of the Gifted line of Magic. As far as anyone knew, Elwyn was the first person ever to bring together two Gifted bloodlines—Solun took great care that the genetic lines never crossed.

From the moment of her conception, her Gifts were dangerous. Her parents hadn't known—how could they? They didn't know they had Gifts, let alone that their Gifts would make their baby a target.

Solun had stalked her parents until the day Elwyn was born, then he came for her. He killed her parents, but before he could get to Elwyn, Astur and Wuervik stepped in. They took her to the Haven and raised her there, supposedly to protect her, but Elwyn knew her imprisonment in the Haven was mostly to protect everyone else from what she would become if Solun had her.

As far as Elwyn understood, Solun thought she was dead. But if he found out she'd survived, he would hunt her and destroy everyone who'd kept her from him. The lie of her supposed death hung over her like an hourglass, the sand ever pouring through. It was only a matter of time before he found out the truth.

If he found her, he would either kill her or make her use her Gifts to serve him. If given an option, she'd pick the first one. She refused to be used to hurt anyone, but she didn't know what kinds of power he had to force her compliance. The only way everyone was absolutely safe from her was if she didn't exist. Or if she disappeared.

The Haven couldn't be the only place she was safe. There had to be somewhere she could go, some way of evading him. Being an Heir of Logic and an Heir of Linguistic, maybe she could figure it out —when her Gifts came to her. They were still dormant, like they were for all her unqualified peers except Neilan.

At the open library door, a figure in a floor-length, hooded cloak appeared and swept in. Elwyn's shoulders tensed. Why a winter cloak? The lucten river under the floor kept the Haven warm. Besides that, it was summer.

The figure, tall with broad shoulders, wound between the study tables scattered throughout the room. The hood slipped, revealing the back of a head with close-cropped black curls, and he turned toward Elwyn and grinned. Her muscles relaxed. Even across the vast library, Neilan's dimples stood out.

With one hand, he pulled the cloak tighter around himself and made his way toward her. What was he doing? He plopped into the chair across the table from her and grinned again.

"What?" she asked, not sure whether she was more curious or

apprehensive.

He opened the front of his cloak. Inside it, he held a thick slice of bread spread with jam. "Happy birthday," he whispered, grinning.

She smacked a hand to her mouth to stifle her gasp and laughed. "Where'd you get that?"

"I have my ways." His dimples deepened, and he held the bread and jam out to her.

She laughed. "I can't eat it in here."

He gaped. "But that's the whole point!"

"We're in the library!" she said, half-laughing, half-aghast.

"We're always in the library. Live a little."

She looked down, trying to pretend that didn't sting. That's what she was trying to do, to find a way to live. To be free.

She wished she could be easygoing like him, but the pressure in her chest never let go. "I don't want to ruin anything," she said, gesturing to the materials on her table. "And I can't risk getting in trouble before my surface trip today."

He looked down and shrugged. "Yeah, I know. Just wanted to do something for your birthday."

Her chest constricted. Why'd she have to hurt his feelings? All she wanted was to not hurt anyone, but here she was, hurting her favorite person in the world. She caught his eye and tried to smile. "Thanks."

He gave a half smile.

She took the bread and jam from him and took a bite. Sweetness burst across her tongue. "So good!"

He laughed, and his dimples showed up again. Then he looked down at the map. "Any luck today?"

Elwyn set the bread on the edge of her study table and glanced at the travel journal. She sighed and said, "Course not."

"What's this one?" He reached for a spiralbound book, opened a page, and folded the rest back along the spiral.

"*Terralum's Crown-Protected Primary, Secondary, and Ancillary Road Systems,*" Elwyn recited.

He scanned the page. "I doubt the Crown-protected roads will be an effective escape route from, you know, the Crown."

She tucked her hair behind her ear. "Solun isn't the Crown."

"Fine, an effective escape route from the Crown's overlord." He caught her eye and smirked.

"Knowing where the roads *are* might be some help," she said defensively.

Neilan flipped through the spiralbound book, but he was only pretending to look. He knew as well as she did that it wouldn't make a difference. They'd been scouring this library for years, but there wasn't enough information here to form a real escape plan, one in which they actually had a destination. The meaningful resources were tucked away in the Treasury in the C.K. Wing, the most restricted branch of the Haven.

If only she could get in. But she couldn't try today, she'd risk her trip to the surface again.

She glanced at the book Neilan held and asked unenthusiastically, "Maybe I could hide in the Tensmon Mountains?"

"Unsafe," Neilan said. "Gangs roam the mountains."

He pulled out another map and unrolled it. The whole continent, Mirterr, glowed from the lucten-light underneath it. He leaned over it and scanned the eastern edge, as far from Terralum as they could get on land. "Maybe the Punipyr Desert?" he suggested dully.

"How could we get there without being spotted?" she asked in the same tone. They'd been through this conversation a million times. It was almost a script, now. They'd probably go on like this for another sixteen years. But maybe by then they'd be Certified Keepers and could get into the Treasury.

Neilan had always said he'd go with her. He didn't have any reason to stay. But she was pretty sure it was just a daydream to him, something fun to think about and plan together.

It didn't keep him awake at night, like it did her.

4

Elwyn watched Neilan trace the map from Terralum toward the Punipyr Desert, crossing the Benetroph Plains. "Any idea what the Plains are like?" he asked.

Elwyn hopped up and crossed to a row of lucten lenses on a shelf labeled "Relinquished Heirs." She followed the row to the section labeled "Benetroph Plains," and she gingerly picked up the first lucten lens, a palm-sized disk of hardened lucten manipulated by Magic to hold memory.

She hustled back to her table, closed one eye, and drew the lucten lens up to her open one. Through it shone the glass table, underlit with silver lucten light, then colors swirled inside the lucten lens and formed a scene.

A woman in the simple, commoner's dress typical of Haveners stood in a half-harvested wheat field watching a man working the field. Unaware of her presence, he lifted an impossibly large sheaf and balanced it across his shoulders. He strolled toward a pile of equally large sheaves across the field, apparently as easily as if it were a single stalk.

The woman followed him. He noticed her, his eyes widening, and he dropped the sheaf. She bowed slightly and approached him. "Excuse me, sir. I'm here to offer you sanctuary. You have power, so you will soon be targeted—if you aren't already."

The man frowned. "Power?"

The woman squinted against the bright sun. "You're an Heir of Magic, as I am."

The man shifted uncomfortably. "Magic? I don't know what you mean."

She pointed to the massive bundle of wheat. "When you prepared to lift that sheaf, what did you do?"

He avoided her eyes. "I willed my legs to be strong, and they were."

She nodded. "You pushed Magic into your legs, and probably the rest of your muscles, whether or not you knew exactly what you were doing. You're powerful enough to be observed as a Magic user. If we can discover you, Solun will too. He tracks the Heirs of the Eudaimonians. Everyone who proves to be powerful or appears aware of their Gifts, he enslaves. If you come with me, you'll be protected and trained. But we need to leave immediately. You can't return home to pack or say goodbye to your family."

The man started, and his eyebrows drew together.

The Keeper continued, "They must believe you had an accident in the fields, or a wild animal dragged you off. You can't tell them that you intend to leave. If you do, they won't grieve properly, and Solun will notice. He will get the information out of them and hold them responsible for your disappearance."

"Hey, now," the man said. "This is a bit sudden. I have nieces and nephews to think of, you know. My sister and her husband need the money I bring in. I can't just abandon them."

The Keeper stiffened. "If you choose not to come with me, I won't come back again. And I trust you won't share this conversation with anyone. If you do, you'll put yourself and your family in even more danger. If you don't come with me, you leave yourself to the mercy of Solun. He will find you, and he will enslave you. And what might happen to your family, then?"

Elwyn squinted past the man into the far distance. The land around the two figures was a wide expanse of flat farmland, checkered with smooth fields. She spun in a slow circle with the lucten lens, so more of the scene took shape around her, but it was just more and more of the same flat farmland. No cover anywhere.

She sighed and pulled the lucten lens away from her eye. The glowing floor of the library seemed dim compared to the bright sunlight of the memory.

"Anything?" Neilan asked.

Elwyn shook her head.

He played with the crinkled edge of the map, his cloak still on. Beads of sweat glistened on his forehead, sparkling silver in the lucten light against his dark brown skin. He wiped his forehead.

"Why're you still wearing that thing?" she asked.

He grinned, surreptitiously reached into his cloak, and dipped his head in. Then he emerged, chewing, and winked. Elwyn rolled her eyes, but a smirk pulled at her lips. Of course, if he was going to go to the trouble of sneaking her a treat out of the K.D. Wing, he couldn't resist getting himself something, too.

"You *just* ate," she said.

"Yeah, but I need extra fuel. I'm an Heir of Magic," he said mock-importantly.

"Along with everyone else here."

"Except you."

Her stomach tightened. "Except me."

He dipped his head in for another bite.

"Don't get caught," she said, trying to make her voice sound light.

"I'm not going down with you this time."

He opened his mouth wide in fake shock. "As though I'm the bad influence here."

She let her hair fall in front of her face. "Fine. But be careful. We don't want to ruin any of these materials."

She turned back to the map, but she didn't take any of it in. Tension pulled at her neck and shoulders, but she tried to keep it off her face.

A boot and the hem of a tan trouser leg came into her line of sight. "Look who it is," Jathdi said, his derisive voice settling onto Elwyn like frost. "Pretending to work again?"

Vacca and her followers giggled.

"Leave her alone," Neilan said, his voice low and angry.

"You do her work for her. Do you speak for her now, too?" Jathdi asked. He stepped closer. "Oh what's this? Ah ah, not supposed to eat in the library."

He reached out and flipped her bread onto the map, jam-side down. Elwyn's heart dropped, and she gasped.

"Hey!" Neilan yelled and jumped up. He lunged at Jathdi.

Jathdi snorted and sprang back, out of his reach. Laughter erupted from Vacca's table.

Elwyn's neck, ears, and cheeks burned. She grabbed the jam-spread bread and shoved it into her pocket, but the damage was done. She wiped frantically at the jam with the long sleeves of her white dress, but it just smeared the sticky mess all over the map. Jathdi strolled away, laughing under his breath.

"Ignore him," Neilan said, glaring at Jathdi's back. "He isn't worth the time."

Elwyn kept her eyes resolutely down, at the sticky map. The corners of her eyes burned and pressure rose in her face as she tried to hold back the tears. She blinked and kept her face averted from

Neilan as she steadied her voice. "Yeah, I know."

That was much easier to say than to do. She doubted he could've ignored it, though he might've been able to hide his reaction. He had plenty of practice with that. He was unusual, like she was. An anomaly, in lots of ways.

He was parentless like Elwyn, but not an orphan. He'd been a Magic user already at six years old—more than a decade younger than anyone else Elwyn had heard of using the Gift. His parents gave him up to Astur and Wuervik, and they brought him to the Haven to be raised with Elwyn as Wuervik's wards.

Usually, at least in the Haven, the dormant Gift was received at the Qualification Ceremony to become a Keeper. Neither of them knew how Neilan had the Gift so young. Plus, he was extremely powerful. Only Wuervik and maybe a few of the most skilled Certified Keepers could come close to combating Neilan.

Elwyn kept wiping at the jam-smeared map, but her sleeves were as sticky as it was. She looked up at Neilan, despairing. He chuckled. "Here, let me help." He waved a hand lazily over the map and her arms, and most of the jam disappeared.

Her dress looked like it'd been laundered, with stains still but no stickiness. The map looked like it'd been wiped with a rag. It was much better than it had been, but it still had a tacky red stain across it. Elwyn wiped at it more with her freshly un-jammed sleeves. Neilan laughed and leaned back in his chair.

A mass of Keepers streamed into the library, and Elwyn's chest tightened. She couldn't get caught, not today. In a flash of panic, she rolled up the slightly sticky map.

Her stomach dropped. She pictured the leftover bit of jam sticking the layers of the rolled map together. The jam would dry inside it and fuse the roll together. It'd be impossible to open without tearing, and the damage would be irreversible. Here she was, yet again, hurting something. She couldn't stop causing harm.

She picked up the map and hustled it back to its shelf, her gut prickling. Neilan watched her return to the table, then he took off his cloak and draped it over her shoulders. She pulled the front closed to hide the stains on her dress.

She started sweating from its unnecessary heat, but she ignored it and kept an eye on the Keepers. There were dozens of them. It had to be most of the Certified Keepers. They crowded around a shelf of spiralbound books, then dispersed throughout the room, looking disgruntled.

Elwyn had never seen this many Certified Keepers in one place. Even at mealtimes, they came in waves. With all of them here right now, the C.K. Wing would be emptier than ever. This was the best chance she'd had yet to get into the Treasury.

She pocketed her notebook, but then she hesitated for a moment. A tingly tug pulled at her chest—a sign of the High King's guidance. Her chest rose. He knew what he was doing. If he was guiding her this time, she might finally succeed.

She stood and whispered to Neilan, "Come on."

He smirked. "Here we go again."

5

Elwyn paused with Neilan in a shadowed curve of the C.K. Wing's main tunnel, the one that led to the Treasury. Neilan's cloak was still draped around her shoulders, but it was more comfortable now because it wasn't as warm in the C.K. Wing.

The lucten vein under the glass floor was thinner here. Rather than one solid river of lucten stretching under the whole floor, the vein here split into lots of thin brooks. Lucten lamps were hung in the ceiling at regular intervals to make up for the lack of natural light, so most of the round tunnel was flooded with silver lucten light. All except for this one curve.

Elwyn took a few steps forward, running her fingers along the smooth cylinders of the roots. Ahead, the bend that led to the Treasury loomed nearer and nearer. She'd never made it this close before.

A tiny thunk rang from up ahead, like the closing of a door. Elwyn froze. Maybe she'd imagined it.

An elbow bumped into her back. She spun around and raised her eyebrows. Neilan stared at her wide eyed and mouthed, "What?"

She put her finger to her lips. A soft *clomp, clomp* grew from around the bend in the tunnel. She waved her arms at Neilan, whispering frantically, "Back! Go back!"

Neilan retreated a few steps then stopped, staring at her with wild eyes. If they ran, they'd definitely be caught. Elwyn's heart raced, but the tingly tug in her chest pulled her toward the shadowed curve. She hurried toward the curve, jamming into Neilan in her panic. He lost his balance and tipped toward the root-lined wall.

He reached out to catch himself on the wall, but instead he fell right through the roots.

Elwyn blinked. She reached out and pushed on the vertically-lined roots where Neilan should have been. The roots swung backward. She pushed the roots apart and squeezed through them into pitch black emptiness. The glass floor gave way to hard-packed mud.

Elwyn listened hard, but she couldn't make out anything through the curtain of roots. She couldn't just stand here and wait to be caught, so she turned away from the roots and felt into the dark emptiness. She took a tentative, blind step, then she felt in the dark for Neilan. She touched an arm, then she found his hand and held on. Keeping one hand in front of her, she pulled on Neilan's with her opposite one. His hand tightened in hers, and he followed her deeper into the pitch black hole.

Engulfed in darkness, Elwyn counted her steps to keep some track of the way. *Ten, eleven.* It was more than a hole. The air was stagnant and heavy, and cold. The lack of lucten made her shiver, inside and out. What was this place? Her mind spun with possibilities.

But Neilan's deep breathing and his hand inside hers grounded her. They were the only real things in the world.

The hand she held out in front hit damp, hard-packed soil. She paused and ran her fingers along it both ways. The tunnel turned. Keeping her fingers on the wall as a guide, she set off again.

Ahead, a tiny murmur rang out in the darkness. She stopped mid-step. Neilan took one step more, but she pulled on his hand to hold him back. He stopped, and she held her breath.

Two voices murmured back and forth, too far ahead to be understood. Elwyn tiptoed toward them. A faint, vague glow showed a curve in the tunnel ahead. Elwyn inched toward it, pulling Neilan's hand with her.

Around the curve, spiderweb-thin lucten veins ran in the wall, growing in density around a door fifty paces away. The thin crack between the door and its frame, lit from behind the door, blazed like a torch in the darkness.

Elwyn and Neilan crept toward it. It was unlike any door Elwyn had seen before. Its dark metal surface was so smooth that it shone like glass. Detailed symbols, like boxy characters, were etched into the frame all around it.

The voices grew louder as Elwyn and Neilan neared the door. They solidified into two voices: Astur's and Wuervik's. Elwyn shivered. She and Neilan held their breath and listened hard, their ears as close as they could get to the cracks around door without touching the door itself.

Astur's voice carried through the cracks, clear in the otherwise silent space. "—changing. It's time to forward her training. We need her Gifts."

Wuervik's voice said, "She doesn't have them yet."

Elwyn's chest trembled. She caught Neilan's eyes, which were wide and tense.

"Yes, but she has the imprints of them." Astur's voice was contemplative. "Only having access to Magic all these years, we're stagnant. We're still in hiding, still incapable of taking action. We need something more, which Logic and Linguistic could give us. I sense that she's supposed to be involved."

"She's unpredictable," Wuervik said. "We can't risk it."

"I am not asking," Astur said, firm and low. Elwyn pictured his silver eyes flashing. "You will inform her of our real situation, and you will train her to use whatever amount of Gifting her lineage has yet provided her to seek the way we have not found."

Elwyn's shoulders tensed. What was the "real situation"? What did Astur want her to do? She breathed as shallowly as she could, straining to catch every word.

"It would be a mistake," Wuervik said.

"We've made a mistake with her already," Astur said. There was a pause, and Wuervik didn't respond. "Though I'm not sure which of our actions was the mistake," Astur continued.

"What do you mean," Wuervik said flatly. It didn't sound like a question.

"I'm not sure what's happening," Astur said, without heeding Wuervik's tone, "but I feel a change coming."

He paused again. A chair creaked, but Wuervik didn't speak. Astur continued, "I've felt the High King pulling my thoughts toward her parents lately, quite often."

Elwyn's arms prickled. They'd barely mentioned her parents all her life. All she knew was that her father was an Heir of Logic, her mother was an Heir of Linguistic, and Solun had killed them. She tried to catch Neilan's eyes, but he was staring hard at the floor.

"What could it have to do with them?" Wuervik asked incredulously. "We haven't seen them in sixteen years!"

The back of Elwyn's mind twinged. She tried to ignore it, to focus on the all-important conversation happening on the opposite side of the door.

Astur's voice grew lower. "That day still pains me to remember."

"We did what we did and it's done." Wuervik's voice was harsh. "There's no point looking back."

Pressure rose in Elwyn's chest. What did they do?

"You're wrong there, young Wuervik."

Elwyn was momentarily sidetracked. Young Wuervik? He had to be in his fifties.

Astur's voice rang out again, "I believe it's time for us to revisit Regsenfrag."

There was a long pause, then Wuervik said in a small voice, "I'm not going back there."

"Yes you are." Astur's voice was even, but his tone was stern. "I must first pay an overdue visit to the Heads. But you will go to Regsenfrag, and you will find her parents. Last I heard, they still lived there. You will—"

Elwyn's heart screamed in her chest and drowned out her senses. Her parents? Her parents *'still lived'*?

They'd lied to her! Her mind flashed with white hot anger, then muddied with confusion. What did they do to her parents?

An image shot through her mind and took root, more vivid and feasible than ever before: a life away from here. A life with her parents. Her chest burned, and her face grew hot. They'd always said her parents were dead. Why did they lie to her?

'Still lived.' Where? She strained her memory for what Astur had said. Regsenfrag, that's where her parents were.

She pulled away from the door. Neilan looked at her, his eyebrows furrowed but eyes wide. She turned and ran back down the tunnel. A hand caught hers before she reached the first curve. She grabbed on tight and bolted into the pitch blackness around the curve.

She smacked into the wall of the tunnel and crashed to the ground, pulling Neilan down with her. The sound of it echoed throughout the tunnel. The distant voices paused.

"We gotta go!" Neilan whispered as he scrambled to his feet.

She reached in the darkness for him and grabbed hold of his hand again. She pressed her opposite hand against the wall and ran, using the wall as a guide. *They're alive!* rang over and over in her mind.

A bang like a door bursting open echoed from behind them. Voices yelled.

Around the next turn, light seeped between the roots ahead, and Elwyn pounded toward it. She burst through the roots, landing on her hands and knees, and Neilan dove through after her.

She jumped up.

"Wait—your boots!" Neilan yelled.

She looked down. Muddy footprints trailed her on the glass floor. She and Neilan yanked off their boots, while footfalls pounded in the tunnel behind the curtain of roots. Elwyn took off, boots in hand, Neilan a step behind.

6

Elwyn's heart and feet raced, but she focused on the single pair of boots thumping behind them. They were getting louder. Neilan's cloak, still tied around her shoulders, flapped behind her as she ran, and the hem of her dress flapped around her ankles.

At the next fork, the left-hand tunnel went to the Concourse. She took the right.

She rounded a sharp turn, and a door ahead stood slightly ajar. Elwyn launched herself through it, and she grabbed Neilan's arm as he nearly ran past it, dragging him in after her.

She shut the door quietly, and leaned her ear against it, holding her breath. She strained her ears. The boots were almost at the fork.

One, two, three seconds passed. The boots pounded down the left-hand tunnel. Elwyn let out her breath, her legs shaking. She sunk to the lucten-lit floor and dropped her face onto her knees.

Neilan's voice whispered, "El?"

"My parents!" she whispered into her knees, voice trembling. "My parents!" She lifted her eyes but couldn't meet his. She stared at his hands, which were clenched in his lap as he knelt facing her.

She turned away. The round room was bare except for a chest of wide, shallow drawers along one wall, covered in a thin layer of dust, and there was a closed door on the opposite side from them. Astur's voice replayed in Elwyn's mind, '—*they still lived there.*'

She stared at her knees and whispered, "They lied." And now they wanted her to help them. They needed her Gifts. They wanted her for the same reason Solun did.

No. She wouldn't do it. Her parents were alive! She had to find them. For once in her life, she'd do what she wanted without worrying about everyone else.

Tension radiated from Neilan, but he didn't speak. Elwyn looked up into his face. His brow was furrowed, and he was staring at his lap with his jaw clenched.

She'd expected a reaction, but not this one. "What?" she whispered.

He shifted.

Her chest prickled. Something was off. "What?" she asked again, louder.

He opened his mouth, closed it, then opened it again. "Are you sure?"

Heat rose in Elwyn's face. "You heard the same thing I did."

"Yeah, but..." He closed his eyes and dropped his face into his hands.

Why was he reacting like this? She'd expected anger, and shock, like she was feeling, not... whatever this was. A thought took form and rose to the surface of her mind. "Wait, you knew?"

His eyes shot to hers. He opened his mouth but nothing came out. His eyes were wide, pleading.

"You knew? And you didn't tell me? How could you?" Her voice broke.

"I didn't!" Neilan burst out. "Well, I thought maybe, but I didn't know for sure!" He held her eyes, his face and shoulders straining.

"When they came for me…" He looked down. "They day they took me, I overheard men—Astur and Wuervik—talking with my parents. They said 'he will be raised with another child, one year younger than him.' My parents asked about the child's family, and the men said, 'Her parents don't live with us. She has no siblings.' That was all they said about you. If your parents were dead, I figure they would've just said so."

Elwyn stared at him, her mind racing. All this time, he hadn't even given her a hint. "How could you not tell me?"

"I didn't know you yet!" He paused, then whispered, "I didn't know for sure… I could've been wrong. And I didn't want…"

"Didn't want what? Didn't want me to have a family!"

"Who wants parents?" he whispered fiercely. Then the heat dropped out of his voice. "Thinking you were abandoned on accident is better than knowing it was on purpose."

Elwyn glared at him. Her thoughts swirled, and she couldn't get a hold of any of them.

"They gave us up," he said so low she could barely hear him. "If they don't want us, why should we want them?"

Neilan met her eyes. His were red, and tears welled in them. His jaw was clenched, and his hands were balled in his lap. Elwyn's chest ached, and her stomach burned. She wanted to scream at him, and to hug him. To punch him, and to hold him. But she dropped her eyes to her lap and sat there, frozen.

The silence stretched, and her own heartbeat pounded in her ears. She squeezed her eyes shut. "I want to know my parents," she whispered. "Even if they don't want to know me."

"I know," he whispered bitterly. He took a deep breath, then let it out resignedly. "What about Solun?"

"What about him?"

"If you surface to find them, he'll find you."

He was right, but she said defiantly, "Maybe."

Neilan's voice rose slightly. "Then he'll find out about the Haven."

"My parents are Gifted. Maybe they can help me avoid him." And actually be free.

The life that had flashed through her mind in the hidden tunnel rose again. A life with her parents, free of the Haven. Free of Solun, free of her fear of hurting everyone. Free of everything she had known.

She'd do it. She'd find them.

Neilan's shaking, whispered voice broke in, "I can't let you leave me, too."

Her stomach knotted. She was all he had in the world. She avoided his eyes as she said, "I have to find them. Now, before they can stop me."

Tension rolled off him, but she kept her eyes down. She wiped the mud from her boots and put them on, then she took off his cloak and tentatively handed it to him.

Neilan sat still for a moment, then rolled the cloak into a ball and clutched it. He wiped his boots and put them on, too. Then, without looking at her, he pushed himself up and pressed his ear to the door. "There's movement out there," he said flatly.

She stared around the room. The door on the opposite side drew her eye. She hustled to it and tried the latch. It was locked. She glanced across at Neilan. "Could you help me?"

He waved a hand toward it, but nothing happened.

Elwyn pulled the latch again, but it remained closed fast. "It isn't working."

Neilan frowned and strode across the room to her. He reached toward the latch, stopping with his hand an inch from it, and closed his eyes. His face tightened, and his arm muscles strained.

But again, nothing happened. He opened his eyes. "It's fortified against Magic."

Elwyn stared at it. "Can you undo it?"

"Fighting Magic with Magic would drain me way more than normal use. This door can't be used much—the Keepers would have to take down the fortification then reinstate it again every time they used it."

Elwyn's mind spun. What were they hiding? But that brought her back: her parents. She hustled to the opposite door, the one to the main tunnel, and she pressed an ear to it.

Silence reigned immediately on the opposite side. Good enough. She raised her eyebrows at Neilan and asked, "Come with me?"

He paused and looked down at his feet.

She couldn't wait for him to decide. She threw open the door and ran into the tunnel.

7

Neilan fought to keep up with Elwyn, who was hustling toward the Concourse. He wouldn't let her leave him.

He clutched his cloak in his fist, which made running awkward, but he couldn't drop it or they'd know he was the one there. A set of muddy footprints were stamped along the glass floor, running parallel with Neilan and Elwyn.

They rounded a curve and the door out of the C.K. Wing appeared. Through the opening, the luctenfall in the Concourse glowed. Elwyn slowed enough to be as inconspicuous as an unqualified trainee coming from the C.K. Wing could be, and slipped through it. Neilan followed her through the doorway and through the wide arch into the crowded Concourse.

The muddy footprints ran on the glass floor from the C.K. Wing all the way to the Training and Recreation Wing, across the Hall. A Certified Keeper yelled out, pointing at Elwyn, and a few more started running toward her.

Elwyn burst into a sprint, heading for the next archway: the Enex staircase, which led out into the wild forestland above the Haven. Neilan sprinted hard to catch up.

He could help them stop her, but his chest tightened. No, he couldn't. She'd never forgive him.

"Stop!" rang through the room. Wuervik burst from the T.R. Wing and reached toward them.

Without thinking, Neilan threw a Magical shield in front of Wuervik. The shimmering, translucently purple shield exploded into being and expanded across the room. Wuervik's Magic slammed into it and reverberated off the walls.

Elwyn paused, looking from Neilan to Wuervik. Neilan hesitated. His chest ached at the thought, but he couldn't force her to stay. He yelled at her, "Run!"

She spun around and sprinted toward the Enex staircase. She was almost to the archway. Neilan surged more power into the shield, then he sped after her, his heart racing.

The Keepers on this side of the shield took off after her, too. One reached forward, so Neilan threw up another shield, blocking Elwyn and him from everyone else. Magic assaulted the shield, slamming into it again and again. Keepers threw all their strength at it. He surged energy into it, sapping him. He stumbled.

Elwyn reached the bottom step of the Enex staircase, and she hurled herself up. Neilan tried to follow, but his legs felt like they were moving through water. His chest and arms shook—holding up both shields was too much. He let go of the one blocking Wuervik, then he dragged his legs into motion, to the first step of the staircase.

Wuervik sped to the second shield and attacked it. Blow after blow weakened it, and the edges wavered. Neilan threw his strength into it, then pushed himself up the stairs. Elwyn was halfway up.

Magic punctured his shield. Neilan strained to close it, but before he could, a wave of Magic flew through the hole. It surged past Neilan, up the staircase. A shimmering, slightly green shield burst into existence ahead of Elwyn. She slammed into it and fell backward, down several steps.

Neilan's heart dropped. He sent a burst of Magic, which buffeted her fall. He dragged himself up the steps between them and pulled her to her feet.

She met his eyes, hers wide. She nodded to him, probably the best 'thanks' she could manage. Neilan's legs shook, and his body dragged. The excessive use of Magic was draining him too fast.

Wuervik's shield held strong ahead of them. Neilan stared down the staircase at his own weakening shield. They were stuck, and he didn't have enough left in him to battle on both sides at once. He took a deep breath, and dropped his shield.

Wuervik and the Keepers streamed up the staircase.

Neilan surged his strength at the shield ahead of them. It wavered. He closed his eyes and yanked at it.

Sprinting footsteps echoed up the stairs behind him. The shield shook, then disintegrated.

Elwyn grabbed Neilan's hand and pulled him up the stairs. He tried to climb, but he stumbled, then fell. She tugged at him.

He pushed Magic into his legs, renewing their strength. Unwise, being so drained already, but what else could he do?

He ran up the steps in her wake, then his mind fogged. The staircase felt like it was spinning.

The Enex hole opened above them, revealing the inside of the hollow, fallen tree trunk that masked the Enex hole. Brightday's sunlight, streaming into the trunk from one side, flooded the staircase.

Elwyn surged toward the hole, Neilan just behind her, but then it started to close. Elwyn looked down the staircase past Neilan, and her face tightened with fear. "Wuervik's closing it!"

Neilan yelled, "Go!"

Elwyn spun from him and squeezed herself through the closing hole. She clambered to her feet, almost able to stand straight up in the massive, hollow trunk. Neilan threw himself into it after her, forcing his arms and shoulders through.

Elwyn yanked his cloak from his hands, grabbed his arms, and pulled, but the hole closed on his waist. He was pinned. He forced his remaining strength into fighting Wuervik's Magic to open the hole. He strained, as stars danced at the edges of his vision.

The hole loosened a tiny bit. Elwyn heaved at his arms, dragging his hips through.

The hole tightened on his legs. His shoulders ached as Elwyn yanked on his arms.

His vision blurred at the edges. Blackness began closing in, and his torso grew heavy. He couldn't hold it up anymore.

He bent forward, close to collapsing. Elwyn grabbed his waist and strained against the hole. Neilan's knees scraped through. She let go of his waist and pulled on one leg, which slipped out of the hole.

Hands closed around the ankle still inside.

Elwyn heaved, but it didn't budge. The hands inside held him fast.

The blackness at the edges of Neilan's vision crept inward. He let go of all caution and threw one last burst of Magic into his leg and yanked.

His boot slipped off, and blackness overwhelmed his mind. He had a falling sensation, then nothing.

8

Elwyn fell back from the momentum as Neilan's bare foot burst out of the Enex hole. He slammed face-down on the ground beside her, limp. She rolled him onto his back and leaned over his face, her hands shaking. "Neil, wake up!"

No response.

"Come on! Neilan!"

Still nothing.

The Enex hole would open again soon. But they'd gotten lucky—a disturbance at the entryway kept the hole frozen shut for five minutes as a safety measure. The Haven's real purpose was to keep people out, not keep them in. Nothing could open it, not even Magic. Especially not Magic. She had five minutes to figure this out.

She pulled his shoulders up, wrapped her arms under his, and dragged him out of the hollow tree. Sunlight seared her eyes as they emerged from the trunk, but Neilan's eyelids didn't even flicker. His warm, dark-brown skin was taking on a gray tinge. Elwyn had to revive him immediately or the Magically-induced exhaustion would kill him.

Her brain spun. What could she do? Her heart thudded, and her eyes burned. No. She forced back the tears—she needed to think. She looked around, but the wild forest on all sides of her offered no ideas.

Wait, a therapeian flower. That could do it.

She looked down at Neilan. The gray tone of his skin was deepening. She covered him with his cloak, then she ran through the thick trees toward the lucten stream that flowed nearby. There might be therapeian flowers in bloom on its bank. There had to be. Please let there be.

A silver glow shone between the trees, and she pushed through the undergrowth toward it. She burst through the trees and scanned the bank. Please.

A gleam of silver sparkled on the bank, reflecting the lucten-light, and Elwyn ran toward it. A mature therapeian flower stood there, bursting with petals which curved backward and down from its center, their tips completing the curve by just touching the stem. A mass of young petal buds sprouted in its center. The mature petals were so densely packed that they formed a globe of light.

She reached for the sacred flower, but her stomach clenched. It felt wrong, but she had to do it. "I'm sorry to pick you," she said aloud. "An Heir needs your help."

The stem snapped, and she clutched the flower and ran. Back through the trees, Neilan shone in the shaft of sunlight. He hadn't moved an inch. Elwyn unceremoniously tore two petals from the therapeian flower and opened Neilan's mouth. She shoved the petals in between his teeth, then she pushed his jaw closed, crunching them. Please, please.

Her skin prickled. For the longest second of her life, nothing happened. Then his cheek began losing the gray tinge, and his jaw muscles responded, chewing the petals.

Elwyn let out her breath. She gave him a moment, then she

opened his mouth and shoved in two more petals. The gray tinge slowly drained from his face. His jaw worked automatically, then his throat contracted as he swallowed.

She breathed freely again. She pushed the rest of the petals into his mouth, and stared into his face. "Neilan?"

No response, but he chewed. A tingly tug pulled at her insides, but she ignored it. She had to help Neilan.

Scraping noises issued from the hollow tree trunk—they were trying to dig it open from the inside, but it wouldn't work. They knew it as well as she did. By her estimation, she still had two minutes.

The tingly tug intensified, pulling her toward the lucten stream. Fine! She obeyed it.

She hustled to the lucten stream, then the tug pulled her up the stream toward Neilan's and her special spot. In a break in the trees, an enormous shape stood facing her. She stopped, her body tensing. The shape moved toward her.

She stood frozen. The tingly tug pulled at her, toward the beast, but she stayed where she was. The shape leaped forward, emerging fully through the trees. It was a massive gray animal with a long head, clawed paws, and enormous wings: a servol—the two-domain animal that supposedly served the High King directly.

Elwyn's chest tingled. Was it here to help her? She stepped forward and reached up. It touched her hand with it's nose, then bowed. It was here for her. It had to be.

She scrambled onto its back. Before she was settled, it bounded forward, along the lucten stream.

"Wait!" she called, and pulled on its neck to get it to turn. She couldn't leave Neilan behind.

It hesitated, but it was clear that it knew what she meant. It tossed its head and grunted. Then it obeyed, bounding toward the spot where Neilan still lay unconscious. Elwyn slipped off its back and crouched next to Neilan.

Voices issued from the hollow tree trunk—the hole was starting to open. Elwyn's heart thudded against her ribs. She reached under Neilan's shoulders and tried to lift him, straining all her muscles. The servol tipped its head under Neilan's back and pushed his torso onto its neck. Elwyn rolled him all the way on and scrambled onto the animal's back as a rush burst from the tree trunk.

The servol took one bound then launched into the air. At the first beat of its massive wings, Elwyn nearly toppled off. She squeezed her legs together around its middle.

Yells erupted behind them, and Elwyn chanced a look over her shoulder. A dozen Keepers stood open-mouthed staring at them. Wuervik reached toward them, his eyes flaming with anger.

A prickly tug pulled at her middle, and she was dragged backward down the servol's back. She wrapped her arms around Neilan's limp body and the servol's neck, and she dug her knees into its sides.

By the second beat of its wings, they were to the tops of the trees. The prickly tug intensified, and Elwyn held on with all her might.

Then the tug vanished.

Elwyn peeked over her shoulder. Astur's arm was held up in front of Wuervik in a placating gesture. Was Astur helping her? But his jaw was set, and he glowered up at her.

Elwyn shuddered.

Elwyn held on as tight as she could. The wind rushing past roared in her ears and yanked at her. She leaned forward, flat onto Neilan's limp body which still laid across the servol's back.

She dared a glance down. The tops of trees carpeted the landscape below, cut through by the many branches of the glowing lucten stream. Somewhere along one of the countless branches of that stream, she'd spent her entire life. But she couldn't tell where—the Haven had already faded into the endless forest.

Even if she looked, she couldn't find it again. The suddenness of that thought made her breath catch. She couldn't go back if she wanted to.

A small part of her ached at the idea of leaving behind everything she knew—it had all happened so fast.

She would be forced to go back if the Keepers caught her. That same small, traitorous part of her was relieved by the thought. But she couldn't let that happen—her parents were out there somewhere.

No, not *'somewhere.'* Regsenfrag.

Astur and Wuervik probably knew where she was going, and they knew exactly the path the servol would take. She'd been taught that servols stayed near lucten, and so far it had held true. The servol flew over the treetops above the many-branched lucten stream, following every bend.

In the distance in front of them, the lucten streams connected into Lucaedter, the larger lucten river that flowed from the mountains looming ahead all the way to the sea far behind.

Elwyn reached into her right-hand pocket and pulled out her small spiralbound notebook. She flipped through the pages on which she'd spent hours painstakingly documenting the path the Keeper had recorded in her travel journal. She'd worked so hard for so long, but even if they landed, there was no way she could find her way from here to the Keeper's safe path. All that work was a waste.

She squinted at the trees and lucten streams speeding below her, then to the mountains up ahead. The servol would probably continue northeast, following Lucaedter. But Regsenfrag, the dot she'd seen countless times on maps without the smallest hint of what it held for her, was east.

She had a head start at least—Keepers couldn't fly. But they would come after her. They knew where she was going, and how she'd get there. What should she do? She was sure the High King had sent the servol, and it had helped her. But what now? Did she have to stay on it?

She couldn't carry Neilan, so she had to wait at least until he woke up. And what about the mountain gangs, Solun's servants, and the Keepers who'd be after her? Elwyn couldn't have handled any of it on her own. The High King had provided for everything.

Why was he helping her?

She reached into her left-hand pocket for her sancan, but her fingers met a sticky mess. She started and looked down. The jam-spread bread was all smushed up but still there.

Elwyn stared at it. This morning in the library felt like a thousand years ago.

She pulled out the smashed, sticky mess and examined it. Still edible. She reached for Neilan's cloak, which was still draped over him, and felt around the pockets. Several of them had lumps of some sort. Even her hunger was taken care of, but again not by her.

She squinted into the distance, tracing Lucaedter with her eyes. The glowing lucten river flowed bright for miles and miles and disappeared into the mountains far to the north. Her insides tightened. North, not east. It must be where she was supposed to go, but it wasn't where she wanted to go.

9

Neilan's mind dragged through mud, clawing itself to consciousness. No, back to sleep. It couldn't be morning yet, he was so tired.

His determined brain kept working its way through the mud against his will. His whole body ached. Why did he hurt so bad? It didn't matter, he just wanted to sleep. But his brain refused to sink back into oblivion.

Memory flooded back, and his heart dropped. Elwyn! Where was she? What had happened?

Why was it so loud? It occurred to him that his eyes were closed and he fought to open them, unsuccessfully. Why was the bed moving like that? His head and his legs, with one boot on, were dangling off it. And he was face-down. Why? He tried to roll over.

"No!" a voice screamed right by him—Elwyn's voice—and hands clutched at him.

He strained to open his eyes. Her panicked face was close to his, and she held onto him as though for life.

"What's—" he tried to say.

"Stay still!" she screamed.

He fully opened his eyes, and nearly passed out again. The ground sped by a hundred paces below him. He was flying. Flying? What was he laying on?

A massive wing beat into view then out of it again. Neilan tried to sit up.

"Stay still," Elwyn said again, a bit calmer this time. "Stop moving. Just give me a minute."

He couldn't look back down, he'd lose it. He met her eyes and held them. Their deep, clear blue, so familiar but still so striking, grounded him. He took a slow breath and looked around him. It was already almost sunset, and he was laying draped over the back of some animal, some flying animal. He turned toward the head. A servol?

Elwyn pulled his cloak off him and tucked it under her leg, then she wrapped her arms all the way around him and held on tight. "Okay," she said. "Now sit up."

He wrapped his fingers into the servol's feathers, so fine they were almost like fur, and pulled his legs up. He leaned into Elwyn's grip and balanced himself with his arms, pushing up to a sitting position. The wind pulled on him, so he leaned into it.

Elwyn loosened her grip tentatively. His back was to her, so he couldn't see her. That wouldn't do. He gripped the feathers again, switched the sides his legs were on, and turned around to face her fully. Her face was bright pink. He burst into laughter.

She frowned at him and said testily, "What?"

"Look at the backs of your hands," he said, pointing to her aggressively pink skin.

She held one up and stared wide-eyed. "What is that?"

"You're sunburnt!" he said, laughing.

"What?"

"Too much exposure to the sun can burn skin," he said, trying to stifle his laughter.

She stared at the back of her hand, touched it tentatively, then looked up into his face. "But you aren't red."

He pointed to the cloak that was tucked under her leg and shrugged. "I was under that. But also I have darker skin than you."

"So?"

"Color in the skin is a barrier against the sun," he said. He took in her bright pink face which used to be so pale and laughed. "You didn't stand a chance!"

She glared at him, but a smirk turned up one side of her lips. Then she looked down at her hands contemplatively. "So you'll never get sunburnt?"

"No skin can withstand the sun forever. I had my fair share of sunburns before—" Memory flashed across his mind: Mama cooling his hot, throbbing cheeks with a wet cloth. He turned away from Elwyn, his eyes burning.

Her hand settled on his arm, and the feel of her touch nearly did him in. He squeezed his eyes shut and clenched his jaw. His whole face tensed with the strain of holding it in.

He kept his eyes shut and his face averted until the tension released, then he took a slow breath and turned back to her. Her bright pink face startled him again. What was he thinking, letting her keep sitting in the sun like that?

If only he could heal with Magic. But he hadn't been trained in that yet, and he could make it worse if he did it wrong. He reached for the cloak and pulled it out from under her leg. "Wear this," he said and draped it over her. "It'll keep the sun off you. You don't want to get more burnt." He pulled the hood up over her head and adjusted it so the slanted, evening sunlight couldn't get onto her face.

She drew it close around herself, then she reached into the pockets and pulled out a mushed-up lump. She shoved it into his hand and commanded, "Eat."

He stared at it suspiciously, but his stomach rumbled at just the thought of food. He took it from her and sniffed it. Bread, smashed up but good enough.

He shoved it into his mouth. The texture of the first bite was off, but by the second bite he didn't care anymore. He scarfed it down.

Elwyn stared into the sky, and he followed her gaze. The Brightday sunset had set the sky on fire above, below, and on all sides of them. The whole sky was lit with a shocking pink. The treetops were tipped with gold, and the Tensmon mountains, so close now, shone deep purple.

Lucaedter below glowed silver and purple, twisting through the trees to the ravine that cut through the mountain range. Neilan looked back into Elwyn's face, and her eyes were wide with wonder. His insides warmed.

"I've never seen one," she said.

"Seen what?"

"A sunset."

"Never?" he asked, aghast. But then again, when would she? They only had surface trips during the day, since Wuervik had never let them stay out past mid-afternoon. And she'd been in the Haven her entire life.

She smiled at him: a sad, thoughtful smile, and his insides fluttered.

The last bit of the sun disappeared into the sea behind them, and the sky faded to purple. A minute later, the planet Fainor rose over the mountains. The rust-colored ball hung in the sky, so much larger than the sun, but so much softer. Fainorlight spread over the landscape, bathing it in red-gold.

Elwyn reached up, as though she could touch it. "It's so... big."

Neilan laughed. "You've really never seen it before?"

She frowned and looked at him. In a hurt voice, she said, "When would I have seen it?"

He looked down. "I know."

He stared back at Fainor, which was filling Brightnight with mild, warm light, but purple-gray clouds swept toward it from the north. Oh no. He recognized those clouds from when he was a kid. Elwyn had never faced a storm before, either. How could he protect her all the way up here? The mountains weren't far away, now. Maybe they'd get to them before the storm hit.

A drop landed on his head. No.

Elwyn turned her face up, eyes closed, mouth open wide.

He couldn't help but laugh. Had she ever felt rain before? It hit him that the world in her mind was formed by things she'd read. She'd had almost no experience with the real world. He hadn't seen these things in years, but at least they had already existed for him. For her, the world as it really was didn't exist in her mind until now.

His mind caught. He'd only had a six-year-old's view of the real world before coming to the Haven. Until now, he'd trusted his understanding of it. But watching her discover for the first time things that had always existed, it hit him: what was out there that he didn't know about? How would he protect her from all of it?

The raindrops grew heavier by the second, and the wind grew chillier. Bumps covered his skin. He reached for Elwyn and pulled the cloak tighter around her.

She looked up at him and started. "No, you take it! You still need to recover."

"I'm fine," he said and squinted into the storm. The mountains loomed ahead, pretty close now. The wind picked up and buffeted them, making the servol swerve. No! How could Neilan help?

The servol righted itself, but Neilan had to do something. He closed his eyes and threw up a Magical shield to block the wind and rain.

The servol tipped, and Neilan's heart dropped. The shield interrupted the airflow too much. He let it go.

His body ached already, from using Magic so soon after regaining consciousness, but he had to do something. He stared around: they were flying over the foothills, and the mountains rose into the sky ahead of them. Elwyn curled in on herself, her jaw clenched and her eyes closed.

The rain pelted them, so thick now that the foothills racing below were almost invisible. The servol was buffeted back and forth by the wind, losing control. He had to do something. He reached out with Magic, feeling the wind.

"Please don't," Elwyn said, her voice muffled.

He leaned in so she could hear him. "It's okay, I'm gonna fix it."

"Don't," she said, pleading. "You aren't strong enough yet."

He reached into the wind, pulled on it with Magic, and slowed it down. For a second, the servol flew smoother. But more wind came at them. He grabbed it with Magic, slowing it.

Gust after gust hurtled toward him. Panic rose in his chest—he couldn't handle this much. He had to let it go, but his instincts kept responding, sending more and more Magic into the wind.

His muscles strained, the strength draining from him. He couldn't keep going like this, but it'd gotten out of his control.

He couldn't stop himself, couldn't hold in his Magic. It was flowing from him, desperately trying to keep up what he'd started.

Elwyn grabbed his face and pulled, forcing him to look into her eyes. "Stop," she said, calm and firm.

He couldn't. He tried to turn back into the wind that was sapping him.

"No," Elwyn said, gripping his face. She grabbed one of his hands and pressed it to her own cheek. "Please," she said, staring into his eyes. "Look at me. Breathe with me."

He looked into her eyes and finally began to see them. Their blue depths sunk into him, and his chest ached. He felt her slow breathing, and he intuitively matched her, breath for breath. His heartbeat slowed, and his panic subsided, then his Magic ceased to flow from him.

The wind smacked into them, and the servol tipped.

Neilan tried to grip Elwyn, but his muscles felt like goo. Elwyn wrapped her arms around his middle and held on tight. The servol fought the wind, and the mountains loomed closer. Neilan's body sagged.

The servol dove. Neilan had the sensation of falling, but Elwyn's arms tightened around his middle. He leaned into her, his head dropping onto her shoulder. The servol pulled up, nearly knocking them off. Its claws clicked on stone, and it lunged forward.

The pelting rain disappeared, and the wind ceased, while darkness engulfed them. The servol stopped, and Elwyn pulled Neilan off it's back. He tried to catch himself with a foot, but he tipped. Elwyn steadied him then laid him down on uneven stone. His eyes closed.

Heavy paw beats pounded away from him, then there was a whoosh, and Elwyn screamed, "No!"

Neilan tried to open his eyes. "What?" His voice came out slow and weak.

Elwyn sat down next to him, and he could feel her shaking in the darkness. "It's gone."

10

Neilan awoke and rolled onto his side. His whole body ached from sleeping   on the uneven, rocky floor of the cave. His stomach grumbled painfully, and his bootless foot was freezing. Slanting, Twilitday morning light streamed into his face. He scanned the cave. "Elwyn?" he whisper-yelled.

No answer.

He pushed himself up from the floor and called again, louder, "Elwyn?"

Nothing.

She wouldn't have left him. Would she? He staggered over the rocky ground further into the cave. Something behind a boulder caught his eye—a bent elbow in a dirty, white sleeve.

"Elwyn?" he whispered. The elbow didn't move.

Neilan rounded the boulder, and the sight of her stopped him short. She lay on her side with one arm bent under her head. Her legs were tucked up toward her chest, with her other arm draped over them as though she'd fallen asleep hugging her knees.

Even in her sleep, her face was taught with anxiety. He'd never seen her asleep before, so vulnerable. He finally saw how scared she was.

Awake, she hid her emotions. She kept them locked up inside, trying to always be collected and self-controlled, to be perfect. Seeing her so unguarded was jarring. His heart ached for her.

He couldn't take it. He nudged her with his bare foot. "Hey," he whispered. She didn't move.

"Hey, Elwyn," he said a bit louder and nudged her again. Still nothing.

He bent down and shook her shoulder.

She sprang up into a sitting position and scooted away from him. "What're-you-doing?" she shrieked.

He jumped. His heart pounded, and his limbs tingled with a burst of adrenaline. "You wouldn't wake up," he said defensively.

She glared up at him. He couldn't think of what to say, so he backed away. He picked up his cloak, the fabric stiff from the dried rain, and made his way to the mouth of the cave.

The Twilitday sky was bright, but the morning shadows were purple down here. Their cave opened just above Lucaedter Scar, the ravine where the lucten river, Lucaedter, cut through the mountain range. It threaded between the mountain ridges ahead and disappeared around a bend.

Lucaedter flowed strong in the center of the ravine, about twenty paces away. Its glowing light danced on the cliffsides, and piles of mud and debris scattered the ground from the rainstorm yesterday.

Elwyn came up and stood a little away from him with her arms folded. Her hands were bright red still from the sunburn yesterday. Neilan looked closer at her face. "Your skin is starting to blister."

Her eyebrows drew together questioningly.

"Your sunburn—it's blistering. Does it hurt?"

She touched her cheeks gingerly. "Yes."

He handed her the stiff cloak. "Be careful to stay out of the sunlight today. You're lucky it's Twilitday, so the sun isn't as strong, but it could still get worse."

"Ick." She threw the cloak over herself and climbed down the short descent to the ravine floor. She scanned the ravine, then walked to the nearest cliffside where the shadows were deepest.

Neilan followed her, clomping awkwardly with one booted and one bare foot. His exposed big toe slammed into a sharp rock, and pain shot through his foot. He grabbed hold of his ankle, hopping on the opposite foot, and looked down at it.

Blood dripped from a wide open gash in his big toe. The exposed flesh inside made his stomach clench, and the world spun. He lost his balance and dropped to the ravine floor.

He closed his eyes and breathed deep, but the smell of blood made it worse. He opened his eyes and held up his injured toe. His head spun again. Blood flowed from it without any sign of stopping. It throbbed with every beat of his pulse. He should put pressure on it, but the thought of touching it made his stomach clench again.

Elwyn bent down and examined it. Her brows came together in concentration, and she pursed her lips. How she could look at it that closely was beyond him. She looked around the ravine for a second, then she reached down and tore a strip of cloth from the hem of the cloak. "This is gonna hurt."

"Wha—?" Neilan began, but Elwyn yanked the strip of cloth tight around his toe. Pain surged through his foot and up his shin. His stomach turned over. For a second, he thought he might actually throw up. "What was that for?" he demanded.

"We have to stop the blood," she said matter-of-factly.

She was right, but he still had to resist the urge to kick her.

"We need to cover your foot."

That much was obvious. He tried to summon as much sincerity as possible into his voice and asked, "With what?"

She squinted at the storm debris scattered around them. After a second, she picked up a chunk of tree bark which was roughly the size of Neilan's foot. She tore a few more strips from the bottom of the cloak and used them to tie the bark onto the sole of his foot. She bunched some in the front to add extra cushion to his toes and secured it behind his ankle.

Neilan stood to test the makeshift shoe. Pain ran through his foot and up his leg, but at least it was better than the rocky ground. It would have to do.

He wished he could heal it with Magic, but that training was still years away. And even then, there was no guarantee he'd be able to heal with Magic alone. If he attempted to heal without knowing exactly what he was doing, he could make it worse than it was now. He didn't know how each skin layer came together, each muscle, each tendon, each blood vessel. If he got it wrong, he could cause irreparable damage.

Very few Magic users managed to become medics, and even fewer to heal the body with Magic alone. Most Medic-Keepers relied on a blend of Magic, drafts, and the body's own healing processes. It was better to let his body heal itself than to try to do it with Magic—his body knew what it was doing. But he resented the wait.

He took a tentative step with the makeshift shoe, and pain shot through his foot again.

"Well?" Elwyn asked.

"It'll work." He took a few steps, his toe throbbing. He could already see a red blotch seeping through the bandaging. He wondered how long it would hold up.

"Do we know where we're going?" Neilan asked. Perpetual wandering on his bleeding foot did not sound good.

"Regsenfrag," she said. Her eyes clouded, and she looked away from him. "I hope they're still there. I don't know where else to look."

He knew that brutal combination of fear and hope. He wished he could make things better for her, but for now, "That's at least a few days away. What about before then?"

She glared at the ravine floor.

"What is it?" he asked.

Her shoulders drooped. "All that time I spent mapping the Keeper's route, and we went a different way. All that time was a waste, and we have nothing to go on."

Neilan shrugged. "We'll figure it out. You wanted to avoid people, but people can be helpful." He caught her eye and grinned. "People make food."

She sighed. Then she buoyed herself up with forced optimism and said, "We should be less than a day from Torlum. We'll stop there tonight for dinner."

"And a place to sleep, too." He rubbed his back. "I don't like the idea of another stone bed."

She pursed her lips.

He asked, "Do you think Astur and Wuervik know where we're going?"

Elwyn squinted up into the sky. "Yeah."

They probably wouldn't make it, but the pain in Elwyn's face was too much for him. He said, "Well, let's get there first."

Neilan's toe throbbed with every one of his heartbeats, and pain shot from his toe to his ankle at each step, but he and Elwyn trudged on for hours.

The Twilitday sun was starting to set. The pink sky and deep-purple shadows contrasted sharply with the bright, liquid-crystal lucten river surging next to them through Lucaedter Scar.

Lucaedter's moving, silver glow reflected off the ravine walls, making it feel a little like the Haven.

At the end of the mountain range, the Scar widened and Torlum rose on a hill in the center of Lucaedter. The island city glowed with lucten-light. The moving, silver light from Lucaedter met the motionless silver glow of lucten-lamps stationed throughout the city. Narrow, dirt roads wove between tightly-packed, single-story wooden buildings. Sparkling lucten accents adorned the front of nearly every building. Lucten even gilded the bridges that surrounded the city.

In the midst of the beauty, something was off. Neilan couldn't make out any movement in the city from where he stood on the opposite bank of Lucaedter. No one moved through the roads or came and went from buildings.

"Where is everyone?" he wondered aloud. Was the place abandoned? He'd thought this was a densely populated city, a hub of commerce as the center of lucten-craft.

Elwyn squinted at the city, her face taut. "Maybe they're already inside for Darkday tomorrow? There's still enough sunlight, though. I'd think they'd be out till dusk."

Neilan's stomach rumbled. There better be something to eat, even if there weren't people there anymore. They reached the nearest bridge and climbed up toward the city. Elwyn ran her fingers along the hardened lucten that gilded the railing. Its light wasn't as strong as Lucaedter's flowing below it, since it had been separated from the source, but it still sparkled with the sunlight it had absorbed during the day. "Do you think they used Magic to make this?" she asked.

Neilan considered. "Maybe, but I doubt it. Torlum is full of lucten craftsmen."

As the sky darkened, windows began to glow with firelight. So there were people here.

They reached the end of the bridge and paused. Neilan looked up each road that branched from the bridge. What now?

"This one," Elwyn said and she set off down one of the roads.

"Wait," Neilan said, trying to catch up with her. "Why?"

She shrugged without slowing her pace.

Neilan's toe ached horribly. "Slow down," he called to her as she pulled further ahead.

She glanced over her shoulder, her mouth open and ready to retort, then she caught sight of his foot. Her face fell. "Oh, yeah. I'm sorry." She came back and walked next to him, making an effort to stay at his pace.

Neilan tried to keep his "oofs" to a minimum as he limped beside her. "Where are we going?"

"I don't know." She looked up a turn then said, "This way."

"Hold on," he said, grabbing her sleeve to get her to pause. "How do you know?"

She grudgingly stopped and faced him. "The same reason I followed the tunnel in the C.K. Wing and same way I found the servol in the woods."

Neilan frowned at her. "Which is?"

"The tingly tug."

"The what?"

Her eyebrows drew together, and she studied him. "From the High King."

Tension pulled at Neilan's shoulders. What was she talking about? She'd never met the High King. They'd been taught about him, but Neilan didn't even know where he lived. As far as Neilan knew, the High King hadn't been seen in centuries. But his heartbeat sped a little, sensing the tingly presence of power he always felt when he thought of the High King.

"Haven't you felt it?" she asked, her blue eyes boring into him.

Tingly, maybe. But a tug? "I don't know," he said, recoiling from her intensity.

She tipped her head to the side. "Would you follow it if you did?"

His chest burned. Follow it? When he didn't know where it was leading? He met her eyes and opened his mouth to speak, but he couldn't think of what to say.

Her eyebrows drew down, and she stared at the road for a long moment. "Well, I do. And it's showing me the way. To… somewhere." Her voice trailed off at the end, and she looked down the road.

He wished he could be sure like that, to have something guide him and have the confidence to follow it. They had nothing else to go on at this point, so he may as well follow whatever leading she thought she had. "Okay," he said, trying to sound optimistic. "Where to?"

Her face brightened, and she set off down the road. He limped after her through the deserted streets, and a breeze began to pick up.

Two turns later, Elwyn pointed at a building far down the next street. "There," she said.

He squinted to make out the sign: "Senphon Inn." He still didn't get how she'd found it, but it looked decent enough. Even so, he didn't trust it. "You wait outside. I'll go in and see if I can work for the evening in exchange for some food and a night's sleep."

She raised an eyebrow at him. "I can work, too. You don't have to do everything."

"No, I'll do it. You don't have to."

"I *want* to," she said irritably. "I'm capable. You don't have to take care of me."

He didn't know what to say. He cared about her, so he had to take care of her. That was just how it was.

Elwyn huffed and set off toward the inn. Neilan limped to catch up to her, but a figure in his peripherals caught his eye. A person was up ahead—a teenage boy with short, straight, black hair, sitting on a bench in front of a shop a few doors down from the inn, staring at his feet. He seemed out of place in the empty street. Neilan's whole body tensed.

<h1 align="center">11</h1>

Sitting on the bench outside the Torlum herbalist shop in the fading light, Hosev Eument counted the minutes. Tinol was still inside the shop.

Tinol's father had been inspecting it when they'd found him. He'd been irritated that they'd interrupted his work and made them wait. But they couldn't wait 'till the inspection was over—they had to leave before Twilitnight set in.

It was safer to travel together, so Hosev had gone with Tinol to Torlum after visiting Father in Regsenfrag. But he'd only agreed on the condition that it wouldn't add more than two days to the trip. He should've known.

Tinol had promised he'd only be in the shop a few minutes, but it had already been two hours. Twilitday was darkening and a breeze pulled at Hosev's tunic. A few leaves skittered down the dirt road, and Hosev's chest tightened. They were losing time—malaps would be here soon.

Hosev was the only person to be seen. It was foolish to be outside tonight.

The breeze picked up. Leaves swirled and flew up into the air.

Wind whipped Hosev's short hair and chilled his ankles. He thought he could already hear distant screeches. His skin crawled, and a shiver ran down his spine.

If he was still in Torlum when the malaps arrived, he'd be stuck here till Dawnday morning. His sixteen-year-old sister Manell was in charge of Mother and all seven of their younger siblings while he was gone. He couldn't make her wait two extra days before he returned. He wanted to burst into the herbalist shop and force Tinol to leave, but he didn't know what Tinol's father would do. Hosev knew better than to cross him.

Maybe he should just leave. Tinol could find his way back on his own.

Hosev's stomach turned. He couldn't leave. Tinol probably wouldn't survive alone. Hosev might not make it either.

Footsteps on the road caught his attention, and his eyes snapped up. Two teenagers trudged up the road. The boy, around his own age, limped on a foot wrapped with tattered rags. The adrenaline that had burst through Hosev's limbs relaxed. These kids were no threat. He was more dangerous than they were.

The boy glared at Hosev distrustfully. He moved the girl to the opposite side of the road and switched places with her, putting himself between her and Hosev. The girl sighed and trudged on wearily, while the boy kept an eye on Hosev, glaring at him as they passed.

Hosev chuckled to himself.

The teenagers stopped at an inn a few doors down from the herbalist's. The boy approached the side door, the servants' entrance, then looked back at the girl. "Wait here?" he asked, pleadingly.

She glared at him.

"Please?" he asked.

She huffed and dropped onto the bench outside. What were they thinking? She needed to get inside!

The servants' door opened, and the boy entered. An eerie screech, definitely not imagined this time, echoed from far down the ravine. The malaps were getting closer.

Hosev's window of time was closing fast. The wind grew stronger, pulling at his clothes. The trees that dotted the road swayed in the wind. Up the road, toward the western bridge, a clump of men lumbered into the city. They wore wolfskins draped over their shoulders, characteristic of the Lupos gang, one of the ones that dominated the mountains.

Hosev tensed and his heartbeat sped. He couldn't bolt—moving too quick now would draw their attention. He stared resolutely at the ground and willed himself to blend into the shop behind him.

The men strode nearer.

Hosev kept his eyes down, but he watched them in his peripheral vision. They approached Senphon Inn. The girl on the bench openly glared at them. What was she doing? Hosev wanted to scream at her, but he held his breath.

Most of them ambled past, but the last three stayed back. When their comrades turned down the next street, they smirked at each other and faced the girl. Hosev's stomach dropped.

One of them approached her. "What's a girl like you doing out on a night like this?" he crooned.

The girl just glared up at them irritably.

The man spoke again, "Up to something, no doubt. Looks like you need to be taught a lesson."

Hosev's chest burned. He couldn't watch. He felt the hunting knife sheathed at his hip and the two short blades tied to his ankles. His hands tingled to grab them, but he couldn't. He clenched his fists and sat on them. He ached to scream at the men, to scream at her. Why was she just sitting there? Didn't she understand?

He couldn't do anything. If he tried, they'd turn on him. He had to make it back home. Mother needed him, and so did Manell.

The girl stood up and faced them. "Leave me alone," she said with more confidence than Hosev could've imagined.

The first man grinned. He stepped closer and reached a hand up to her cheek. She jerked back and stepped away from him.

The man chuckled under his breath. He advanced again, and she backed away again. She was moving further and further from the inn's door, which was exactly what the man intended. The girl's eyes grew wider—reality was starting to sink in.

Hosev ached to do something. But he couldn't! He had to stay alive for his family.

Screeches echoed closer, and the hair rose on Hosev's arms. The rising wind caught a wooden sign in front of the herbalist shop, and the sign slammed against the wall. The men turned toward the sound.

In that brief opening, the girl turned and sprinted down the road. Fool! Run inside!

Tinol's blonde head poked out the door. Finally! "What was that?" he asked.

The men took off after the girl, and Hosev's heart slammed into his ribs. Ignore them! But he couldn't. He jumped up and ran after the men.

Without a word, Tinol sprinted after him.

12

Elwyn's lungs were on fire. Her legs felt like they'd give out any second, but the catcalls and footsteps behind drove her on.

She pounded down the street. Between two buildings ahead, a narrow space appeared, and Elwyn ran for it. She skidded into the alley, then sprinted on. The footsteps behind her dulled.

A wall rose in front of her. To the right, there was a deep shadow. Another alley, she assumed, so she aimed for it. As she approached, the shadow enveloped her, and her eyes adjusted to the dim light just in time. A solid, stone wall rose above her. A building connected to the wall, ending the alley.

No.

She ran headlong for the wall and jumped. She clawed at stones that jutted from the masonry, but she slipped and tumbled back down to the ground.

She hurtled up a pile of garbage and reached up the wall again. She dug her fingers into the spaces between the stones, and the toe of her boot caught an edge.

She dragged herself up the wall a foot. She gripped the wall with her other boot and pulled herself up one more foot. Then her boot slipped, and she careened back down to the garbage pile.

A menacing chuckle echoed down the alley. Elwyn's neck prickled, and a shiver ran down her arms. Her brain screamed at her to run. She scratched desperately at the wall. There had to be a way out.

Soft footsteps approached, but Elwyn refused to turn around, clutching at the stone wall.

"Nice dress you got here," a deep voice crooned. "I know someone who'd like it." Cold metal touched Elwyn's leg.

A shiver crept up her body, and she spun around. The man held his sword out like a limb and lifted the hem of her dress. The gray head of a wolfskin was pulled down over his forehead like a hood. The skin's forelegs draped over his shoulders as though the wolf was part of him, and he had fangs tattooed around his eyes.

His two companions stood a few steps back, smirking at her. They had the same pattern of fangs around their eyes, but their gray wolfskins were slung across their shoulders like unsettling shawls. The men's bulky bodies blocked most of the alleyway.

She pulled her skirt away from his sword and backed away, edging higher up the garbage pile until she was flat against the wall. Her defense training flicked through her mind, but she'd never fought more than one person before.

The man with the wolf-head shroud grinned without mirth, showing blackened, broken teeth. Elwyn grimaced and squinted over his head into the darkness. There had to be some way to escape.

"Don't like what you see?" the man crooned, with a venomous edge to his voice. "Think you're too good for me, eh?"

Elwyn turned back to the man, and the look in his eyes stopped her short. His sleet-gray eyes, rimmed with fang tattoos, were murderous and hungry. Her mind went blank. Those eyes bored into her and ate away at her soul. She tore her eyes from his, but they were burned into her mind.

His two companions stepped closer, and Elwyn pressed her back into the cold, hard stone. The first man chuckled under his breath. Elwyn couldn't think. She spat at him.

"Ooh, she's got fire," the man on the right said.

The one with the sword clucked his tongue at her. "Ah ah, girlie. Don't wanna go gettin' yourself in trouble, now." He swished his sword in her face menacingly. The flash of metal made her flinch. He chuckled.

The man on the left took a step forward, and the other two shifted. Their joviality disappeared, replaced by anticipation. Elwyn peered from face to face, studying them. They stepped slowly toward her, climbing the garbage pile.

She darted to the right.

They boxed her in.

She spun to slip between them.

They closed the gap.

She stepped backward to the wall again and pressed her back into its unyielding surface. The stone snagged her dress. The man nodded, and his two companions darted at Elwyn.

She screamed and bolted. The back of her mind registered the sound of a rip, but all she thought of was escape.

They caught hold of her arms and held her there. Elwyn twisted and flailed, but they held her fast. Her sunburned wrists and hands stung in their grip.

She kicked at one of them, then he stamped hard on her foot and held it down. Pain shot through her instep and up her leg.

The second one held down her opposite foot, too. The third man moved toward her, and the hairs on her neck stood on end.

He towered over her. Filth coated his face, and his long, ratty hair and beard obstructed most of his features. The only distinguishable part of him was his sleet-gray eyes, rimmed with fangs, gleaming with brutality.

Elwyn's internal alarm shrieked in her chest. She instinctively tried to wrap her arms around herself, but the men held them tight. She yanked and twisted against the men's holds, her shoulders straining, but she made no difference.

The man approached until he was inches from her face. He reeked of sweat and alcohol, and his breath smelled like rotting meat. She gagged, and her gut tightened. She turned her face away as far as she could.

Hot breath grazed her neck, and a shudder ran down her spine.

She tugged harder on the men's grips, but they didn't budge. Her skin stung, but she pulled harder. Her joints creaked. She screamed and twisted, but it made no difference.

A cruel voice whispered in her ear. "You may be the prettiest one yet."

Fingers made contact with Elwyn's neck, and her whole body raged against the touch: her stomach heaved, and vomit rose into her throat. Her arms jerked in a protective reflex.

Hatred and disgust welled up inside her. It filled her heart and overwhelmed her mind. The world was a vile place. She hated everything in it.

A low, malicious chuckle shook Elwyn's soul, and she flailed. She had to get away.

But she couldn't escape. She couldn't move.

The man grabbed hold of her chin and pulled her face toward his, crooning at her.

Elwyn screamed and thrashed, drowning out the man's muttering. Her skin burned cold where he had touched her. It was tainted. She wanted to slice it off.

His other hand grabbed her cheek to hold her face hard, and

reality hit her full force: she couldn't stop him. There was nothing she could do.

Despair overwhelmed her. His hands clutched her face, forcing her to look at him, and her sense of self disintegrated. She could do nothing—she was nothing.

She yanked again at the men's grips, fruitlessly. She hated herself for being unable to move, unable to do anything to stop them. For being so weak. She hated her body for drawing his notice. She wanted to tear it off, to leave it behind. To float away, unencumbered by her contaminated body.

He was disgusting. She was disgusting, having been touched by him.

A sharp thud reverberated through the alley.

The man stepped back from her and turned slowly away. Something shiny stuck out of the back of his arm. He reached around to it and yanked out a small, bloody knife. His arm bled freely from the wound.

Two teenage boys stood about twenty paces away, staring at the men and Elwyn. The shorter, blonde one with wiry limbs held his arm out, following through from throwing the knife. His other hand held a short sword.

The taller boy with short, black hair had a hunting knife in one hand. He reached down and pulled a dagger from a sheath tied to his ankle.

The wolfskin-shrouded man with the bleeding wound smirked, and Elwyn's skin went cold. He took a step forward, and the blonde boy yelled out and ran toward him.

The two men holding Elwyn's arms let go to pull their weapons from their sheaths, and Elwyn collapsed onto the garbage heap.

The men sprinted forward, and Elwyn pushed herself to her feet, her heart pounding.

Metal flashed. Blade on blade clashed.

The five people twisted and swung and spun. One of the men charged, which opened a gap to the right, along the wall. Elwyn bolted for it.

Metal whooshed past her ear and she ducked, then a heavy, wooden knife-hilt clipped her in the shoulder. She stumbled, but her momentum kept her going, so she tumbled out of range before she fell to the ground.

She rolled over and jumped up, then she took off again, running with all her might.

"Oi!" the leading man's voice rang out. "Alfis, go get 'er!"

13

Elwyn spun around a corner. Her heartbeat pounded in her ears, and footsteps hammered behind her, echoing up the narrow street. The wind whipped her hair around her face and blew dust into her eyes. She rubbed her eyes while she ran.

Sleet-gray eyes and fang tattoos flashed through her mind. Her face burned where he'd touched her skin.

The wind rang with high-pitched screeches, which brought Elwyn's mind back to the present. She rounded another corner, and the street opened up to a view of the ravine, glowing with lucten light. High above, soaring between the mountaintops, huge, black shapes blocked the stars.

High-pitched, maniacal screeches echoed through the ravine, and a shiver ran down Elwyn's spine.

She sprinted down the street until she reached its end, where two more streets broke off it. She stopped mid-step and looked down each street. She didn't recognize either of them. She peered frantically down both options, gasping for breath.

Footsteps echoed up the street behind her, and those heart-stopping screeches flew down from above. A split-second impulse brought Elwyn running down the left-hand street. Her lungs ached.

She came up on another fork and impulsively picked the right-hand turn. Elwyn's ears rang with the screeches—they were getting closer fast. She tried to listen for footsteps, but she couldn't make anything out through the blood-curdling sounds above.

A screech immediately above reverberated through the narrow street. Elwyn instinctively backed flat against a building. A massive, black, winged shape swooped down from the sky. The man following her ran for cover, and the sight of him made Elwyn's insides twist.

The winged beast swooped toward him. Still in mid-air, it lifted him off his feet in its massive, bone-crushing beak. The man screamed.

The beast swooped back up into the sky with the man flailing in its beak. They disappeared into the darkness, but the man's horrified, pained screams echoed into the night.

Elwyn's insides burned, and her heart pounded. As though to urge her to move, more screeches echoed down from above. She looked up and down the street. She had no idea where she was. Fear rose in her throat and prickled down her arms. Her brain started to spin. Before it could overwhelm her, she took off running up the street.

Above the horrifying screeches, another sound pricked Elwyn's ears, coming from far up ahead. She instinctively ran toward it. As she got closer, Neilan's voice became distinguishable, screaming her name into the night. With renewed energy, she sped toward Neilan's voice.

She rounded one last corner and there he stood, glowing in firelight at the door of the inn. He spotted her, and his eyes went wide. He burst into movement, sprinting toward her, limping with each step on his wounded foot.

"No!" she yelled, barely able to squeeze enough air from her lungs to make a sound. She waved him back. He ignored her, of course, and kept limp-running straight toward her.

An eerie screech, too close, echoed around Elwyn. She looked up even though she knew what she'd see. A black, winged shape swooped down toward her from a side street. Neilan didn't see it. He only had eyes for Elwyn.

"Go back!" she screamed at him.

The beast swooped closer.

"Neilan, run!" she screamed with all her might.

He turned toward the winged beast, and his eyes went wide. He paused, glanced horrified from the beast to Elwyn and back, then started running toward her again. She yelled in frustration and pushed her already exhausted legs even harder. She had to get to him, that was the only way he'd go back.

She was steps from him, reaching out for him. He reached out too, and their hands clasped. He pulled her to him and reached toward the beast with his opposite arm. It was five paces from them, its person-sized beak gaping open.

Neilan swung his arm up, and a gust of wind launched the beast upward. It soared over them, twisting and screeching angrily.

Neilan squeezed Elwyn's hand and let out a breath, but the beast beat its wings against the wind and spun in the air. It swooped toward them again.

Elwyn took off toward the inn, dragging Neilan by the hand.

14

A man appeared in the inn's wide open door, silhouetted by the yellow firelight spilling onto the dirt road. Elwyn flew through the door, pulling Neilan in after her, and the man slammed the door behind them.

His terrified, sincere eyes caught Elwyn's. An image of sleet-gray, fang-rimmed eyes flashed across her mind, and her insides tightened. The man gave her a small, grim smile and moved into the room.

A fireplace roared at one end of it. Tables were scattered about, lit with candles. Most of the tables were full of people with goblets, and there was a counter at the far end. Elwyn scanned the faces: no wolfskin-shrouds or fang-tattoos met her eyes, though they kept flashing through her mind.

A small table sat empty in the corner. Elwyn wound her way to it, while Neilan followed close. She picked a chair facing the room, her back and side protected by walls like in the library at home. Home? She'd never thought of it that way before.

She sank into the wooden chair, and her legs melted with exhaustion. The man who'd let them in called out, "Lyra?"

A head popped up behind the counter. The woman, dark-haired, pale-skinned, and green eyed, looked delicate but strong, like a taut harp string. She grinned and poured out two steaming mugs. She brought them over and set them in front of Elwyn and Neilan. "Drink. You two look like you've had a rough day." Her melodious voice washed over Elwyn.

Elwyn took the mug mechanically. The smell of spices reached her from what felt like a long way away, and she took a drink. It was some sort of cider. Warmth flooded her stomach and her limbs.

The man who'd let them in came up behind Lyra and put an arm around her waist. Elwyn's skin crawled with the memory of the man's hands on her face.

The man smiled kindly, and the edges of his eyes crinkled. "Can we get you anything else?" he asked.

Screeches still rang outside, and Elwyn's mind flashed with the image of a dark, winged beast swooping toward her, beak open.

"What are those things?" Neilan asked.

"The malaps," the man said.

"The what?"

"Malaps—Torlum lies in their flight path. Every Twilitnight to Darknight they fly overhead. Anyone outside when they show up will likely be taken."

Elwyn asked, "What are they?"

His brows came together. "Haven't you heard of them? Most people don't live in their path, but I figured everyone knew of them. Where are you two from?"

Elwyn hesitated. "Far."

The man cocked his head to the side, studying her. She shrank down in her chair and avoided his eyes. Lyra answered, "They're sky-dwellers, whose only limbs are wings. They can't land. If they do, they can't get back up into the air and they starve.

"They follow an air current that flows through Lucaedter Scar and around the mountains to the north. The current brings the first of them here every Twilitnight, but most of them fly overhead through Darkday. They'll take anyone who ends up in their flight path. They prefer man-meat to livestock. They take the livestock too, but only if there are no people around."

Elwyn shuddered. She'd seen a few one-domain animals before, in the forest by the Haven. She'd been wary then, since one-domain animals were averse to humans. But those were land-only, so their malevolence toward humans was the mildest.

She'd never heard of a sky-only animal. The hostility must be strong between malaps and humans. Why would people live here? "Why doesn't everyone move to outside of the malaps' path?" she asked.

Lyra looked down, and the man smiled sadly. "It's not so simple." The tiny lines around his eyes deepened, and his eyes shadowed. Then with a forced smile, he asked, "Would you two like something to eat?"

"Of course they do, Reid. They're half-starved," Lyra said and sprang away. Reid gave them a quick nod, then he strolled to other tables.

Elwyn felt Neilan's eyes on her. She turned to him, and his face was taut with anger. She avoided his eyes and tried to make her voice light. "What?"

"What were you doing out there?" he asked with an edge to his voice. "I told you to wait on the bench for me."

Elwyn glared at the table.

Neilan went on accusingly, "I was only gone a couple minutes, then I came back and you'd disappeared."

"It's not like I wanted to go. Those men wouldn't leave me alone." Her heart thumped, and her eyes shot to Neilan's. She wished she could pull the words back into her mouth.

Neilan's eyes widened, and he sat up straighter. "What men?"

Elwyn glared at her lap. Wolfskins, blackened teeth, and fang tattoos crowded her mind. A hand on her face. Hot, rotten breath on her cheek. Her skin crawled.

She squeezed her eyes shut, and a gentle hand touched her shoulder. She winced, and her eyes flew open.

With eyebrows drawn together, Neilan was peering into her face. He looked like he was right on the line between concern and anger. "What happened?"

Elwyn looked down at her lap and laced her fingers together. "Some men came up to me when I was outside and said some things. So I ran away."

Neilan kept staring at her with his eyebrows drawn together. "Why didn't you call for me?"

"I didn't know where you were. It was so fast. I did what I thought I needed to do."

He scowled at the floor. "I—"

"It's done," she cut across him harshly. She couldn't keep talking about it. He had to stop. She glared at him. Neilan looked away, still scowling, then he took a sip from his mug.

Elwyn focused on the hard, warm mug in her hands and stared at the rest of the guests. She kept her thoughts only here, only now. The room hummed with quiet chatter. Everyone seemed comfortable, but there was no festivity or laughter.

Lyra hurried back to Elwyn's and Neilan's table, arms laden with dishes. She laid them on the table, each of them receiving two full plates and a bowl. "Eat up!" she commanded, bouncing on the balls of her feet.

"Thank you," Elwyn said quietly and ate a spoonful of stew. Her empty stomach groaned. The warm bowl, the meat and vegetables—

this was real, nothing else.

Neilan said, "Thanks," and scooped a huge spoonful. Lyra nodded and bustled away.

15

Hunger satisfied, Neilan scanned the room. The couple who owned the inn seemed kind—they'd even offered food and lodging for the night with his promise of working tomorrow, rather than making him work first. But that made him nervous. These people definitely had a secret.

He couldn't let anything hurt Elwyn. He wouldn't let her out of his sight, not again. He'd only been away from her for a couple minutes, and—what had happened out there? He watched Elwyn out of the corner of his eye. She was always reserved, but he'd never seen her shut down like this. Her eyes were vacant, and she ate mechanically.

Reid moved across the room and seated himself at a large, stringed instrument, then Lyra came and stood next to him. As soon as she reached him, the room hushed, and all heads turned toward them.

Reid slowly drew a bow across the instrument. The sound rose and became rich. He fell into a tune, using the bow as well as plucking the strings with his fingers. A sweet, higher sound mingled with the instrument's deep tones—Lyra had begun to sing. She'd started in slowly, as the instrument had, and built until the two were equally powerful.

Warmth spread through Neilan's insides, and there was a pressure in his chest as though his heart was reaching toward the sound. He felt light. His worries faded, and his burdens lifted. A few, blissful minutes passed. His heart threatened to reach out from his chest, but it was strangely pleasant. He relaxed for the first time in days.

As Neilan's spirit floated within him, a deeper, fuller sound joined the other two. Reid was singing now, too. While Lyra's voice had made Neilan feel light and carefree, Reid's voice contained the sorrows of the world.

Neilan's heart constricted with memories: Papa's booming laugh, Mama's warm arms around him. Climbing trees with his cousin, her mischievous eyes sparkling. The day *they* came. The overwhelming fear and anger, the helplessness. Elwyn, eyes flashing with a smirk on her lips. His heart reaching out to her. His frustration with her, and his fear of losing her. His fear *of* her and her power over him.

The pain that Neilan kept in a deep, secret place all welled to the surface at once, but somehow it didn't overwhelm him. Reid's voice took Neilan's heartache and softened it. The pain didn't disappear, but it became lighter, even sweet.

Lyra's voice rose again to meet her husband's, which she'd lowered as her husband took over. Now, the two joined sorrow and joy into one confusing, beautiful reality.

Neilan's heart broke open inside him, reliving a lifetime of pain and insecurity. The feelings he'd kept buried for years were confronted and somehow soothed. He forgot the world around him, forgot even the music itself, experiencing only the emotions it drew out.

Slowly, he came back. The music quieted then disappeared, and the room was left in heavy, contented silence. His cheeks were wet—he was crying. Not just crying, weeping. He hastily wiped his eyes, nose, cheeks, and chin, and glanced around.

Elwyn was staring at her lap, tears streaming freely down her face. Her cheeks were splotchy, and her eyes were puffy and red. Neilan's eyes welled up again. He wanted to reach for her, but she seemed so far away. He wiped his eyes and looked around the room.

Two teenage boys and a man stood just inside the doorway. The boys looked dazed, like Neilan was, but the man eyed the couple suspiciously. Throughout the room, faces were solemn but contented, eyes swollen and red.

What had happened? How had two people broken the entire room?

No one else seemed surprised. Neilan eyed Lyra, who'd returned to the counter and was refilling drinks. Reid had sat down at a table with guests and was engaged in conversation. Were they trying to sell more food and drinks? Or was it something else? He needed to investigate, to protect Elwyn from whatever this was.

He glanced at Elwyn. Her tears had stopped as she turned inward again. He whispered to her, "Be back in a minute."

She tightened her lips and sat more stiffly.

Neilan pushed his chair back and stood up. Pain shot through his foot, and his leg gave out under him. He fell back into the chair and inspected his foot. He'd almost forgotten about it—he'd gotten so used to the pain, but now it smacked him hard. His toe ached and burned. An impulse in the back of his mind told him to cut it off. He looked closer. Swelling bulged through the makeshift bandaging.

Lyra cried out and hustled over. "What happened to you?"

"I cut my foot," he said blankly.

Elwyn's eyes went wide, and some presence bled into the vacancy behind them. "When did it get like that?"

"I dunno." Heat rose into his cheeks. "It's not that bad."

"Not that bad!" Lyra said, exasperated. "It needs treated at once! I'll be right back." She hurried away to the back of the room. Neilan sat staring at his foot for a moment, not really seeing anything. His neck and ears were hot.

"Why didn't you tell me it was so bad?" Elwyn said accusingly.

Neilan shrugged. "There was nothing we could do."

Elwyn straightened. She must've known he was right. Her eyes softened, and she said quietly, "I just don't want you to be hurt."

His chest warmed, and a smirk pulled at the corner of his lips. "Me neither."

She stared at him, with that vagueness still lingering behind her eyes. "Do you think you'll be okay?"

"Hope so," he said, turning back to his foot.

Lyra appeared again with a large bag slung over her shoulder. "Scoot your chair back." She knelt in front of him and said, "Put your foot up on my knee."

He did as she said and watched. She gently unraveled the ratty, makeshift bandaging and the shreds of bark that were still tied up inside it. It was crusted with dried blood. Neilan didn't really want to look, but curiosity locked his eyes on his injury. The bandaging stuck to the wound, which felt like it was being stabbed.

She poured some water on the bandaging and let it soak for a moment, then she yanked it off. Pain shot through Neilan's foot and up his leg. "Ow!" he yelled and pulled back his foot.

"I know," she said. "I had to."

Neilan glared at her but eased his throbbing foot back onto her knee. His newly exposed wound stung as it met fresh air. The gash in his toe lay wide open, and his stomach heaved. He covered his mouth to hold down his rising dinner. The cut seemed even larger than at first. It was puffy and ringed with purple, and the flesh within looked wrong, mutilated. On the other side of Lyra, Elwyn's eyes were wide. She sat stiff and still, staring at his toe.

Lyra put an empty bowl under it, and she poured thick, warm liquid over the wound. "Hold it up right here."

While he held up his foot to drip into the bowl, she poured steaming water into a larger bowl then crushed herbs between her palms. There was a light, melodic sound—she was humming. It seemed out of place compared with her intensity a second before. She sprinkled the herbs into the bowl of hot water and grabbed a handful of a different kind of herb.

Neilan watched transfixed as her expert hands worked on the concoction while her mind seemed occupied with the song in her head. A small smile even played on her lips. Hopefully she wasn't too distracted to do it right.

She pushed the bowl toward him. "Soak it in here."

He thought the hot concoction would sting, but it was pleasant. A gentle sensation flowed through the wound and up to his ankle. He imagined the medicine soaking into his skin like a sponge. Lyra laid out a few layers of white cloth and began to hum again, a different tune this time. She spread salve on the cloth, then she crushed herbs into a second salve and spread it over the first one. Her movements flowed in rhythm with her song.

Once she'd filled the cloth with salve, she set it aside and turned her attention back to the bowl Neilan's foot was in. Her tune switched back to the one from before, but it was richer this time and more urgent. There was a change in the water that matched her tune: the sensation flowing through his foot quickened and intensified. It was as though her song had a direct effect on the healing power of the herbs.

Neilan stiffened. Her song *did* affect the herbs. She must have the Gift of Music. Music could influence plant and animal behavior, as well as human emotion, and she was using it on him.

Sure, she was using it to help him, for now. But when she—and her husband, did he have Music too?—had sung and played, it had broken him open to the most raw place inside him. A shiver ran down his spine. He'd always thought Magic was the most powerful Gift, but this—this was world shattering.

And this couple was using their Gift on unsuspecting listeners. The people here had expected the effect, but did they know such power was being used on them? Would they've been okay with it if they did?

Neilan had always been told that the Heirs on the surface didn't know who they were, but this couple used their Gift intentionally. Did they know what it was?

How had two Heirs of Music ended up married? Elwyn had been in trouble since conception because her parents were both Heirs of the Eudaimonians. Reid's eyes, when Elwyn had asked why they stayed here, came back to him. Maybe the malaps were enough to keep them hidden.

Lyra lifted Neilan's foot out of the water and dried it off, careful not to touch the wound itself. The swelling and pain had receded some, and relief washed over him. She wrapped his foot in the bandages she'd prepared, taking care to coat his split open skin with the salve.

After she'd finished tying the bandages, and had made sure every bit of skin was thoroughly covered, she looked back at the blood-soaked shreds of cloth and tree bark he'd been wearing. "Why was this tied around your foot?"

"To stop the bleeding," Elwyn said, a little defensively.

Lyra blinked. "Of course. I meant, where's your other shoe?"

Neilan shrugged. "I lost it. A while ago."

"Ah, hence the wounded foot." She considered for a moment, then spoke as though to herself. "His feet are larger, but with the bandaging, it should fit." She looked up at Neilan again. "I'll be right back," then she disappeared through a door at the back of the room. In a few minutes she was back, carrying a pair of boots and a mug. She handed the mug to Elwyn. "Drink."

Elwyn stared blankly at her. Pointing to Elwyn's hands and cheeks, Lyra said, "It'll help the sunburn."

Elwyn bowed her head and obeyed. While she drank, Lyra bent down and held the boots up to Neilan's feet. "We'll stuff them with cloth and bandages, so they should fit."

Neilan nodded, hoping she wouldn't try to put them on just yet. The thought of anything pressing against his toe right now made his insides squirm. She put them down next to him and turned to leave. She headed for the counter, saying over her shoulder, "Elevate that foot."

Elwyn scooted her chair closer to Neilan and said, "Here." She lifted his leg to rest on her lap. "You okay?"

"Yeah. It's starting to feel better already." He scanned her face. The sunburn was already fading, leaving behind dry, peeling skin as though the burn was a week old. He leaned closer to her and lowered his voice. "They're Heirs of Music."

Elwyn's mouth opened in an "oh," then she nodded. "Makes sense."

Neilan whispered, "Don't say anything. I think it's dangerous for them."

"I'd imagine so," Elwyn whispered back. "Two Heirs of Music, married? How'd they slip through Solun's grasp?" She paused, and the vague look in her eyes became sharp. "Can we hide here, too?"

Neilan's heart gave a jolt. Could they? These people were using their Gift on purpose, a sure way to attract Solun's attention. But here they were, and here he wasn't.

Elwyn stared wide-eyed at Neilan, but it was clear she wasn't seeing him. He could almost see the thoughts spinning behind her eyes.

16

The shrieks outside reached Elwyn as though through a haze. Her mind was spinning, but slowly, as though she was trying to dance in mud. She was almost excited—Lyra and Reid were safe here, enough to use their Gift unchecked. This could be the place. Her parents were still out there, but what if she could make it without them? They obviously didn't need her, maybe she didn't need them.

Her mind flashed with fang tattoos around sleet-gray eyes, a malicious smile of blackened teeth. Her cheek burned with the memory of the touch, making her stomach turn. A soft hum floated to Elwyn from across the room. Her mind eased and the tightness in her chest relaxed. She searched for the source.

Lyra stood at the counter, apparently humming to herself, but every few seconds she glanced up and scanned the room, monitoring her guests. She caught Elwyn watching her and smiled, continuing to hum.

Elwyn took in a deep breath, what felt like the first real breath she'd had since… Since…

Here and now. Focus on here and now. She studied the room, and two faces stood out: the boys who'd helped her in the alley sat at a table with a man who looked like the blonde boy. In her mind, the dark alley surrounded her again. Her breath caught. She'd been helpless, entirely helpless.

Her eyes and fists burned. She wanted to scream, to rage, to punch something. To prove to herself that she wasn't weak and worthless. That she didn't need anyone's help.

But she had needed help. She forced herself to face that fact. She wanted to yell, to deny, to claw at the faces swimming in her memory, but the constant humming floated through her mind and body, pacifying the rage and easing the humiliation. She took another deep breath.

The boys caught her eye. She had to do something, to talk to them, before she began to hate them for existing in the place in her mind she wanted to burn down. She lifted Neilan's foot from her lap and stood, setting his leg back on her chair. He raised his eyebrows at her.

She waved off questions. "Just a minute."

His eyebrows contracted, but he didn't try to stop her. She slipped between the tables and crossed the room, presenting herself at the boys' table. They looked up at her, but the man with them ignored her. He watched Reid and Lyra intently, almost hungrily, as they bustled around the room, and he took notes in a small journal.

Elwyn met the boys' eyes and said, "Thank you."

The taller boy with straight, black hair nodded. The blonde one grinned and gave her a deep bow. "At your service mi'lady."

She inwardly rolled her eyes. They looked at her expectantly, and she stared back, shifting her weight. "I'm Elwyn," she said to break the silence.

The boy with black hair raised a hand and said, "I'm Hosev. And he's Tinol."

Tinol swept his arm out for an embellished bow, and there was a flash of shining red. Elwyn started. A long gash ran across the inside of his upper arm. "You're hurt!" Once again, she'd hurt someone. She'd been a force of destruction.

"A minor wound, I assure you," Tinol said in his mock-courtly tone.

She swept her eyes over Hosev. A deep red welt ran across his cheek, and the arm of his tunic was torn, revealing a laceration on his forearm and dark bruise spreading around it. "You both need medical attention."

She turned to get Lyra, but halted. Tinol's father was still watching Lyra and Reid, taking notes. Elwyn glanced again over the boys' injuries. They needed help to keep from catching an infection. She had to do something. She couldn't let her impact on them be worse than it already was.

Elwyn scanned the room for Lyra, who was at the counter refilling mugs, and she caught her eye. Lyra nodded and wound her way toward Elwyn, dropping off mugs at tables along the way. "What can I do for you?" she asked.

"These two are injured. They…" She glanced back at Hosev.

He sat up straighter and cut in, "We had a mishap trying to get inside when the malaps showed up."

Lyra's eyes narrowed, but she nodded and hustled away. Elwyn's mind flashed, and her heartbeat quickened. She touched the hard, deeply-grained wood of the table. She traced the pattern of the rings, smooth and irregular, like the roots in the Haven. She was here now. Nothing existed except now. She took a deep, slow breath.

The boys were staring at her inquisitively, but she avoided their eyes. Only here, only now.

Lyra returned with her medical kit, and Elwyn let out her breath. She stepped back and dropped into a chair to give Lyra room. Lyra hummed as her practiced hands made quick work of Tinol's cut, then Hosev's laceration. Tinol's father watched her every move closely, but she appeared unconcerned. She gave each of the boys a mix of herbs steeped in hot water to drink.

In the corner of Elwyn's eye, the door to the outside opened. Two men, one with a wolfskin wrapped around his shoulders and the other with a wolfskin over his head like a hood lumbered in. Elwyn's heart lurched, and her throat tightened.

"That's them!" Tinol whispered to his father.

The men dripped blood and put pressure on various wounds.

"Oh my!" Lyra burst out.

Tinol's father stood and approached the men. He pulled a thin scroll from inside his cloak and deftly flicked it open. "As the Crown's Inspector, I place you under arrest for—"

Lyra jumped between him and the men. "Every person who enters my establishment is under my protection." She turned to the men. "You are welcome here."

Elwyn's insides burned.

The Inspector glared at Lyra haughtily. He pulled out his journal and made another note, then looked at her with a raised eyebrow. "You have no authority here. But I'll give you a chance to reconsider this fruitless attempt to interfere. I assure you, you will not wish to harbor these men when you hear the charge against them."

The room hushed, and all eyes turned toward them. Elwyn's arms and neck prickled. She felt like sprinting out into the night to face the malaps rather than stay there, but she couldn't move, as though she'd grown roots.

Glaring at the Inspector, Lyra pointed to an empty table and said loudly, "Sit there and I'll bind up your wounds."

Elwyn's heart pounded. The one whose wolfskin was draped over his shoulders caught sight of her and nudged his companion. He eyed her with a malicious smirk. His companion, with the sleet-gray eyes, made a noise deep in his throat almost like a growl. Her mind flashed: a dark alley, rotten breath on her cheek.

The Inspector stepped in front of the men again. "You are arrested for the attempt of forced, unsanctioned union," he paused and looked haughtily at Lyra.

Lyra froze, her eyes widening.

He continued, "With this girl," and he pointed at Elwyn. Elwyn's insides clenched.

Lyra started and stared at Elwyn. A yell and a crash resounded across the room—Neilan had burst out of his chair onto his injured foot and fell.

The Inspector, glorying in his triumph, gestured to his son and Hosev, saying, "As accused by these young men."

Elwyn trembled and the room spun. She squeezed her eyes shut and reached into her pocket, expecting to find the smooth, wooden head of her sancan, but her pocket was empty. Her heart dropped. No. She reached further. The whole bottom of her pocket was torn open. The sound of fabric ripping in a dark alley played in her mind as though from a distance.

The wave she'd been holding back crashed over her. Tears rushed into her eyes, and she dropped her head into her hands and shook with sobs.

The haughty voice of the Inspector said, with an air of gesturing toward Elwyn's sobbing form, "Any more objections, hostess?"

The room was silent.

Footsteps approached where the men stood. A shuffling noise came from the men, and the Inspector's voice said, "I wouldn't try that." There was a sharp clamp, and a gruff cry of pain. "We'll head for the southeast watchtower. I suggest you cooperate, or I'll leave you outside with the malaps." Heavy footsteps moved toward the door.

From the door, the Inspector's voice rang out, "The Crown will be interested in your method of entertaining your guests." He paused, and his voice lowered. "You'll regret standing in my way."

Screeches pierced the room, louder now through the open door. In the midst of her sobs, Elwyn automatically looked toward the sound. The Inspector, with a metal device wrapped around the wolfskin-shrouded men's wrists, arms, and chests, pulled out his sword. Holding it up toward the malaps, he stepped out the door and pulled the men out after him.

Elwyn dropped her face back into her hands, her whole body shaking. A low, deep humming moved toward her, and strong arms lifted her to her feet. The arms and voice led her across the room, through a door, and down a hallway.

Neilan's voice called after her, and Lyra's spoke softly to him.

The arms holding Elwyn up led her through another door and set her on the edge of a bed. Neilan came in and sat next to her, putting an arm around her. Reid left the room and shut the door, taking his Music with him.

As soon as his voice was gone, Elwyn's pain crashed over her. In the darkness, her mind replayed the night, again and again. Her chest tightened, and her insides clenched. Her lungs seized up, making it hard to breathe. She hugged her knees to her chest, shaking.

Neilan kept his arm around her. His presence was a streak of warmth in the dark coldness that threatened to swallow her up, while her traitorous mind forced her to see it all. To feel it. Over and over. And over.

17

Early in the morning, Elwyn sagged in a chair in the inn's kitchen, waiting for her job assignment for the day. Screeches rang through the walls from the malaps outside, and she stared through the small, kitchen window. Nothing was distinguishable in Darkday's near-blackness, but she imagined the faint stars blocked by dark, winged shapes.

Neilan stared at her with wide, searching eyes, but she kept hers turned away from him. She couldn't think about him—she could barely stay upright. He'd stayed with her the night before until she'd fallen asleep. But her sleep, if it could be called that, was full of terror. The wakeful darkness had been saturated with memory. When she slept, wolfskin-shrouds and massive, winged monsters plagued her. She'd wake up afraid to fall back to sleep, but terrified of being awake. Both were nightmares.

Across the kitchen, Lyra spoke with the cook, a solid, good-natured looking woman. Reid walked in from the dining room and approached Elwyn and Neilan. "To cover your expenses from last night through tomorrow morning, it'll be a long day. Are you prepared?"

Elwyn nodded, staring at the floor. Reid pointed to a tub full of water and said to Neilan, "As you shouldn't be on your feet today, you'll be in charge of washing."

Neilan nodded assent.

Reid turned to Elwyn. "And you'll bring the dishes out to patrons, clear them away afterward, and handle any coming-and-going Lyra needs done in between."

Elwyn nodded, but Neilan burst out, "I'll do the work for both of us." His voice grew tense. "She needs to rest."

"Working will be good for her," Reid said calmly.

"Then can't she do something in here?" Neilan's tone had a tinge of panic.

Reid smiled, but said firmly, "We'll look after her."

Elwyn glared at the floor. She resented being talked about as though she wasn't there, but she couldn't bring herself to care enough to interject.

Lyra said across the room, "Focus on what you can do right now, and let us do what we can."

Feeling smothered, Elwyn mustered the energy to stand and said, "Is anything ready to go out?"

The cook pointed to a few plates piled high with breakfast fixings. "These are for the long table in the back." Elwyn picked them up and hustled out of the stifling room.

Entering the dining room, her mind flooded with memory and her breath caught. Focus. She held her breath and hurried to the long table. She set down the plates and half-ran to the counter across the room. She ducked out of sight behind it and knelt, wrapping her arms around herself and closing her eyes while her memory spun.

Gentle humming floated to her ears, and her lungs opened. She took in a long, shaking breath as Lyra rounded the counter and sat down next to her on the floor. Elwyn tried to get up, but Lyra put a hand on her shoulder and said gently, "Tell me what happened."

Elwyn stammered, "No, I'm okay, I'm sorry, I'll get back to work."

Lyra shook her head and said again, "Tell me what happened."

Elwyn stared into nothingness. Fine, she'd get it over with. She closed her eyes and gave Lyra a quick summary—the most she could face remembering. Lyra listened, then sat silent for a long time.

After a while, Elwyn felt the impulse to move. She stood up, and Lyra stood too. Lyra squeezed her shoulder, then handed her a few plates that had been sitting on the counter. "These are for that table by the door."

As Elwyn wound toward it, Hosev's and Tinol's faces appeared at the table next to her goal. Tinol called out cheerily, "Morning!"

She tried to smile, and Tinol glanced at the plates in her hands. "What're you doing?"

She dropped off the plates at the next table and said, "Working off my debt."

Tinol raised his eyebrows. "We did something for you, too." He scanned her body with his eyes, and his voice took on a sinister tinge. "What are you gonna do for us?"

Elwyn's insides clenched, and her neck prickled. Hosev glanced at her horrified face and smacked Tinol. "Stop it, man."

"What?" Tinol protested. "She's paying them back. Why not us?"

"I don't have money," Elwyn said in a small voice, hoping she misunderstood his meaning the first time.

"I know," Tinol said ominously. Elwyn's mind flashed with the hand gripping her face, the hot breath on her cheek. She started shaking.

"Elwyn," Reid's voice called. "There's another load for you."

She turned to him, barely seeing her surroundings. The dark alley insisted on taking form instead, as she hurried toward Reid's voice.

"Hey! What about us?" Tinol's voice called after her.

"Stop it!" Hosev whisper-yelled at him. "That's enough."

"Mind your own business," Tinol said harshly, and his chair legs scraped the floor as he stood.

Reid's strong, sorrowful voice burst into song, different than the one last night. The sound of this one had an edge to it, a hardness, almost an accusation.

Elwyn reached him, and the dark alleyway melted back into the inn's dining room. In the corner of her eye, Tinol slumped back into his chair and dropped his face into his hands. Reid's song faded to a hum, with a gentler tone now. Elwyn's constricted insides relaxed.

She reached for the plates piled on the counter, but Reid put out a hand and said, "Leave those." He gestured to the back of the counter, so she followed him, apprehensive.

"What happened last night?" he asked.

The scene flashed before her, and she started trembling again. She wrapped her arms around herself and said, "Lyra knows. You can ask her."

"I'd rather hear from you."

She squeezed her middle. "Please don't make me."

He nodded patiently. "I won't." He began humming again, a gentle, understanding tune, as though it felt her pain.

She let it wash over her. The tune wasn't insistent, but it made her feel more capable. The scene in the alley flashed through her mind again, less overwhelming this time. Half-consciously, half-instinctively, she launched into her story.

She shared more detail than she'd given Lyra. Not on purpose—she remembered more now. Then her mind inexplicably focused on something she hadn't been aware of at the time: the feel of a rock jutting into her back while the men held her against the wall. Her mind replayed that detail over and over again. Then it began to fade.

The tightness in her chest relaxed, and her breathing steadied. Her real surroundings took form again, and she remembered where she was. She looked around, surprised, and met Reid's eyes. He was looking at her, but his look felt passive. Not aggressive or needy, just patient.

Self-conscious, Elwyn reached for the plates on the counter. "Where do I take these?"

Reid pointed at a table in the far corner, where four men leaned close to one another, speaking quietly. Something about them gave her a chill, but she picked up the plates and headed to them.

"A day to Regsenfrag," one of them, a man with ice-blue eyes and sandy-blonde hair, was whispering. Curiosity piqued, Elwyn strained her ears.

The man went on, "We'll meet with Nineveh and make our contract on Brightday. Nineveh's an old friend—he'll pay well. And we'll move in at first dark on Twilitnight. The Sovereign wants her transferred 'unobserved.'" The man unrolled a small parchment.

The rest of the men leaned in closer. Under the pretext of putting plates on the table, Elwyn glanced at the parchment. It was a sketch of a face, a woman with dark hair, around forty years old. It was strangely familiar.

She finished setting the plates on the table and turned away. The face on the parchment filling her mind's eye. In her peripherals, the man who'd spoken glanced at her suspiciously. Before he could say anything, Elwyn grabbed an empty plate from the next table and hurried to the kitchen.

Her mind spun. That face—it was her own face. Except not. Older, with dark hair. But so much like her own reflection she couldn't get it out of her mind. It must be—

She burst through the door to the kitchen and half-threw the plate into Neilan's washtub. "They're here!" she whispered at him, panic rising in her voice. "They're going to Regsenfrag! They're looking for me—I mean for her!"

Neilan stared up at her with wide eyes, obviously not understanding a word she said. She tried to grab hold of her thoughts, to settle her mind enough to make sense. "Solun's men are here," she said urgently.

Neilan started. "Wh—how do you know?"

"I heard them talking. They're—they're going to take my mother!" she said, her voice growing shrill.

Neilan dropped the plate he was washing and stared at her in blank shock. "What do you mean?"

Elwyn shook herself and related what she'd seen and heard. Neilan's shock hardened, and he set his jaw. In a low, grave voice, he said, "What can we do?"

His seriousness quieted her panic. She took a breath and considered. Was it worth it? Maybe she could disappear here, make a life for herself without worrying about anyone else. Her mother would be watched by Solun's servants—if she went to her parents and helped her mother, she'd put herself in Solun's way. Even if she managed to get them away to safety, all chance of disappearing into the shadows and living free of Solun's eyes would be gone.

She didn't have to help. She could flee, be free the way she wanted to be.

But her chest constricted. Deep inside, she felt that the time for that kind of thought was over. She couldn't let her mother be imprisoned by Solun, not if she could help. She'd never forgive herself otherwise. She let out her breath and said resolutely, "We'll have to get to her first."

Neilan looked down at his bandaged foot and nodded slowly. She tensed—his injury would slow them down. His eyes met hers, apprehension and guilt rolling off him. He *would* slow them down, but she couldn't let him feel bad about it. She put a hand on his arm and said, "We can't leave till Dawnday tomorrow anyway, but neither can they. There's still some time to heal. Maybe Lyra can speed up the process."

He gave a half-hearted smile and looked down at his foot again. Elwyn's mind spun. Her mother—she had to get to her. But she had to wait, too. She itched to get moving.

Her mind flashed with fang-rimmed eyes, and a dark alleyway. No. She shoved it down. She filled her mind with her mother's danger. She had to help, that's what she wanted to think about.

She focused on the new knowledge: her mother needed her. She made it fill her mind, pushing down the rest of her thoughts—the ones she couldn't face.

Muffled screeches from the malaps rang through the room. They'd been so constant that she'd nearly gotten used to them, but when the sound broke through her consciousness, she shivered. A winged mass of darkness flashed across her mind.

No. Her mother needed her. She held onto the thought. She couldn't just sit here, waiting and thinking. She had to do something.

"These plates are ready," the cook said across the room. "Take them in and Lyra will let you know which table they go to."

Elwyn picked up the plates and headed into the dining room. The task to focus on helped divert her spinning thoughts.

18

On Dawnday morning, before first light, Elwyn sat with Neilan in the dining room of the inn. It bustled with people, all ready to get moving as soon as the sun rose after the long darkness and rest. Screeches had continued through the night, and they still rang through the walls every once in a while as the last malaps flew overhead. Lyra had said that they'd be gone by first light, they always were.

Lyra re-bandanged Neilan's foot carefully after working on it again with her herb concoction and Music. Elwyn had watched her work, feeling the Music even though it wasn't being used directly on her.

The nightmares had come again last night. Monsters in the sky and on the ground, chasing her in the dark. But through each nightmare, a strain of Music played, giving her a thread of courage and peace in the midst of the terror.

Lyra slid Neilan's foot into a boot that would've been too large for him normally, but the bandages made it snug. She tied it up firmly, making sure his injured foot wouldn't slide around inside it. She held up the opposite boot and said, "I'm going to bandage your uninjured foot too, to fit in this one, so your stride will be even. This isn't ideal, but having one shoe so much bigger than the other will alter your stride, which could cause more problems in your knees and hips." She paused and looked at him firmly. "This is a temporary solution. As soon as your injury is well enough to remove the bandaging, you'll need properly fitting boots."

He nodded. She wrapped his uninjured foot and stuffed the toe, then she fit his foot into the boot and laced it tightly. "How do they feel?"

He shrugged. "Fine."

She had him get up and walk a few paces. His boots flopped, and his normally smooth walk was awkward, but his gait was even at least. Lyra nodded in relative satisfaction and cleaned up the bandages and herbs. She hustled away to meet the many guests' last needs before leaving.

Elwyn finished the toast, eggs, and soup she'd been eating. She wrapped up the bread and hard cheese Lyra had given them for later and put them in her pocket. She'd sewn up the hole the night before, but even full of food, her pocket felt empty. She couldn't accept that her sancan was gone.

Neilan leaned over his bowl of soup, scarfing it down. He scraped the bowl with his toast, soaking up the last bits. Elwyn's insides warmed. Somehow, the familiarity of watching Neilan's voracious eating made her feel at home.

It hit Elwyn that she hadn't heard a screech for a few minutes. Instinctively, she looked toward the door, just as Reid opened it. The faintest, pre-dawn light shone through the open door, and Elwyn let out a long sigh while a joyful tremor ran through the room. The light felt like a restoration, a revival of what was good and life-giving.

The guests burst into movement, packing up their belongings and hurriedly finishing their meals. They flooded toward the door, while the pre-dawn light grew. Elwyn and Neilan stood, too, but Reid motioned for them to wait. Neilan shrugged at Elwyn, and they sat back down.

In the throng heading for the door stood the men, Solun's servants, who were going to catch her mother. Elwyn's neck and shoulders tensed. She couldn't wait here, she had to get moving. Her eyes darted from Solun's servants to Reid, and back. How long did he want them to wait? And why? Had they not earned enough yesterday to cover their expenses?

Reid beckoned to them. They grabbed their last bits of food and hustled to meet him at the door.

"I'm going to accompany you," he said, "at least to the border of Torlum. The Lupos gang will be seeking revenge for the arrest of their comrades, but they know better than to attack the Crown's Inspector. It's likely that they will lay in wait for you, an easier target."

Elwyn's stomach clenched. Her mind flashed with wolfskins and fang tattoos. How many of them were there? Reid was only one man, what could he do? She couldn't let them kill him for her sake. "Won't that just put you in danger, too?"

"I have what I need to deter them," Reid said. "They won't hurt us." He pulled out a small flute and held it up. Neilan frowned, and Elwyn couldn't blame him. A flute?

Lyra jogged over from across the room, calling out, "Get moving! You're losing daylight." She herded Elwyn, Neilan, and Reid toward the door. Before she could push him out the door, Reid wrapped his arms around Lyra's middle and pulled her into a kiss. When he pulled away, she wobbled a little and said with a grin, "Out of here."

Elwyn's heart swelled, absorbing some part of the love they shared. She and Neilan stepped out into the cool morning, the dawn sky icy blue with a band of gold glowing just above the rooftops.

The lucten accents on the building fronts reflected the morning light like glass. They no longer glowed, since they gave up the light they'd absorbed last Twilitday over the course of Darkday. They'd absorb more light today and reflect it back into the night once the sun set.

The narrow road was packed with people and horse carts, bustling in every direction. Elwyn barely believed it was the same place she'd walked into two nights ago, when it had seemed abandoned. Her mind flashed with a dark alley and winged shapes, and her breathing sped up.

It was memory, she wasn't there anymore. Focus on here and now —she was safe. The words felt hollow, but the memory didn't overwhelm her this time.

Reid wound his way through the crowded roads in a steady incline, up the hill that Torlum sat upon. Elwyn followed a step behind him, and Neilan limped after her. As they crested the hill, at the highest point in Torlum, Reid pointed southeast. "Look out over here."

Elwyn followed his finger, and the countryside opened up before her. Farms and pastureland southeast of Torlum sloped down to the edge of a lush forest. Lucaedter flowed toward her from its source, the Amplum lucten-river that flowed south from Nasclum. Just northeast of Torlum, the Amplum branched into two: the strong, surging lucten-river Lucaedter flowed southwestward around Torlum and through Lucaedter Scar, and a thin lucten-creek, the Filuc, flowed south along the inland edge of the Tensmon mountains.

From the maps she'd pored over, Elwyn knew that Filuc flowed right past Regsenfrag, just a day and a half's journey away. Her breath caught—she was a day and a half from her parents' town. Would that be fast enough?

A tune burst into existence right next to her. Elwyn's chest constricted and her heart pounded as dread descended on her. Adrenaline coursed through her body, intensifying and sharpening her vision. Sweat beaded on her upper lip and ran down her back. Her breathing quickened, nearly hyperventilating. Instinctively, she dropped into a crouch and covered her head.

In the corner of her eye, Reid was standing tall and firm, blowing hard into the flute. He glared across the narrow road at a group of men wearing wolfskin shrouds, cowering and covering their ears.

Elwyn's own ears ached. Her senses were so heightened that even the early dawn light was piercing. She panted for breath. She couldn't handle it. All her instincts told her to bolt, but she didn't know where to go. Her ears rang. She covered them with her palms, pressing as hard as she could, but her head pounded with every note.

The wolfskin shrouds in her peripheral vision fled. They stumbled down the next road and disappeared into the crowd. Instantly, the tune stopped.

Elwyn's breath and heartbeat slowed. Her senses sunk back from heightened awareness, and her body temperature returned to normal, but her ears still rang in the comparative silence.

She tentatively dropped her hands and stood back up. A hand gently touched her shoulder. Her heart thumped and adrenaline bounded through her again as she spun around, but it was Neilan, his eyes wide and face tense.

She followed his gaze to Reid, who was standing erect, holding the silent flute to his lips, ready to blow into again should he need to. Power radiated from him, almost as visible as light, dimming the surrounding street in comparison.

The pressure of Neilan's hand on her shoulder increased. She didn't have to look at him to know that he was scared. And when he was scared, he was even more protective of her than usual.

"What was that?" he asked tremulously.

Reid didn't move. He stood staring at the spot where the Lupos gang had disappeared. Then he blinked and turned to Neilan. The power that radiated from him dimmed, and his shoulders sagged. "This flute," he said wearily, "when used by one with a certain ability, emanates the impression of power and fills its hearers with fear."

Well, yeah. That's exactly what it had done. But the simple words didn't match the horror Elwyn had just experienced.

Reid continued, "The Lupos gang does not have the courage to fight in the midst of such fear." A shiver ran down Elwyn's spine, but her fear ebbed. Those men weren't all-powerful.

Keeping a hand on her shoulder, Neilan squinted up and down the street. "I think they're gone," he said, but his voice didn't sound convinced. "Won't they come back?"

"Lupos territory extends through the western half of Torlum, and it ends at the next road," Reid said, looking back to where the wolfskin shrouds had disappeared. "The Poli gang will retaliate if they act past Midifrag Road. They won't risk a war over you."

Some of Elwyn's tension released.

"Let's get moving," Reid said, and he took off up the road at a quick pace.

Neilan caught her hand, and they hustled after him. As they got closer to Reid, Neilan shivered. Elwyn whispered, "What?"

"I feel Magic," Neilan whispered back.

Elwyn started. "Does Reid have it?"

Neilan frowned. "I've never felt it near him before. I think it's the flute. Made by Magic users, for Music users."

Elwyn's skin prickled. How could that be—weren't the Heirs on the surface unaware of their Gifts? Did Reid know about Magic? Did he know what Music really was? She ached to ask.

They turned a corner, and Reid slowed down. Elwyn and Neilan nearly ran into him. Reid continued up the road at a leisurely pace, all appearance of haste gone. Elwyn followed, her chest tense, with Neilan's hand in hers. The switch was nearly as unnerving as what may have been behind them. The crowd bustled around the road, heedless of them.

"We're in Poli territory, now," Reid announced.

Elwyn looked behind her, unable to let go of the feeling that wolfskin shrouds hid in every shadow. Distracted, before she knew what she was doing, she blurted, "Did a Magic user make the flute?"

Reid's eyes went wide, and Neilan's grip tightened on Elwyn's hand. Reid asked in a low voice, "What do you know about Magic?"

Elwyn froze.

Reid considered her, then he hummed gently, and Elwyn's tension eased. The Music settled over her, conveying peace. But there was also a subtle urgency, a drive toward openness.

She resisted. Was he trustworthy? She could only decide from her own observations of and interactions with him. Her mind replayed them: his help with her overwhelming memories and with the Inspector, his kindness in feeding and housing her, his willingness to fight to protect her.

She considered. She might be wrong, but all her observations communicated the same message about him: that he was trustworthy. She leaned into the Music that quieted her fear and took a steadying breath. "I'm an Heir, too," she said softly.

Reid met her eyes, his round with concern and understanding. He turned to Neilan, eyebrows raised in question, but Neilan looked away, hand tight on Elwyn's. Reid turned back to Elwyn. "It's a heavy load," he said. A lump rose in Elwyn's throat, and she nodded. He gestured for her to walk close alongside him. She drew to his side, Neilan keeping close to her opposite one.

"Our marriage was arranged by the Sovereign," Reid said. A shock ran through Elwyn's chest. Did Reid serve Solun? He continued, "He offered each of our families money should we marry, for the sake of, as he called it, protecting hereditary transmission. He didn't threaten, but Lyra and I both understood what was at stake. If we agreed, our families would be taken care of. If we refused, our families as well as we would be eliminated."

Elwyn nodded slowly. The busy road seemed to sink into oblivion around her as her whole attention focused on Reid's voice.

"What we didn't anticipate," Reid continued, "was how much we would connect. Our Music helped us access one another's hearts, and we love one another more deeply than we could have imagined possible even had we fallen in love before we were married.

"The Sovereign intended to use our joint Power to bolster his army, as well as test the Power output of our children. So far, we have not had children. Even so, we would have been useful to him had the Sovereign's plan worked. What *he* didn't anticipate is the courage and gumption our connected hearts have given us. Each of us on our own had only an average amount of courage—not enough to stand against the Sovereign. But together, we build one another up and give one another the capacity to do what is terrifying and difficult but we know is right. We wouldn't be his tools anymore, so we fled. We've lived in hiding from him ever since."

Elwyn's mind flashed with a dark shape against the stars. So that's why they stayed in the malaps' path.

"But why do you sing?" Neilan asked. "You gave yourself away, to us at least. And I think to the Inspector, too."

Reid stood tall. "We help people. We won't stop out of fear."

Elwyn's chest swelled. His courage was infectious. Elwyn wanted to be part of it somehow. What did she do that was hard but right?

She was going to help her parents. But what then? All she wanted to do was flee, to get away from Solun and to be unable to hurt anyone. Her heart sank. That felt somehow less than the dream of courage, of impact, that had sparked with Reid's story.

The road opened to a wide bridge over Lucaedter, and Reid stopped. "Here is where we part," he said smiling, but his eyes were turned down.

Elwyn started. He'd become familiar and safe. She didn't like to leave him.

"Have a good journey," Reid said. "I feel sure, somehow, that we'll meet again. A long time from now."

Elwyn's heart rose at the thought, but her arms prickled. Something about his prediction felt ominous. She forced down the feeling and smiled at him. "Thank you."

Neilan nodded. "Thanks."

Reid smiled and turned away from them, heading back up the street, while she and Neilan ascended the bridge.

Filuc glowed ahead, a thin silver ribbon winding southward toward Regsenfrag. Elwyn's skin began tingling. She was a day or so from Regsenfrag, from her parents. But then what?

19

Elwyn hustled through the forest along Filuc in Dawnday's strong midday sunlight, searching for edible plants. They'd had to take a break to rest Neilan's foot, but she couldn't sit still. Her mother was closer to being arrested every moment. They didn't have time to waste.

Neilan was sitting against a tree trunk a few hundred paces away, out of sight now. His foot was healing remarkably fast, but it was still painful, and it slowed him down. A lot.

The journey from Torlum to Regsenfrag could be done in one day if they moved fast and didn't take breaks. Elwyn's heart drummed with the reminder that time was running out for her mother. The men had said Twilitnight, but plans could change.

Part of Elwyn's mind acknowledged that some of her anxious hurry was to keep her mind on the present, so that she wouldn't remember. Then her memory flashed: a dark alley.

They couldn't get to her. They'd been arrested, and they were far away now. Even so, her skin crawled. She couldn't talk herself out of the anxiety. If only she could take Reid's soothing Music with her, but he was far away now, too.

"Elwyn!" Neilan's voice screamed through the trees. "Run!"

Sleet-gray eyes and blackened teeth slammed into her mind, and she burst into a sprint. She bolted with all of her might, with one thought alone: flee. Get away from those eyes at any cost.

A massive tree in front of her had branches low enough for her to reach. She grabbed one and swung herself up. She barely registered the bark scraping her arms and shins as she scrambled higher and higher.

As she neared the top of the tree, movement between the trees a hundred paces away caught her eye. She squinted through the leaves. Three people were struggling in a mass on the ground.

Two pulled away, nearly collapsing in exhaustion. The third rolled on the ground with his wrists latched together—it was Neilan. He thrashed, and the cuffs on his wrists shot to the ground, as though they were magnetized to it. As the mass separated, Elwyn recognized two Certified Keepers from the Haven. It wasn't the Lupos gang. Relief flooded her body.

But they'd caught Neilan. She had to help him. How? What could she do? If they'd overpowered Neilan, then they were far stronger than she was, and she'd never sparred more than one person at a time.

Her mind screamed, *Help him!* But what if she was caught, too? What about her mother?

Her stomach tightened. The Keepers wouldn't hurt Neilan, but what would happen to her mother once Solun had her? What could Elwyn do?

She couldn't do anything—her mother needed her more. Her face grew hot and her chest burned.

The Keepers spoke to one another, then one of them grabbed hold of Neilan's cuffs and pulled him to his feet. Neilan yanked out of her grip, and his cuffs dropped him to the ground again. The Keeper lifted him to his feet again and pulled him into motion, back the direction they'd come from. Shoulders sagging, Neilan followed her lead.

The second Keeper nodded to the first one and moved off through the trees in another direction, no doubt looking for Elwyn. A pang shot through Elwyn's heart. Neilan was really going. In her mind's eye, she saw him in the dining hall, alone—shoulders hunched and the light in his eyes dimmed. And of her, somewhere unknown, without him.

Neilan slowly faded into the forest: just his trousers and boots were still visible. It felt like part of Elwyn was being pulled away, as though that portion of her soul was attached to Neilan instead of herself. The last of his boots disappeared, and Elwyn's soul tore into two, one part going with him.

She sat still on the branch, stunned. It couldn't be real. Neilan was part of her, he couldn't be gone. But he was, and she'd let it happen.

She sank back into the leaves, trying to make herself face the truth. It couldn't be real—it had happened too fast. Her mind reeled, spiraling with imagined versions of the future, without Neilan. How would she find him again? She didn't know where the Haven was. Her breath caught, and she nearly fell off the branch.

She pressed her back into the tree trunk and forced herself to calm. She pushed down thoughts of the future and considered the present. The second Keeper was still down there somewhere, looking for her. She adjusted her position on the branch, then she tucked the hanging edges of her dress in between her shins, making sure she wasn't visible from below.

Then she sat still, waiting. She needed to get moving, she was her mother's only hope. But she'd be useless to her mother if she was caught. Just a little longer, then she'd go as fast as her legs would take her.

20

Neilan's wrists ached. The Magical cuffs that held them together were as heavy as lead. He tried to adjust where they sat on his wrists, and he regretted it immediately. The device tightened and shot toward the forest floor, yanking Neilan down with it. His elbows smacked the ground, and his injured foot throbbed.

The cuffs held him to the ground, unable to move. The Keeper rolled her eyes and gestured toward them. They disengaged from the ground, returning to the comparably manageable weight of lead.

Neilan stood and tried to roll his shoulders, then he closed his eyes and projected his focus into the cuffs. The second his Magic brushed them, they clamped tight again and dropped him to the ground. Neilan pulled as hard as he could, but he couldn't drag them even an inch.

"Are you going to do that every two steps the whole way back to the Haven?" the Keeper asked.

Neilan glared at her, and she glared right back.

He looked away from her and waited. She sighed and released the cuffs from the ground. "Nirep will meet up with another pair of Keepers and pursue Elwyn, but my orders are to take you back immediately."

"Great," he mumbled, voice heavy with irony.

She eyed him for a moment, then she took off. He tried to keep up, foot aching with each step. He grunted, and the Keeper turned around and raised an eyebrow.

"It's my foot. I hurt it," Neilan said, trying not to sound pathetic.

Her eyes softened. "Sit down."

Neilan obeyed, glad to do it on his own instead of the cuffs making him drop. The Keeper reached for his boot. "May I?" she asked.

Neilan nodded, and she pulled off the boot. She inspected the bandages, then closed her eyes and put a hand over the bandaged foot, feeling the wound with her Magic. Tingling ran through Neilan's toe and foot as her Magic brushed his skin.

She opened her eyes and looked at him. "The care that has been taken has kept infection away, so this wound is well within my expertise. May I heal you? It'll hurt a little."

Neilan nodded and braced himself. Prickling entered his toe, increasing to a burning sensation. The skin on his toe pulled as though it was being stretched. The burning sensation grew, and his whole foot ached. He took deep breaths, trying not to visualize what was happening.

The burning eased. Neilan waited a second to make sure, then he opened his eyes. The Keeper smiled and unwrapped the bandages. His gash was closed up and his toe was back to normal, just a little shiny where the wound had been. The Keeper looked closely at it and touched the shiny part. "Does this hurt?"

Neilan shook his head and let out a sigh of relief. All those years with a perfectly functional toe, he hadn't appreciated it. He'd never take it for granted again.

The Keeper glanced at his oversized boot and touched it. The leather squeezed tighter, shrinking the boot a bit. She tried it on his foot, then adjusted it some more. "My son is around your age," she said while she worked.

Neilan nodded but didn't say anything. The last person he wanted to think about right now was Jathdi.

"You two don't seem to get along," she said. He nodded again. What did she want him to say, that he and Jathdi were great friends? That her son was a nice kid? He wouldn't lie.

She just nodded back and started working on his opposite boot. She hummed while she worked, and it felt peaceful. It didn't have the Musical power of Lyra's, but it was sweet and normal and grounding. Just a mother humming while she cared for a kid. Not her kid, but a kid all the same.

Like Mama's humming voice while she washed up after a meal, or while she swept. His chest tightened. The Keeper put Neilan's boots on him and felt the toes. "How do they feel?"

Neilan stood and took a few steps. They fit almost as well as his old boots. "Good," he said. "Thanks."

"You're welcome." She stood too and faced him. "We'll be traveling together for a while. Will we be companions or will I have to treat you like a prisoner?"

Neilan glared at the ground. He didn't want to go willingly, but it was no use pretending he could escape from her with these cuffs on. He said to the ground, "I'll come with you."

She smiled. "I'm Sharah. Glad to be with you, Neilan."

He gave her a half smile, the most he could muster. She glanced at his wrist cuffs, considering. She touched them, and they separated into heavy bracelets. Neilan swung his arms and rolled his shoulders.

"They still work," she said warningly.

He frowned. Fine. At least he could move his arms. They headed off through the trees, retracing his and Elwyn's steps from this morning. The thought of her twisted his stomach. Where was she? Had she been caught, too? No, he'd know if she had—she'd be with him.

She was going to help her mother. He knew why she thought she had to, but she'd chosen her mother over him. His gut clenched. Would he ever see her again?

Neilan's whole body sagged as he trudged toward a small settlement in the Tensmon Mountains while the Dawnday sun set ahead of them. Elwyn was gone. That fact had been circling in his mind all day. It was the only concrete thought he had.

She'd needed to help her mother, he told himself again and again, but his chest ached with emptiness. She'd picked them—her parents who'd abandoned her—and now he may never see her again. He couldn't protect her. He wouldn't even know if something terrible happened to her. What was his life worth now?

Sharah walked beside him in silence. She'd tried chatting with him throughout the day, but he hadn't felt very conversational. He'd barely responded to her each time, and she'd apparently decided to leave him to his thoughts.

The settlement, a mere dozen cottages which were nestled in a sheltered hollow of the mountain, loomed closer in the twilight. "We'll stop for the night," Sharah said, breaking the silence for the first time in an hour. "We have a safehouse here."

Neilan scanned the tiny cluster of homes. "Are these people Keepers?"

"No. And they don't know who we are," she said quickly.

"Will they take us in?"

"They take in anyone who needs it."

Neilan paused. "Why?"

She approached the nearest cottage and knocked on the door. "They choose to," she said simply.

The door opened and an elderly man with a genial smile stood before them. "Come in, come in," he said, waving them forward and opening the door wider. He shuffled out of the doorway, unsteady on his feet, and called into the cottage, "Visitors!"

Neilan followed Sharah through the door, into the cottage's single, square room. Half a dozen cots lined one wall, and a table with some mismatched chairs was set in the middle of the room. At the hearth sat a young boy and a graceful, middle-aged woman stirring a large pot.

The woman smiled, though the corners of her eyes remained turned down. "Wonderful timing. The stew's just about ready, Papa." The father and daughter bustled around the room, setting the table and herding their guests into chairs. The boy scurried behind them, helping where he could.

They ate in relative silence. The elderly man and his daughter asked no questions, and Sharah avoided chatter as much as basic politeness would allow. Neilan didn't speak at all, what was the point? His mind was full of Elwyn—full of the lack of her. He had to get back to her.

The boy sat next to him, shoulders curved and eyes down. Neilan's heart stirred in spite of himself. He turned to the boy and asked, "What's your name, little man?"

The boy looked up at him and quickly back to his bowl. "Menee."

"How old are you?"

"Six."

Neilan's heart heaved. When he was six, his whole world had turned upside down. He tried not to think about it and looked around for something to say. "Is this your grandpa?"

"No," Menee said, sitting a little straighter. He started kicking his legs under the table. "I was all alone so they took me in."

"Of course we did, little one," the woman said.

The elderly man winked at Menee. "Didn't know what we were getting into."

Neilan smiled down at the boy, who was growing more personable by the second. He lowered his voice secretively and said, "You know something?"

Menee whispered, "What?"

"You're worth it."

Menee beamed at him and whispered back, "I think so, too."

Neilan laughed. The sound of it startled him. How long was it since he'd done that?

Quite comfortable now, Menee asked, "Do you like beetles?"

Neilan shrugged and said, "Enough. Do you?"

"They're my favorite. I have a collection." And Menee launched into a recital of every beetle—shape, size, and breed—he'd ever found.

Neilan nodded and interjected comments and questions, enjoying the boy's prattle. It gave him something to focus on. All the time, though, an ache loomed just below the surface of his mind. Elwyn's face kept swimming into it unbidden. She was out there somewhere, and he wasn't with her. It gnawed at his insides.

He'd find her. He had to. There was nothing else for him to do.

21

Elwyn took a deep breath to calm her racing heart as she stood at the edge of the forest. Regsenfrag sprawled before her, shining in Brightday's strong sunlight. The town was bounded by Filuc on the east and a freshwater river on the west. Between the rivers, the place was packed. Most of the buildings were two-stories with flat roofs which had seating, gardens, and all sorts of things on top.

Elwyn wrapped her arms around her middle. She felt so small here, and so alone. She felt like only part of herself, as though the rest of her was somewhere else.

She'd wanted to be alone, she reminded herself. She'd wanted it as long as she could remember, and now was her chance. She didn't have anyone to perform for, anyone to pretend for, anyone to hurt. If only it didn't hurt *her* so much.

She could handle it. But did she want to? The thought came unbidden, and she pushed it down. She had to handle it. There wasn't another option. Time was running low, and the Keepers had to be here by now. So did Solun's servants, and they were going to take her mother tomorrow. She had one day. One day to... to do what?

A pang hit her chest. What could she actually do to help on her own? She didn't know, but she had to do something.

She gathered herself and took off, toward Regsenfrag's main road. As she hustled into the town, there weren't many people in sight. An occasional voice rang between the tall, square houses, and domesticated two-domain animals ran up and down the alleys. The distant roar of many people bustling about came from further up the road—that must be the town marketplace. She hurried toward the sound, watching warily for Keepers and Solun's servants.

A young woman passed by and looked back at Elwyn quizzically. It hit Elwyn that she was drawing attention to herself by her obvious anxiety. She slowed her pace to a casual walk, held her head high, and looked straight ahead. Her instincts strained against her will, desperate to keep scanning for those she feared, but her will was stronger.

She kept moving toward the sounds of people. The closer she got, the busier the streets became. She rounded a corner and found herself in the middle of the marketplace, a wide road lined on both sides with stalls selling what looked like everything imaginable. The road was flooded with more people than Elwyn had seen in her life, moving in all directions.

In her mind's eye, she brought forward the image of the face on the scroll, and she scanned the faces that passed her. The crowd moved so fast she couldn't check all the faces before they were gone. A couple glanced at her, frowning, and Elwyn saw herself as they saw her: a figure standing still on the edge of the bustling crowd, staring intently into it. She stood out too much.

She waded into the crowd, trying to keep her head down and search the faces around her at the same time. She tried to move with it, but the flow of people parted around her like a boulder in a stream. She didn't understand the trick, the system they all apparently worked within in order to function so densely-packed together. The faces around her were a blur, and she was too conspicuous. This wasn't going to work.

She drifted with the flow as much as she could until she reached the edge of the crowd. She hovered near the covered stalls that lined the side of the road, pretending to browse.

The nearest stall, selling elaborately-crafted jewelry, glittered in the sunlight. It burned her eyes, like staring into the Brightday sun. She turned away quickly.

Elwyn wandered carelessly, she hoped, down the row of stalls. She glanced at the wares as she passed, trying to pretend she was interested in them, while all the time scanning the faces nearby with her peripheral vision.

The minutes went on. And on. They turned into what felt like an eternity. Her eyes ached from straining her peripherals. The sun had already moved halfway across the sky, and still no one she passed looked anything like the scroll—anything like *her*.

Too much time had passed, and still she'd done nothing. Unless she counted not-getting-caught-yet as something. What if she didn't find her mother in time?

While she wrestled with her failure, her eyes passed across a stall selling vibrant, embroidered fabrics. The seller sat on a stool in the middle, and behind her hung a massive tapestry. Before her conscious mind caught up, she had stopped and was lost in the tapestry.

It was a view of Regsenfrag and the surrounding valley from the nearby foothills that lay before the Tensmon mountains. The town, overwhelming and chaotic from up close, seemed small and insignificant from so far away. Actually, not even that far away. The valley spread into the distance, vast and placid. The forest north of Regsenfrag was a mere carpet of green, with cloud shadows and sunlight playing over it.

As Elwyn stared, she felt as though she were seeing deeper and deeper into the scene. She made out the main road through Regsenfrag, individual rooftops, even the marketplace. It was full of people, but from that distance the crowd felt quaint and unassuming. It seemed as though Elwyn could see the very merchant's stall she was standing at now, one of the many in the sweet, amiable market.

A long, slow breath filled Elwyn's lungs. The tension and immediacy of her hunt faded into the largeness of the world around her. She felt her place within the broader reality, the shared world. It steadied her, made the present feel manageable. Her problems hadn't destroyed the world—the world still existed. Her problems still existed, too, but they were smaller than they'd seemed.

A voice broke through, "You like it, yes? It's a bargain."

The stark worldliness of this statement pulled Elwyn out of the experience. She stumbled a step, dazed, and the busy, loud marketplace imposed itself on her senses again.

The seller said, "You want it? Of course you do. It's ten perivits, eight clavids."

"I, um," Elwyn stammered, "I can't buy it."

The seller threw up her hands. "Every time! I don't get it! They stare, they gape, but they don't buy! I should've known when that witch sold it so cheap." Her voice grew bitter. "It must be cursed. I'll get her back for this."

Everything inside Elwyn stepped up in contradiction. It wasn't a curse, it was beauty! Such beauty that she couldn't imagine owning it. Possession would be a taint to something so genuine.

Who could've made it? Elwyn's mind raced. Was the weaver an Heir of Aesthetic? Elwyn didn't want to be the reason this woman confronted an Heir, or anyone for that matter. What could she do?

She stammered, trying to come up with something to say. The seller glared at her with one eyebrow raised. The tingly tug pulled at Elwyn's middle, directing her away from the stall. She resisted, trying to figure out how to dissuade this woman from being angry with the unknown Heir because of her.

The tug intensified. Her mind was torn, half of her was still contending in her heart with this woman, but the rest of her was distracted by the insistent sensation in her middle. The seller's eyes bored into Elwyn, as though to intimidate her into buying the tapestry. Elwyn didn't know how to extricate herself from the mess she'd somehow made.

But the tug persisted, so Elwyn finally gave in. She simply walked away from the stall, in the direction the tug pulled her.

A few stalls away, she glanced at a pile of fruit. A voice rose nearby, chatting cheerily in a language Elwyn had never heard before. The words washed over her from the next stall, where a woman with long, dark hair talked with the merchant. The woman's voice flowed over Elwyn in a way the merchant's didn't, though they were speaking the same language.

Elwyn drank in the melodic rhythm of the woman's voice. She felt the emotion of it, even though the words meant nothing to her. The woman shifted, and her face came into view. A shock ran down Elwyn's spine. It was the face from the scroll—Elwyn's face, but with dark brown eyes and hair, and olive skin. She was Elwyn's mother, she had to be.

Elwyn froze. What now? Should she approach the woman and introduce herself? *'Hi, you're my mother.'* No, she couldn't do that. What then?

The woman waved at the merchant and turned away, while Elwyn's mind screamed at her to do something. The woman walked away.

Panicked, Elwyn followed, her mind spinning. What could she do?

In the edge of Elwyn's vision, a stationary figure stirred. It was a man with long, straight, black hair that was tied into a tail at the back of his head and hung to his waist. He wasn't looking at her, or her mother, but he moved at exactly their pace and direction.

The back of Elwyn's neck prickled. She couldn't have told why, but she was sure he was following her mother. Was he one of Solun's servants?

Elwyn's mind fought between fleeing for her own sake and keeping her mother in view. She kept following, as he did, for a minute or so, then he melted into the crowd. Elwyn paused, scanning for him, but the back of her mother's head was barely visible, far ahead, so she surged after her.

The man with the waist-length ponytail burst into view, running full-speed at Elwyn. Her stomach dropped. Figures with familiar faces emerged from the crowd and converged toward her and the man. Keepers! She bolted.

Running in the thick crowd was like moving through water. She dared a glance over her shoulder. Wuervik! He was pushing his way through the crowd toward her, but his eyes were on the man. The man! He was gaining on her.

Elwyn pushed her way onward. The road opened up, and her mother was there, not far ahead, walking up the steps to a house. A blonde man came out of the house and gave her a quick, familiar kiss. A shock ran down Elwyn's back—was that her father? The couple turned to enter the house.

"Wait!" Elwyn yelled with burning lungs.

The couple turned toward the sound and started. The man put a hand protectively on her mother's arm. Elwyn reached toward them as she ran, and the man stepped back toward the house, pulling lightly on his wife's arm.

"Wait… please!" Elwyn called between breaths. They paused.

Footsteps pounded behind her. Elwyn sprinted the last few steps as fingers closed around her wrist. "I'm your—!"

The grip on her wrist yanked her backward, cutting her off. "No!" she screamed, and spun toward her captor.

Wuervik glared at her, his hand tight on her wrist. "Come with me," he commanded.

She whipped her arm around to loosen Wuervik's grip, but she was useless against Wuervik's Magically-enhanced strength. Her chest heaved, and her heart rose into her throat.

"Come on!" Wuervik yelled and pulled on Elwyn's arm. She resisted and opened her mouth to yell, but another person stepped into her field of vision. Astur's blazing eyes shocked her into momentary stillness.

"It's too late for that I think, Wuervik," Astur said coldly.

Wuervik glared at Astur, then jumped. Elwyn spun to follow his gaze. Her mother had come up behind her and put a steadying hand on Wuervik's shoulder.

"What is this?" her mother asked, looking at Astur.

Astur broke her gaze and looked down. A shiver ran down Elwyn's spine. Astur, cowering? But she took her chance. "I'm Elwyn —your daughter."

22

Elwyn's mother's eyes widened, and she stepped back. Elwyn's heart dropped.

The man came up behind her mother. "What are you doing here?" he asked aggressively, looking at Wuervik. Wuervik's eyebrows came together, and he glared at the ground.

"What do you mean, Theon?" Elwyn's mother asked. She turned intently to Wuervik, and her eyes shadowed. "Medic Vin?"

"You remember him, Cuinn," Astur said in a low voice.

"Of course I do, that was the worst day of my life," Cuinn said, then she studied Elwyn's face. "You *are* Elwyn. You have to be." Elwyn nodded slowly, not sure what to make of that.

"That's not possible," Theon said harshly. "Our daughter is dead."

Elwyn's insides tightened. She stared open-mouthed at the man she'd believed was her father.

Shouts reverberated up the street. A group ran toward them, the man with the waist-length ponytail in the lead and the men she'd seen in Senphon Inn in his wake. "Take the girl, too!" the leader yelled to his comrades.

Wuervik pulled Elwyn behind him protectively. Behind the group,

Keepers fought to catch up to them.

"What—?" Cuinn burst out.

Astur cut across her and yelled, "Inside!"

Wuervik whipped around and dragged Elwyn by the wrist toward the house. She stumbled, trying to get her feet under her while straining against Wuervik's grip.

Cuinn ran after Elwyn, yelling, "Wait!"

Wuervik pulled her through the front door. In a whirl, bodies bounded in after her. Wuervik slammed the door and latched it.

In a blink, Elwyn stood with Wuervik and Astur in the entryway of a neat, little home, staring into Cuinn's and Theon's shocked faces. Was she wrong—were they not her parents? Neither Wuervik nor Astur had contradicted her when she'd claimed them.

"What's going on?" Theon yelled.

Shouts and booms poured in from outside the door. Wuervik sped to the window, Elwyn in tow. Outside, Keepers were ineffectively trying to hold off Solun's servants, who fought hard. Elwyn had thought Keepers were powerful, but they could only do so much without exposing themselves as Magic users. Solun's servants surged through them and surrounded the house.

Astur shouted into the air, "Please!" Then he bolted through the house and disappeared into a room at the back. A second later, his voice called out, "Wuervik! Here!"

Theon grabbed Wuervik's arm. "Hold on! Tell me what's going on!"

Wuervik twisted out of his grip and followed Astur's voice, again pulling Elwyn with him. She obeyed his pressure, her mind in a whirlwind. In the back room, Astur pointed eagerly at a spot in the clay floor.

Wuervik closed his eyes and reached toward the spot. A second later, his eyes popped open and he gaped at Astur, who nodded excitedly. Wuervik closed his eyes again and heaved both his hands upward. The clay floor erupted.

Elwyn's parents burst into the room and screamed. Where the floor had been, there was now a gaping, pitch-black hole. Wuervik pulled Elwyn toward it.

She dug her heels into the floor and called out, "No, wait!" She turned to Cuinn. "They're coming for you!"

Wuervik paused. "For them?"

Elwyn nodded frantically. "For Cuinn. I overheard them in Torlum!" Then to Cuinn, she screamed, "You can't stay here!"

Astur and Wuervik shared a look, wide-eyed.

"Hold on," Theon said firmly with hands raised, as though with some rational conversation he could make the situation make sense. "Tell me what's going on."

A boom hit the front door. Then another.

Wuervik stopped pulling on Elwyn's wrist and grabbed her with Magic. The prickling tug yanked her to the edge of the hole. Or, not just a hole: it disappeared into dark emptiness to the east and west—a tunnel. Astur was somehow already in it.

Elwyn strained against the Magic holding her to look back at Cuinn. "Please! You can't stay here!"

Cuinn stared hard at Elwyn for a second, then turned to Theon. Her face was set but her eyes were kind. "I'm going." He opened his mouth to speak but she held up a hand. "I'm going," she said firmly. "And I want you to come too."

The intensity of their eye contact made Elwyn squirm. More was being communicated than the simple words.

A crash resounded from the front of the house. "Now!" Wuervik yelled.

With a quick glance at Cuinn, Elwyn jumped into the hole, and Wuervik followed her. Shouts rang down the hallway, coming closer.

Cuinn bounded toward the hole and dropped into it. Theon followed, face set hard.

The man with a waist-length ponytail burst into the room. Wuervik gestured to him over Elwyn's shoulder, and the chunks of hard-packed clay that had been the floor flew at the man. He ducked, and the clay chunks crashed all around him. Voices shouted down the hall.

Astur took off down the tunnel to the west, and Elwyn and the rest followed him into pitch darkness.

A voice in the room above said, "Watch the house, keep the ones outside from coming in. I'm going after them." Then a thump dropped into the tunnel behind her.

$$\triangle$$

Elwyn hurried dazedly in the darkness, aware of the bodies around her though none of them spoke. The muted footfalls behind them drove them on.

Once her eyes adjusted to the darkness, an indistinct, faint light seemed to move with them through the tunnel. She searched uneasily for the source, but she couldn't figure it out. It was enough light to walk by, that had to satisfy her for now.

She had a million questions. Her parents were right there! She'd dreamed about them her whole life, fought so hard to get to them, and here they were. But were they? Everything had been a whirlwind, then it had stopped and left her spinning instead.

Were these her parents? Astur and Wuervik would've contradicted her right away if they weren't. Wouldn't they?

Could she count on anything she'd known, or thought she'd known, before? All she could go on was what she'd seen herself. She searched her memory. Her parents had recognized Wuervik—they'd met before. But then, why did Theon say their daughter was dead?

Was that how he dealt with giving her up, telling himself she'd died instead? But he'd been so earnest. Overwhelmed and irritated, and earnest. Nothing made sense. Elwyn's mind reeled.

Wuervik reached over his shoulder, and a Magical shield expanded across the tunnel behind them. Cuinn and Theon jumped.

"What was that?" Theon asked. It was a whisper, but in the silence his voice thundered.

Wuervik whispered curtly, "It'll hold him off for a while."

From the front of the group, keeping his face forward, Astur said, "Much will be explained and will make sense, but not now. You must wait."

"Wait?" Theon burst out. "You're asking me—"

Astur spun around to face him, silver eyes blazing in the pitch black tunnel. Theon froze, and Elwyn's skin prickled. Astur's irises were lit up, two tiny circles searing the darkness, glowing silver like lucten.

He glared at Theon with those glowing eyes and spoke in a low, grim voice. "You will wait."

He turned forward again. The glow moved with him, continuing to light their way in the tunnel, but the two circles were seared into Elwyn's vision, floating in front of her. How did he do that? What was she missing?

A crash rang in the darkness behind them, then a yell. Elwyn jumped, and they all burst into a run.

Solun's servant couldn't break through: the shield would weaken as Wuervik got further away, but it was strong for now. But really, what did Elwyn know? So much of what she'd thought she'd known had flipped upside down.

As they ran, the banging and shouting grew further and further behind.

But now what? They'd take her back to the Haven. She was a

prisoner again, and so were her parents. How was she ever going to be free? Even so, her heart stirred. That had to be where the Keepers had taken Neilan, too. She should be able to make it on her own, but how could she be free if part of her was always somewhere else?

She had to find another way. The option she'd always counted on, to flee and disappear into the outer world without Solun noticing her, was gone. She'd put herself in his sight the moment she approached her mother knowing that his servants were watching. He'd know who she was. If he didn't already, he'd soon find out, and then he'd hunt her harder than ever before.

Something clicked in her mind: she had to go to the source. The only way to truly be free was to be rid of Solun. She had to find a way to beat him. No one else had—not the Keepers, not Wuervik, not even Astur.

She couldn't do it, she had nowhere to start. How would she do what no one else had been able to do? Her skin echoed with the tingly tug that had directed her into the tunnel in the C.K. Wing, brought her to the servol, and guided her to her mother. The High King was guiding her. She'd find the way.

23

Hosev and Tinol descended into the rocky valley of their hometown, Gravusfrig. The deep purple shadows of Twilitday morning were lightening as the sun rose higher. Hosev had traveled as fast as he could, much to Tinol's annoyance. Hosev was fine with him being annoyed, as long as they got home fast. And they'd made it, finally.

In the center of the city, Phaemin Fortress jutted far into the sky, atop a craggy hilltop. The coal-black stone towers shot into the sky at angles like a natural rock formation, except that the depth of its blackness and the height of the structure contrasted sharply with the dull, gray rock of the hilltop. Plus, natural rock formations gave Hosev a feeling of awe, whereas this one gave him only dread.

Its windows—long, narrow, and pointed like natural fissures in the rock—were darker even than the towers. Hosev had never seen light from within. The windows of the lower levels were hidden behind the tall, stone wall which surrounded the fortress. The few inhabited areas must be on the ground floor. Not many of the Sovereign's servants stayed there, and the Sovereign himself rarely came.

The dark fortress stared down at the city, menacing all that fell at its feet. The force of it bore down on the people of Gravusfrig.

It felt as though a heavy load landed on Hosev's shoulders, growing heavier with every step. Usually, the weight was there but he didn't notice it. Now, after being away from it for eight days, it weighed him down like lead. Even Tinol had stopped talking as it bore down on him, too. Welcome home.

They crossed the bridge into town, spanning over one of the many empty riverbeds. Useless bridge, really, but no one dared step into those empty riverbeds. Hosev didn't either, though he couldn't explain why. They felt eerie.

He and Tinol sped down the narrow road, between the city's closely-huddled buildings. At the first fork, Tinol paused. With a tense face, he waved at Hosev and said, "See you."

Hosev tried to smile, but the weight bearing down on him made it hard to do so. The burden of Gravusfrig and worry for his family consumed him. He waved back and turned away without a word. Tinol took the road to the right, and Hosev set off down the one to the left.

Ahead, a small, rocky hilltop rose a story above the surrounding cottages. As he approached the hill, he shielded his eyes from the rising sun and squinted at the thick trees that ran around the top of it. He climbed the hill and rounded the line of trees to a little cottage. The wooden structure, gray from years of weather, nestled into the hilltop surrounded by an orderly vegetable garden. Manell's small flowerbed, usually pristine, had grown some weeds, and the flowers drooped.

Hosev reached the door of his family home and paused with his hand on the latch. He took in a deep breath, doing his best to fight the pressure bearing down on him. He released the breath, stretched his lips into an unfelt smile, and bounced on the balls of his feet in forced peppiness. He threw open the door and called out in a falsely jovial voice, "Hey family!"

Manell, who was on the floor playing with their four-year-old brother Refwah, jumped in surprise. Reffie squealed and ran at Hosev. He slammed into Hosev's legs and wrapped his little arms around him in a tight hug.

"Hey bud," Hosev said and lifted him from the floor. He gave him a quick squeeze while he watched Manell over Reffie's shoulder. Manell stood up and tried to smile, but it didn't reach her eyes. The strain of the last eight days showed in her tense face and the circles under her eyes.

Hosev set Reffie down and wrapped an arm around Manell's shoulders. "How is she?"

Manell shrugged and looked down. "The same."

A stampede from the back door drowned out any response Hosev could make. Five of his siblings all pounded into the house at once. They pushed, jostled, and climbed over one another to get to Hosev first. He was assailed with chatter and hugs and chaos. Two-year-old Faell bounced up and down behind her older siblings, trying to find a hole she could push through. The corners of Hosev's mouth turned up. The tension that plagued him faded some, and he let out a genuine laugh.

Mother appeared in the doorway from the back room, holding the baby. She met his eyes for the briefest moment, then ambled to her rocking chair, their one luxury.

She lowered herself slowly, so disengaged from the act that it looked like she was just giving into gravity. She sunk into the chair and looked up at Hosev, her vacant stare making his chest burn.

"Father is coming home soon," Hosev said.

The children whooped, and Manell grinned. Even Mother's face stirred.

"Something is finally happening with his assignment," Hosev

said. "He said he'll be in Gravusfrig by Darknight, and once his assignment is complete, he thinks the Sovereign will let him come home for a while. Maybe permanently."

The children jumped up from the floor and ran in circles around Hosev, cheering.

Some of the pressure in Hosev's chest released. It finally sank in and he let himself believe it: Father was coming home. He'd be here, to take care of Mother, to take care of all of them. Hosev wouldn't have to be the man of the house anymore.

As Reffie and Faell ran in circles with the rest of them, Hosev imagined what it was going to be like for them. Faell had only seen Father once since she was a baby, Reffie maybe three times, but they would get to grow up with him here, actually living at home with them. Father hadn't lived at home for the last sixteen years—ever since Hosev was one year old, when the Sovereign had assigned Father to the post in Regsenfrag.

Mother slowly stood with baby Vey and ambled out of the room. Hosev's heart sank. Even the younger children were silent as they watched her walk out. A moment later, they dispersed.

Manell dropped into the rocking chair. Hosev sat down on a stool next to her and asked, "How's it been? How're you holding up?"

Manell glanced up at him and shrugged. "I'm fine. Just tired." She paused. "He's really coming home?"

"That's what he said." Hosev looked at his lap. "I'm sorry it took so long. We got stuck in Torlum."

Manell's hand rested on his arm. "I'm just glad you're back safe. I wasn't sure…"

Hosev met her weary eyes, and his stomach tightened. She'd thought something had happened to him. How could he make up for the weight she'd borne? All by herself, taking care of Mother and their seven siblings while fearing for Hosev's life on top of it all.

From the back of the house, the baby cried. Weariness flashed across Manell's face, then she forced on a smile and hurried into the back room to help Mother with baby Vey.

Hosev went outside and took a deep breath. Back to routine. That's the best he could do to help Manell, and Mother, and all of them. He crossed to their small garden and pulled up some onions and potatoes, then headed back inside to prepare them.

24

Through uncountable hours, the tunnel was the same. Elwyn couldn't remember how many times they'd rested in between long stretches of walking. She'd fallen asleep hard at the last rest, only to be woken what felt like a second later.

She'd entirely lost track of time. It might be the next day for all she knew. They were still moving, thanks to the flatbread with nuts and dried fruit Wuervik had packed, but her body felt wobbly, like she might collapse at any time.

Still, she trekked on—there was nothing else for her to do. Her mind wandered far, to wherever the rest of her heart was. What was he doing right now? Had he made it back to the Haven yet?

Was he hurt? Was he angry with her? Her stomach twisted.

The air in the tunnel began to change, growing less heavy and stagnant, and Elwyn's mind pulled to the present. Ahead, a faint light bloomed, and they hustled toward it. As they approached the light, the tunnel opened into a cave. Through the mouth of the cave, rain fell in a thick sheet. Wind blew in Elwyn's face, sticky and wet but blessedly fresh. Astur kept moving, pacing toward the wall of rain.

"Hold on," Theon said, determination bleeding into his tone. It was clear he'd been holding it in for a long time, and he wouldn't be put off any longer.

Astur turned around, his eyes still faintly glowing. "Wait here."

Theon's voice rang through the cave, "Who are you?"

Astur ignored him, but Elwyn turned to Theon, trembling. It was time to have it out. He hadn't been speaking to her, but she wouldn't wait for them anymore. "I'm your daughter."

Astur paused, and Theon's face hardened. "We buried our daughter. Please stop torturing us."

His words hit her like a punch to the chest. Buried? Astur's voice rumbled with the rainstorm. "No you didn't."

Theon's eyes flashed. Rage welled in his face, and he opened his mouth.

"That was not your daughter." Astur's voice was even and calm, but the sound of it sent a strange, blazing tremor through Elwyn's body.

Cuinn stepped to her husband's side and asked sharply, "Who was it?"

"No one," Wuervik said. Cuinn frowned at him. "It wasn't a person," he added hastily.

Elwyn's mind whirled. None of this made sense. Theon glared at Wuervik and took in a breath to speak, but Wuervik cut him off. "It wasn't a baby, I—"

Astur put up a hand and Wuervik ceased. All eyes turned to Astur. His shoulders sagged, something Elwyn had never seen him do before. In a low voice, vaguely in Wuervik's direction but mostly to himself, he said, "The servol showing up to help Elwyn destroyed me. He sent it against me to tell me I'm wrong. But which part of what I've done was wrong? Everything? What am I to do now?"

Astur paused, then he said aloud, "It is time, but we must begin earlier." He collected himself. "You both are Heirs of an ancient people, the Eudaimonians, and have inherited their Gifts. Solun, who rules here—"

"The Crown?" Theon interrupted.

"No. The Crown is merely his puppet. Solun you may know as 'The Sovereign.'"

Theon frowned. "The petty lord in the south?"

Astur shrugged. "That may be what he has presented himself to be, in order to more easily fulfill his plans, but that is not what he is. He is the unhuman, undying ruler of Terralum, and he is spreading his tendrils throughout Alloidem."

Cuinn shivered.

A shadow passed behind Astur's eyes. "Solun has tracked the Heirs as the Gifts have been passed from generation to generation over the past nine centuries. Those who are powerfully Gifted or show conscious mastery of their Gift are taken in order to serve him —he will not let powerful Heirs remain outside his control.

"He distrusts humanity, so he retains a tight hold on it. He believes that if all five lines of Heirs were to ally against him, he would be overthrown, and all he has built would crumble. So he keeps Heirs from joining one another, except of course in his service. He has developed a system to prevent Heirs marrying one another or procreating together. Marriages must be officially sanctioned, and unsanctioned union is punished harshly, with either death or indentured servitude of both parties."

Fang-rimmed gray eyes flashed across Elwyn's mind, and her chest tightened. The sound of rain filled the humid cave.

"Occasionally, Solun allows Heirs of the same line to marry," Astur continued. "Most likely this is to test how much power their children will inherit, but he watches them closely to retain control over them."

An image of Lyra and Reid, his arm around her waist, passed in Elwyn's mind's eye. How many more couples had Solun forced to marry? Were they the only ones who'd escaped from his control, or were there more?

"Your marriage is historically unique," Astur said, "in that you are Heirs of two different ancestral lines. I do not know how that oversight happened. Was your marriage sanctioned?"

Cuinn nodded contemplatively. "The Regsenfrag clerk couldn't find a record of Theon's birth, so he assumed Theon was the child of a farming family who'd forgotten to register the birth of their eleventh or twelfth child. He'd seemed annoyed and unwilling to deal with the investigation he would need to make, so he registered Theon as a local farmer and sanctioned our marriage." Cuinn paused. "I felt sure, somehow, that we shouldn't contradict him."

Astur's eyes narrowed thoughtfully.

Cuinn continued, "He's from—"

Theon grabbed hold of her arm, looking at her with wide eyes.

She met his eyes calmly and said, "We've come too far." She turned back to Astur and continued, "He was a merchant's apprentice from Ordoc, near the northern border. He came here to deliver goods, a trivial trip which he didn't bother to register with his local clerk. We met, then he decided to stay."

A small smile lit the corners of Astur's lips. Elwyn's heart stirred despite the strain on her nerves. Cuinn paused and grew tense. "What did you mean by different ancestral lines?"

Astur said, "You, Cuinn, are an Heir of Linguistic. Theon, you are an Heir of Logic. When you two conceived, your child would be both an Heir of Linguistic and an Heir of Logic. As far as we know, she is the first person in history to inherit more than one Gift. That child could be powerful. As Solun will not let himself be challenged by such power, he prevents it. If it cannot be prevented, he enslaves it. If it cannot be enslaved, he kills it.

"Around the time your pregnancy was registered with the clerk, Solun discovered that an Heir of Logic had disappeared from Ordoc. That person was tracked to Regsenfrag, and discovered to be married and with child."

"How do you know?" Theon interrupted, distrust staining his tone.

Astur met his eyes, challengingly. "We watch him."

Theon didn't respond, but his jaw was set firmly. "What happened when he found us with child?"

Astur paused and looked at his feet. The hammering rain echoed in the otherwise silent cave. "It appears that Solun decided to let your pregnancy remain, in order to see if he could possess the power your child would inherit. He posted his servants to watch you and intercede when you gave birth. My Keepers noticed Solun's interest in a pregnant couple and investigated. When we understood the situation, we interfered."

"I thought you said you already knew," Cuinn said, eyes narrowed.

Voice strained, Astur said, "Not at that point."

"You said you watch him," she pushed.

"We," he said evasively. "I did not say who is contained within that 'we.'"

She raised an eyebrow. "Who is 'we'?"

"I am not going to share that, yet."

Cuinn narrowed her eyes at him. She seemed to understand more of what was going on in the conversation than Elwyn could hear. Elwyn's neck and shoulders strained with the palpable tension in the cave. "You interfered," Cuinn said. "How?"

Astur looked down, and Wuervik shifted his weight uncomfortably. Cuinn turned to Wuervik and said angrily, "You posed as a medic?"

"I am a medic," he said hastily. "Or—I was. You and your child had the best care available."

"Yet she still died," Theon said quietly.

Wuervik stared at his feet. "No, she didn't," he said. "We couldn't let Solun have her, but we weren't sure how we were going to do it. We couldn't tell you, or take you all with us. If all three of you disappeared, it'd alert Solun. There had to be something for him to believe was the child, so in preparation I bought a realistic-looking baby doll, and Astur and I waited for the circumstances to offer an opportunity. Then, when you were in labor, the baby went into distress."

Cuinn squeezed her eyes shut. "We remember. Please don't describe it."

Wuervik shifted again. "Okay. Well, then you were unconscious, and the midwife made Theon leave the room. So we made an impulse decision and sent the midwife out, too. I delivered the baby with the help of my Gift—Magic. She would've died otherwise.

"Then I used Magic to make a small casket and to change the appearance of the doll I'd bought into a lifeless imitation of the child you bore. I disfigured it enough to preclude the need for an autopsy, as well as to have a reason to seal the casket and to insist that the family not see the child even if the casket was opened. I sealed the disfigured doll into the casket, then I concealed the live child and left with her. Astur told the midwife that the child was a girl and was stillborn, showed her the casket, and gave instructions for burial." He paused. "After you buried the casket, I came back and read the name on the gravestone, and we gave it to her."

The cave was silent.

"You had to believe the child was dead," Astur said, a tinge of pleading in his voice. "If you didn't, Solun would know someone had taken her. He would have searched for her mercilessly. He would have found us and ruined any chance we have to defeat him."

A sob burst from Theon, as though he'd been trying to hold it in with all his might but now it exploded out of him. He dropped to his knees and whispered, "So you're saying my baby, the one I cried over and buried, who comes back to me in my dreams, isn't real?"

Elwyn's chest constricted. She instinctively stepped back, wanting to fade into the cave wall.

Astur's voice broke as he said, "Yes."

Tears streamed down Cuinn's face. "How could you do it?"

Astur whispered, "I thought we had to. I've since realized that we should've found another way. I am sorry, for all of it."

Silence stretched. The rain, falling lighter now, still echoed through the cave. Twilitday sunlight filtered in, a little brighter now that the storm was easing.

Cuinn whispered, "And now?"

"Now?" Wuervik asked.

Astur cut across him. "She came to find you."

Cuinn met his eyes, then looked at Elwyn. "Why now?"

Astur opened his mouth, but Elwyn said, "I thought you were dead. Then I found out you weren't."

Cuinn's eyes snapped to Astur, anger radiating from her. He dropped his gaze to the floor. "Yes, that's what we told her. I am sorry for that, too."

No one moved, the silence heavy around them.

Wuervik glanced over his shoulder, back down the tunnel, and shifted his weight. "We need to get moving," he said tentatively.

Astur straightened, forcing resolve into his tone. "Yes, we do." Then he said apprehensively, apparently unwilling to command them now, "Cuinn? Theon?"

Theon rose to his feet. "First," he said, and he looked at Elwyn.

Tears rose into his eyes again, and she squirmed under his gaze. He wiped the tears away and came toward her.

He held out a hand. She took it, trembling, as he said softly, "It's nice to meet you, my Elwyn."

Trudging through the rain, Elwyn's hair and clothes dripped, her fingertips were wrinkly, and her feet sloshed inside her boots.

She watched the strange man and woman walking through the forest a few steps ahead of her—her parents. They had a contented way together. They flowed, responding to one another's movements unconsciously. They seemed aware of one another even though they weren't interacting. They were used to one another, lived one life together.

It was the opposite with Elwyn. They glanced over their shoulders at her, curious and unsure. They were constantly aware of her, too, but it was a different awareness. It was overt, like an intrusion. She didn't belong. She wasn't *family*.

Of course she wasn't—they'd never met her before. They hadn't even known she existed. Elwyn tried to hold on to her rationalization, but her chest still constricted.

She watched the woman in front of her and imagined calling her Mother. No, it didn't feel right. As a child, Elwyn had dreamed of sitting curled in her mother's lap, saying *'I love you, mama,'* and her saying *'I love you, my girl.'* But now, faced with her for real, it couldn't be. The years of absence stretched between them like a river. Elwyn could see across it, but she couldn't come closer or she'd get swept away. Her parents were Cuinn and Theon, and they'd have to remain so.

The rain eased to a light sprinkle, just enough to keep Elwyn soaking wet, but she could see further now. Where were they? The cave had opened into a forest clearing, and they'd set off into the trees. But which forest? They could be anywhere.

She looked over her shoulder. Foothills rose behind them, with rocky peaks looming behind those. The sun was moving away from the peaks, toward the horizon ahead. Had the tunnel taken them under the whole Tensmon mountain range?

She squinted through the sprinkling drops at Astur. Tension pulled at him, and his lips were set in a thin line. Behind her, Wuervik's jaw was set hard.

"Where are we?" Elwyn ventured to ask.

Without turning around, Astur said, "Too close."

"What do you mean?" Theon asked. His face was turned to Astur, but Elwyn felt him watching her out of his peripherals.

"That tunnel we found runs under your house and under the mountain range, in a straight line toward the safehouse your daughter has lived in all these years. It doesn't bode well."

Elwyn's arms prickled. Everyone was silent.

Theon looked over his shoulder at the mountaintops behind them and started. "Are we in the Forbidden Lands?"

Astur said stiffly, "Yes."

Theon considered him. "Is that why you put your safehouse here? Because no one else will come near it?"

"The reason this land is forbidden and the reason the Haven is here are unrelated to one another, but they both branch from the same original fact about the location," Astur said.

"Which is?" Theon asks.

"Nothing of your concern," Astur said harshly.

Theon opened his mouth to retort, but Cuinn put a hand on his arm. He met her eyes and she shook her head. Theon changed tactic. "What if we're caught here?"

"If we're caught here," Astur said, "we'll have bigger issues to worry about than punishment for being in the Forbidden Lands."

Theon's eyes widened. "What about our footprints?"

"Wuervik is taking care of them," Astur said. Elwyn looked at the muddy ground behind them. There were only a few steps' worth of prints visible. Wuervik flicked his hand, then the footprints smeared and broken sticks straightened.

Cuinn watched his work. "What did you call your Gift?"

"Magic," Wuervik said, an edge to his voice.

Cuinn nodded contemplatively. She opened her mouth to speak, then shook her head. "How far are we from your safehouse?"

"Less than half a day," Astur said, his voice tight.

Elwyn's stomach felt strange. The cold had been sinking in since they entered the storm, maybe that was why. But it wasn't a cold feeling. Instead, she felt a little hot. But also cold? Maybe. She couldn't exactly tell.

Her head was getting fuzzy. She squinted at Astur again, and his clothes weren't sticking to him like hers were. He didn't even look wet.

No, that couldn't be. Maybe her vision was hazy from the rainwater that still dripped into her eyes. Her limbs grew heavy.

"How'd you know the tunnel was there?" Theon asked, his voice prickly.

"We didn't," Astur said evasively.

"Even worse," Cuinn said, eyes narrowed at Astur. Astur whipped around and faced her, eyebrows raised.

"How did you find it?" Theon asked in a challenging tone.

"Heirs of Magic have an awareness of what matter surrounds them. Wuervik could feel space below the floor," Astur said, looking away. Elwyn's feet dragged. She felt so heavy. It was hard to keep her head up straight.

"But he didn't find it. You did," Theon said aggressively. "Tell us the truth."

"I was directed," he said with defensive aggression.

"Directed by whom?" Cuinn asked, but her eyes were on Elwyn.

Elwyn closed her eyes, it was too hard to keep them open. The toe of her boot caught on a tree root.

"Elwyn!" Cuinn's voice screamed.

Elwyn crumpled, landing on hands and knees in the mud. Her head lolled, it was so, so heavy. Strong arms reached under hers and tried to pull her to her feet.

"I just need to sleep," she said, but her voice barely made any sound.

"Don't touch her," Theon's voice said as he moved closer. Different arms from the first scooped her up. She shook her head and tried to say she's fine, but no voice came out. "It's okay," Theon's voice said gently. "I've got you."

The sounds around her were blurring. Her body sagged, and she couldn't think anymore.

25

Neilan sat alone in the huge, underground cave the Haveners had adopted for dining, staring into empty space. There was nothing worth looking at. With unfocused eyes, he scooped bite after bite of gruel into his mouth.

His wrists were still stuck in the wrist locks, but they were disengaged—for now—so he had free movement of his arms. But if he went within five paces of the Enex staircase, they'd re-engage. The cuffs would snap together and hold him down. His wrists still burned from how he'd found that out. Even disengaged, they were heavy as lead. His forearms ached.

Across the dining hall, Jathdi eyed Neilan. He tried to pretend he was just glancing by accidentally, but his eyes lingered on Neilan too long. Jathdi didn't need to pretend—his stares didn't matter to Neilan in the slightest.

Only one person mattered, and he would probably would never see her again. The thought punched him in the gut, just like every time it crossed his mind. It left a pit in his stomach, and he wanted to hit something. Instead, he just ground his teeth and smashed the gruel with his spoon.

Where was she now? Had she found her parents? Jealousy stabbed through his chest, but he wasn't sure if he was jealous of them, or of her.

An image flashed across his mind, his father's laughing face as he swung four-year-old Neilan high over his head. Neilan's lungs caught. Then it was his mother's cool hand pressed against his feverish forehead, her gentle voice humming. Tears burned in the corners of his eyes, and his chest ached, like a hole that was on the verge of caving in. He couldn't stay here like this. He wouldn't.

Maybe if he moved fast enough, he could pass the Magical boundary at the Enex staircase before the wrist locks triggered. Neilan's heart pounded, awakening his senses for the first time in days.

He stood and carried his bowl, still half-full, to the dish cart, then he left the dining hall. Once he was out of sight, he bolted for the Concourse.

Rounding the last corner of the K.D. Wing, the luctenfall glowed through the archway. He burst into the Concourse and nearly smacked into a group of Keepers. They were circled around a few people, who were hidden in the middle of their mass.

They were all turned toward the people in the center, so Neilan sidled around them. Maybe he could slip past without being noticed. As he side-stepped the last Keeper, she shifted, showing the people in the center of the group: a woman standing anxiously next to a man holding an unconscious form. A mess of blonde hair tumbled down and a pale hand hung limp from the form.

Neilan's heart jolted. "Elwyn!" he burst out, and he shoved through the crowd of Keepers.

She didn't move, and Neilan's heart hammered. "What's wrong with her?" he yelled at the people all crowded around her.

Wuervik came up behind the man holding her, and his jaw

muscles were tight. "Give her space."

"What happened to her?" Neilan asked, panic rising in his voice. Elwyn's head lolled. Her formerly white dress was almost completely brown with mud.

Wuervik turned toward the Medical Ward, leading the man holding her, and Keepers closed in around her. Neilan pushed through them, his whole body shaking. He wanted to scream, but nothing came out. The world was crumbling.

The woman pushed closer to Elwyn, squeezing Neilan out in the process. His fists and eyes burned. He glared at the back of her head and hustled to regain his place. He'd shove that woman if he had to.

He squeezed into the tiny gap between the woman and Elwyn, and set himself firmly by Elwyn's side. The woman's eyes widened, then her eyebrows furrowed and she stared contemplatively at Neilan. He kept his face forward and his jaw set.

At the door to the Medical Ward, Wuervik gave the crowd of Keepers a nod and they dispersed. He opened the door and held it wide. Astur went in, leading the man holding Elwyn. Neilan stayed close by her lolling head, and the woman followed, eyeing Astur. Wuervik came in last and shut the door firmly.

The expansive main room of the Medical Ward was full of movement. Medic-Keepers hustled back and forth across the glass floor, lucten surging beneath their feet. The glowing, silver light glinted off the equipment that filled every available space of the main room.

Chief Medic-Keeper Pena gestured toward a row of beds against the far wall. "Lay her there." As the man laid Elwyn onto the bed at the end of the line, Med. Pena came over and asked, "Illness or injury?"

The man opened his mouth, but Wuervik said over him, "Illness, we believe."

Med. Pena asked, "Circumstances?"

Wuervik said, "Out in a rainstorm, she collapsed." Pressure rose in Neilan's chest. How sick *was* she?

Med. Pena nodded and leaned over Elwyn. She opened Elwyn's eyelids, pressed her fingernails, felt her forehead, checked her pulse, and listened to her lungs. Neilan's skin prickled, sensing the Magic that assisted her examination. After a few seconds, she nodded and hurried off to a large counter next to shelves and shelves of drafts and raw ingredients. She spoke to two medics, who began working immediately, grabbing herbs and liquids from the shelves.

A junior medic began grinding a piece of hardened lucten into powder. Med. Pena snatched it from him and worked it into a fine dust. The medics handed her ingredients, and her practiced hands ground them, tore them, measured them, and poured them into an impossibly complicated draft. Again, Neilan sensed the Magic that flowed from her to emulsify the ingredients.

Astur caught Neilan's eye and said, "You should get to know these newcomers." He gestured to the man and woman. "Cuinn and Theon Hakon, Elwyn's parents."

Neilan started and looked at them fully for the first time. With a shock, he saw Elwyn's face on the woman's body, with dark brown eyes and hair instead of Elwyn's blue and blonde. It was different, but weirdly the same.

"Cuinn and Theon," Astur continued, "this is Neilan, Elwyn's co-ward and closest friend. They have been raised together under Chief Keeper Wuervik's supervision, as they are the only two children in the Haven without parents present."

The two of them looked back at him, and Neilan saw his own apprehension reflected in the man's face. The Elwyn-lady had a warm smile, but her eyes were sad. She looked at him like she understood him completely. His insides squirmed, and he instinctively stepped away.

The Elwyn-lady turned back to Astur and asked, a bit aggressively, "Co-ward?"

Wuervik tilted his head, confused by the question, but Astur looked at his feet and shifted uncomfortably. "Heir of Linguistic," Astur said, "it has been a long time since I've had the privilege of spending time with one of your line with the Gift. I must be more conscientious about my communication."

The woman—Cuinn, Elwyn's mother, he had to get that through his head—narrowed her eyes at him. "Ward?" she asked. "Not daughter? Not sister? You took her from her family and didn't have the decency to give her a new one?"

Astur's shoulders tensed, and Wuervik looked at the ground.

Half-angrily, half-tenderly, Cuinn said, "She's a daughter now, if she wasn't before."

Neilan's eyes drew to Elwyn like a magnet. Her pale skin was almost see-through. Blue veins stood out on her hands and her closed eyelids. Her skin didn't look strong enough to protect her. It looked so fragile it might tear at the slightest touch.

Her nose was still peeling from the sunburn, and he had a bizarre, manic urge to laugh. He turned it into a cough.

"Are you feeling okay?" Cuinn asked.

Wuervik looked closely at him. "Medic Pena, Neilan was out with her for part of her journey. He may have caught whatever she has, too."

"I'm fine," Neilan said quickly, waving away Wuervik's scrutiny, but Med. Pena was already hurrying to him.

She looked Neilan over, then headed back to the counter. "There's no point pretending you're okay when you aren't," she said. "You don't have what she has, but you could use some help still."

What was she talking about? He was fine. Well, he was exhausted and tense, and completely drained. But that was because of his emotions—it didn't mean he was sick. Did it? Could his emotions affect his body? Or his body affect his emotions?

Med. Pena pulled down a large, half-full, hexagonal bottle of silver liquid from a line of three. She poured a dose of the healing draft into a metal cup and brought it to him. "Drink," she commanded.

He obeyed. He'd always wondered how it tasted. The silver liquid was like fresh spring water.

"I don't think you need these anymore," she said, pointing to his wrist cuffs. "Wuervik?"

Wuervik nodded absently and reached toward them with Magic. They loosened and slipped off, sailing through the air to Wuervik's outstretched hand. Neilan's arms felt like they'd float, they were so light now.

Med. Pena hurried back to the counter with Neilan's empty cup and finished Elwyn's draft. She poured it into a narrow, glass tube and corked it, then she grabbed another draft from the counter and poured a small dose into another glass tube.

"What's that?" Cuinn asked.

"A vitamin mixture to support her immune system," Med. Pena said. "Her immunity to the illnesses of the outside world is limited, since she has lived down here so long." She hustled to Elwyn's bedside and opened her mouth. She poured the vitamin mixture into Elwyn's mouth and waited for the swallow reflex, then she poured in the draft.

"So this is your fault," Theon said, glaring at Astur.

Astur blinked in surprise. Wuervik said, "What do you mean?"

"You brought her down here and took away her body's ability to protect itself." He looked like he wanted to fight them. Neilan did too, for that matter.

Astur stood expressionless, except for a bend in his typically straight back. He probably blamed himself, but it was Neilan's fault more. He'd helped her escape. Neilan's chest constricted. He couldn't lose her. There had to be something he could do.

He felt so helpless. His eyes drew back to Elwyn's form laying flat on the bed, and her eyes were open. His heart leapt, and his pulse pounded in his veins. No one else seemed to have noticed.

She looked dazed, and her face was expressionless, but she held Neilan's eye contact. He raised his eyebrows and gave her a small smile. A corner of her mouth twitched up for a fraction of a second. Still flat on her back, she glanced around the room slowly from person to person.

In the background of Neilan's consciousness, Theon's voice said, "What about you all? Do you have sufficient immunities to the outside world?"

How could they still be talking about that when Elwyn was awake! Didn't they see? Didn't they care?

Astur said, "Yes. Once they become Qualified, Keepers start regularly taking the vitamin mixture and have short surface missions, which helps their bodies adjust to the surface illnesses through small exposures. Each time they return, they first come here to spend time under observation and receive medical aid if necessary."

"'They'?" Cuinn asked quietly. "What about you?"

Astur and Cuinn stared at one another. The ferocity of their eye contact made Neilan's hair stand on end. "What about you?" Cuinn repeated, a suspicious gleam in her eyes.

Astur's silver eyes intensified, and his face hardened. "I am not human."

A shiver ran down Neilan's spine, and a tremor ran through the room. Not human? What was he?

Astur continued, "So I am not subject to the limitations of the human body."

Cuinn raised her eyebrows at him.

"I have… different limitations," he said bitterly.

"You look human," Cuinn said, combatively.

"My kind have cloaked our appearance to blend into this world. We are made of light, or at least that's the closest thing here to what we are. We've taken on the appearance of humans in order to complete our assignment here, but we do not have physical bodies, in the way humans do. What you see is merely illusion."

Astur balled a fist and swung at Wuervik. But rather than punching Wuervik in the face, as it looked like he would do, his arm slipped right through Wuervik's head. The room gasped in unison, but Wuervik didn't react at all.

"I cannot touch the physical world, and it cannot touch me," Astur said. "There is a way I may become temporarily physical, which some of my kind have used, but I have not and will not use it."

Cuinn's eyes narrowed. "What are you?"

Astur paused, then he said, "I am one of the Ansomafin."

Med. Pena jumped and stared at him. Astur glanced sidelong at her and kept speaking. "I'm known here as a Protector. My kind is divided: my fellows and I are Protectors, and we work in opposition to the Others, led by Solun."

Med. Pena stared wide-eyed at Astur. "You're his kind?"

"Yes," Astur said simply, but firmly. Bumps rose on Neilan's arms.

"Why didn't you tell us?" Med. Pena asked angrily.

"Those to whom the information was pertinent have been told. For the rest, it has not been deemed wise to share the information. To medics, who are not asked to heal Ansomafin because we require no physical healing, the information is irrelevant. You did not need to know," he said with finality.

Med. Pena looked at the floor silently, but tension rolled off her.

After a minute, Cuinn asked, "Why do we need to know? Why is it 'pertinent' now?"

Astur frowned. "I'm unused to Heirs of Linguistic. I must be more careful."

Her eyes narrowed, and her voice dropped lower. "Why is it pertinent now?"

Astur glared at her, but his eyes were pleading, too. Neither of them blinked. He said, "I believe this is all as it was meant to be."

Neilan had the uncomfortable impression that more was being communicated than the words Astur was saying. Their eye contact was so intense it seemed like it should be private. It felt like Neilan was intruding. He looked back at Elwyn. She was dazed and obviously exhausted, but there was a little bit of life in her eyes. She watched her mother and Astur languidly.

"Elwyn was meant to seek you out, and to find you," Astur said. "Something larger is happening, which will alter the future of more than just Terralum, of Alloidem as a whole. You are meant to be part of it, so you must understand it. But," he paused and shifted. "We've put off confrontation for so many years." He looked down. "We don't know how to proceed."

Neilan cringed. A helpless tone in Astur's voice was terrifying. If Astur couldn't figure it out, how could anyone else?

"The only advantage we had was surprise," Astur continued, "for Solun didn't know that I am still here. That's gone, now."

Elwyn was part of something bigger. Of course she was. Her face was expressionless, but the light in her eyes had sharpened.

"We'll need your help, the help of all Heirs of the Eudaimonians," Astur said. "We don't know how to rid the universe of the Others.

You see," he trailed off. Then he met Cuinn's eyes again with the same hard intensity as before, as though trying to force Cuinn to understand and find the answer. "My kind cannot die."

Neilan's skin crawled, and Cuinn squeezed her eyes shut. "Cannot die," she said under her breath. "*Cannot.*"

Theon said in a low tone, "You can't die, so neither can Solun. We can't kill him. Solun knows you can't die, but he thought you were no longer around." His voice hardened. "There's somewhere else to go, somewhere we can send Solun."

Astur blinked in surprise, then his eyebrows came together. Fury and fear rose behind his eyes. "No."

Theon glared at him suspiciously, and his eyebrows drew together. Cuinn watched each of them, then she put a hand on Theon's arm. He glanced at her, and she nodded to him. Theon's rising anger ebbed.

"So Solun can't be exiled," she said. "Or killed." She squeezed her eyes shut again. "*Cannot* die. It's a burden." She turned to Astur. "How long have you been here?"

Astur stiffened, but he answered, "I've run this Haven for four hundred thirty-five years, and I've been in Alloidem for nearly nine hundred years."

Nine hundred years? Astur was that old?

On the bed, Elwyn's eyelids fluttered, approaching the edge of exhaustion. Then her eyes closed, and her head lolled. Neilan's chest tightened. Was she okay? He scanned the room, but no one seemed to be paying attention to Elwyn—everyone was too wrapped up in her parents and Astur.

Cuinn's jaw was tense as she faced Astur, but her eyes softened. "I can't imagine living in this broken world for that long. In my forty years, I've had enough pain for eternity."

She put her hand in Theon's and leaned against him, then she looked at Elwyn's form laid out on the bed. "What can we do for her?"

The group of Medic-Keepers shook themselves, as though waking from a daze. Med. Pena approached the bed and checked Elwyn's pulse and breathing. "For now, what she needs is time."

Time? Wasn't Med. Pena supposed to be a powerful Magic user? Neilan's fists burned. "Can't you heal her with Magic?" he burst out.

"Her body will do a better job than I can do, given the proper conditions." Med. Pena said calmly. "We'll provide those conditions."

"What if—?" Neilan stopped himself. Elwyn was strong. She'd pull through. She had to.

26

In the morning, Neilan sat next to Elwyn's bed in the Medical Ward. She hadn't woken up or even moved since last night, and Neilan's insides felt permanently twisted.

Astur stood a few paces away with Elwyn's parents. "Your specific Gifts relate to mental processes," Astur was saying, "which can be honed to more enhanced effect. You must learn to discern which lines of thought are vital and which ones are periphery, which you may ignore. To do that you must first understand the Gifts, both your own and the rest of them."

Neilan couldn't believe they were talking about something as trivial as the Gifts with Elwyn laying there so sick. How could they even think of something else? She was all that mattered.

Uncaringly, Astur kept speaking. "There are five: Linguistic, Logic, Magic, Music, and Aesthetic. Each Gift grants the Gifted a specific, natural capacity in an area of human need, which contributes to human flourishing. Heirs can use their Gifts without training, but the Gifts are more powerful and effective with intentional training."

Astur gestured to Theon and said, "Logic is the Gift of order, which grants the ability to understand the mathematics and reason of the world and to bring order to the chaos. Logic helps humans function within and bring order to the world."

He gestured to Cuinn. "Linguistic is the Gift of communication, which grants the ability to effectively communicate with another, both verbally and nonverbally. Linguistic aids in both interpretation of another's meaning as well as conveying of one's own meaning. Linguistic helps living beings connect with one another.

"Magic is the material Gift. It grants the ability to manipulate matter, to affect change in and exercise dominion over the physical world. Magic helps humans steward the physical world. All Haveners, except you two, Elwyn, and me, are Heirs of Magic," he said, gesturing at Neilan.

"Music is the Gift of the internal, which grants the ability to understand the impact and nature of sound, and to create sound to affect the emotion and health of living things. Music enters into a being's inner world, into that which is individual, and brings that which is within into relation with what is without—that is, community. Music helps living beings access and thrive within their deep internal worlds.

"Aesthetic is the Gift of the external, which grants the ability to internalize the meaning of what is seen and to create visuals to convey meaning. It engages what is external, therefore shared, and brings the individual into relation with the external and communal. Aesthetic helps individuals meaningfully connect with that which is outside of self.

"Together, the Gifts build community and give humanity the tools to flourish."

Both Theon and Cuinn stared at Astur, thoughts whirling behind their eyes. After a moment, their expressions relaxed.

Neilan glared at them. They were unbelievable. The Gifts didn't matter, not with Elwyn laying there. Her face was thinning, and the blue veins on her eyelids stood out sharply.

"But they didn't," Theon said, as though continuing a thought from before. "They were part of the Eudaimonians' downfall. Weren't they?"

Astur raised his eyebrows, then slowly drew them down and together. "The Gifts are blessings, but in themselves they cannot fix the brokenness of human hearts."

Cuinn's eyes narrowed thoughtfully. Neilan turned resolutely away from them, his eyes and fists burning. He could still feel them behind him, as though his anger was a fiery rope that pulled his focus to them even though his eyes were on Elwyn.

"In the nearly nine-hundred years since the Gifts were given," Astur said, "I have yet to see them used solely for good."

"The Sovereign has been in charge that long?" Cuinn asked.

"Solun fell about six-hundred fifty years ago. He has ruled and oppressed Alloidem ever since—"

"You say oppressed," Theon said. "But we've lived supposedly under his rule our entire lives and have barely felt his presence."

"Solun is not omnipresent," Astur said, "so he can only be in one place at a time. He must rely on the eyes, ears, and abilities of his servants to carry out his will, a fact which brings him unending anger. He resents relying on anyone but himself, especially humans."

Cuinn shifted, turning toward Elwyn. As though she cared. "Is there anything else we can do?"

"The Medic-Keepers have done all they can at this point," Astur said. "She's in the hands of the High King. We must wait for her healing to be complete."

"The High King?" Cuinn asked. "I've never heard the Crown called that."

Despite his annoyance, Neilan looked at her, surprised at her ignorance.

"The Crown is not the person to whom I referred. Follus, Crown of Terralum, is merely Solun's puppet," Astur said with an odd sadness to his voice. "The High King reigns over all kings of this and all worlds." Neilan's chest tingled with the presence of power that came with thoughts of the High King.

"But that's just a myth," Theon cut in.

Astur's silver eyes pierced him. "Is he?"

Cuinn's eyebrows drew together thoughtfully. "Stories are powerful. Myths reveal the yearnings of our hearts. In a way, they are true, even if they aren't real."

Astur's lips quirked. "I appreciate your point. But there is still a significant difference between a myth and a real person, don't you agree?"

"Of course," she said, frowning at him. "But that's not what we're dealing with here."

"Isn't it?" he asked, with the same look he'd just given Theon.

"What are you saying?" she asked sharply.

His lips quirked again, and his silver eyes sparkled. Was Astur enjoying this? Neilan would never understand him. "What do you think I'm saying?" he asked with an inviting tone.

Theon glared at him outright. "You're saying the High King is real."

Astur grinned. "Yes."

"But how could you know?" Cuinn asked.

"How much do you remember of our conversation yesterday? Consider: how long have I been in this world, Heir of Logic?"

"Nearly nine-hundred years," Theon answered automatically. "Assuming your time has aligned with the years of the Eudaimonians, you've been here exactly eight-hundred ninety-seven years, as it's y.e. 897."

Astur nodded, a grin on his lips. "Correct." Then he looked at

Cuinn. "What can you infer?"

She frowned, but understanding seemed to be growing behind her eyes. "You were somewhere else before," she said, cocking her head to one side.

"Correct," he said. Astur was from another world? Neilan's mind reeled.

"Where were you?" Theon asked, his voice tinged with both suspicion and awe.

"Where the High King is," Astur said, his eyes glowing. Astur's already straight back seemed to straighten more. "The High King is the one who sent me here." The room reverberated with the delight charging his words.

Cuinn visibly trembled, but then she frowned. "How can he help Elwyn?"

"The High King is a powerful user of all five Gifts," Astur said. "He doesn't need to be geographically close to apply them, as humans do, and his skill is immeasurably beyond that of any Gifted human."

"Then why have Magic-using medics here?" Theon asked. "Why doesn't the High King just take care of it all without the need for Gifted humans?"

"He desires for humans to work together, to use the tools he has given them to serve one another. When possible, he directs them toward one another. When humans are incapable of handling the situation, often he intervenes. But you must understand, there is far more at stake here than just Elwyn's life, though her life *is* important to him. The High King's work here is far greater than humans or Ansomafin can understand. That being said, I believe he will heal her. His blessing is on her."

Cuinn narrowed her eyes at him. "Then why not just say he will, rather than that explanation that spins in a circle just to end up at the same place?"

Astur's lips quirked again. "It's more complicated than that, which I know you already understand. You cannot fool me, though you do surprise me, Heir of Linguistic."

Cuinn stared at Astur for a long moment, then her eyes unfocused, and she stared at nothingness. "My mind is fuzzy," she said.

"Yes," Astur said. "It's your Gift. Every individual with a Gift has a threshold of the Gift's capacity to work. Once that threshold is reached, the Gift begins to be harmful rather than helpful. As yours is Linguistic, which functions within the mind, when it is overused it will slow down your brain. If you continue to push it, it will eventually take away your capacity for communication. You will lose the ability to speak and to understand speech and other communication.

"Usually, rest in darkness and silence will refresh your body, but if you refuse to stop using the Gift, it could be catastrophic. It would eventually interrupt the communication between your brain and the rest of your body, shutting down your major bodily systems, which would be fatal."

Silence reigned for a moment, then Cuinn wobbled on her feet. Theon wrapped an arm around her waist and held her up. She sank into him, and Theon looked at Astur wide-eyed.

Astur gestured to the next room of the Medical Ward, where private rooms branched from it. Theon held Cuinn up and half-carried, half-dragged her toward it.

They only spared one glance at Elwyn before they left. Neilan clenched his jaw. Why were they here, since they obviously didn't care about her? It'd be better for everyone if they just left.

27

Elwyn's mind woke slowly, as though it was being dragged to the surface of a deep pond. She tried to open her eyes, but they wouldn't budge. Her mouth tasted terrible.

For a long time, or maybe a second, she stayed still with her eyes shut. She became aware that she was on her back, on a firm surface. Her muscles ached, and her joints hurt. The taste in her mouth was distracting. She wished she could chew some mint.

Her throat was dry, too. She tried to reach around for water, but her arms wouldn't respond. She strained to lift her head, but it was too heavy. This was getting annoying. What was she doing here?

Sounds began to take shape around her. They were indistinguishable at first, but she listened hard. They slowly divided into voices, but she couldn't make out any words. The strain of trying to understand them exhausted her, so she gave up and let the voices blend back into a low din.

She wanted to relax into whatever surface she was laying on, but her body hurt too much. She wished she could roll over.

Light pierced her closed eyelids. She squeezed her eyes tight against it, and her eyelids responded! She was able to roll her face away from the bright light, then she opened her eyelids a crack. She was staring at a root-lined wall. She rolled her head over to the other side and made out a few people-shapes moving around the room.

"She's awake!" someone said above her, holding a lucten lamp over her face. Shapes rushed closer. Elwyn forced herself up into a sitting position and looked around. She was on a bed in the Medical Ward, and Med. Pena stood over her with the lucten-lamp.

The two people Elwyn had just met, her parents, stood next to her bed, eyes wide and faces taut, staring into her face, while medics bustled around the room. Neilan stood a few paces away, with his arms crossed. His face was worn, with circles under his eyes.

A medic rushed out of the ward. Med. Pena came back to Elwyn's side and tried to lay her down again. She didn't want to, the bed hurt. Med. Pena pushed gently but firmly on Elwyn's shoulders until she gave in.

"How do you feel?" Med. Pena asked.

Elwyn cringed from the scrutiny of so many people. "I'm okay," she said in a croaky voice. "Just thirsty."

Theon burst into a shaky, stress-tightened laugh, and tears welled in Cuinn's eyes. "We were so scared," Cuinn whispered, covering Elwyn's hand with one of hers and trying to wipe her tears with her opposite one.

Med. Pena held a mug of water to Elwyn's lips. She leaned up a little to drink, trying not to dribble it all over herself in that awkward position. Why wasn't she allowed to hold the cup herself?

Wuervik and Astur burst through the door, trailed by the medic who'd left the room a moment earlier. Astur's face was etched with relief, and Elwyn recoiled. Such an open expression on his face was off-putting. Wuervik's eyes were wide, with circles around them like Neilan's, and his jaw muscles were tight.

All the people looking at her made heat rise in her face. She scanned the room to avoid them, and her eyes met Neilan's. What was he doing over there? She frowned at him, and he slowly, apparently hesitantly, came toward her. "What happened to me?" Elwyn asked, her voice crackly.

"You caught a surface illness on your… trip," Astur said, a touch of irony in his voice.

Self-conscious, Elwyn looked away from him. "Am I better?"

"Nearly better," Med. Pena said. "You'll need to take it easy for a few days, and you'll need to spend time in the sunlight today to strengthen your body." She turned to Wuervik, "Bring her to the surface at midday today, for the strongest sunrays."

Cuinn faced Astur. "I want to take her up. By myself."

Wuervik's eyebrows shot up. "Absolutely not. She already fled once, and that man will still be looking for us."

Astur looked from Cuinn to Wuervik and said sadly, "We took her from her parents. I cannot forgive myself for the time I've stolen from all three of them. Her mother should be allowed time with her."

Wuervik retorted angrily, too low for Elwyn to hear, and the two of them whispered sharply back and forth.

"You okay?" a tense voice asked. Neilan stood at her bedside, with his shoulders curved in and his hands clasped nervously in front of him.

"Yeah, I'm fine," she said reflexively, trying to hear what Astur and Wuervik were saying. She looked vaguely at Neilan, but something about his face made her stop and look closer. He looked awful. His face was tight and thin, and the circles under his eyes looked worse up close. His normally glowing skin had a dull tone to it. "What's going on with you?" she asked.

He glared at her.

She tried again. "You look sick, too." She didn't know how to say what he actually looked like.

"I've just been worried," he said, looking at the floor. "You were really sick."

"I'm sorry," Elwyn said. She didn't know what she meant by that, but the pain in his face made her heart ache.

He looked at her, and tears pooled in his eyes. "I didn't know if you were going to make it."

Elwyn's heart lurched. She reached toward him, and he reached out, too, taking hold of her hand. At his touch, a tingle ran all the way up her arm. Having him so close made her feel like she was whole again. She leaned into the comfort of his nearness.

"Fine," Wuervik said loudly and irritably. "But I think it's a bad idea."

Wuervik, Astur, and her parents approached Elwyn's bed. Neilan let go of her hand and hastily retreated to a spot behind them, glaring at their backs. Elwyn frowned at him. Why'd he leave her?

"You need sunlight to help your body get stronger," Cuinn said, "so you and I will go to the surface at midday for an hour, if you feel up for it. What do you think?"

Elwyn's heartbeat sped. Alone with Cuinn? Yes, she wanted to, but also not at all. What would she say? They barely knew one another.

"As if she has a choice," Neilan said under his breath, frowning resentfully at his feet. What was wrong with him?

"That sounds good," she said to Cuinn, hoping to cover up Neilan's attitude. It hurt her feelings. He was her favorite person, and she wanted everyone else to see him like she did, but he was making himself seem mean. That's the last thing she wanted Cuinn and Theon to think of him.

Why couldn't he just be his normal self? He was so frustrating.

28

Elwyn sat in a ray of fresh Dawnday sunlight with Cuinn, at the edge of a freshwater stream, in a small clearing twenty paces from the hollow tree trunk that hid the Haven's Enex hole. It was almost as though she was a normal Haven kid, visiting the surface for her monthly trip, chaperoned by her mother.

The air was warm and sweet, full of the forest. Two-domain animals sang in the trees and skittered around the forest floor, out of sight. A slight breeze cooled Elwyn's face, and she breathed deep.

She couldn't think of anything to say, but Cuinn sat next to her with her eyes closed and face turned up to the sun, breathing in the forest just like Elwyn. Apparently she was content to sit in silence, if that's what Elwyn wanted.

Silence was easier, but Elwyn wanted to talk. Despite knowing it was impossible, her mind kept replaying the image from her dreams as a kid, of sitting in her mama's lap, feeling comfortable and cared for. What could she say to get to know this person who was supposed to be her mother?

Her chest was still tight with frustration about Neilan. Why'd he have to be like that? Why couldn't he show his best self to these people?

Elwyn didn't like admitting it to herself, but she wanted to make a good impression on them. She wanted them to like her, and she wanted them to like her best friend. Her only friend. Ugh, why did she have to care?

As though she could tell the bent of Elwyn's thoughts, Cuinn said, "Tell me about your friend, Neilan."

Would Elwyn be able to do that when she had Linguistic? She hesitated. "What do you want to know about him?"

Cuinn opened her eyes and turned to Elwyn. It felt like she was reading Elwyn's soul through her eyes. Elwyn turned away, pretending to be interested in a bird taking flight.

"What do you want to share about him?" Cuinn asked. Elwyn couldn't tell exactly how, but she sensed that Cuinn was giving her an opportunity to share her heart, to help Cuinn see Neilan as she did.

What should she say? Her mind reeled. How did she see Neilan? Her mind filled with the image of him, eyes sparkling as he laughed at her sunburn. Her heart swelled. "He's comfortable," she said, without really knowing what she meant. She frowned to herself. What did she mean?

She tried again. "He's easy to be with." Well, not always. "Except when he thinks he has to protect me."

She couldn't get her thoughts together. She tried to get a hold of something concrete to say about him, to explain his behavior. "His parents gave him up," she said finally. "They let Astur and Wuervik take him to the Haven, when he was a kid—six years old. It hurt him." She paused. "He didn't want me to go find you." Why'd she say that? That wasn't going to help Cuinn like him.

But Cuinn sat silent, her face peacefully contemplative. After a long moment, she said, "He's afraid we're going to take you from him."

"Well, yeah," Elwyn said. That was it, wasn't it? Why couldn't he just say that, instead of being mean?

"What's he like normally?" Cuinn asked.

Elwyn considered. "He laughs a lot. He eats a *lot*." She grinned to herself. What else? "He looks out for me. He helps me not take everything so seriously." She shrugged. "He feels like home."

Cuinn smiled, a gentle but radiant smile. "I know just what you mean."

Elwyn's heart warmed, but then a shadow passed over her mind. "But why's he acting so strange?"

Cuinn picked up a stick and rubbed its rough edges. "Does he know he's your home?"

Elwyn opened her mouth to respond then started. How could she answer that?

Cuinn continued, "It appears as though you're his home, too. And he's afraid we're going to take his home—you—from him."

Elwyn ached inside. What would that be like for him? "But you won't."

"How does he know that?" she asked gently. "Does he know how important he is to you?"

Elwyn frowned to herself. "I don't know." How was she supposed to tell him that?

Cuinn looked at the stick in her hand and said, "When your father and I were first married," then she paused. "'Your father!' I've imagined myself using that phrase a thousand times, but it still feels strange." She smiled sadly and reached out to put a hand on Elwyn's cheek. Elwyn started but didn't pull away. Cuinn's touch sent a tingle through her face and down her neck. "My daughter," she whispered. "It's still so hard to believe you're real."

The corners of Elwyn's eyes burned. She looked down but leaned into Cuinn's touch.

They were silent like that for a long moment. Then Cuinn said again, "When your father and I were first married, I thought I had to be strong. I thought I had to hold everything in, to keep my inner mess from being a burden to him." She rubbed Elwyn's cheek with her thumb. "I think you're a lot like me."

Elwyn's heart warmed.

Cuinn held up the stick she'd picked up. "Your father taught me something. He got a stick and stood it up, like this." She stood it on the forest floor on its end, and it immediately fell over.

"He told me I was like the stick, trying to stand on my own. Then," she picked up another stick, "He did this." She stood up both sticks, balancing them by leaning their top ends against one another. She let go, and they stayed upright, holding one another up. "'We're like these,' he told me. 'If we lean on one another, our leaning holds one another up.'

"Then he did this," Cuinn continued. She stood one stick up straight and tried to balance the second one against it. The uneven pressure made both of them collapse. "And he told me, 'If you don't lean on me, I can't lean on you.'

"Neilan needs a safe place to lean into. You used to be one another's safe place, but he's afraid you're going to lean away now that we're here. He can't stand on his own, no one can. So instead of risking leaning on you when he feels like you're going to let him fall, he's leaning on his anger instead."

Cuinn paused. "Anger can't hold us up long, but it feels safer sometimes than leaning on a person we think will drop us."

Elwyn's chest tightened. Was that really how he felt? But what was she supposed to do about it? What if when she tried, he dropped her instead? She wasn't sure she was willing to lean on anyone, even him. She wanted to be able to stand on her own, so she couldn't hurt anyone. If Neilan leaned on her, what if she dropped him on accident?

"I wish I couldn't hurt him," Elwyn said. "I don't want to hurt anyone. That's all I want, to not hurt anyone. I've been told my whole life that my existence is dangerous for everyone around me. There's nothing I can do to help that, except be alone. Then I couldn't affect anyone. If I didn't affect people, I couldn't hurt them."

Cuinn stared out into the stream, which flowed so slowly that they couldn't see its movement. She picked up a pebble and tossed it into the stream. It's tiny plunk sent ripples of concentric circles in all directions. She tossed in a few more pebbles, and their ripples ran into one another.

"We all make ripples," Cuinn said. "We affect one another. It's part of living."

"Then what if I stand really really still?" Elwyn said under her breath.

Cuinn smiled. "See that rock sticking out of the surface? Watch." She tossed in more pebbles. Their ripples circled and collided, but when they reached the rock, they stopped. "Even staying still affects people. It blocks their ripples."

"Then what if I disappear?"

A shadow passed over Cuinn's face. "You already did that. And it was the worst thing that ever happened to your father and me."

Elwyn's shoulders tightened, and she looked down.

"You can't avoid affecting people," Cuinn said and put her hand on Elwyn's. "Your existence, once begun, will always affect people."

Tension pulled at Elwyn's neck and face. She'd just have to find a way around it.

Neilan's tense, resentful face swam back into her memory. She was already hurting him. How could she stop? As though sensing her thoughts, Cuinn put a gentle hand on her shoulder. "All he needs right now is to know you care about him."

Elwyn considered. Absently, she reached into her pocket for her sancan. Finding nothing, her heart dropped. That's right, it was gone.

How could she show Neilan she cared about him? She scoured her mind. The sancan!

"I think I have an idea," she said. "But I need some time over there to get it ready." She pointed the direction of Neilan's and her special spot.

Cuinn smiled sadly and patted her arm. "Don't go far."

Elwyn nodded and stood up. Cuinn scooted into the shade and laid back on some moss. "I'm here if you need me," she said.

Elwyn smiled and took off through the trees toward their special spot. A minute later, the trees opened up to their small clearing.

At the edge of the clearing, the ground dipped into a boulder-edged crater. Moss covered the crater's floor, and there were two flat boulders near the center. Broken sticks, dried leaves, and bits of debris strew the space between the two boulders. The familiar sight lightened Elwyn's heart. Their years of play had left their mark on this place.

She searched the ground at the crater's edge until she found a chunk of wood large and solid enough for her purpose. She picked it up then descended into the crater and settled onto the mossy ground between the flat boulders.

She squinted under one of the boulders and found Neilan's whittling knife. She wasn't nearly as good at it as he was, but he'd taught her enough to make do. Hopefully the thought was more important to Neilan than the execution.

She visualized her sancan, the one he'd made for her right here all those years ago, and she held the image in her mind. She made a few tentative marks with the knife, then set to work.

She sat for a long time, lost in her labor. The lump of wood became a smaller lump, with vaguely wing-shaped lumps coming off the sides. She shaped the wings, then moved onto the large, beaked head. The body was sleek. She didn't bother to detail the feathers—that was beyond her skill. So were the webbed claws: this sancan's feet were round blobs. But Neilan would know what it was supposed to be.

There was a rustle in the trees. Her eyes shot up to the trees beyond the crater, a shiver running down her arms. Why had the sound struck her? There were animal sounds in every direction.

But she should be getting back to Cuinn. She held up the sancan and looked over it. A few more adjustments and it'd be ready. She turned it in the light to look closer at the wings. A shadow moved behind a clump of trees.

Was Cuinn watching her? No, she wouldn't stalk in the shadows. Would she? Elwyn pretended not to see and carved texture lines into the wings.

The shadow shifted. Half of a face flashed into the light and back into the shadows as the watcher adjusted his position. It was a him, that much was clear. He was familiar. She held the flash of his face in her mind while she pretended to focus on the sancan in her hands. She hadn't seen enough to identify him for sure.

Her heart pounded, and her throat burned cold. Adrenaline pumped through her body, but she kept her eyes down, so he wouldn't know she'd seen him. She picked up the longest stick she could see on the crater's mossy floor and found a long, pliant stem for twine. She tied the whittling knife to the end of the stick and hid it under her arm.

Elwyn picked up the nearly-finished sancan, careful to keep her makeshift spear concealed under her arm, and she stood up. She made a show of brushing off her dress, stalling to see what the man would do.

He perked up at her movement and kept watching closely. There was a greedy glint in the man's eyes, sending a shiver down her spine. The expression brought back a flash of memory: wolfskin-shrouded men sizing her up. Her limbs shook with adrenaline, and her breath came faster.

As nonchalantly as she could, she climbed the crater's bank and left their special spot, keeping the corner of her eye on the man. He waited until she was a little way away, then he stepped from behind the clump of trees and sneaked to the next tree trunk. His waist-length black hair was tied into a tail at the back of his head.

Her heartbeat sped. Cuinn was nearby—Elwyn couldn't lead him toward her. Where should she go?

She took a few steps the opposite direction from where she'd left Cuinn, away from the Haven's entrance. The watcher moved again.

She walked slowly toward the bank of the lucten stream, trying to seem unshaken. Her heightened senses registered every leaf the watcher shuffled and every breath he took.

What now? She could run, but her legs were already wobbly from being so sick. He'd catch her immediately.

He was too close to the Haven. She couldn't let him know how close. What could she do? Lead him away. But if—when—he caught her, would he kill her or take her prisoner? Could she resist torture?

She walked beside the lucten stream, keeping her spear pinned under one arm and the sancan in the opposite hand. She picked up her pace, and he sped up, too.

Her legs shook, already tired from the exertion. Why couldn't this have happened when she was at full strength? She had to do something before she lost her energy and all her nerve. A pair of brutal, sleet-gray eyes swam into her mind's eye, along with the helplessness when those men had caught her, held her, taunted her.

Her skin crawled as though they'd just touched her.

Then came the emptiness and the desire to abandon her tainted self. The rage, the desire to scream, to thrash, to destroy the entire world. The fury and disgust at herself for being unable to do anything at all. Her stomach clenched. She would not be helpless again.

She took off in a full sprint, away from the Haven. The watcher ran after her, all pretense of stealth gone.

Hot, animal rage boiled up inside her. Her makeshift spear scratched her arm as she ran, and she gripped it, flexing her fingers around the shaft. She would do this. She was capable.

Her heart raced, and her muscles shook, threatening exhaustion though they still pulsed with adrenaline.

A thrill ran through her whole body. She breathed in deep, then she whirled around to face him. A deep, guttural yell issued from somewhere inside her, and she raised her spear.

29

Neilan burst out of the Enex hole into the hollow trunk. Where was Elwyn? Her hour was past, and she hadn't come back down. He couldn't believe they'd let her go up with only that woman.

Wuervik's yells issued from the hole as he ran up after Neilan. Who cared? Neilan had to make sure Elwyn hadn't run off again. He wouldn't let her leave, not this time.

At least Wuervik didn't try to fight him with Magic. After last time, he probably knew it wasn't worth the energy it wasted.

Astur appeared, slipping up through the ground right in front of him, at the end of the hollow trunk. Neilan jolted back, a shock running down his arms. Astur was full of tricks all of a sudden. Apparently he didn't care about hiding his non-humanness anymore. "Leaving without permission is forbidden, Neilan," he said calmly.

Astur's body filled the trunk. But he wasn't really a body, was he? "I have to make sure!" Neilan said, bolting straight through him. Astur stared after Neilan, unable to stop him, and his face was strangely calm.

An animal scream echoed through the trees, and a shiver ran

down Neilan's spine. Instinctively, he ran toward it.

A few moments later, there was a flash of movement between the trees along the lucten stream. He sprinted that way.

Long blonde hair swung into sight. A few steps more and there she was, facing a man, pointing a spear at him. The man held a dagger and a hunting blade, ready to strike.

Her eyes were blank, as though her soul wasn't behind them anymore. Neilan froze, and the hairs on the back of his neck stood on end. She dropped a small lump onto the ground, bared her teeth at the man, then lunged.

Neilan wanted to call out to her, to help her! But his body wouldn't respond. He stood paralyzed, partially hidden behind the last clump of trees, watching his worst fears realized.

The man dodged her spear and swiped toward the back of her leg, but she spun away from his blade.

In what seemed like one continual motion, he twisted his hand and swung at her head with the dagger's wooden hilt. She ducked, but he clipped her shoulder. The velocity of his strike knocked her over.

Mid-fall, she rolled toward a tree trunk. She jumped up and spun around the trunk then swung at him with her spear, missing him. Before she could bring it around for another swing, the man threw both his arms out wide and tackled her.

They landed hard at the base of the tree, and she cried out. He landed on top of her, holding her down. She screamed and thrashed in his grip, her spear flailing from where he pinned her arm at her side.

He yelled and rolled off of her, with a slice all the way through his cheek. His skin hung open, and Neilan's stomach turned over.

She jumped up and turned, so Neilan got a full view of her face. That person wasn't Elwyn. It couldn't be. Those eyes were cold and alien. Not his best friend, not his Elwyn.

Yells behind him vaguely registered in Neilan's ears, as the Elwyn-ish person hefted her spear with a terrifying, self-satisfied smirk that sent new shivers down Neilan's spine. She pointed the spear at the man on the ground, who was groaning and holding his bleeding cheek.

He flipped onto his hands and knees and his arm flashed, his dagger sweeping across the back of her ankle.

She screamed, and her leg buckled. Her spear shot downward as she fell, toward the man's back. She tried to catch her fall with it, and her bodyweight heaved it into his back. The point disappeared, lodged deep.

The man collapsed. His body jerked, then he ceased to move. Blood poured from Elwyn's ankle.

She sat up and grabbed her ankle, but blood squeezed between her fingers. Her empty eyes settled pitilessly on the lifeless body. Then her hands began to shake. As if she sensed Neilan's presence, her blank eyes turned in his direction, and his neck prickled.

Running footsteps came up behind him. Wuervik yelled, and Cuinn screamed. They sprinted past Neilan, toward her.

Life bled back into Elwyn's eyes, but they looked years older. She half-glanced at Cuinn and Wuervik, then her eyes rolled back. She flopped backward and lay flat on the ground.

Cuinn dropped to her knees next to Elwyn, Wuervik a step behind. But Neilan stood still as though rooted to the spot. He couldn't go to her, and he couldn't run away. He couldn't move at all.

Wuervik rolled the man's body over, and Cuinn gasped. "That's him," she said, "the one who followed us. Now that I look closer at him, I've seen him around Regsenfrag for years."

Wuervik touched Elwyn's ankle. The tendon and skin knitted

back together, and blood ceased to pour from the wound. Cuinn shook Elwyn's shoulder and spoke in her ear, but it made no difference.

"She's lost a lot of blood," Wuervik said. "We need to get her back to Med. Pena."

As Wuervik lifted her, Neilan tore his eyes from Elwyn's limp form. A lump on the ground caught his eye—the object she'd dropped just before she'd attacked.

His legs suddenly moved of their own accord, entirely unconnected to his volition. They moved mechanically to the object, while his mind was dazed. It was a carved piece of wood laying in the underbrush, roughly the shape of a sancan, like the one he'd made for Elwyn so long ago. It was freshly whittled, in Elwyn's style.

He stared at it, his mind curiously blank. The world didn't make sense anymore. It was as though his brain had shut off.

He stared at the wooden object, then stared at Elwyn's unconscious form. He should say something, *do* something, but nothing occurred to him. He was hollow.

30

Hosev sat outside the cottage skinning two small robbes. Would there be enough meat here for all ten of them? He'd have to see how much meat these yielded, then maybe he'd have to grab an extra cabbage from the garden to add to the meal.

Next to him, Manell sat scrubbing potatoes. Through the open door came the sound of Mother's rocking chair creaking as she rocked with baby Veylas, back and forth, back and forth, while she stared blankly into the empty hearth.

A lump rose in Hosev's throat, and he swallowed hard. Where was Father? It was already Dawnday. He was supposed to be back to Gravusfrig by last night, Darknight. The Sovereign must not have released him yet.

Hosev squinted above the trees at the coal-black towers of Phaemin Fortress, rising out of the center of the city. Was Father there right now? How long would this part of his assignment take? What if the Sovereign didn't release him to come home afterward?

"Leave it alone," said Alarrin, Hosev's thirteen-year-old brother, working in the garden. "It's fine like that."

"But the rows need to be further apart," their eleven-year-old sister Seralie retorted with a whine in her voice.

"I like these ones, they need more room to get big," piped up Keinta, their eight-year-old sister.

Reffie ran past, chasing a bee. "Careful, Reffie," Seralie said. "Those ones hurt."

"Jaeveh!" Alarrin called out to their seven-year-old brother. "Grab that stick, we'll use it to make these rows even."

"But they're still too close!" Seralie whined.

Manell sighed and put down the potatoes, starting to get up. As usual, she thought she had to take care of everything herself.

"Leave them," Hosev said. "They'll figure it out."

She gave him a half smile. "But we need those vegetables to grow well. If they don't plant them properly—"

"It'll be fine. They can do it." He smiled what he hoped was an encouraging smile. "We handled it ourselves when we were much younger than they are."

"But we're… I don't know. We had to do it by ourselves. They don't."

"We already have most of it planted. If this part doesn't thrive, we'll make do. Let them try. They have to if they're ever going to be able to do it on their own."

Manell huffed and dropped back down. She picked up a potato and scrubbed it aggressively, taking out her antsy impatience on it. Hosev chuckled to himself.

An indefinable rush flew into Hosev's chest, then up to his head. He froze, and the knife from his hand clattered into the bucket. Behind him, Manell's scrubbing halted.

In the garden, sudden silence reigned.

The only sound now was the slow creak of Mother's rocking chair, echoing in the eerie silence. Without meaning to, Hosev tracked it, calculating at what point in the rock it creaked, therefore which pieces of wood within it were creaking.

"What was that?" Keinta said.

"Oh!" Alarrin yelled. "Here we go, this one is the right width. Take this stick and make the rest as wide as this notch."

"I told you they had to be further apart!" Seralie said triumphantly.

"No, not at that angle," Alarrin said. "The sun moves across here during the growing season, they have to face this way so these ones don't shade those ones."

As Alarrin spoke, Hosev's mind pictured exactly what he was pointing out, and how they'd planted the garden inefficiently all these years. It seemed so obvious, now.

How? What had happened?

Hosev's mind spontaneously planned a pattern of planting, unlike the uniform rows they'd always done, that would ensure each plant got the optimum spacing and sunlight while maximizing space efficiency.

He shook himself and picked up his knife. He reached for the robbe he'd been skinning and immediately his mind calculated how much meat a robbe of this size, shape, and weight would yield: three portions by itself as a main dish, six portions if mixed into a stew.

His gut clenched. Something wasn't right. He raised his eyebrows at Manell. She stared at him with wide eyes and shook her head, shrugging.

Dread prickled the back of Hosev's neck—what was going on? Did it have to do with Father's assignment?

31

Elwyn lay for a moment in black stillness, her body aching. Sounds took shape around her: whispers and shuffling.

She opened her eyes and bright light seared them. She groaned and pulled herself up into a sitting position, then she opened her eyes.

Her parents, Wuervik, Astur, and Med. Pena were hovering over her, and she was in the Medical Ward. Again. Why was she back here? Her whole body ached, especially her ankle.

Memory flashed across her mind: searing pain as a knife swiped her ankle. Her weight landing on her spear, slight resistance as it slipped between ribs. Elwyn's body started trembling.

Another memory flashed, sleet-gray eyes and fang tattoos. Her shaking increased. She pulled her knees up to her chest and wrapped her arms around them.

"Elwyn?" Cuinn's voice asked quietly.

Elwyn held her legs tighter and squeezed her eyes shut. Med. Pena draped a blanket over her shoulders as she rocked back and forth, shaking. Her mind kept flashing: the man's face, his knives, wolfskins, a dark alley.

She opened her eyes. She had to find something else to fill her mind with. Neilan stood five paces away, staring at her with wide eyes. His arms were crossed across his chest protectively. She tried to catch his eye, but he looked down and took a step further away from her.

Why wouldn't he come closer? Her body kept trembling. She wanted him near, to put an arm around her and make her feel safe. The sticks Cuinn had leaned together came into her mind. If there was ever a time she needed him there to lean on, it was now.

Her chest constricted, and tears welled in her eyes. She had to find something to do, to think about. She scanned the Medical Ward. On the opposite side of the room, a shape lay on a bed, covered with a blanket. A medic had her hands in the air over the blanket, moving slowly.

"What's she doing?" Elwyn said quietly.

Med. Pena followed Elwyn's gaze. "Preserving the body until burial can be arranged."

"Body?" Elwyn's insides tightened. "Is that..." She couldn't finish the thought.

Cuinn did it for her, in a gentle voice. "The man you encountered on the surface."

"He's..." Elwyn said.

Cuinn nodded and said softly, "Dead."

A prickle ran down Elwyn's arms. "Did I... kill him?"

Cuinn gave her a tiny nod.

Elwyn's breath caught. She'd killed someone. Her mind replayed the scene, the feel of the spear slipping between his ribs. She'd trained in sparring enough to know he hadn't been trying to kill her, just to incapacitate her. She was the only one trying to give fatal blows. The final thrust, after he'd sliced her ankle, had been partly gravity. But she'd wanted to kill him, and she'd killed him.

She'd done it. She'd had to—right? He was the enemy. Wasn't he? She'd had to do it to protect Cuinn. And Neilan and Theon, and everybody.

Her eyes drew back to the shape under the blanket. She could make out the legs and the head. The man's face swam into her memory, his waist-length ponytail swinging.

She'd had to do it, she told herself again. He was the enemy. But her stomach squirmed. He'd served the enemy, but he wasn't the enemy himself. Her mind reeled. "What now?" she squeaked out.

"We will return the body to Regsenfrag," Astur said, "for proper burial."

Wuervik's eyebrows furrowed. "You can't be serious."

"Those who love this man deserve to know what happened to him," Astur said firmly, "rather than be left wondering."

Silence reigned in the room.

"There are many things about which I am unsure," Astur said, "but this I know."

Wuervik stared at him for a second, then he turned to a junior medic and said, "Get Oktoh." The junior medic nodded and scurried away.

Those who love this man. Could he have had loved ones? Facing him, she'd only seen the enemy. But what if he'd had a family? A weight settled in Elwyn's chest. She'd killed someone. He was dead, and he wasn't coming back. It was so… final.

How could she fix this?

Astur looked hard at Elwyn. "Much has happened around you that I don't understand. You were in the tunnel in the C.K. Wing just at the moment I was talking about your parents, after I'd sent every Keeper except Wuervik out of the Treasury to protect the privacy of that conversation. You found a servol the moment you fled from this Haven, which was willing to bear you on its back. You were in

Torlum at the same inn with those who were going to arrest your mother, giving you warning of it. This man," he gestured to the shape under the blanket, "made it to this area at the exact moment that you were up there. How did you end up in these places at these moments? Please explain what you can."

Elwyn couldn't stop trembling. Too much had happened, could she explain it? Some, maybe. "In the C.K. Wing, I followed the tingly tug."

"Tingly tug?" Wuervik asked, but Astur's eyes went wide.

"From the High King?" she said sheepishly, as though asking for their approval, but she didn't know why. She knew it was the High King, but what she knew to be true with every part of her being was somehow hard to say out loud. It was too close to her heart to be spoken.

"Yes," Astur said in a low voice, but it resounded through the room.

"The same tug brought me to the servol. And in Torlum, it guided me to that inn."

Astur looked long at her, face unreadable. After a long moment, he asked, "And today?"

"Today, I don't know. I didn't feel anything. Well, I felt angry. And afraid. But I didn't feel a tug."

Astur stood stone-faced for a long minute, and Elwyn's heartbeat sped. Was he angry with her? "I see," he said finally.

The Medical Ward door opened and red-haired Oktoh, one of the highest-ranking Certified Keepers, rushed in. Astur turned to Wuervik and said, "Post guards at intervals in the trees around the Haven's entrance."

Wuervik nodded and turned to Oktoh, speaking to him in a low voice. Oktoh's eyes went wide and flashed to Elwyn, then back to Wuervik. The look in his eyes brought back the weight of what she'd done. The pressure in her chest made it hard to breathe. She'd *killed* someone.

Astur stepped between her and Oktoh and caught her eye. "The High King is doing something here, with you. I can't see what, but I do see that you need guidance—you're floating on whatever wind comes your way. You must figure out what it is he has for you to do, so you have something to ground you before you follow a foul wind so far you destroy yourself and the work he has for you without knowing it."

Elwyn stared. How was she supposed to do that? She just wanted to avoid hurting people. Her eyes drew to the shape under the blanket. So far, she'd done a terrible job.

The image floated into her mind of Cuinn tossing pebbles into the stream, of their ripples colliding. Elwyn wanted to be free, to live without affecting or being affected by people. She didn't want to make ripples or feel people's ripples. But everything she did and didn't do seemed to make ripples. Cuinn had said she couldn't avoid affecting people, and she'd been right.

Elwyn stared at the figure under the blanket. She had to fix this, to find a way to undo it.

Astur caught her eye again, and his were burning with intensity. "Will you commit to doing so?"

Elwyn looked away from his burning eyes. If she committed, she'd have to abandon her own way, and they'd all be leaning on her. It was too much. "How would I even figure it out?"

"That, I'm not sure. But I believe he will guide you if you're actively listening. I'm going to bring you somewhere I think will aid you."

She frowned. "Where?"

In the midst of his stern face, a tiny smirk lit a corner of Astur's lips. "A place I'm told you've tried to break into, several times."

She started, and Wuervik looked up from Oktoh. "No," he said flatly.

Astur turned toward him calmly, but authority rang in his voice. "I have decided."

Wuervik's eyebrows drew together, and he glared at Astur, but he didn't object again.

Astur faced Elwyn. "Will you commit to searching for and acting on the High King's work for you?"

Elwyn set her chin on her knees. She wanted to figure out how to be free from Solun, free from everyone. To flee, so she couldn't hurt anyone else.

The sticks Cuinn had leaned against one another floated into her mind. People needed one another to lean on. They couldn't make it alone. Maybe people couldn't, but Elwyn had to. She wouldn't hurt more people. Her ripples had started moving—she had to stop them from touching more people. That's what she needed to do.

What if the High King wanted her to do something else? Her chest tightened. That wasn't a comforting thought. Couldn't he just make what she wanted to do work out instead?

She dropped her forehead onto her knees. That wasn't how he worked. She had limited sight, and what she wanted was as limited as her sight. He had far sight, and his plans were as far-sighted as he was.

Whenever she'd trusted the High King before, he'd proved trustworthy. Resisting only hurt her and everyone else. She sighed, but her insides tingled in response to her growing conviction. She met Astur's eyes and said in a small voice, "Yes."

He nodded. A small smile lit his mouth, but it didn't reach his eyes. He turned to her parents and Neilan. "I believe you three are meant to be part of this with her. Will you help her?"

Her parents nodded, but Theon's jaw was tight and Cuinn's eyes were turned down at the edges. Neilan stared at his feet. After a second, he gave a tiny nod.

Astur looked back at Elwyn. "Are you ready?"

A shock ran down her arms. "Now?"

32

Winding through the C.K. Wing, Elwyn's instincts told her to hide, to keep close to the root-lined walls and be ready to flee, but she forced herself to stand tall, to stride behind Astur as though she believed this was real.

Moving light from the thin lucten-brooks under the glass floor met the stationary light from the lucten-lamps hanging above. Her mind trailed back to the sparkling lucten accents that adorned the buildings of Torlum. These rough blocks of hard lucten were coarse in comparison.

They passed the shadowy corner where Neilan had fallen through the wall. How much had happened since then! She glanced over her shoulder at Neilan, who was trailing behind the group.

He was watching her with wide eyes, but as soon as she looked at him, he turned away. She turned back around and tried to ignore the sinking feeling in her chest.

They rounded the end of the tunnel, and a wide, blank, latchless door loomed ahed. Her heartbeat sped. Astur stopped in front of the door and looked over his shoulder expectantly. A huff came from behind Elwyn, and Wuervik stepped forward. He pressed his hand to the blank door and closed his eyes. There was a scraping noise inside the door, then a click.

The door thunked open a crack, and Wuervik heaved it open. Astur strode in, and Elwyn took a deep breath to slow her pounding heart, then she stepped into the Treasury.

She found herself on steps that descended at least ten feet, to the floor of a massive, ancient library. The ceiling, far above, was hidden in shadow. In the center of the room stood a single pillar of dark wood, so thick her arms probably couldn't reach around it. It rose into the shadows of the ceiling, disappearing from view at the top.

Three streaks of lucten circled the base of the pillar, about standing height. A tube of glass surrounded the bottom of the pillar, from the floor to a few feet above the streaks.

The walls were lined with shelf after shelf of dark wood, packed with material: scrolls, lucten lenses, leatherbound books, and stacks of loose parchment wrapped in ancient leather. Elwyn's boots echoed on the glass floor, under which thousands of thin veins of lucten ran in a twisting web.

On every side, countless archways revealed more rooms leading from this one. Elwyn spun in a slow circle. Every wall was filled with shelves as far up as she could see. The shelves disappeared into a haze near the ceiling, far out of the glow of the thin, winding lucten veins below.

Large tables were scattered throughout the room, made of dark wood like the pillar and shelves, rather than glass ones like the T.R. Wing library. The tables, some at standing height and some lower with chairs around them, were topped with lucten lamps.

At a few of the tables, the light in the lucten lamps had drained. Their light could be fully renewed by reconnecting with their source, or partially renewed by absorbing sunlight. The dim lucten lamps sat on the tables like large, crudely-cut, crystal centerpieces.

Two far tables were piled with materials, and a group of Certified Keepers hovered over open leatherbound books and unrolled scrolls.

Astur turned to face Elwyn, his hands clasped behind his back. In the low light, his silver eyes glowed faintly. The rest of the group formed a loose semi-circle facing him. The door thunked closed and Wuervik hurried over, placing himself stiffly right next to Elwyn.

Astur's gaze bored into Elwyn, and she strained to hold his eye contact. Her eyes burned, and she widened them to keep them open, but they watered mercilessly.

"I don't know what the High King intends for you, Elwyn," Astur said. "But you are meant to be part of this. I don't understand why, or even how you are to be involved, but the High King's blessing is on you." He paused, considering, then he said, "You have free rein here."

Wuervik started. "You can't be serious."

Astur's eyes flashed to him. "I am."

Wuervik glared at him and closed his mouth, but he eyed Elwyn. She tried to focus on Astur, but she felt Wuervik's stare like a beam of heat.

"This Treasury contains the collected knowledge and records of Haveners over the last four-hundred years," Astur said. "Sift through as much information as you can. Find your work in the world and the answers that have eluded me for so long. Listen for the tingly tug you described. Cuinn, Theon, and Neilan, help her. There is a lot of information here, too much for one person to search by herself. Listen for the High King's leading, as she has, and help her find answers."

The room was deathly silent. One of the Keepers across the room coughed, then everyone around Elwyn stirred. Cuinn gave Elwyn a quick smile, and Theon nodded at her, then they crossed the cavernous room to the nearest archway and disappeared through it.

Avoiding her eyes, Neilan wandered to a far wall.

Elwyn uneasily scanned the room she was in. She had no idea where to start. She walked to the nearest shelf of leather-wrapped parchment and scrolls.

Wuervik followed her and watched over her shoulder as she scanned the rows, his gaze boring into the back of her head. She didn't take in any of the titles she read, she was too conscious of his eyes on her. The hairs rose on the back of her neck.

"Wuervik," Astur said, and Elwyn jumped.

Wuervik turned to him.

"Leave her be."

Wuervik glared at him, hesitating, then he tore himself from Elwyn's shadow. She breathed in relief.

She turned to a row of lucten lenses, on a shelf etched with the label, "Descriptions of Known Servants of Solun." She carefully lifted one from its place, closed an eye, and held the lucten lens up to her open one.

Colors swirled. A small room took form, with an unadorned bed in the center. Two girls sat on the bed, both with auburn hair and freckles, and they wore matching nightdresses. The older of the two sat behind the younger, brushing her hair.

The younger sister was weeping. Between sobs, she said, "And he pushed me! And then I yelled at him and then he swung to hit me so I ran away."

Tears welled in the older sister's eyes, and they fell silently down her cheeks as she brushed her little sister's hair. "He used to be the best brother. What happened while I was gone? What changed?"

"It's ever since that man with the rings came. He's mean now."

The older sister started. "What man?"

The younger sister shrugged. "I don't know who he is. But he came back with Ralsim from the regional market last month. Ralsim took an extra day to get home, and when he showed up, there was a man with white hair, a green tunic, and gold rings on every finger in the cart with him. He didn't seem old enough to have white hair, but he did. Ralsim had a funny look on his face, and he was all jittery and excited. The man stayed the rest of the day and when he left Ralsim turned grumpy and he's been mean ever since."

The older sister's eyebrows furrowed. "Did you talk to this man? What did Papa say about it all?"

"No, he made me nervous. I watched from up in the tree. Papa was really angry. He even yelled at Ralsim, and Ralsim tried to hit him. Papa caught his fist and I ran away and hid in the bushes by the creek until the yelling stopped."

The older sister clenched her jaw. Fury rose behind her eyes, but she kept quiet and continued to brush her sister's hair. After a long pause, she whispered, "I'm sorry I wasn't here for you."

The younger sister shrugged. "You couldn'tve done anything. And I'm glad you weren't here, the man might've stayed longer if he'd seen you. He had that look about him, like the men in town who watch you and say things."

The scene swirled and disappeared. The Treasury's dark shelves and lucten web shone through it again, and Elwyn's neck tensed. What had happened to those girls? Did Solun's servant come back?

Her mind flashed with sunlight glancing off metal and a waist-length ponytail, sleet-gray eyes and fang tattoos. She wrapped her arms around herself and shoved down the images. Focus. She had a job to do.

Eyes bored into Elwyn from across the room where Astur and Wuervik stood, and the hairs on her neck rose. She couldn't take this. She replaced the lucten lens and hurried through the nearest archway. The center of the room beyond it had two empty study tables, and shelves ran along every wall. Two more archways branched from the opposite end.

Alone for the first time, reality sunk in, and Elwyn's heart started to race. She was here, actually in the Treasury. Her old goal rose up again. She could search for an escape route: figure out where Solun and his servants were least likely to be, and where she could go to be free of him forever.

But her heart constricted. There was nowhere she could go to escape him now that she'd shown herself. And she'd made a commitment. She'd agreed to follow the High King's sight instead of her own. She couldn't see the end, but he could, so she had to trust that he'd get her there. She couldn't break her word and abandon everyone, now.

Sure she could.

Her chest burned. No, she couldn't. Solun would outlive her no matter what, so she had to do her part to *defeat* him. That was the only real way to be free of him. She hoped that's what the High King would show her.

33

Elwyn ran a finger along a shelf of leatherbound books in a side room of the Treasury, trying to look like she was doing something important. It was Twilitday already—the third day she'd been searching, and she'd found nothing. There was something she was supposed to do, and if she didn't do it, she'd *follow a foul wind* as Astur had said. She had to figure this out, before she ruined it.

Everybody needed her. She was supposed to be able to do this, to find her work, but she was failing.

Wasn't the High King supposed to be helping her? How could he let her down like this? She sighed and turned to the next shelf, but emptiness gnawed at her. If she couldn't rely on the High King, who could she rely on?

"Why won't you help me?" she whispered. Then it struck her, she hadn't asked him to, yet. She'd expected him to help automatically, so she hadn't even thought of asking him. She took a breath and whispered, "Please help me find what you want me to do. I need you."

Confidence and peace flowed into her. She took a deep breath, and some of the tension that constantly pulled at her released. "Thank you," she whispered.

A tingly tug pulled at her middle, and adrenaline shot through her. It was finally happening! The tingly tug pulled her through an archway into a long room beyond. A section of lucten lenses glinted just inside the archway, with a label that read, "Evidence Prompting Disciplinary Action." The tug drew her to it. She picked one up and held it to her eye. Colors swirled.

Bright light smacked her in the eye from the surging lucten under the floor of the Haven's T.R. Wing, in the medic-training room.

A Keeper strolled between the cauldrons of a small group of Keepers-in-training, and he leaned over a cauldron. "Good. Then the redimere snake venom, yes, good. Now increase the heat." The Keeper-in-training added a chunk of wood to the fire under her cauldron. The liquid in her cauldron rose to a boil and turned milky-white.

The Keeper nodded and moved on. The next one was boiling, too, but it was thick and brown. "Olin, did you add the ground mycaud bone?"

Olin's thick eyebrows came together. He looked into his cauldron, and his shoulders tensed. The Keeper pulled a cloth from his pocket, grabbed the handle of the cauldron, and picked it up. He swept it to a side table and grabbed an empty cauldron. "Begin again."

Red crept up Olin's neck and face. "You do it!" he yelled.

The Keeper started. He paused, and his eyebrows drew together. Olin, who'd widened his stance, glared at him with clenched fists.

The Keeper turned to the rest of the Keepers-in-training. "That's enough for today. Pack up. I'll see you Dawnday, same time." He leaned toward Olin and spoke low. "Wait here, please."

Olin frowned. The rest of the group glanced at one another, then they hurriedly packed up their work tables. They grabbed their things and glanced at Olin out of the corners of their eyes as they fled from the room. Olin glared at them and held his ground.

When the room was empty, the Keeper walked over to Olin and sat down facing him. He looked up into Olin's face. "Are you okay?"

Olin started and looked at his feet.

"That didn't sound like you," the Keeper said.

Olin glanced at him, then back down. He stepped backward to the nearest chair and sat down.

"You seem tense," the Keeper said. "What's going on?"

Still looking at his feet, Olin muttered, "Pa hit me again this morning."

The Keeper started, and his eyes widened. He leaned toward Olin. "I'm so sorry. Does that happen a lot?"

"Sometimes."

The Keeper sat back. After a moment, he said, "I need to speak with the Chief Keeper about this."

Olin's face jerked up, and his eyes widened. "Don't! Chief Gadira'll say something and Pa'll get angry. Just let it be."

"It's not okay for him to hurt you. I will not let it be." The Keeper caught his eye and held it. "You do not deserve to be hurt."

Olin looked down.

"I'll talk with Gadira later today. But for now, I'd like you to stay here a little while."

Olin kept his eyes on his feet. His shoulders were still tense, but his fists were no longer clenched. He sat back in his chair.

The Keeper stood up and went to the nearest full cauldron. He pulled a small bottle from his pocket and pulled out the stopper, then he let one drop fall into the cauldron. It sizzled, then the contents condensed and solidified into a rock at the bottom of the cauldron.

He wove through the tables, putting a drop of the bottle into each cauldron and gathering up the leftover ingredients. He carefully divided and left out one portion of each ingredient. He brought the rest to the side of the room, where jars sat in a row. He unlatched the jars and poured each leftover ingredient into its appropriate jar. He brought the cauldrons to the side table, removed the rocks, and stacked the cauldrons. Then he set them aside and turned back to Olin.

Olin was supporting his chin with one hand, his elbow resting on the table next to him. The opposite arm was crossed under it, his fingers tapping a beat.

The Keeper asked, "How are you feeling now?"

Olin shrugged. "Okay."

The Keeper nodded. "Let's try the draft again."

Olin grumbled something under his breath, but he stood and picked up the parchment that had the instructions carefully inked. He looked at the Keeper out of the corner of his eye. "I'm sorry for yelling at you."

The Keeper turned to him and gave a small smile. "Thank you for that. I forgive you."

The scene dissipated, and the Treasury's lucten web reformed. Elwyn set down the lucten lens and stared for a while at the web of lucten veins under the glass at her feet. Her mind spun. An image returned of the two sisters from the memory she'd watched on her first day in here. This memory felt so different from that one. Why?

After that one, Elwyn had felt tense and full of fear for those girls. Nothing truly terrible had happened to them, yet, but it felt like something was coming. They were vulnerable, and anything could've happened to them after that memory ended. In this one, something terrible had already happened to Olin. But by the end of the memory, it felt peaceful.

What was the difference? The girls were unprotected. They obviously cared for one another deeply, but they couldn't do anything about the circumstances that could hurt them. Olin had an adult in his life who both cared for him and could help him. Olin wasn't unprotected. He was cared for by someone who was capable of improving his circumstances.

Elwyn's chest swelled. This was… something. What was it? What could she do with it? She didn't know, yet, but something was brewing.

Her mind still full of the Olin memory, she picked up the next lucten lens in the row, pulled it up to her eye, and colors swirled.

The T.R. Wing's sparring room took form. The glowing glass floor was covered in places by thickly padded rugs, and duos sparred throughout the room. Olin stood in a fighting stance, facing a teenage girl in a tunic and trousers, the uniform for defense lessons. Her long, brown hair was braided down her back.

The girl lunged at him, and her long, dark braid swung, but Olin spun out of her reach. She crouched and ran at him, shoulder aimed at his stomach. He bent forward, wrapped his arms around her middle, and lifted her from the ground.

She twisted in his grip, so he dropped to one knee and flattened her on her back on a padded rug. She screamed, her eyes widening in terror. She writhed and flailed in a frenzy, all sparring technique abandoned.

His eyes widened. He sat on her legs and pinned her arms to her sides to stop her from kicking and punching him.

She froze, and her eyes went blank. Olin froze too, staring into her face. She lay perfectly still, eyes staring up toward the ceiling, unfocused. Her face was expressionless.

"Hey," Olin said, his eyes narrowing.

She didn't move.

"Hey, Jevienna, are you okay?" He tapped her arm. "Jevs!"

She stayed entirely still.

He put a hand to her forehead. "Jevs, come on. What's wrong?" He bent close to her face, squeezed her hand, and shook her shoulder. Her head wobbled a little as he shook her.

He backed up off her legs and let go of her arms, all the time staring into her face with wide, terrified eyes. A second later, she blinked and looked up at Olin. Her eyes widened, and she backed away. She pushed herself up to a sitting position, pulled her knees up, and wrapped her arms around them.

Olin sat down facing her. His eyes were wide, and his arms were tense. "Did I hurt you?"

She dropped her chin onto her knees, hugging herself. "No," she said quietly.

"What happened?"

Her hands trembled, and she tucked them behind her knees. Her face was tense, as she shook her head. "Nothing."

"That wasn't nothing." Olin scooted closer and tried to catch her eye. "What's going on?"

Jevienna ducked her head, her forehead on her knees. She curled in on herself in a protective ball and rocked back and forth. Olin reached out to touch her arm, but hesitated and pulled back.

She lifted her eyes. "I felt, it felt like…" She hid her face again, muffling her voice. "You holding me down like that. It reminded me of… of Kaelstom."

Olin started, then his eyes narrowed. His jaw tensed, and his voice lowered. "What did he do to you?"

"Just forget it."

Olin's eyes shadowed. Red crept up his neck and face and he opened his mouth, then he paused and closed it. He took a deep breath, then he put a hand gently on her elbow. "I'm here with you."

She lifted her face. Her eyes were red.

"It's not okay for him to hurt you," Olin said. "It isn't your fault."

A teardrop slid down her cheek.

"We'll deal with this together. You aren't alone."

The scene dissipated. The dark shelves and lucten web took form once again. Elwyn pulled the lucten lens from her eye and replaced it on its shelf, her stomach clenching.

The girl's face flashed through her mind, then sleet-gray eyes and a dark alley. Her skin prickled, and her insides roiled. Olin's face came next: his calm, confident demeanor in this memory, the transformation from the first recorded memory to the second.

Somehow, the end of this memory felt hopeful. Olin could help, probably by leaning on the Keeper who'd helped him. Just like the Keeper had cared for him and been able to help him, now Olin could do the same for Jevienna.

How had that happened? How had Olin gone from an angry, vulnerable kid to a caring friend who was capable of helping another?

34

On Darkday at midday, Elwyn sat in the cavernous dining hall across the table from Cuinn and Theon. She stared down at her plate of roasted meat, potatoes, and toast, avoiding their eyes.

Even though she wasn't looking at them, she felt their eyes boring into her. They were watching her, wanting to talk to her, but she couldn't think of anything to say, and their intensity made her insides quaver. She took a bite of toast for something to do.

If only it was Dawnday already. Darkday, the day of rest, grated on her nerves. She wanted to get moving, to get working. To do something. To focus on something that would distract her from her internal world. Resting made her think and feel too much.

She had work to do. It was important work, at least according to Astur. And he should know—he was more than nine-hundred years old, apparently. Couldn't she skip resting today and keep working instead? Wasn't time running low?

"What's on your mind?" Cuinn's voice asked softly.

Elwyn poked at a potato, then she met Cuinn's eyes. "I can't just sit here and wait. I have work to do. Shouldn't I get to it?"

"Rest is as important as work," Theon said gently. "Without rest, we cannot work. Without work, we cannot rest."

Elwyn glared at her potatoes. "I don't want to rest."

Trying to conceal the laughter in his voice, Theon said, "Sounds like someone else I know."

Cuinn laughed outright. "Like mother like daughter." She put a gentle hand on Elwyn's arm and asked mildly, "What've you found in the Treasury so far?"

Elwyn considered. The nervous tension in her body eased a bit, having something concrete to focus on. The memories of Olin came back to her. They felt vital, but she couldn't exactly say what she'd learned from them. She sighed. "Well, I saw a couple lucten lenses," she said. "I think they're important, but I don't know how."

"Can you describe them?" Theon asked.

"I guess," Elwyn said. She told them all she could remember of the two memories of Olin, then she described the memory of the sisters. "At the end of it, I felt so different than the ones with Olin. After the one with the sisters, I was anxious, but after the Olin ones I felt peaceful."

Cuinn nodded. Theon asked, "What do you think was the difference?"

"In the Olin ones, there was someone there who cared about them and who could help them."

"And the sisters?" Theon asked.

"It didn't seem like they had anyone to help them. Their father had tried but the brother was still mean and angry, and the man with the rings had left but I don't know what happened afterward. He could've come back, 'cause there was nothing to stop him. It seemed like any number of terrible things could have happened to the sisters after the end of that memory. Thinking about it, I still feel nervous for them."

"You don't know exactly what happened after the Olin memories, either," Theon pointed out. "Can you explain how it feels different?"

"I guess I don't know what happened with Olin and Jevienna and the people who'd hurt them," Elwyn said. "But for some reason I don't feel nervous. I feel sure that something good did happen, that they were taken care of."

"What about their situation was different from the sisters?" Theon asked. Thoughts in Elwyn's mind began to line up. It felt like Theon was leading her somewhere, but he wanted her mind to get there, too, instead of him just telling her what to think.

"They had someone who wanted to take care of them and who *could* take care of them," Elwyn said.

"Can you be more specific? What do you mean by 'take care of them'?"

Elwyn stared at her toast, her mind whirling. There was something concrete there, but she couldn't grab hold of it. Every time the thought got close, it spun away from her again.

She closed her eyes and concentrated, replaying the memories in her mind. In the Olin memories, the person who was hurting was taken seriously. Their experience was treated with respect, communicating that their suffering was real. The people who were hurting were told they weren't alone, and it wasn't just words. The person who was with them communicated strength and resolve, showing that he was capable of entering into the situation and improving it, and that he would do so. She felt sure that he wouldn't leave the hurting person to suffer alone—he was now irrevocably in it. He was committed to all the struggle and pain that will come with being involved in the terrible situation, and he wouldn't leave in the middle of the struggle, for the hurting person to deal with the consequences alone. He was in it, from this point onward. Not because he had to, but because he cared.

How was that different from the memory of the sisters? The older sister treated the younger sister's experience with respect, too. But in this case, both of them knew the older sister couldn't do anything about the suffering. She could sit in the suffering with her sister, but she couldn't change it.

"There was a person hurting, and a person who cared about that person," Elwyn said, as the whirling in her mind began to settle. "The person who cared did so enough to sacrifice his own comfort or safety, and maybe more, by entering into the hurting person's situation in order to provide real help. The caring person would suffer with and help the hurting person, so the hurting person didn't have to hurt alone. It made a real difference to the hurting person, enough that one hurting person became no longer just a hurting person but also a helping person for someone else."

Theon sat back and smiled approvingly. Cuinn sat forward and asked, "Do you remember the sticks I showed you?"

Elwyn nodded. "The hurting person was alone, but then another person picked him up and leaned toward him, so he had someone to lean on."

"So what does that mean for you?" Theon asked. "What can you do with this idea?"

Elwyn considered. "Um, lean in?"

Theon smiled. "What do you mean by that?"

Elwyn huffed and stared back at her potatoes. It was easier to keep the idea general and vague. Specifics were hard.

What could she do? The first thing the Keeper in the memory did was to recognize that Olin was suffering. Instead of getting angry with Olin for his burst of anger, the Keeper realized that it was a sign that Olin was suffering.

The Keeper responded with patient kindness, giving Olin a safe place to share his suffering. Then the Keeper communicated to Olin that Olin mattered and that the Keeper was now part of the situation and would take steps to help. Then he gave Olin space to calm down.

So what could Elwyn do? "I could try to do what the Keeper did—recognize the signs that someone is suffering and instead of getting angry with them for hurting, enter into their suffering with them."

A clank rang from the next table as Neilan dropped his tray onto it. He slumped into a chair, facing away from them. His shoulders curved, and he leaned over his plate. Elwyn's insides roiled. Why was he acting like that? He was so frustrating.

Something had broken between them. He'd been grumpy and avoiding her for days. She had so much going on right now, she wanted him with her. He grounded her. Now she felt off-balance, like the floor had dropped out from under her feet. Why couldn't he just be normal?

Her memory flashed with the image of Olin, the self-protective anger radiating from him. She could almost picture him sitting just like Neilan was right now. Her mind twinged—was this Neilan's way of showing that he was suffering? Her chest constricted.

But then, what now?

She stared at Neilan's back. He hadn't looked at her a single time since he'd sat down. What could she do to help him? Where could she start?

She could try to catch his eye, but he wouldn't look at her. She could go sit by him, but every time she'd gone near him in the last few days he'd walked away. Even if he didn't walk away, then what? What would she say?

The idea of entering into people's suffering seemed so much clearer and easier when she was thinking of imaginary people, but this was different. Too close. Neilan was too—real. Real people were harder than imaginary people.

35

Hosev rolled away from the Dawnday morning light that streamed through his window. Alarrin, Jaeveh, and Reffie were already up, but Hosev couldn't get himself out of bed.

Mother's rocking chair creaked in the front room. Creak, creak. Creak, creak. Unending. She'd done almost nothing else for days.

Creak, creak.

Hosev stared at the ceiling.

Creak, creak.

Silence.

Why'd she stop? Hosev sat up, listening hard.

The baby screamed, and Hosev's stomach dropped. He flew out of bed, bolted through the door, and knocked over a stool left in the passage. Through the clatter, the baby's wails still pierced the air. He threw the stool out of the way and barreled to the front room.

Mother sat in her rocking chair, still as stone, staring toward the front door, while baby Veylas wailed in her arms. Hosev followed their gaze.

A man stood in the open doorway. Well, not a man, really. He was tall—too tall. His face was a pale, sickly white, like dingy wool. His hair was a dull black, like soot. His eyes were jet black orbs: no whites, no irises, no pupils, and his features were twisted with a hunger Hosev couldn't place. As soon as he caught sight of Hosev, he smirked, and his black orbs glinted. What was the Sovereign doing here?

The Sovereign turned back to Mother. "Your husband is dead."

No. Hosev's insides twisted, and the hair on his arms rose. Mother stared back at the Sovereign, unblinking. Then her shoulders drooped, and her head bowed. She leaned forward, her head lowering toward her knees, slowly collapsing.

Hosev ran to her and lifted her shoulders, then he pulled baby Veylas from her arms. He balanced Vey in the crook of one arm, then supported Mother with the other.

"It'll be okay," Hosev whispered. He wrapped his arm around Mother's shoulders and held her. Mother leaned into him. Hot tears welled in the corners of his eyes and a lump rose in his throat. He choked it back and blinked to clear his vision.

In a rush, his siblings burst into the room. They piled around Hosev and looked to him wonderingly. Manell ran to him and put an arm around Mother. She caught Hosev's eye and raised her eyebrows.

Hosev opened his mouth to speak, but his throat couldn't form the words *Father is dead*.

"He was murdered," the Sovereign said.

Hosev froze, and heat shot through him. His hands, arms, and chest burned. He held Mother's shoulders tight and slowly turned to the Sovereign. The Sovereign watched him with a greedy glint in his black orbs, and Hosev's neck prickled under that stare.

"You descendants of Nineveh will have inherited your father's," the Sovereign paused, searching for a word, "specific skillset. As the eldest, I'm here to offer you a position, to replace your father in my service."

Hosev started. His stomach lurched at the idea of serving the Sovereign. He'd been angry with Father as long as he could remember for doing that same thing. He glared up at the tall figure looming above while he crouched next to Mother.

The black orbs bored into him, and fury brewed behind them. Hosev's eyes burned, but he couldn't look away. What would the Sovereign do if he said no?

But really, what else could he do? Father was dead. His siblings and Mother would starve if he didn't figure out a way to provide for them. And if he refused, the Sovereign would make sure he never got another job—that was, if he let him live at all. He didn't have a choice, and the Sovereign knew it. That's why he'd come.

Hosev met the black orb eyes. He let go of Mother's shoulders, handed baby Vey to Manell, and stood. He picked his way through the pile of his siblings, approached the Sovereign, and faced him. The corners of the Sovereign's mouth curved up, and he said, "Your first assignment is to find your father's killer."

Hosev's heart jolted. His father's killer—he'd never get used to that phrase. But he could bring Father's killer to justice. "I will," he said. His voice cracked in his dry throat.

The Sovereign's mirthless grin grew. Hosev dropped to one knee in front of the Sovereign and bowed his head. He said the words he'd hated and feared as long as he could remember, "Sovereign, I pledge myself to you."

His stomach knotted, and his face and arms drained of blood, leaving him cold. The Sovereign nodded in satisfaction. "We leave immediately."

Hosev started. Right now? Manell stifled a sob. What had he done? He couldn't leave Manell here, in charge of Mother and everyone else, especially now, now that...

But he couldn't say no, they needed him to support them. It was either leave them but support them, or stay and watch them starve. Or be killed for refusing the Sovereign, and let Father's killer get away with it. He had to find Father's killer. That person had broken Hosev's world. He would find whomever it was, and he would make that person pay.

But after that, how long would he belong to the Sovereign? He knew: the rest of his life.

Λ

Hosev stared at the top of Senac's sandy-blonde head as he bowed over Hosev's right hand. The blood dripping from the back of his hand was streaked with black ink. His hand ached, but Senac was only halfway done with the semastud, the identifying tattoo of the Sovereign's servants.

It began at his pinky. When it was done, it would extend all the way across the back of his hand and circle around his thumb. Apparently Senac and Father had been friends of a sort for years, but this was the first time Hosev had met him.

"Sorry about your father," Senac said conversationally as he continued to pierce Hosev's skin with a needle. "I knew him well. I'm the one who found him dead, you know."

Hosev started, jerking his hand.

"Hey, don't do that! You'll mess it up." Senac's ice-blue eyes glared at him.

"Sorry," Hosev said mechanically. "You found my father? Where was he?"

"In that room with the hole, back in Regsenfrag."

"What?"

"The house he was assigned to watch. That man and woman's house."

Hosev stared at him. He knew the house—the one Father had showed him when he'd visited him in Regsenfrag.

Senac looked up, shrugged, then looked back at Hosev's hand. "In the back room there was a big hole, right in the middle. Nineveh went in after the people and he told me to stay back and keep watch so I did. I stayed there for a couple hours and he didn't come out so I left, but I came back every day to check. About three weeks later, the hole was closed up and Nineveh was laying there dead."

Hosev's shoulders tensed. He opened his mouth, but no sound came out while the gears in his mind began to turn. That room was the key he'd needed.

36

Elwyn leaned over a wooden, standing-height table in the Treasury, reading a leatherbound book—a long-ago Keeper's travel reflection of the northern tundra titled *Soli Vaccord, an Exploration*. Well, the book was open on the table in front of her, but her mind was across the room, where Neilan stood facing away from her unrolling a scroll. She'd tried to catch his eye, but he wouldn't look at her.

How was she going to do this? She lost the sancan she'd made for him, so now what? That question had kept her frozen since yesterday.

She couldn't even read anymore. Her mind was focused on him and this problem she needed to solve. She smiled grimly to herself. If only it was just a problem she needed to solve. This was way harder.

Reconnecting with Neilan and helping him through his hurt was the first thing she was supposed to do. That conviction had been settling into her heart more and more since the conversation with her parents yesterday.

But why this? Connecting with a person who was hurting didn't seem like it would make that big of a difference in the fight against Solun. Plus, it was ambiguous. She'd rather do anything else, even stick a sword into the immortal Solun. It wouldn't make a difference, of course, but then at least she'd know what to do, and she'd know when she'd done it.

The High King must have his reasons. But why her? It was such a simple thing, so simple that anyone could do it. But also, it was so, *so* hard. It wasn't a task, it was a person, and not just a person, a relationship. It required two people. If it was a task just up to her, easy—she could make herself do anything she thought she had to do. But it wasn't just up to her. How was she going to get him ready to, wanting to, and willing to lean on her? How could she make him connect with her?

She didn't know how. She didn't have the steps to follow, or even the first step to start moving in the right direction.

Couldn't she start with someone else, someone who didn't matter so much to her? This was Neilan, her closest person. He could cut her to the heart faster and deeper than anyone else. But then again, if she couldn't make this thing work with him, how could she make it work with anyone else?

The lucten-lamp on the table had faded without her noticing. The words on the pages she'd been attempting to read for so long were dim in shadow. She leaned closer and could just make out the first lines on the right-hand page: "I sat alone in my tent with my flameless fire, chewing my relative feast, gutted. Why was I here? Why was I doing this? Information, at what sacrifice? Soli Vaccord —'Alone Empty-Heart.' Only then did I understand what the ancients meant when naming this forsaken place."

Elwyn's eyes drew back to Neilan of their own accord. Now he was sitting at a table flipping absently through a loose stack of parchment. The words she'd just read floated back into her mind, "Alone Empty-Heart." It seemed like an equation: alone = empty heart. Sitting alone, shoulders bowed, Neilan looked like that:

empty-hearted. Elwyn's heart stirred.

What now? Well, she could go over there. But what then?

She closed the book and returned it to its shelf, then she walked toward Neilan, her footsteps on the glass floor eerily loud. Her chest tightened as she approached him.

As she got close, she panicked. What should she do? What should she say? She looked down at him as he sat alone and said the first thing that came to mind, "Hey."

He started and looked up. Her heart gave a jolt when his eyes met hers, it had been so long since that had happened. But he looked back down and said in a small voice to the parchment on the table, "Hey."

Neilan fiddled with a corner of the parchment uncomfortably. Elwyn shifted her weight, then she huffed to herself. This was ridiculous. She sat down and leaned over the parchment. The handwritten scrawl was informal, much different than the precision of the book she'd just been looking at. "What's this?" she asked in as light of a voice as she could muster.

Neilan shrugged, keeping his eyes averted from her. "A travel journal."

"Of what?" Elwyn asked, trying to keep her voice light.

"The Punipyr Desert," he said, his voice flat.

Elwyn bristled, and annoyance bled into her voice. "Care to elaborate?"

"Not really."

She huffed, out loud this time. Why'd he have to make this so difficult?

He glared at her. "It's just a Keeper crossing the desert, going from tribe to tribe for supplies. Not very interesting. What do you want me to say?"

Her neck tightened, and her insides grew hot. What did she want him to say? She didn't know. Something. Anything, as long as it wasn't mean. But she didn't know how to say that. She stared at him, no words coming.

He asked aggressively, "What?"

"What is your deal?" she burst out.

He glared at her, anger radiating from him. "I'm just trying to help like Astur said I have to. This isn't helpful, so there's no point telling you about it. Do I have to tell you about everything I read?"

Ugh, he was so frustrating! He knew as well as she did that she didn't care about what he was reading. She just wanted to talk to him. But he was going to make it as difficult as possible. Why was he being like this?

"I'm just trying to make conversation," she said defensively.

"Aren't we supposed to be working?" he asked with an edge to his voice.

Fine! Heat pulsed through her, rising up her chest and neck to her face. She shoved back her chair and stood up. Her mind flashed with a dark alley, then a sunlit wood, a spear in her hand. She blinked hard and shook away the memories. She was here, not there. Be here.

She looked down at Neilan, but he wouldn't look at her, so she stalked away. He knew how to irritate her better than anyone. She crossed to a shelf of scrolls and picked one up at random. She unrolled it and pretended to study it, but her mind was reeling.

Slowly, the heat in her neck and face ebbed away, and her heartbeat slowed. She looked back over her shoulder at Neilan, who still sat glaring at the parchment in front of him refusing to look at her.

She didn't want to leave it like that. But now what?

<h1 style="text-align:center">37</h1>

Neilan scanned a Treasury shelf lined with scrolls. It felt as though the ground had been pulled out from under him, and he couldn't get his footing.

He couldn't look at Elwyn. Every time he did, his spine crept with the memory of her empty, pitiless eyes while she fought that man. He wanted to forget it, but it kept coming back. He felt the distance between them expanding, and his Elwyn was slipping away.

Yesterday, when she'd talked to him for the first time in days, he'd pushed her away. What was wrong with him?

He had to fix this. How, though? There had to be something here that could help him figure out what was wrong with him. He peeked over his shoulder, through the archway to Elwyn in the next room. She was deep in a large volume, intent on her goal as always.

Her empty, pitiless eyes floated into his mind's eye, then her eyes rolling back and her body going limp while Neilan had just stared at her.

She'd needed him, and he'd frozen. He was supposed to be there for her, but he hadn't been then, just like he hadn't been when she faced those men in Torlum. If he couldn't protect her, what was he good for?

Nothing, that's what.

And now he couldn't even look at her. He'd pushed away his best friend, the only good thing in his life. Just like with his parents.

He didn't know what he'd done to make them stop loving him, to make them want to get rid of him. That's what he needed to figure out. He had to know why he was unlovable, why people left him. If he could figure that out, maybe he could change. Then maybe he could fix things with Elwyn.

His first day in the Treasury, he'd noticed a wall of lucten lenses labeled "Heir Acquirements." Maybe Wuervik or Astur had recorded the day they took him. Maybe Neilan's parents had told them why they didn't want him.

Neilan hustled through the archway to the main room where the wall of "Acquirements" was. Rows of lucten lenses glinted from countless shelves, from the floor to just above Neilan's head. Each lens had a tiny year etched into the wooden shelf in front of it.

He leaned close to a low shelf. Two in a row were from the year of the Eudaimonians 472. Then three from y.e. 490. This was way off. He skipped a few rows. Y.e. 608. Closer. A few rows up: y.e. 837. He stood on tiptoe for the second to last shelf: y.e. 872. Whoa, there were a lot from that year.

Down the row, y.e. 880, the year he was born. Almost. None from y.e. 881, the year Elwyn was born and brought here. Y.e. 883, y.e. 885, then two from y.e. 886. Finally!

He picked up one of the ones from y.e. 886 and held it to his eye.

Colors swirled. The inside of a small, wooden hut took shape. A younger-looking Oktoh, hair as red as ever, with his arm around his wife, a younger-looking Chel, faced a woman with a round, protruding belly. She looked like the Certified Keeper Baeliti, but different. Younger, but broken. Now, she had more life in her eyes.

"I'm sorry," Chel was saying. "I know it's scary, especially now. Your husband's sacrifice to save you has left you alone. You escaped from Solun once, but he'll keep coming for you. We can protect you. And you must remember, your child will be born of your bloodline, so she'll be in danger, too."

The woman's eyes went wide. "She?"

Chel's face softened. "You're having a daughter."

The woman looked down and put a hand on her belly.

Neilan pulled the lucten lens away from his eye. He replaced it and reached for the next one, the last recorded of the year he'd been taken. His fingers shook as he picked it up, and a shiver ran up his arm. He closed one eye and drew the lucten lens up to his open one.

Colors moved inside it. Neilan's childhood home formed around him, the knotted wood of the walls, the packed-dirt floor, the homeyness that seemed to hang in the air like incense.

In the west-facing window hung the meticulously-crafted colored-glass figurines Papa had made for Mama before Neilan was born. On the windowsill below them sat the wooden animals and trees Neilan had watched Papa whittle for her, little by little over the years. One tiny bird, blocky and mottled, was Neilan's single contribution to the gift.

The late afternoon sun shone through the window, reflecting the scene on the opposite wall. The shadows of the wooden figures created a complete woodland scene silhouetted on the wall, and the glass figurines refracted the sunlight to create an intricate sunset over the scene, ever-changing as the sunlight moved through the sky. Papa had given Mama a piece of her home, the woodlands to the north, and he'd given her a perpetual sunset, extending the time of day she said made her heart swell with peace.

Seated at the table, Mama leaned forward holding her face in her hands, while Papa rubbed her back slowly. Tears streamed freely down his cheeks and off his chin.

Neilan spun slowly with the lens to his eye to see the rest of the room. His parents sat across the table from a younger-looking Wuervik, and Astur who looked exactly the same as always.

"You're certain?" Papa asked.

Astur nodded. "You bear the surname of the original Eudaimonian Magician, which draws attention already. But also, your son's Gift is strong—his power is potent. If we were able to discover him this young, there's no doubt Solun will notice him soon."

Wuervik leaned an elbow on the table. "It's unusual for children to be able to use their Gift. Only one generation can use a Gift at a time—typically the parent would retain the Gift until the child has reached adulthood at the least. Most often when the Gifts are unknown, the Gift transfers from parent to child when the parent reaches elderhood or dies. Obviously," he said, gesturing to Neilan's parents, "that's not the case here. Sometimes, a Gift is unused so it leaves on its own. Or, the Gifted parent can willingly let go of it to give it to his or her children."

Papa leaned back in his chair. His eyes narrowed as they always did when he was contemplative. "I think I had something like what you describe, years ago. But then, when Neilan was born, I was so scared I wouldn't be able to protect him, to care for him, to train him in all the ways a child would need. I wanted to give him everything I possibly could. In the middle of the night one night, while I held him, I was overwhelmed with that fear. Then it felt like my heart left me through my hands and sank into my son's tiny body. I wasn't as strong or capable after that, but it somehow felt like Neilan would be."

Astur's silver eyes softened, and he gave Papa a sad smile. Wuervik nodded in understanding.

"Can we come, too?" Mama asked, her voice muffled from holding her face in her hands. She glanced up hopefully.

Wuervik shook his head. "One child's disappearance can be covered by the idea of an accidental drowning. But an entire family's disappearance is much more difficult to explain away."

A sob burst from Mama.

"If all three of you disappear," Astur said, "it'll alert Solun. He'll investigate, through his own effective means. He'll learn of Neilan's exceptional power and search for him. Our plan is that when Neilan is grown, he will be a Keeper of the Way, who will covertly interact with the outside world. But if Solun is actively searching for him, he'll be confined to the Haven indefinitely. If you were to come, too, his life would be a prison."

Mama dropped her face into her hands again. "Can we visit him?"

Wuervik shook his head, and Mama sobbed.

Astur bowed his head sadly. "Once he's under our protection, we can't sacrifice his safety and that of the rest of the Haven by revealing its location for visits, and we can't bring him back here to visit you or he may be discovered. You will tell your family and friends that he disappeared while playing by the river. Have a funeral for him, and live as though it was authentic."

Mama's body racked with sobs, and tears streamed down Papa's face as he wrapped his arm around Mama's middle and leaned down to her. He said gently, "We can't protect him. We aren't equipped."

"I know," came Mama's muffled voice. Tears leaked out the sides of her hands, and Papa resumed rubbing her back.

Mama pushed herself back up and faced Astur. "We want to give him his best chance for a good life." Her wet cheeks glistened. "There is only so much we can do for him, here. I don't want him stuck here, and I won't let him be enslaved by Solun." Her voice faltered. "If he's given the chance, he can make a difference in this world. He's capable of so much. I won't prevent that."

Wuervik nodded. "We'll train him to use his Gift effectively. He'll grow in power, and his future will be open wide."

In the corner of the room, six-year-old Neilan poked his head around the door. "He will be raised with another child, one year younger than him," Astur said.

"Does that child have family?" Papa asked.

"Her parents don't live with us. She has no siblings."

Mama noticed Neilan. She stood slowly and walked to him, taking obvious effort to keep from running. She wrapped her arms around him tightly.

Neilan tore his eye from the lucten lens. He couldn't watch the rest, how his parents had told him to be strong, had hugged and kissed him, and how they'd disappeared into the distance as Wuervik carried him away.

How they'd never appeared again.

He mechanically replaced the lucten lens in its spot on the shelf, hands shaking, and sunk to the floor. He wrapped his arms around his shins and dropped his head onto his knees. His chest burned, but his limbs were cold. Hot tears leaked out the corners of his eyes and streamed down his face.

He rocked back and forth, reliving Mama's sobs and Papa's free-flowing tears. He cursed himself, he didn't know what for, but was even emptier now than before.

And he still didn't know how to fix things with Elwyn.

38

In the purple haze of Twilitday morning, Hosev walked the streets of Regsenfrag that he'd so recently walked with Father. Ahead loomed the house Father had watched for the past sixteen years, which was surrounded by the Sovereign's servants. Hosev's shoulders tensed, but he was one of them, now.

As he approached the house, a large, square, hard-looking woman with three silver slashes on each of her arm bands stood up from the front step. "Halt," she said in a gruff voice, and she held a hand out in front to stop him.

"I'm here on the Sovereign's orders," Hosev said, his voice coming out weak and shaky. Get it together.

"None may enter," the woman said.

A lanky man hurried over and bowed low to her, holding out a sealed letter. "For you, Maena," he said in a querulous but self-important voice.

She eyed him and tore it open. She scanned the page, then grunted. Her eyes fell on the man still bowing in front of her, then she raised her eyebrows and said, "Dismissed." He scurried away.

Turning back to Hosev, she asked "Semastud?"

He fisted his right hand and held it to his heart, just as Senac had instructed him. His skin all around it was red and puffy, and parts of the tattoo were scabbed over. The woman inspected it and narrowed her eyes. "New?"

Hosev nodded. "Two days old," he said. The woman eyed him suspiciously. "I'm Hosev, Nineveh's son," he said quickly.

She grunted, then she sat back down on the step, taking up most of it, and nodded to him. "Proceed."

For a second he waited, but she didn't seem inclined to move, so he edged around her and pushed the door open. He scanned the small, simple room. There was a door to a back room, like Senac had said. For a second, he froze. He didn't want to see the room Father had been found dead in. Then heat roiled inside him. He was going to find the people who did it.

He ran to the door and threw it open. The back room was ordered, exceptionally so. There was no hole, and no indication that there ever had been one. Senac had said the hole was closed up, but that made Hosev expect to see a mound of dirt, or some mark to indicate where it had been. Was Senac lying?

As he studied the room, an impression grew that it was *too* ordered. It felt inauthentic, falsely imposed. The back of his mind twinged: it wasn't right.

He reached for his belt sheath. His fingers found his hatchet's smooth wooden handle, then he pulled it out of its loop. He knelt, swung the hatchet up over his head, and slammed it down at the floor. The metal point sunk into the packed dirt of the floor, deeper than he'd expected.

Hosev swung it again, and it stuck in the floor this time. He yanked it out, and dirt crumbled around it. With another four swings, it punched a hole straight through the floor. He reached through the hole and felt around. His hand waved in empty air, and his heartbeat quickened.

He hacked at the hole he'd made until it was wide enough to fit through. How deep was this hole? He couldn't see the bottom, just empty darkness. He stowed his hatchet, tightened the strap of his pack over his shoulder, and lowered himself into the darkness. Only his fingers still gripped the edge of the hole by the time his feet touched ground. He let go of the edge and squinted into the darkness.

"Hey!" he shouted, and his voice rang in the empty space around him. The echoes moved east and west. Which way?

He stood for a moment, indecisive, then he shook himself. There were two ways, he had to pick one. He hefted his pack and set off to the east.

⋀

Hosev walked for an hour, or maybe seven—it was hard to tell in this perpetual dark. It felt like he was the only person in the whole world.

A faint light glimmered ahead, and he hustled toward it. It grew as he got closer, until he could make out shafts of light glowing in lines on the tunnel walls and floor. Just past the light, the tunnel abruptly ended. The ground sloped upward toward the light, which shone between wooden slats of an angled wall.

He stood on the lines of light and squinted through the slats. The air was less stagnant—it was almost moving here, seeping between the slats of wood. This was it, the end of the tunnel. Father's murderer must be on the opposite side. Heat grew in his chest and radiated outward, his fists burning.

He groped at his side for his hatchet, pulled it out, and gritted his teeth. The heat inside him pulsed through his limbs and sped his heartbeat. He swung the hatchet at the wooden slats, and the boom reverberated through the tunnel. Light poured into the tunnel from the hole now open in the slats.

A woman's voice screamed, and Hosev's breathing quickened. He was so close. He swung the hatchet again, and the slats shattered. He yanked on the remaining pieces, pulled himself through the hole, and found himself in the middle of a bright, comfortable home. A plump woman cowered against the far wall, screaming.

Rage flashed through Hosev's mind, blinding all but one thought: Father's killer. He ran at the woman, hatchet raised, and screamed, "What happened to my Father?"

She crumpled, dropping to the ground with her arms over her head, and disintegrated into sobs.

A thread of reason broke into Hosev's blinding rage, opening his eyes to the figure quaking on the floor. Light flooded his mind again, and he saw himself in his mind's eye: rage boiling in his eyes, holding a hatchet raised over a helpless human being.

Heat drained out of him, leaving him cold and wobbly. He dropped his arm and sank to his knees. As the heat sapped from his body, his mind drained of thought. The woman's sobs rang eerily in his rapidly emptying mind.

He sat there, unthinking, barely blinking, for who knew how long. After a while, he became aware that the woman had quieted down. She'd stood up, and she was stepping toward him tentatively with a hand reaching out to him, as though she were approaching a wild animal. With his emotions so raw, the sight made him burst into a laugh. The woman flinched and fled back to the wall.

Hosev hushed his maniacal laugh and took a deep, quavering breath. When he mastered his voice, he looked at the woman and said quietly, "I'm sorry."

Her eyebrows went up, and her eyes were round. She slowly approached him again, even warier than before. She got within an arm's reach of him, then backed up a step. "Who are you?" she whispered.

The bizarre normalcy and yet unanswerability of the question hit Hosev in the chest, and he chuckled. She started, but held her ground.

"I'm..." Who was he? He wasn't sure. He sighed and shrugged. "Hosev." He had no better answer.

The woman leaned toward him, her eyebrows drawn together in concern. She clearly thought he was insane. Which, if he was honest with himself, wasn't far from true.

She crouched down to meet his eyes. "How did you get in that tunnel?"

Hosev started, and a tremor ran from his chest down his limbs. "What do you know about it?"

"Well," she said, shrugging. "It was my great uncle who dug it, you know."

Hosev just stared at her open-mouthed.

"He was an eccentric, they say," she said, settling into her story. "He had the house back when he was alive. Or maybe he's still alive? No one really knows. Anyway, he muttered a lot. Said something over and over again, something about 'Edna. Get to Edna.' At least I think that's what he said. I'm not sure. I only saw him once, when I was a little girl. Everything I know is from my mama. He was her uncle, you know. Anyway, he spent a lot of time inside the house. Wouldn't come out for weeks at a time. No one knew why. Then mama's papa realized it had been months since he'd seen his brother. He came over to check on him, but he didn't answer the door. So my Pop, that's my mama's papa you know, broke the latch and searched the house. He found this wall here, except it wasn't a wall then it was just an opening and behind it was all dug down and out. He went in and figured out it was a tunnel and went on a long way. He followed it for a bit, calling out and such, you know, but no one was there. He left and checked back a few times, but he figured out pretty quick his brother wasn't coming back. So the house was his now, and he moved in with mama and Gram and me, boarded up the hole, and we lived here ever since," she finished with a nod.

Hosev's mind spun like a top, set to motion by her story and still reeling afterward. A few moments later, it finally settled, and he grabbed hold of a thought. "It's been boarded up since then? No one has come through recently?"

"Nope, not a one," she said, hands on her hips. "Until now, of course."

Habit told him not to trust her, she could be lying, but somehow he knew she was telling the truth. She had nothing to do with Father or his killer. She was wrapped up in her own world, which only collided with his from the inexplicable behavior of a distant relation.

The tunnel had gone two directions, east and west. He'd tried east —it was time to follow it west.

"Thank you, ma'am," he said. "I'll be off."

She started, seeming reluctant to let him go now that he'd calmed down. "So soon? I was gonna get some lunch started in a moment," she said, bustling to the kitchen.

"Thank you, but I need to get going. I'm sorry about… all of this." He gestured to the mess and the hole in the wall.

"Nah, don't mention it. It'll make quite the story at market next week. No one will believe me."

Hosev quickly grabbed his hatchet and his pack and backed toward the hole.

"Maid Melia thinks she's so interesting. Talks so much she doesn't let anyone get a word in."

"Thank you," he said again, nodding to her. She didn't seem to notice.

He fled back into the tunnel, her voice trailing behind him: "She'll take a step back at market next week when no one cares to hear about those naughty chickens of hers when…"

39

Elwyn sat at a table in the Treasury watching Neilan through an archway. It was Twilitday afternoon, two days since she'd last tried talking to him. For two days, she'd been pretending to work while her mind spun in circles. Cuinn's sticks floated back into her mind. They both had to lean together in order for them to be able to support one another. If only one leaned, they'd fall, so why wouldn't Neilan lean in?

Her mind twinged. What did it actually mean to lean in?

She imagined one stick leaning in. The act was putting itself in the hands of another, giving up the chance to hold itself up for the sake of connecting with another. It was also giving another stick a chance to drop it.

It struck Elwyn that she was trying to pull Neilan in without leaning toward him herself. How was she to do that? The leaning— or in another word falling—stick was putting itself in a vulnerable position. But still, one stick had to lean first. Is that what she had to do with Neilan? What if he dropped her? She couldn't risk it. She didn't want to.

Her eyes drew back to him, sitting just inside the next archway.

His foot bounced on the glass floor over the spiderweb of lucten veins, antsy energy finding an escape even though his shoulders were bowed and he stared into space. The table in front of him was empty—he wasn't even pretending to work anymore.

She had to try. She stood up and walked toward him. What was she going to say? What did it mean to lean first? Be vulnerable, but what did that mean? She scanned her mind for a formula, a clear, logical series of steps for her to follow, but there was nothing.

She reached Neilan's table and sat down. He started and leaned back in his chair, away from her. She sighed to herself. Good start.

He looked away from her, at nothing in particular. She watched him, while his eyes and posture were as far from her as he could get without running away. She missed the old way, when he wanted to be near her and sought her out. She needed him near her, so she could tell him all she was feeling and feel him draw even closer as she did so. So she could *lean* on him. It finally made sense.

"I miss you," she whispered through her thick throat.

His eyes widened and shot to her. He stared at her without saying anything.

She swallowed and tried to get control of her voice. "I don't know how to do what the High King wants me to do. I'm scared."

He didn't move, didn't even blink. Just stared at her with wide eyes, leaning back in his chair. It was almost as though he was frozen.

Her face tensed as she tried to hold back tears. She met his eyes again, but he still didn't speak or lean in. He just stayed there frozen.

She jumped up and ran away, through the arch to the opposite end of the next room, until she was out of his line of sight. Tears flowed, and her chest heaved. Sobs burst from her uncontrollably. It felt as though she had been holding a door shut against a flood then she'd opened it a crack. Now all of it was bursting out, and she couldn't get the door shut again. Her mind flashed with wolfskin shrouds, closing in. A lifeless body under a blanket. No.

She pressed her back against a shelf and dropped to the ground, pulling her knees to her chest. She tried to take deep breaths, but they shook and kept getting interrupted by sobs. She squeezed her shins with her arms and pressed her face into her knees.

Eventually, the sobs subsided. She took a few deep, shaky breaths and wiped her face with her sleeve. She leaned her head back against the shelf and looked toward the archway to the room Neilan was in. He was supposed to lean in, to catch her as she made herself vulnerable. But instead, he'd just watched her fall.

Why couldn't he work with her? She was trying to do what she was supposed to do, and he was making it even harder. Except this was worse than that. It wasn't just a task he wouldn't accomplish with her. It was her heart that she held out to him, and he didn't reach for it.

Why did people have to be so messy?

She couldn't go back over there. She looked around the room. At the opposite end of this room, an arch led to another one. Through a small archway at the far end of that room, Cuinn stood at a wooden table, feverishly scanning a scroll.

Elwyn stood up. There was a big wet spot on the front of her dress, where she'd wept into her knees. She shook her dress out, but it didn't make much difference.

Elwyn tiptoed through the arch and the next room, taking deep breaths and fanning her face to cover up the signs that she'd been crying. She slipped quietly through the archway into the room with Cuinn and watched her mother.

This room was much smaller than the last, with a ceiling Elwyn could reach if she stood on tiptoe. The shelves held some lucten lenses and many rolled scrolls and maps, but nothing here was bound. Dust coated the scrolls and the shelves themselves.

Across the room, a dark metal door was framed between shelves. It was as smooth as glass, and it shone in the thin veins of glowing lucten. All around it, odd, boxy characters were etched into the frame. Chills ran down her arms. It felt like years ago that she'd seen the back of that door, when she'd first heard of her parents' existence. Now, on this side of the door, her mother stood in the flesh.

Cuinn took down a map, and it left behind a clear outline of dust where it had sat on the shelf. A few spots on the shelves were empty, with dust-outlines of what had been scrolls laying on them. All the scrolls that had been moved seemed to be piled on Cuinn's table. Cuinn unrolled the map hurriedly. After a second, she shook her head and rolled it back up. She turned to return it to it's nest of dust and noticed Elwyn standing just inside the arch.

Cuinn grinned and beckoned excitedly, bouncing back to her table "Come see!"

Elwyn's skin tingled. She hesitated, then she stepped tentatively to the table. She stood next to Cuinn, staring down at the chaos splayed out before her. Five scrolls were laid flat, held open by rolled-up maps to weigh down the edges.

Cuinn pointed to three of them. They were covered with boxy characters like the ones framing the door. These were occasionally interrupted by a different type of character, less boxy but with similar features.

"I've never seen this language before!" Cuinn said excitedly, as though this were a special kind of treat. "Here," she pointed to a place where the boxy characters gave way to the more flowing characters, "it switches to one of the more ancient languages I'm familiar with, Aznya. Then it switches back.

"If you look close here, this character looks like one in Aznyan."

She reached for a charcoal pencil and scratch parchment. "The Aznyan one, katolofou, looks like this." She drew a crossed section at the top with small crosses interlaced over it, and met it with a waved line that curved up from the bottom.

"Katolofou is a family of trees which grow in the hills around the Tensmon mountain range. This one here," she pointed again to the character in the unknown language, "has an indicator at the top for a similar tree, but with a wide, flat base. It could be a related type of tree that grows in an area of flat land."

Elwyn stared at the scrawl and nodded slowly. "I think I see it."

Cuinn bounced on her toes. "Now if you look here," she pointed, "here, here, and here, there are more land features. A mild coast, a well-established forest, a lucten river, and a wide stretch of uninhabited land."

Elwyn nodded, hoping she looked like she understood why that was so interesting.

Cuinn's eyes gleamed. "It describes the land we're standing under right now. I think this is a scouting report from when they were deciding where to build the Haven."

"Whoa," Elwyn said. It was strange to think of this place before it was a Haven, when this underground world was just an idea.

"Here," Cuinn said, pointing to a two-part character that stood out starkly against the rest of the characters, "is the best part. It's positioned as part of the description of the coast close to where the Haven was built, but it isn't in either Aznyan or the primary language here."

Elwyn leaned in. The strange character made her neck tingle.

"It draws me in. I can't stop looking at it," Cuinn said, leaning closer to the page to drink in the image. She traced it gently with her finger. "These lines here, and this area right here, are close to these ones over here," she pointed to some of the unknown language's features.

"Based on Aznyan, I can piece together some of these characters' meanings. And if I use that assumption for this character, I think it's a name." She squinted at it. "I'm not sure if it's the name of a being or a thing. But that's the part that draws me in. Based on the context, it doesn't seem like a being, but the name holds life. Sounding it out based on some similar characters' pronunciation in the Aznyan dialect, it's pronounced Ed-na."

The hairs on the back of Elwyn's neck stood on end. There was power in that name.

"Ed-na," Elwyn whispered. The sounds felt sweet on her tongue, like a decadent dessert that was too rich to have too much of. She wanted to repeat it, but it felt too sacred to speak flippantly. She craved to know what it was. "Should we ask Astur about it?" Elwyn asked.

Cuinn pursed her lips but nodded. "I guess he's the only one who'd know about it, since he was around when this place was built." She carefully picked up the scroll that held the two-part character, Edna.

Elwyn led the way through the series of arches to the main room. When she approached the spot where Neilan still sat, his face in his hands, she looked straight ahead and kept walking. She was still too raw.

In the main room, Astur stood alone, staring at a scroll laid out on the table below him. He looked up expectantly.

"I've been translating some scrolls in the far room through there," Cuinn said and pointed over her shoulder. "I've found an unusual character. I'm not sure why, but it feels crucial."

Elwyn helped her unroll the scroll and hold it open. "If I've translated it correctly," Cuinn said, "it's pronounced 'Edna.'"

Astur jolted. It startled Elwyn so much that she nearly let go of the parchment. Astur stared at Cuinn in open shock. A second later, his shock dissolved. His face hardened and his jaw clenched, his eyes blazing. Elwyn stepped back reflexively.

"What—" Cuinn started.

"Put that back where you found it," Astur commanded, his voice hard. He stared down at the scroll as though it were a weapon. He looked like he wanted to snatch it from Cuinn's hands. He probably would have, if he could.

"Put it all back. All research on that topic must cease. You are forbidden to enter that room again."

Cuinn's eyes narrowed. "What are you hiding?"

Astur stared at her open-mouthed. They both seemed to balloon with rising wrath.

The door to the Treasury burst open. Nirep, a Certified Keeper with a puff of white-blonde hair on top of his head, sprinted down the steps. "They're mobilizing!" he yelled, his eyes wide. "Solun's servants, they're mobilizing like I've never seen!"

Theon strode in from a side room. "What do you mean?" he said in a low, even voice, as though to calm Nirep enough to make him speak rationally.

Nirep took a deep breath and made an effort to calm himself, but he stared at Theon with brows furrowed. "Who are you?"

Wuervik stepped forward. "What do you have to tell me?"

"I've been scouting in Gravusfrig, like you told me to. Solun's servants are swarming to Phaemin Fortress and organizing in numbers I've never seen before. They're preparing for something."

Wuervik's jaw clenched. He hurried to Nirep and spoke in a low voice. Elwyn's neck and arms prickled.

Neilan burst through the side archway, scanning the room with wide eyes. He found Elwyn, then he looked down and curved in on himself.

40

A faint light appeared far ahead in the tunnel, and relief flooded Hosev. He didn't know how long he'd been in this formless darkness, keeping a hand on one side of the tunnel as a guide, but based on how many times he'd gotten hungry, he estimated it had been a day and a half. All that time, the tunnel had gone in a straight line.

The thing growing in his brain reared up: he visualized the maps he'd studied, and his mind traced the line he'd walked. If his estimation was correct, he was all the way through the Tensmon mountains by now.

The light grew, and he hustled toward it. The formless dark took shape, and the rough, dirt walls opened into a stone cave. Through the cave opening, faint light from Dawnday morning glowed.

He tiptoed to the cave mouth and stood there, looking into a forest. The map in his mind told him this was the coastal forest on the west side of the Tensmon mountains: the Forbidden Lands.

Crowndom law forbade anyone from entering this forestland, and the punishment was death. But the Sovereign himself had told Hosev to find Father's killer. Could he risk it? Manell and everybody needed him, but Father's killer was out there. Heat boiled up inside him, clouding his mind. Father's killer was out there.

But where? This forest stretched for miles to the western ocean, and many more than that to the north and to the south. The heat drained out of him—how was he going to search this whole land? Well, the tunnel had gone straight the whole way, and straight was as good a direction as any. He hefted his pack higher on his shoulder and set off.

△

By Dawnday evening, Hosev sagged on his feet. The map in his head told him he was approaching the coast, but he'd found nothing. Why had he followed that childish plan to 'walk straight'?

A few hours ago, the hairs on the back of his neck had pricked, and he'd felt as though he was being watched, but he hadn't been able to find anything that could've been watching him except for some small, one-domain beasts which had fled once he'd taken a step toward them.

A distant roar broke into his consciousness, like that of a large animal, and a shiver ran down his neck and arms. He stopped and listened hard. It was coming from up ahead, but not just straight ahead: from the north and south, too. Was it a whole pack of beasts?

He took a tentative step and listened again, but the sound didn't change. He took another step. The beast, or whatever it was, didn't seem to notice him, yet. He tiptoed forward, ready to dart up a tree at the first movement he caught.

A minute later, a breeze washed him with the smell of salt. He tiptoed further. The trees thinned, and something bright sparkled between them. The roaring continued, uninterrupted but growing louder.

Hosev squinted between the trees. A broad, flat space opened past them. He couldn't see any beasts, which would've had a difficult time hiding in that open land, but the roar grew overwhelming. He burst through the trees and ran into the open space, adrenaline pulsing through his limbs, and he spun to catch sight of anything coming toward him.

No beasts appeared. As his adrenaline subsided, his surroundings took form. He stood on a stretch of undergrowth that gave way in twenty paces to a strip of flat whiteness, then blue. Dark, bright blue, which stretched to the horizon.

Tales of the sea gave it a sinister personality, bent on swallowing any who attempted to cross it, or they made it sound romantic and gentle. Standing here, all he could think was it was massive. More water than he could believe existed in the whole universe lay before him. It made him feel small.

Small, that wasn't exactly the word—there was more to it than that. The massive, dense blue in front of him gave off a sense of power, of timelessness. He became starkly aware of his weak, human body and his comparatively short life. He was no more significant than a grain of the sand in front of him, and he was far shorter lived.

It seemed like that thought should be unsettling, but it was somehow comforting. All his strivings, which had felt so important, were tiny compared to the breadth of the universe. His cares still mattered to him, but they were dulled, made manageable.

The sky, hazy and thick, lit up orange and pink as the sun sank down toward the horizon. Hosev watched it, breathing deep. His mind was blank, and he was okay with it.

Way out in the ocean, a vague form began to grow visible. As the sun set, it lit the edges of what looked like two mountains. The sun began disappearing behind the two shapes, well above the horizon line. Was there an island out there? The hairs on the back of his neck rose.

He'd studied maps for years and none showed an island off the western coast of Terralum. What was that place? And why wasn't it marked on maps? His insides prickled. He knew, somehow, that it was not a question he should ask. He shouldn't even mention to the Sovereign that he'd come this far west.

Weight descended on him again, and his cares settled back into his heart. What was he going to do now? His mind formed the map he'd been following, keeping a straight line. He had to go back to the tunnel's opening again and start a real search, sweeping in a snaking curve to make sure he covered every inch of this ground.

On the way back, though, he'd search a little more where he'd felt watched.

$$\Delta$$

Hosev's body ached while he trudged through the endless forest. He crunched the moss and dead leaves carelessly as Brightday's mid-morning light filtered through the trees, giving the forest a green-gold glow. He'd slept late, the overwhelming feeling of defeat keeping him from rising early like he ought to have.

But what was the point of rushing? It could take years to scour this whole forest. Then, of course, what if he was looking in the wrong place altogether?

As he neared the place he'd felt watched before, a sharp rustle up ahead hit his ears like a thunder clap. His heart jumped, and he backed up and crouched behind a tree.

The sound moved further away. He crept out from behind the tree, bending low, and stalked toward the noise. Muffled voices hissed through the trees, and his heart leapt. He held back the impulse to dart at the voices. His heartbeat pounded in his ears, dimming the sound he strained to keep track of.

A few paces ahead, a footprint stood out starkly in the

underbrush. More footprints rolled on behind it and in front. They appeared out of nowhere about five paces to the left, and they continued toward the voices. His mind twinged, but he shoved it down. His thoughts were too full—he'd finally found Father's killers!

He crept after the prints toward the voices, and the footprints turned. The back of his mind asserted itself again, saying something was off, but he could almost taste his victory. In a small clearing ahead, a flash of limbs disappeared behind a pile of boulders. He ran to the pile and peered around the side, but nothing was there.

He looked closer. In the space between the bases of two boulders, a small hole lay open, exactly the size of a crawling adult. He dropped to his hands and knees and stuck his head into the hole. It was a rock cave which tunneled steeply underground. Inside it he caught the low hum of voices.

He squeezed through the opening and crawled downward. Sharp pebbles dug into his hands, and his knees ached, but he barely registered it. His whole body trembled with excitement.

The tunnel gradually grew taller. About fifty paces in, he raised himself to his feet, though he still had to hunch over nearly in half. He felt the way with his hands in pitch blackness, and the voices ahead grew faint. He sped up, stumbling in the dark.

The tunnel turned, and a tiny light glowed far ahead. Hosev darted toward it, and the voices became louder and more urgent. Hosev sped into a hunched-over jog.

Then the floor dropped out from under his feet, and he fell through open air. Light seared his eyes, and his stomach turned over. It felt like it would fall out of his body altogether, then his fall slowed. People stood all around with arms reached out toward him.

He dropped gently onto something firm, and in one movement, he rolled off it and pulled his daggers from his ankle sheaths. He threw one, then the second.

The daggers hit a translucently blue wall in front of the people and clattered to the ground. Hosev drew his hunting knife and ran at the people, but there were bars in the way, or what stood like bars but looked like tree roots.

He darted at the roots and pushed, but they were immovable, solid as steel. They stood in a circle all around him, closely spaced. In the center of the ceiling high above him, a hole gaped. He was caged in.

No. Not now. He'd found them. He had to make them pay. He couldn't fail now.

Something inside him broke. Heat filled his insides and obscured his vision. A growl-like scream exploded from deep in his chest, and he ran at the roots and slammed into them. He flung his hunting knife, but it hit the translucent wall and landed out of his reach. He swung his arms through the gaps in the roots and screamed until he ran out of air. He swiped and clawed at the people on the other side of the bars, who were far out of his reach.

His ribs ached from straining against his cage, but he couldn't stop. They stared at him with wide eyes and open mouths while he slammed his body against the roots again and again. He tasted blood, and it spurred him on. He slammed his head against the roots.

Pain exploded through his forehead. He braced against the tree roots to hold himself up, and the heat seeped out of him. He wobbled on his feet as people backed out of the room one by one, sharing furtive glances and urgent whispers.

When the room emptied and the pounding in his head settled, he spun in a slow circle. He was in a round cage in the center of a circular room, which had packed-dirt walls and floor. His cage had no door, only a place in which the roots were tangled rather than straight and vertical like the rest. He pushed against the tangle of roots, but it didn't budge.

He slumped to the ground and sprawled out flat on his back. Small stones poked into him, but he couldn't summon the energy to care. He'd failed.

41

Brightday afternoon, Elwyn stood in the middle of the main room of the Treasury. There was nothing to glean here, now, but she had to keep trying, or at least look like it.

Neilan sat in the next room, framed in an archway. He kept staring at her, then looking away when she'd turn toward him. She couldn't take it. She had to get out of Neilan's line of sight. Another archway caught her eye, and she hustled toward it.

She wandered through that room, and the next one, and the next. Full shelves lined every wall, rising from the floor to the ceiling of each room, but none of it could help her. Information was one thing, people were another. She could absorb all the information in the Treasury and still be stuck in these uncomfortable feelings, and still not be able to force Neilan to be easier to deal with.

She couldn't stay like this. She had to do something to distract herself. Through the last arch was the room she, Cuinn, and everyone else had been banned from. It drew her in, and she followed the impulse. Outside the arch, she glanced around. No one was within sight, so she crossed the threshold.

Just inside the ancient room, a row of lucten lenses lay covered by a thick layer of dust. She ran her finger along the row, and her fingertip gathered dust, leaving behind a line of sparkling lucten. She picked one up, brushed it off, then lifted it to her eye.

Colors swirled. The Haven's massive Concourse took form, but it was different. The floor was packed-dirt, and torches flared from brackets along the walls.

People were moving in all directions, but a few in the center of the room stood frozen, staring up at the ceiling. The tiniest glowing bead squeezed between the roots in the center of the ceiling and fell, sparkling, to the floor, where it joined a few more glowing droplets.

As the people watched, horror-struck, more beads formed in the same spot, faster than the first one, and fell to the floor. The beading drip grew to a thin stream. The droplets on the floor joined up into a tiny pool of glowing lucten.

People backed away nervously as it grew, careful not to step in it. Liquid lucten was so thick a person could get stuck in it. This much wasn't a big deal, but people couldn't float on it. If the lucten got deep enough, it would overwhelm them completely.

The stream thickened, pushing between the roots of the ceiling. The roots bowed and pushed apart as the force of lucten grew stronger. The pool on the floor spread, expanding quickly. People screamed and fled to the walls.

Astur appeared in the C.K. Wing archway, with brows knit as he observed the chaos. Then his eyes fell on the rapidly-widening stream of lucten falling from the ceiling, and his face lit up.

While Haveners screamed and fled through the archways, away from the widening lucten-pool, Astur ran toward it. He laughed aloud and raised his arms triumphantly. The fleeing people stared at him with wide eyes as though he were insane.

"Thank you!" Astur yelled, his voice booming over the chaos.

The scene dissipated, and Elwyn put it back in its nest of dust.

Lucten hadn't always flowed in the Haven? Her thoughts wandered back to the torchlit Concourse, seeming so forlorn without the moving glow of lucten filling every nook. She'd thought the original builders of the Haven had directed it there with Magic. If not that, what had brought it there?

Her mind spun, but she couldn't answer her own question. To distract her spinning thoughts, she picked up another lucten lens, brushed off the dust, then drew it to her eye.

Colors swirled.

A cavernous, stone ballroom took shape, glowing silver with lucten light. Countless sparkling strands of delicate chain links made from hardened lucten were strung from the center of the ceiling to the edges of the room, like a massive, sparkling tent. Liquid lucten glowed from long channels along the edges of the room, rimmed with ornately carved stone.

Music surged through the room, gentle but strong. In the center of the ballroom, hundreds of people danced, swirling into circles, into pairs, back into circles. Then they wove through one another in graceful, geometric patterns. Jewels that were woven into the fabric of the dancers' clothing reflected the light from the lucten pools, scattering it on the walls in ever-moving, sparkling swirls.

Across the ballroom, five thrones stood on a platform. On the thrones, three women and two men sat dressed in flowing, silver robes, serenely watching the dancers. Each had a silver circlet resting on her or his head. Next to the thrones, two younger women and three younger men stood in flowing, silver robes identical to those on the thrones, but their heads were bare.

Surrounding the raised platform, armed guards stood shoulder to shoulder. Their smooth armor shone in the lucten light, and their breastplates and shields were etched with the Eudaimonian crest: the therapeian flower with five mature petals and five young petals. The etchings were filled with lucten, so they sparkled silver.

Behind the platform and thrones, windows stretched from the floor to the high ceiling. Through them, wide lucten rivers ribboned into the distance. Around the stone building that the ballroom was in, the lucten-rivers converged into a wide pool of liquid lucten. Twilitday's evening sky was purple, but it glowed orange just over the setting sun. The glowing-crystal lucten rivers were tinged purple, reflected from the sky.

Just outside the edge of the dancers, watching the people on the thrones, Astur stood next to a man with sleek, shiny, black hair, cream-colored skin, and eyes as silver as Astur's. They both wore sparkling, blue robes. Three women stood a few paces away in the same blue robes with the same lucten-silver eyes.

"We've made little progress," the man with Astur was saying. "Or at least less progress than I had expected by this point."

"I agree," Astur said. "Their nature as mortals makes this work inefficient. Each generation must be re-taught all that is and has been, and all that needs to be."

The man stared out over the sea of dancing figures. "There must be a better way."

Astur followed his gaze, and he was silent for a long moment. "Humans are changeable, inhibited from clarity by their limited age and experience."

The man folded his arms and tapped his elbow with his forefinger. "Yes. But that is not the only problem. They disagree with one another, causing strife and inconsistency even between the five ruling at one time."

"True," Astur said. "Their opinions are as inconsistent as they are, and their differences from one another add another layer to the chaos. Perhaps one single ruler would provide clearer vision, give better opportunity to pursue one goal consistently. Each additional person involved in the ruling process makes it that much less efficient. Yet the problem would still remain of beginning again with each new generation."

The man sighed, looking toward the thrones. "I wonder, should mortals be the decision-makers? Or should an immortal guide them more directly?"

Astur's eyebrows came together thoughtfully. "I do not believe that's what the High King intended. Though I begin to wonder the same. Mightn't he have overestimated humans' abilities?"

The man's eyes flashed. His pupils dilated abruptly, taking over his silver irises. They kept dilating, taking over the surrounding whites, too.

Astur, who still looked toward the thrones, didn't notice. After a second, he shook himself. "Our role was clearly defined. I apologize for letting my mind be carried off." He turned to the man and started. His eyebrows shot upward.

The man turned away, and his pupils receded. But they remained eerily large, with only the slightest ring of silver around the wide, black pupils. "I'm not sure it is out of our place to consider such things. We were sent here to help them. When they fail, shouldn't we intercede? Where they are incapable, because of limitations and inconsistency, shouldn't we guide them?"

His pupils began dilating again, slowly, while he continued, "Where they lack order because of the inability of a group to agree, shouldn't one mind order them, guide them in a singular direction?" The whites of his eyes slowly succumbed to his ever-widening pupils. "Doesn't it make more sense that one being, unlimited by age, untainted by strife, direct all? Mightn't it be good for that one being to be alone at the head of humanity?"

Astur took a step back. His eyes were wide and his face tense. "What are you suggesting?"

The man's eyes flashed, then he forced calm onto his face. "Nothing." He waved a hand nonchalantly, his black-sphere eyes cast away from Astur. "Merely philosophizing."

Astur's eyes narrowed. "There is no such thing."

The scene dissipated.

Hands trembling, Elwyn pulled the lucten lens from her eye and stared at it. Who was that man? She thought she knew, but she hoped she was wrong. Had Astur triggered Solun's idea of ruling mortals?

She needed to talk to Astur. She tucked the lucten lens into her dress pocket and hurried out of the room. She wove her way back to the Treasury's main room, climbed the stairs, and pushed open the heavy door.

While she wound through the hallway toward the main tunnel of the C.K. Wing, Chel and Oktoh hustled down the hallway, tense. At a fork, they took the right-hand tunnel, the same Elwyn and Neilan had taken so long ago when they'd fled from the hidden tunnel.

Elwyn paused at the fork. In the corner of her vision, Chel and Oktoh reached the door to the same room Elwyn and Neilan had hidden in and opened it a crack. They slipped through, then closed it firmly behind them. What was that about?

She looked up and down the tunnel. It was empty, so she crept up to the door and pressed her ear against the cool, hard wood. Voices vibrated through the door.

"What has he told you?" Oktoh's voice asked.

"Very little of note," Cuinn's voice replied, and Elwyn jumped. "But I'm close to breaking through. I need a break, then I'll try again."

Keepers mumbled and boots shuffled against the floor, as they all prepared to leave the room. Elwyn spun around and bolted to the nearest doorway. She threw open the door of what turned out to be a small room with a long table, lined with chairs. A shelf full of scrolls and stacks of empty parchment ran along one side.

She shut the door and pressed her ear to it while footsteps shuffled past her doorway and disappeared down the tunnel. She waited another minute, and the silence stretched, so she opened the door and crept out into the hallway.

She approached the door they'd come out of and leaned her ear against it, holding her breath. The room beyond was silent.

She tried the latch, and it clicked. She opened the door a crack and peeked in. It was as empty as the last time she'd been inside— emptier even, because the lucten veins under the floor were thinner than before. There were two more differences: the chest of drawers was free of dust, and the Magic-fortified door on the opposite side was wide open.

Elwyn slipped inside the room, closed the door, and tiptoed to the open door across from her. She poked her head through the open doorway, but two Keepers stood mere feet from her. Elwyn darted back through the doorframe and hid behind the door that stood open.

Thankfully, they'd been facing the other way, looking through large windows. What were those for? She'd never seen windows inside the Haven before.

She peeked through the crack on the hinge-side of the open door. The Keepers were in a small, narrow room with another door on one side. On the opposite side of the glass was a circular room, only faintly lit. No lucten at all ran under the floor. Crude-cut hardened lucten, like the informal lucten lamps on the tables in the Treasury, lay on the floor in a wide circle. In the center of the room stood a cell of free-standing tree roots.

A cot sat in the center of the cell. Sitting on the floor next to the cot, with his head bowed, was a teenage boy with straight, black hair. Elwyn's neck and arms prickled. She stood frozen, hiding behind the open door. What was going on here?

<h1 style="text-align:center">42</h1>

Elwyn's legs ached from hiding behind the door. How long was it—ten minutes? Half an hour? Through the crack of the door, the room with the cell glowed even more dimly than before.

One of the Keepers turned to the second one and said irritably, "It's time to replace the lamps again, already. They're losing light faster and faster."

The second Keeper nodded and said, "Best to have the room ready when she comes back." She sighed. "Back to the luctenfall, yet again."

They walked past the door Elwyn hid behind and through the main room. Elwyn held her breath. A few seconds later, the outer door thudded shut. Elwyn crept out from behind the door and into the windowed room, her knees creaking as they bent for the first time in so long.

She peeked out the window. The boy hadn't moved—he was still sitting on the floor with his head down. Across the windowed room, the door to the cell-room stood open a crack. She slipped through it, dropped to the ground, and crawled on her hands and knees until she was below the windows so the Keepers wouldn't see her if they came back.

The boy stayed seated there with his head on his knees. He might've been asleep. She coughed to get his attention, but he didn't move. She coughed again, louder.

"What?" came a muffled voice. It was slightly familiar.

Elwyn sat on her knees and leaned down almost to the floor to try to see his face, but he still didn't look up, so she tried speaking. "Hello?"

The boy lifted his head and raised his eyebrows at her derisively. Once his eyes met hers, Elwyn jumped and her heartbeat sped. His eyes widened, then he squinted at her. "You," he said quietly.

"Hosev?" she asked.

His eyebrows drew together.

"What're you doing here?" Elwyn blurted.

"It's not like I want to be. What are *you* doing here?"

"I live here," she said, and his eyes narrowed further. She looked at the cell and asked, "But how'd you get here?"

He glared at her. "I was sent to find you people, and I did." His eyes flashed, then he paused and looked down. "But then I got caught."

"Why'd you come after us?"

"Why?" He leaned forward. "Justice! You're criminals."

Elwyn sat back on her heels. "Says who?"

"You're murderers."

"What?" She stared at him, bewildered.

"You murdered my father!" A vein pulsed in his neck, and his voice grew quiet. "And you'll pay."

A shiver ran down her spine. Suspicion seeped into her mind, but it couldn't be true. There was no way his father could be the man she… No, it couldn't be. "Why do you think that?"

"He followed you people through a tunnel from Regsenfrag," he said, his voice dripping with anger, and bumps rose on Elwyn's arms. "Then you people killed him. You stuffed his body back into the house and closed up the hole, as though we're stupid enough to fall for that."

Elwyn's stomach knotted. Astur's words about the man she'd killed came back to her in a paralyzing rush: *those who love this man.* They were supposed to be nameless somebodies, distant and vague, so she didn't have to imagine them. How could it be Hosev? She stared at him, the boy who'd risked his life to help a stranger, who'd saved her.

Who's father she'd killed.

But the man she'd killed had served Solun—she'd done what she had to do. Her brain held onto that idea as to a lifeline. But her skin crawled, as it had done when the fang-tattooed man had touched her, the man Hosev had saved her from. Just like in that alley, she wanted to float away, to disappear. But this time, she was the loathsome one. She couldn't escape from herself.

She stared at the floor—she couldn't meet Hosev's eyes, couldn't face what she'd done to him. She wanted to throw reality away, to toss it from her.

A tingly tug pulled at her chest, but it didn't draw her to action this time—it pulled her inward. It tightened her chest and spoke to her heart: reality was reality. She'd done it, and she had to face it, to accept responsibility for what she'd done.

She closed her eyes and took a deep breath. "It was me."

"What?"

She opened her eyes and braced for whatever was coming, then she said in a quavering voice, "I killed your father."

He stared at her for a long moment. Then his eyes shadowed, and his voice grew dangerously low. "I should have let them kill you."

A shiver ran down Elwyn's back.

Hosev leapt up and flew at the root-bars. He screamed and cursed her, then he reached his arm through the bars and swung at her.

She dodged his fist and moved further away from the cell, out of his reach. He clawed the air at her. He screamed and punched the root bars, his fist cracking against the wood. He howled in pain and grabbed his hand. He crumpled to the ground and screamed, whether in pain or rage she couldn't tell.

He was so different from the person she'd met not long ago. Her mind stirred. In the Olin memories, she'd seen another stark transformation: Olin had gone from an angry, aggressive kid to someone compassionate, who was willing and able to help another person.

Hosev had changed just as drastically, but the opposite way. He'd been hurt by someone—by *Elwyn*—who'd thought only from her own perspective. She'd seen that man only as the enemy, not as a person, and she'd killed him. She hadn't had to—even at the time, she'd known he wasn't fighting to kill. She could have called for help, could have incapacitated him, anything else. But she'd killed him.

She couldn't have known that Hosev would be the one to suffer for it, but someone was going to suffer. The fact that she'd hurt someone she knew instead of a stranger made it feel more real, but it didn't change the reality itself. She'd hurt someone, and that someone had always mattered whether or not she had to face the person she'd hurt.

She hadn't considered that her actions could have such far-reaching effects, such terrible ripples. She'd sent Hosev straight into Solun's hands.

She needed to fix it. Her mind scrambled for ideas. She could help him, be like the Keeper in the Olin memory, then maybe he'd stop serving Solun. Yes, that was it, it had to be. She needed it to be. She couldn't be the problem, she was going to be the solution. She had to be—she couldn't face herself otherwise.

Solun couldn't do everything himself, so he needed people to work for him. If his servants stopped serving him, he couldn't do much, could he? That was the answer. She knew it deep inside.

But what about Hosev? The first thing she could think of was to free Hosev from the cell—that she could do, it was way easier than fixing things with Neilan. Her mind twinged, but she shoved down whatever it was telling her. She couldn't let her mind free or she'd have to feel too much. Action, that's what she needed to focus on.

Hosev's screams faded, and he flopped flat on the ground. His chest heaved, and his hands shook. Elwyn stood and circled the cell. There was no door, so she circled again. In the center of the cell's high ceiling stood a square trapdoor, but it was far out of reach.

She squinted at the cot and tried to judge the distance. It might work. She ran back into the window room and the one beyond, to the chest of shallow drawers in the outer room. She yanked one out and turned it over, dumping its contents onto the ground. Loose parchment and lucten lenses scattered across the floor.

Her stomach clenched at the wreckage, but she couldn't worry about that now. She yanked out and dumped several more drawers, then stacked them into a teetering pile in her arms. She sprinted back to Hosev's cell and dropped them all on the floor.

He started.

"I'm going to help you get out," she said flatly.

He glared at her, fire burning behind his eyes. She stepped back, at least an arm's reach away from the cell just in case, then she pointed up to the trapdoor. "You need to go through there. I can't find another way out."

His eyes narrowed at her, then they flicked to the ceiling.

"Turn your cot up on its side," she said.

His eyebrows drew together. Then he looked over his shoulder and glanced from his cot to the trapdoor. He took one more probing look at Elwyn, then he pushed himself up and hustled to the head of his cot. He heaved it upward until it balanced on the foot's wooden frame.

He clambered up the vertical cot frame, balanced on the top, and reached for the trapdoor. His fingers were still at least two feet from it.

Elwyn snatched up a shallow drawer from her pile. "Stack this on top," she said as she shoved it between the root-bars. Halfway through, it got stuck, so she leaned her weight into it.

The drawer squeezed through and dropped to the ground inside the root-cell, and Hosev jumped down.

One by one, Elwyn shoved the rest of the drawers through. Hosev grabbed them and dumped them onto his upended cot. He climbed back up then stacked the drawers. He carefully stepped up onto the teetering tower.

She peeked over her shoulder through the windows. The room beyond them was still empty. The seconds took years as he tried to find his balance. Finally, he steadied himself enough to stand upright and reach for the trapdoor.

His fingers brushed it, but he couldn't get a grip. There wasn't a handle or anything to pull it down. He stretched to reach into the grooves around it, but he couldn't get enough of a hold to prise it open. He raised himself onto his toes and reached with one hand.

Elwyn's heart hammered. She wanted to scream at him to hurry. She checked the windows again—still empty.

He got his fingertips into the groove and pulled. It fell open, but Hosev couldn't reach in far enough to pull himself up. Elwyn ran back into the narrow room and ripped out another drawer. Lucten lenses and parchment sprayed the room. She sprinted back to the cell and shoved the drawer through the roots.

"Catch!" She tossed it to Hosev.

Hosev reached for it, but her aim was way off. It smashed against the opposite side of the cell and clattered to the floor. Her stomach dropped. Hosev looked at her with wide eyes, then he launched himself into the air. The cot and pile of drawers crashed to the floor, the sound echoing through the room.

But he'd gotten a hold. She held her breath while he dangled from the hole in the ceiling. One of his hands slipped—the one he'd punched the bars with. Elwyn's body trembled with adrenaline.

He reached that arm back up and caught hold again, then he swung his legs and heaved his head and torso through. He swung his legs again, and he got a knee up, then he pulled both legs through.

Just as his final boot disappeared, a familiar, authoritative voice reverberated through the room. "What is this?" Astur yelled.

"Run!" Elwyn screamed.

Hosev didn't need the advice. Desperate scratching came from the ceiling, and the sound sped away from the hole and faded from earshot.

Elwyn spun to face Astur and planted her feet. He stalked toward her, a sinister fire burning in his eyes. Bumps rose and prickled along her arms as he asked in a low voice, "What did you do?"

His words shot through her, but there was no going back from here. She stood up straight and held her chin up. "I helped him escape."

Astur's eyes narrowed, and his jaw clenched. "Why?" His voice was so low she barely heard it, but the tone sunk into her bones like ice.

A cold fury built within him. Icy waves of anger radiated from him, and his eyes bored into her. As she held his eye contact, the rest of the room began to get hazy. Everything around him faded into a harsh, bright blur. Then even he faded—all that existed was Astur's livid, glowing eyes.

Elwyn's brain screamed at her to run away, but she held Astur's gaze. Her eyes burned, but she refused to back down. She had to fix what she'd done.

"I killed his father," Elwyn said. Her voice rang in the sharp brightness around her and Astur. "That's why he's serving Solun, why he came for us. It's my fault, so I have to help him."

The burning haze around Astur's eyes eased some, and he began to take shape again.

She pulled the lucten lens out of her pocket and held it up. "If I send someone down the wrong path, I don't run away. I do what I can to fix it."

Astur started, then his eyebrows drew together, and he studied her for a long time. Slowly, the harshness of the light around him calmed. The haze dissolved, and the room took form once again. His eyes were still narrowed and his jaw was still set, but the cold fury had dissipated.

Elwyn let out a long breath. "We can't kill Solun. And if Hosev is any indication, killing Solun's servants just helps him get more. We can't win that way."

Astur held her gaze.

"You told us that Solun has to rely on his servants because he can't be everywhere at once. If he didn't have servants, he wouldn't be able to do very much. We have to find a way to take away his servants without killing them. If people had something better to turn to, so they didn't need Solun, they wouldn't serve him. We have to offer that better option, give people a reason to abandon Solun."

Astur's gaze was so strong it burned. It was like staring into the sun. Elwyn squeezed her eyes shut, then a crash resounded from behind the windows. Nirep and Oktoh burst into the cell room, then froze.

"What happened? Where is he?" Nirep yelled, his shock of white-blonde hair flopping around in his panic. He sprinted to the section of mangled roots and Magically spread them into a wide hole. He bounded into the cell, reached up, and jumped futilely for the trapdoor.

He clambered onto the fallen cot and leaped. He missed the trapdoor by several feet and slammed hard onto the floor. He jumped back up and yelled, "Help me!"

Oktoh shook himself and reached toward Nirep, Magically lifting him up and through the open trapdoor. In seconds, Nirep disappeared in pursuit of Hosev. Muffled scratching sped away from the trapdoor, and Elwyn's insides clenched.

43

"Oktoh, please summon Wuervik," Astur said. A chill ran down Elwyn's arms. Oktoh dipped his head and slipped through the door into the windowed room. Astur stared Elwyn straight in the eyes, expressionless and unblinking. Her eyes burned, but she fought to hold his eye contact. The outer door thunked closed, then silence reigned.

Elwyn couldn't hold his eye contact anymore, so her eyes drew to the cell. The lucten lamps had dimmed so much that the open trapdoor in the center of the ceiling was nearly invisible in shadow.

"I have a conundrum, Elwyn," Astur said. Her eyes shot back to his, and his unblinking stare gave her chills.

He tilted his head slightly. "I've been unable to catch my balance since your sixteenth birthday." He paused. "Actually, long before that. Since the day I became aware of your existence. You are a mystery to me."

Elwyn froze.

"The High King's blessing is on you," he said. "That is the problem I face."

Elwyn started and squinted at him. Had she heard him right?

"Nearly every action you've taken since your birthday has been unforeseeable and problematic to me, and I have been unable to discern the High King's intentions in it. That, as you may expect, leaves me in an uncomfortable position."

Elwyn nodded, because it felt like he expected agreement, but her mind was spinning.

"Until a few moments ago," Astur continued, "I was at a loss to understand what you were meant for, but I'm beginning to understand." His gaze bored into her, and he seemed as though the knowledge disturbed him. She raised her eyebrows—it was all the response she could muster.

Astur continued, "Much is still veiled to me. I am unable to foresee how this will play out, but I can see the shape of it."

Elwyn looked down, and she was surprised to find the lucten lens still in her hand. She was absently turning it in circles.

"What's contained there?" Astur asked. "You implied it's noteworthy."

Elwyn held the lucten lens firmly. "It's a memory of yours, I think."

Astur stiffened. His eyes narrowed, and his eyebrows came together, as he stepped closer. "Hold it up, please."

Elwyn met his eyes, then she lifted it up and held it there. He approached her, leaned forward, and looked through the lucten lens, standing entirely still.

He stayed like that for a long time, and Elwyn's arm grew heavy. Finally, he leaned back. Elwyn let her arm fall, and slipped the lucten lens back into her pocket. His face was tense, and he worked his jaw. "I'd forgotten I made the mistake of recording that memory." His eyes were hard.

Elwyn looked down but watched him out of the corner of her eyes. "Was that who I think it was?"

"That was my colleague and close friend, Ohr," Astur said. Elwyn frowned. Had she been wrong?

Astur continued, "He's now known as Solun."

Her limbs went cold. She'd expected it, but it still hit hard. She glared up at him. "So, you gave him the idea."

Astur closed his eyes and bent his head. "Yes."

She shivered. Everything that Solun had done could be traced back to that conversation. But her mind twinged—that couldn't have been all of it. Her mind replayed Solun's eyes dilating into black spheres. The transformation was so fast that it couldn't have started there. She paused, then she said, "That wasn't the start of it."

Astur frowned.

"He'd already entertained the idea," she said. "There's no way he could have fallen so deep so fast."

He blinked, and his eyebrows came together.

"That conversation may have tipped him over the edge, but he was already near the tipping point on his own. You just gave him the last push."

Astur bent his head and stood frozen. She played the memory in her mind again. "What was that place?"

Astur stirred. "That was the main ballroom of Montri Castle at Merlum, the seat of the Eudaimonians while they reigned."

Elwyn's chest prickled. "So I'm related to the people on the thrones?"

"Four individuals on that platform, two of whom sat on thrones, are your ancestors," Astur said.

Her mind drifted back to the memory. Which ones? In her mind's eye, she saw Astur and Solun watching them. "Why were you there with Solun?"

"That was our assignment," Astur said. "Well, one manifestation of our assignment."

Elwyn frowned. "What do you mean?"

Astur laughed wearily. "That question requires a long answer."

Elwyn raised her eyebrows. "Okay."

Astur gave her a wry yet solemn smile. "Once again, you keep me off balance." Then he steeled himself and said, "Nine centuries ago, humans across Alloidem had nearly wiped themselves out. The High King interceded to save humanity from itself. He sent my brethren and me of the Ansomafin to assist humanity's recovery."

A shiver ran down Elwyn's back.

"The High King, the source and powerful user of all Gifts, selected five humans on whom to bestow them, one Gift to each. The Gifts were a blessing that was meant in turn to bless all of humanity, which he made and loves. Those five Gifted humans became known as the Eudaimonians."

Elwyn's stomach warmed, but her insides tensed.

"My brethren and I understood our role to be: help the Eudaimonians reorder Alloidem. We gathered the the five Eudaimonians into Terralum to rule one nation first, intending to afterward spread their influence throughout the world. They ruled Terralum as benevolently as humans could."

He paused, his eyes on his far-away memories, then he continued, "They each took care to conceive one child, only one, to be each Eudaimonian's Heir. We thought that was best, to prevent war over succession. The Heirs were fiercely protected, and they were raised to take their parents' thrones when the ruling generation should pass beyond the gate. They did not blend the Gifted lines. At the time, my brethren and I believed that this was the correct course of action: the Eudaimonians holding power to control the chaos of humanity."

He closed his eyes and looked down. "This worked, at least to the degree of the Eudaimonians retaining command, for five generations. But in the sixth generation, not long after that memory took place, it fell apart. Ohr, now called Solun, led a faction of my brethren whom we now refer to as the Others. They manipulated the ambition of the sixth generation of Eudaimonians, whom you saw on the thrones, to believe that their static rule of Terralum wasn't enough."

Elwyn shuddered.

"These Eudaimonians then pursued more power and more far-reaching control, which imploded the system. It was simple, then, for Solun to undermine their rule and take over. Solun killed the Eudaimonians, and their Heirs fled." Astur squeezed his eyes shut, as though to block out his memories.

"The Heirs concealed their identities and disappeared into the populace. Solun has taken great pains to track the descendants of the Eudaimonians without their knowledge, in order to use their Gifts for his purposes as well as to destroy potential threats. He lives in constant fear that the Heirs will join one another and rise up against him."

Astur looked into the space above Elwyn's head and continued, "The rest of my brethren and I fled. For centuries, I have felt the burden of responsibility. You are the only human alive, the only human for three centuries, to know why. Even my own brethren don't know about that conversation. It is my second-deepest shame."

Elwyn's chest burned. "What's the first?"

Astur bent his head. "My cowardice ever since."

Her limbs went cold.

Astur stayed silent for a long moment, then he met her eyes. "The High King intends for something to happen, something you are to be involved in. It is against my instincts to trust a human, especially one so unpredictable to me as you are. But therein, I think, lies the point."

Elwyn held her breath. She considered, her mind rolling through what she'd learned in the Treasury, and what Astur said now about the Eudaimonians. There was something there. All at once, it clicked together in her mind. "You were wrong."

Astur started.

"About the Eudaimonians," she said, "and about humanity. You said you were sent to assist humanity's recovery, but you set up a system of subjugation instead. Your job was recovery, not domination. Recovery requires healing. Healing doesn't come from the top down, but from the inside out."

His eyebrows knitted, and he looked down.

"We *can* heal," she said, her chest warming. "And we can beat him."

He met her eyes, hope and fear warring behind his.

"I think I found a way," she said. "In the Treasury, I watched more lucten lenses than just yours. They were memories of a kid named Olin."

Astur's eyes widened.

"He went from angry and quick to lash out to compassionate and willing to help another person."

"Yes," Astur said contemplatively. "He did."

"You remember him?"

"Of course I do." Astur's eyes gleamed. "By adulthood, he had built a strong community within a small group of Haveners. They were a mixed bunch—they all grew up in the Haven, but they had drastically different childhoods. What united them was intentionally caring for one another. Their presence here was a source of unlimited joy to me. When they grew old and passed beyond the gate, the Haven was left a darker place without them."

Elwyn's chest tingled, and her hands trembled. That was it. "It starts with caring for individuals, like Olin did, with both our hearts and our actions. But doesn't have to be just a small group of

Haveners. We can expand the community, spread it throughout Terralum, and the whole world."

Astur's eyes went wide as he stared at her, and his eyes sharpened and grew bright.

This was it. It warmed her, permeated her whole being. Solun needed servants to bolster his power, so she needed to give people something better. This was how they'd do it.

A crash reverberated through the room, and Elwyn jumped. Wuervik burst through the outer door, sprinted through the windowed room and into the cell room. "What happened?" he yelled. "What'd she do?"

Astur turned to him calmly. "We must prepare defenses. Solun will be here soon."

Elwyn's stomach dropped. No, Hosev was supposed to turn away from Solun. She'd helped him, so he was going to change. He wasn't going to show Solun how to get to them. Right?

Wuervik blinked, and his face paled. He gaped from Astur to Elwyn, and back. "What did she do?" he repeated.

"She helped the prisoner escape," Astur said, and his face was as serene as Elwyn had ever seen it. "Nirep has gone after him, but I don't expect him to recapture the prisoner. We must prepare the Haven for Solun's arrival."

Wuervik's jaw hung open, and his face flushed. He turned on Elwyn and breathed in. She prepared herself for his anger.

"Desist," Astur said, holding up a hand.

Wuervik's face reddened even more, but he closed his mouth.

"Take a deep breath," Astur said. "And listen to me. Solun and his army are coming. It is not a question anymore of if, but when. I believe he will act as soon as the prisoner returns to Phaemin Fortress to report."

"No," Elwyn broke in. "He won't tell Solun. That's what I was saying, help people and give them a reason to turn away from Solun. Then Solun won't have as much power. He can't tell Solun!" Her voice broke.

Astur looked down on her with compassion in his eyes, and he said, "It's not so easy as that."

It had to be! Hosev couldn't tell, she couldn't be the one to bring Solun here. She just wanted to not hurt anyone. Was this what came of trying to help?

A vein in Wuervik's forehead pulsed. He took a breath and held it for a second, then he let it out slowly. "Can't we do anything to stop the prisoner from reaching him?"

"Our best hope for that is Nirep, since anyone else would be far behind pursuit at this point," Astur said. "I cannot foresee the outcome, though I have a feeling Nirep will not succeed."

Wuervik's mouth tightened into a hard line, and he glared at Elwyn.

"I have made the decision," Astur said, "to accept Elwyn's actions."

Wuervik's mouth dropped open, and the vein in his forehead pulsed again. His voice lowered. "I said, didn't I, that she could topple the whole Haven."

Astur stared serenely at him. "Yes." Wuervik's eyes narrowed. Astur kept his eye contact and said, "I believe that's what she was intended to do."

Elwyn and Wuervik started. Astur said, "I'm beginning to perceive that toppling the systems I have set up is part of what the High King intends her for."

Heat rose in Elwyn's chest and up her face. What had she done?

Some of the redness drained from Wuervik's face, turning it splotchy. The vein in his forehead eased, and the tension in his face smoothed. The intensity in his eyes mellowed, and he turned to

Elwyn. It had been a long time since she'd seen his eyes so calm when looking at her. His eyebrows narrowed contemplatively as he said, "Okay."

Astur nodded approvingly, and Wuervik turned back to him. "Can we keep Solun out indefinitely?"

Astur's lips tightened, and he looked at the floor. "No, I believe not."

Elwyn's heart dropped, and Wuervik's face drained of color. "Then what do we do?"

"I'm open to your suggestions."

"We have to leave," Wuervik said. "Abandon the Haven."

"Yes." Astur's eyes deepened sadly. "I believe you're correct."

Heavy silence bloomed in the room, seeming to absorb all the oxygen.

"Where can we go?" Wuervik asked quietly.

"I'll search the mountains for a temporary refuge. Before that, though, we must prepare the Haveners and the Haven itself. We cannot abandon it as is, for Solun would gain access to our records. More would be in danger than just the Haveners—he would hunt anyone we have ever come into contact with. And the Haven serves another purpose, a purpose greater than protecting and training Heirs. It is the last line of defense."

"For what?" Elwyn asked.

"That is restricted information," he said sternly, and Elwyn jumped at the change of tone. What did the Haven defend besides Heirs?

"Okay," Wuervik said, accepting Astur's evasion. "What do we need to do?"

"Empty the Library and the Treasury, and scour the rest of the Haven for scattered informative materials. As much as we can carry, pack up to take with us. The rest must be destroyed."

Elwyn imagined centuries' worth of information burned, never to be recovered. Her chest constricted.

"And we need to prepare defenses," Astur continued. "Solun will most likely come to this entrance, where the prisoner entered and exited. Only a Certified Keeper should understand the locking mechanism in order to open it. If the cell remains locked, it will hold in Solun's human servants. Without them, Solun can cause only limited damage. Strengthening this cell must be our first priority."

Wuervik nodded. "We'll fill in the tunnel to delay them, and post guards outside like at the main entrance."

Astur nodded, his face tense. Wuervik kept talking. "I'll establish a Magical boundary at the entrance to keep anyone from crossing."

"Good," Astur said. "Make it so that when it is broken or crossed, it will set off an alarm throughout the Haven to signal immediate flight."

Elwyn's heartbeat sped, and she asked "'When?'"

"He will find a way," Astur said, and silence reverberated in the room. "My hope is that we'll be able to flee before Solun and his servants arrive, but that may not be possible. Timing will be key. We don't want Haveners caught in the open when Solun's servants arrive. We must either be long gone by the time they get here, or flee while they are held back in this cell. That should give us time, but it will be limited. This cell cannot detain Solun himself."

Wuervik pressed his lips together in a hard line, then nodded resolutely. "Anything else?"

"Post a guard here, too," Astur said. "We must be warned the second Solun comes through the bars, and we must hinder him as much as possible from coming further into the Haven. Once I find a refuge in the mountains, I'll direct as many Haveners there as can be spared from preparations." He paused. "I fear any preparations we can make will be insufficient. Solun has powerful Heirs of all five

Gifts. We are outmatched."

Wuervik nodded. "Yes, but we'll do what we can. I'll inform the Certified Keepers and get to work." He paused for one last second, eyebrows raised at Astur, waiting in case there was more.

Astur nodded firmly, so Wuervik spun on his heel and hustled out of the room. Astur stood still for a long moment, then he turned to Elwyn. "Help with the preparations to abandon the Haven, but at the same time, follow your instincts. Because you are so unpredictable for me, I don't understand the specifics of what you're supposed to do. But the High King has a purpose for you here."

Elwyn's chest tightened. That's what she'd been trying to do all this time and she was failing.

44

Hosev crashed through the undergrowth, heedless of the branches hitting his face. He had to get away. He'd found them, he'd succeeded.

The one chasing him was gaining ground—he could hear the man barreling toward him. The path Hosev was plowing simultaneously slowed Hosev down and helped his pursuer move faster. A pinging in his mind finally broke through his consciousness: he had to change tactic.

He was still far enough ahead that he couldn't see the pursuer. That meant the pursuer couldn't see him, he hoped. A massive tree with low branches stood a few steps ahead. Hosev plowed past it, slamming through the underbrush about ten paces past the tree, then he stopped. He back-pedaled toward the tree, careful to place his feet exactly on his first set of footprints.

He swung himself into the tree and clambered up until he could see the pursuer. A white-blonde head charged down the path Hosev had made. The man kept reaching out and swiping the air, and the branches which had smacked Hosev in the face flew out of the man's way. Despite his sweat, bumps rose on Hosev's arms. These people were unnatural.

He couldn't outrun that man forever. He had to stop him. His first impulse came to the surface: kill the man. His insides squirmed at the thought, then his anger rose up in response. Why shouldn't he? They'd done it to Father.

His mind clawed for dominance over his rising anger. They'd done something terrible. Doing the same thing wouldn't make the situation better, it'd just make Hosev exactly like them. If he was a murderer, too, he couldn't blame them for being that same thing.

Okay, he couldn't kill the man, but he had to stop him. The man was forty paces away. Think! What could Hosev do?

The path ran directly under the tree—that was Hosev's opportunity. The man wouldn't see Hosev in the tree, and in his haste to follow the footsteps, he wouldn't be looking closely enough to notice the change in the footprints' weight distribution from Hosev's back-pedaling.

Knock him out, that's what Hosev had to do. His mind calculated the man's height, speed, and the blow that would knock him unconscious without killing him. He paused—Hosev was unnatural, too, ever since Father died.

He pushed the thought away and scanned the area under the tree. What could he hit the man with?

A young branch around the man's head-height grew out into the path Hosev had made. When he'd pushed past it, it had flexed then swung back into place.

The sounds grew closer. The man was only fifteen paces away. Hosev scrambled down lower in the tree and pulled on the young branch. His mind calculated the tension required to deliver the blow he needed. The branch was just supple enough to produce the tension without snapping.

Hosev crouched on a low branch, on the opposite side of the trunk from where the white-blonde man would come by. He braced himself and pulled the young branch toward him, holding it at the exact tension point to deliver the blow.

The man burst into view, attention all focused downward on Hosev's footprints.

Hosev held his breath. Wait, wait, now! He released the branch. It flung at the man and cracked him on the forehead.

With barely a sound, the man crumpled. His body sprawled onto the underbrush, his limbs splayed at uncomfortable angles. Hosev's breath caught. Had he miscalculated?

He waited, holding his breath, but the man didn't move. Hosev quietly climbed down and crept closer. The man stayed perfectly still, body limp. Hosev crept up to the body and leaned over it. His neck prickled at that thought. Him—not it. He couldn't be dead, Hosev couldn't be a murderer.

He watched the man's chest, but he couldn't convince himself there was movement. All Hosev's knives were gone, the murderers had taken them, but the man's own hunting knife was strapped to his hip. Hosev pulled it out and held the flat side of the blade up to the man's nose.

The shiny metal clouded with the man's breath, and Hosev flooded with relief.

He considered the knife, then he put it in his own hip sheath. He arranged the man's limbs into less horrible positions, then took off again through the underbrush. Adrenaline from the chase began to drain out of him, and his body sagged, but he kept moving.

He started on his first track, then he veered out of the way and stepped more carefully to leave behind as little of a track as possible. Granted, they probably knew where he was going.

His mind laid his path over the maps he'd memorized. Gravusfrig was southeast. He didn't need to go all the way back to the tunnel under the mountains and to Regsenfrag, he could head south and cut through the thinner part of the Tensmon mountains.

He'd found them. He was going to avenge Father. Heat rose up inside him.

Elwyn's face swam back into his mind. *She'd* done it. She'd murdered Father, and she was going to pay. Everyone she cared about was going to pay.

But she'd helped him escape. Why? What was her angle? His neck prickled, while heat still bubbled in his chest.

It didn't matter why. She was going to pay.

45

In the main room of the Treasury, Elwyn wrapped a lucten lens in a cloth and slid it into the crate at her feet, then she reached up for another.

She wrapped the lens, deposited it in the crate, and grabbed another. In every direction, Keepers Magically pulled down whole shelves' worth of records at a time. They sent full sacks and crates to the pile in the center of the room and grabbed empty ones.

They eyed her, and some openly glared at her. Their whispers raised the hairs on the back of her neck. Heat rose up her face, but she couldn't blame them. Ever since Nirep had shown up again this morning, he'd been telling the Certified Keepers what she'd done. It seemed like he was trying to deflect his failure to recapture Hosev by blaming her.

Well, he was right. At the time, she'd convinced herself that she'd had to do it, that she was helping. But now she knew she'd been rash, responding to her overwhelming feeling of guilt. She'd wanted to fix it on her own, immediately, to free herself from her guilt. She hadn't considered who else would be hurt.

She'd thought she had to act fast, before anyone could stop her.

But there had to have been a better way to handle it, a way to help Hosev that didn't put all the Haveners at risk. When she'd actually talked with Astur, he'd *listened*. Together, maybe they could've found a way to help everyone at the same time.

How could she fix this, now?

The Treasury's door opened. Wuervik and Astur appeared, silhouetted in the doorway, then they strode down the stairs. Astur paced to the single pillar in the center of the room. "In the building of the Treasury, this pillar was imbued with Magic. When the Haven is compromised, the Treasury must be destroyed, and an Heir of Magic must trigger its destruction. Wuervik?"

Wuervik frowned, but Astur beckoned to him. Wuervik approached the pillar hesitantly.

Astur pointed to the glass tube that surrounded the pillar. "Draw a finger from here, around it, to here."

Wuervik raised his eyebrows, but he complied. The glass melted away, and the rings of lucten glowed. He glanced at Astur and backed away with wide eyes.

Astur nodded. "The process is begun. When the Haven is infiltrated, an Heir of Magic must press all three rings simultaneously, then flee. Twelve seconds after the touch, the room will collapse and everything within it will ignite, so that the information cannot be recovered."

A shiver ran through the room. Elwyn ached at the thought of so much information lost. It was her fault.

Astur spun slowly, making eye contact with each person in the room. "It *must* be done."

The Keepers' faces were tense, eyes wide and jaws set.

"Defenses have been established," Astur said, continuing to circle slowly. "But I am not fool enough to believe that will be enough. Solun has Heirs working for him from each of the Gifted lines." His eyes reached Elwyn's, and he held them sadly. "His capabilities far outstretch our own. Prepare yourselves."

Elwyn's shoulders tightened. Astur turned and strode up the steps, and at the door, he waited. A second later, Wuervik followed and opened the door of the Treasury.

The room stirred. Keepers met one another's eyes uncertainly, then they all burst into a flurry of activity. In the corner of her vision, Neilan edged closer to her, but he kept his attention on the shelves. He didn't look at her a single time. Elwyn tensed. Was he coming to her? Or was he avoiding her? She wished he'd pick one instead of putting her on edge like this.

He was close enough to speak, now, but he still wouldn't look at her. She couldn't take it. She turned to him and said, "Hey."

His eyes flashed to her then away again. "Hey."

Now what? She scanned her brain for something simple to say, something that wouldn't be emotionally charged, but everything was emotionally charged right now.

He reached up to the shelf and curved his arm like he was pulling something in for a hug, and a line of spiralbound books from a high shelf cascaded down into the open sack in his hands.

What could she say to him?

The lucten lens in her hand floated up into the air. She started, then warmth spread from her chest down her arms, and she peeked at Neilan out of the corner of her eye. His hand was subtly turned toward her, a finger pointed at the lucten lens. A tiny smirk played on his lips, and a dimple was just starting to show itself.

She caught the lucten lens, and a smile pulled at the corners of her lips. She sidled closer until her shoulder was inches from his. They both kept their eyes on the shelves, packing up everything they could reach, but Elwyn's whole mind was focused on him, on his nearness to her, and she felt his attention on her.

Tension bled out of her shoulders and neck. They stayed that way for a while, not speaking, just being near one another. The anxiety that had been building in Elwyn's heart slowly ebbed as the peace of his closeness sunk in deeper.

After a few minutes, though, her neck tensed again. They'd made progress, shouldn't she do more? She searched her mind for a conversation starter.

"What've you been up to for the last week?" she asked. As soon as the words were out of her mouth, she wanted to pull them back in. She knew what he'd been doing, grumpily staring into space.

He started at her voice, then is dimple disappeared. "Nothing. Just this."

Now what could she say? She asked, "Have you found anything interesting?" That wasn't what she meant. She wanted to ask about him, not his assignment. But she didn't know how to communicate that.

"No," he said.

The wall was going up between them again. They were just as geographically close as they'd been a minute ago, but the space between them was widening again. Her chest tightened.

How could she fix this now? She had to do something, before they came apart again. She tried to come up with something to say to get them back to where they were before. She opened her mouth, but nothing came to mind.

The shelves in front of them were empty now. Neilan took a few steps away, to the next set of shelves.

Elwyn stood still for a minute, the warmth of his presence draining out of her. Then she went back to the shelf she'd been working on before and packed up more lucten lenses.

Why'd she have to push it? She shouldn't have spoken. Why did she always push?

46

Heaviness descended onto Hosev while he slogged through the winding streets of Gravusfrig. He headed toward the rocky hill from which Phaemin Fortress shot into the sky.

Dawnday sunrise had begun to shorten the shadows, but darkness from the fortress still lay heavy over the western side of the city. Hosev resisted the urge to tiptoe in the shadows. Instead, he made himself walk tall. He'd done his job, he had the right to approach the fortress.

He rounded the hill and up the steep road that led to the main gate. The solid, iron slabs that made up the gate loomed ahead. Hosev's legs strained, exhausted from traveling so fast from the murderers' lair. He was almost there, to the next step of his revenge. His legs felt like lead, and his breathing came in gasps as he neared the iron gate in its high, stone wall.

"Halt!" came a voice from the top of the wall where a guard leaned over. "State your business."

"I'm Hosev Eument," he panted, "son of Nineveh." He breathed deep to reopen his lungs. "I've returned from a mission with information for the Sovereign."

The guard leaned back and spoke low with a guard next to him, then a grinding creak rent the air, and Hosev jumped backward. It had been a prudent impulse: the massive, iron gate swung toward him, skimming the road right where he'd been standing. He backpedaled a few more steps, just in case.

Another guard appeared in the space between the open slabs of iron. "Show your semastud."

Hosev fisted his right hand over his heart. The guard examined the thin, intricate tattoo, less red and puffy now but still scabbed over. Then he straightened and said, "You'll find him in the throne room. May his favor rest on you as you approach him." A shiver ran down Hosev's back.

The guard stepped aside, turning perpendicular to Hosev, and fisted his own right hand across his chest.

Hosev dipped his head in a quick bow, then hustled across the stone courtyard to the high, shiny, black door of the inner fortress. Before he touched the latch, the doors opened inward. Two of the Sovereign's servants appeared between the doors, faces severe. The one with two silver slashes on each of her armbands asked, "Your business?"

Hosev swallowed. "I need to speak to the Sovereign."

"Follow me," she said, and took off. Her boots clomped on the polished, black stone floor.

Hosev hustled after her, eyes adjusting slowly to the low torchlight that shone on the polished, black stone walls and floor. They reached heavy, unadorned doors. Soldiers on either side of it bowed at the woman's approach. Once Hosev reached her, she gave him a quick, stern nod, then she walked back the way she'd come.

The soldiers pulled open the heavy doors, and Hosev's throat tightened. Across a vast room, barely visible in the low torchlight, the throne stood on a raised platform. The Sovereign sat on the throne, hands splayed stiffly on the armrests, staring directly at him. Hosev stood paralyzed.

The nearest soldier pushed Hosev through the doors, and he stepped into the room, then the doors banged closed behind him.

The Sovereign loomed down on Hosev, staring at him hungrily. Hosev avoided his black orb eyes and approached the throne. His brain screamed at him to run, to flee while he still could, but he walked steadily. He stopped twenty paces from the throne and knelt.

"Well?" the Sovereign asked.

Hosev stared at the floor. "I found them."

A bark of glee erupted from the Sovereign. Against his better judgment, Hosev looked up at him. The Sovereign's black orbs flashed, and his mouth twisted into a joyless grin. Hosev's skin crawled.

"Where?" The Sovereign's voice trembled with glee.

Hosev hesitated and stared at his boot. "In the Forbidden Lands," he said in a low voice.

Anger swelled from the throne, emanating from the Sovereign as though it was tangible. Light dimmed, and darkness leaked from him like a shadow that sucked up all the light it touched. The shadow grew, filling the air around the Sovereign. Filling, or emptying?

The black orbs bored into him, and fury brewed behind them. Hosev's eyes burned, and his stomach knotted, but he couldn't look away. As he held the Sovereign's stare, the black orbs widened to encompass everything around them. The Sovereign's face, his body, and the rest of Hosev's world was consumed by complete, light-killing darkness.

The Sovereign's orbs shone in the center of the darkness, glaring down on Hosev. Shivers ran down his spine and arms, and the hairs on the back of his neck prickled. The shadow sapped the room of all light, until Hosev was just a consciousness floating in nothingness. Cold seeped into him from all sides.

"What did you see?" the Sovereign asked, his voice ringing in the darkness.

"A forest," Hosev said. "They're underground."

"Anything else?" The Sovereign's voice was harsh.

Hosev's mind raced. The island swam into his memory, but he pushed it down. "Nothing," he said. Then he added, "They caught me in their lair, but I got away."

The darkness roiled for moment, then pulled back, slowly returning to the Sovereign. The throne room took form once again, glaringly bright in comparison, but the cold remained.

Hosev shivered, staring at his boot as he found himself still kneeling.

The Sovereign leaned forward, bearing down on Hosev, and said, "Show me."

47

In the middle of the crowd, Hosev shifted his weight uncomfortably, trying not to bump anyone. He watched his fellow servants of the Sovereign out of the corners of his eyes, but he kept his face down to avoid eye contact. The courtyard of Phaemin Fortress was packed with the Sovereign's army from the towers to the outer wall.

The Dawnday afternoon sun baked Hosev's head and shoulders, and the stone courtyard radiated with heat. A familiar voice babbled nearby, "Yeah, only a week!" Hosev searched the crowd. Between the shoulders of the soldiers in front of him, Tinol's blonde head was bobbing excitedly. A shock ran through Hosev's chest. What was he doing here?

Another voice rumbled in response. Hosev side-stepped the soldiers in front of him and squeezed past another to Tinol's side.

"Hosev!" Tinol burst out. His face split in a wide grin, but there was an undefinable shadow in his eyes.

"What's going on?" Hosev asked.

"I joined up!" Tinol said.

Hosev tensed and asked, "Why?"

The shadow in Tinol's eyes deepened. "Thought you were special, huh? The only one our age the Sovereign would want?"

Hosev frowned. What was wrong with Tinol?

"Father will be proud," Tinol said, then his bravado cracked. His old emotional frailty showed through, and he looked at his feet. "He hasn't answered my letter yet, but he's busy. Letters take time." He shuffled a foot. "He'll be proud."

A knot rose in Hosev's throat, and his chest was cold. He couldn't think of anything to say, so he shifted his weight and said the first thing that came to mind, "When did you join?"

"Right after you," Tinol said, perking up. "I heard you'd joined, you didn't even tell me." His voice had an accusatory whine, and his bravado surged back. "I thought if you did, why shouldn't I? I went straight to the Sovereign, and he gave me a job right away." His eyes flashed, then he puffed up his chest. "I'm the youngest by far in this position."

What could the Sovereign have Tinol doing? Was he an errand boy?

"I started training already," Tinol said. "The Sovereign said I'll be a valuable asset."

Before Hosev could stop himself, his eyebrows rose in surprise. Tinol glowered. "Why shouldn't I be? I'm just as important as you. More even—I volunteered. The Sovereign said he values eagerness."

Hosev's insides roiled. Why was Tinol being so competitive? He'd always had a caustic edge, but it used to be just an edge. Now it was spreading, taking over the rest of him.

An instinct in Hosev's mind told him it wasn't worth continuing this conversation. It wouldn't go anywhere, and Tinol would just sink deeper into his bravado. Hosev turned away and scanned the tops of the heads around him.

Looking above the crowd for the first time, movement on the walls caught his eye. He squinted. People were drawing on the inside of the outer wall, creating a chalk mural across the whole thing. Hosev's shoulders tightened. Would they get in trouble?

But no one was stopping them. They were evenly spaced, all drawing the same shapes. The shapes took form into a crowd. As Hosev watched, the generic crowd became a mirror image of the crowd of the Sovereign's servants, each artist mirroring the section directly behind her or him.

Hosev was too far from the wall to make out specifics, but he felt as though he saw it all. As he stared at it, he even saw himself—a figure in the crowd. His short, straight hair framed a face that was solemn and intent. Next to him and a few inches lower stood Tinol's light hair, falling around a face that was longing and anxious under a thin veil of eagerness.

Around their two faces, more faces took form. Every one of the Sovereign's servants had a unique expression reflecting that individual's unique emotions. His own face, seen through the eyes of another, meshed into the context of the hundreds of faces around him. The crowd became a collective. The individuals were there, but their individuality blended into unity of being. Even Hosev's own reflection was no longer just his own—he looked like one of the many. The image sunk into his heart, and he *felt* like one of the many.

His individual goals and desires were still there, but they were smaller. They shrunk as the collective's grew. Unity of being drew him into unity of purpose.

The back of his mind registered that he'd had this experience before, at the edge of the sea, but it was different. Then, it had been peaceful and still. Passive, even. Just the quiet of recognizing his existence in relation to the existence of all else. It was the place where striving ceased.

This was pointed, purposeful. Striving didn't cease, it was the opposite. The collective purpose ballooned inside him into single-minded, irresistible drive.

A tall, burly man stood up on the wall, Maar—the Sovereign's most-trusted servant, who held the highest honor in the Sovereign's service: the Sovereign's Subordinate. He was the only one with four slashes on his arm bands. Maar gave the impression of a bear, powerful and dangerous but also protective and devoted. The guards next to him on the wall appeared diminutive in comparison. Maar raised his hands over the crowd, then lowered them slowly and firmly.

The varied sounds from the packed courtyard hushed. It felt like a thick blanket came down on Hosev's head, stifling sound and his breathing at the same time. Silence settled throughout the courtyard.

Maar's hands raised, and it felt like the blanket lifted, so Hosev could breath easily again. The collective purpose still filled most of his consciousness, but the back of his mind wondered what Maar had done.

From behind Maar, the Sovereign stepped forward, his black orb eyes standing out even from so far away. The crowd froze, and Hosev's insides went cold. The Sovereign stared out over the crowd for a long moment, letting his presence sink into the hearts and minds of his soldiers. Then he looked behind him and nodded.

The Sovereign's Communicator stepped forward and looked out over the crowd. His prematurely white hair glowed, and his gold rings glinted in the sunlight as he gestured to them. "Army of the Sovereign," he called, his voice carrying through the courtyard and echoing off the tower walls. "Our cause is needful. Rogues seek to undermine this orderly society the Sovereign has graciously provided us, to dismantle the systems in place. They intend to send us into turmoil for their own ends. The threat must be wiped out before they spread chaos across Terralum."

Hosev's chest heated in agreement. They had to stop the rogues.

"In our swift strike against this brewing storm," the Communicator said, "all must comply with these mission-specific requirements in addition to usual protocol: while our primary goal is to eradicate the threat, our method requires captives. The Sovereign expects that the lair he has found represents only part of the threat. Dead rogues cannot give us information. Death may be inevitable, but as much as possible, capture rather than kill." The words sunk into Hosev's heart, the urgent need to obey rising in response.

The Communicator continued, "We will be entering the Forbidden Lands." A tremor ran through the courtyard. The Communicator waited while order settled back over the crowd. "None may step beyond the track set for us by the Sovereign. Wandering and self-direction are prohibited. As per usual protocol, the punishment for breaking any of the Sovereign's requirements is immediate death. Order must be maintained."

A shiver ran down Hosev's spine, but the Communicator's words rang in his heart and his chest swelled with the desire to obey them. The back of his mind registered a difference in the instructions, reason given for the first but not the second. Curiosity piqued in his mind, but collective purpose overwhelmed it.

The Communicator stepped back, and the Sovereign's Coordinator stepped forward. She shook her long braids behind her shoulders and clasped her hands behind her back. "Order must be maintained," she echoed the Communicator. "We will organize for speed and efficiency. The whole will be divided into four, which will then each be divided into two: Power-wielders and non-Powered. Each group of Power-wielders will be divided by Power. The non-Powered will pair with the senior Power-wielders. Each non-Powered will assist and defend the Power-wielder he or she is assigned to. Movement will be ordered through seniority."

She nodded at a group in the back. They dispersed evenly,

stepped into the crowd, and started shuffling people around. "My deputies are now specifying groups and seniority. Follow their instructions."

They began moving people behind Hosev into groups, and the order molded itself in Hosev's mind like a map. The collective mass of soldiers divided in his mind into clear groups, and clear order within the groups. In his imagination, he saw them setting off efficiently, in peaceful order, rather than a mass surging at once and clogging the gates.

"Power?" a thin man asked in Hosev's ear, and Hosev raised his eyebrows at him. The orderly picture in his mind cracked. It had made sense when she was talking, but now—Power-wielder? What was that?

The man huffed. "Are you a Wielder or non-Powered?"

Hosev shook his head and shrugged.

"Are you new?" the man asked, exasperated. "These last-minute recruits," he grumbled under his breath. "Uninformed, untrained, useless." He squinted into Hosev's face. "You're familiar."

Hosev leaned back from the scrutiny. "You may have known my Father, Nineveh."

"Ah," the man said. "Powered, but untrained. I'll categorize you as non-Powered for now." He tipped his head and appraised Hosev. "Come."

He clutched Hosev's shoulder and dragged him closer to the front, to a soldier with three slashes in the second row from the gate, a woman with hair the orange-red of autumn leaves. Instead of a sword at her hip, a bow and quiver were slung over her shoulder. The man bowed to the woman and pushed Hosev into place beside her. "New recruit. Untrained Logic-wielder. Nineveh's son."

Logic-wielder? The back of his mind piqued.

"He'll be your non-Powered," the man said to the red-haired

woman. He turned to Hosev, "Defend her. Whatever she commands you, obey." He paused. "She's a senior Logic-wielder. Watch her and learn."

Hosev nodded and stood next to the woman, uneasy. She scrutinized him and said, "You look like him."

Hosev nodded. He'd heard it more times than he could count.

"I'm Folia," she said, and she fisted her right hand across her chest.

"Hosev," he said and returned the gesture, then he shifted his weight. Was it worth asking? He pushed down his nerves and took a chance. "What are Powers?"

He expected shock at his ignorance, but she looked at him steadily. "Inherited abilities. The Sovereign is careful of Power-wielders—they're dangerous if unrestrained. To that end, the Powers are not spoken of except to those sworn to the Sovereign's service." Hosev's neck prickled. "There are five. You're a wielder of Logic, inherited from your father."

A chill ran down Hosev's arms, and he considered. "How many of these people have Powers?"

She glanced at the crowd behind her. "Eighty-two percent."

Eighty-two percent? So many Powered. The murderers had something, too, but this had to be more. All these Powered were going to help him punish them. Heat bloomed in his chest and spread up his neck.

The Coordinator's deputies glided through the crowd, instructing each person of their place in the departure order. Then a slow, deep drumbeat began at the back of the soldiers, near the towers. Folia's face emptied of expression and she turned to the gate, staring ahead stonily.

The drumbeat grew in speed and intensity, and several more drums joined in. Voices began to accompany the drums, growing slowly as the drumbeat had. Hosev's chest swelled.

Intensity rolled through the crowd, and it pounded in Hosev's chest with every drumbeat. The collective purpose rose again inside him, pulsing with the drum and surging through his body. His chest burned, and his fists clenched. He bounced on his toes with the beats that throbbed through his whole body. He ached to get moving, to go, to burst into action.

The crowd around him roiled, swelling with emotion right along with Hosev. It ballooned through the courtyard until it felt as thought the courtyard itself would explode.

"Now!" the Sovereign's voice burst from the top of the wall.

The huge, iron gates creaked open, and the crowd surged. Hosev burst into a run alongside Folia. He felt as though he could run forever, his chest floating on the fumes of the emotion that boiled inside him.

The roiling crowd flowed smoothly out of the gates despite the chaos of emotion ballooning in every chest, maintaining the departure order set by the Coordinator. Hosev set his teeth. He was going to get his revenge.

48

Hosev pulsed with the drumbeats in the purple shadows of Twilitday evening. He marched a step behind Folia, right at the front of the Sovereign's army in the forest above the murderers' underground lair. Soldiers wove through the trees behind him as far as he could see.

The Sovereign strode in the shadows ten paces ahead, following the meticulous directions Hosev had given him, and Subordinate Maar stamped along five paces behind the Sovereign. Drums beat behind Hosev, and metal clanked on all sides: weapons shifting as their masters marched grimly to battle. Eyes straight forward, Maena stalked beside Hosev, stony and severe.

Folia readied her bow. Just above the bow's handle, a small flat bar was attached on a swivel. She pulled out two arrows, and positioned them on either side of the bow, resting on the flat bar. Another swiveling bar, thin and round, was attached to the string. She nocked the two arrows onto the swiveling bar instead of directly onto the string.

She squinted into the trees and motioned to the Subordinate. Maar came closer to hear her. "Guards will be in the trees. That's the best vantage point and cover the land offers."

Maar nodded, eyes sweeping the trees.

"They'll have a messaging system," Folia said quietly. "If they're Powered, the messages will be either Musical or Magical."

Something moved in Hosev's peripheral vision. A bright yellow bird zoomed away ahead of them. Maar reached toward the bird, then it spun in the air and flew to him. It settled onto his shoulder and perched there.

Up ahead, another yellow bird shot off through the trees ahead. Maar swiped the air, and this bird also spun around and swooped toward him. It perched on his shoulder next to its twin. A movement jolted in the tree next to him, and the Sovereign gestured casually. "Maena?"

In a flash, Maena surged forward. She barreled toward the movement, and launched herself at the tree trunk. She caught the trunk mid-air and shimmied up. Hosev's heart pounded.

From higher in the tree, a woman jumped out of it, over Maena's head. Maena threw herself off the trunk at the woman. The woman faced away, legs thrashing as though she were running, but her body slid backward toward Maena, who tackled her and held her down.

The woman flailed, but it made no difference against Maena's practiced hands. She glanced up at the Sovereign with raised eyebrows.

"Capture," he said.

Maena's hands flashed, and ropes slid from a coil at her back, twisting around the woman's body from her upper arms to her feet. The woman squirmed, but Maena still held her down. A drummer from the next row of soldiers approached with a cloth in his hand. He placed the cloth over the struggling woman's mouth, and she went limp. The back of Hosev's neck prickled. A soldier broke off from the group, lifted the woman, and slung her limp body over one shoulder.

Twenty paces ahead, a man jumped out of a tree and sprinted toward the murderers' lair.

"Raenin?" the Sovereign said.

Maena's twin brother Raenin took off after the man. The man's eyes bulged, and he gestured toward a branch where a brown bird was perching. The bird turned crimson and sped off toward the lair. Maar gestured, and the crimson bird flew to him as the yellow ones had done. It squeezed between the two yellow ones on his shoulder.

Raenin caught up to the man and tackled him. Solun gestured to the drummer, who approached with the cloth as before, and the man ceased moving.

A voice from above screamed, "Go!" Five people, scattered throughout the trees, jumped down and took off running.

Quicker than Hosev could follow, Folia shot her arrows. They soared at the running figures, hitting two of them at the bases of their skulls. They dropped to the ground, limp.

Another pair of arrows released, and two more runners dropped. One more arrow, and the last runner dropped with an arrow in his spine. His arms kept moving, dragging himself slowly onward.

A woman in a tree held onto a branch and reached across the army's path. In the tree opposite hers, ten paces away, a man reached back toward her. A translucent wall appeared and stretched between them, swirling with faint orange and fuchsia. Maena, Raenin, and Maar pushed against the wall, but they couldn't get through.

The Sovereign nodded at Maar, who reached toward the people in the trees, and they fell. Their bodies crunched as they slammed to the ground. Bumps rose on Hosev's arms. The woman lay still, her body limp. The man rolled over with difficulty and tried to crawl.

"Won't last long," Folia said. "Impractical to keep as a captive."

The Sovereign nodded. Maar surged forward and came down on him. Maar's hands flashed and the man ceased to move, neck at an odd angle.

Hosev shivered, and he kept his eyes straight ahead as he passed the body.

Boulders flew at the soldiers from two directions, and Hosev threw himself to the ground. The Sovereign stood tall and strolled through the boulders' path. They flew right past him. Hosev could have sworn they flew right *through* him.

Folia raised her bow, tipped both swivels, and fired. As she let go, Hosev's mind anticipated their paths: to two trees up ahead. A second later, two bodies dropped from the trees, arrows through each of their right eyes.

Hosev's skin crawled, but he walled off the emotions rising within him and shut them out.

As they neared the man with an arrow in his spine, still trying to drag himself onward, the drummer covered his mouth with the cloth, and the man went limp.

In a small clearing ahead stood a familiar pile of boulders. Hosev ran toward it and rounded the pile. At their base, the hole that had been there before was tightly packed with fresh mud. Hosev sat back on his heels and looked up at the Sovereign, not knowing what to do. The Sovereign eyed him, and his black orbs flashed. Hosev's heart dropped.

The Sovereign gestured over Hosev's shoulder and Maar stepped forward, the three birds still on his shoulder. He reached out to touch the wall of mud, but his arm stopped a few inches from it as though hitting a wall.

He felt along the space, maintaining the same distance of a few inches from the packed mud. He pressed against the invisible wall and closed his eyes. Then he opened them and barked, "Keirsh,

Wana, Aiol!"

Three soldiers broke off from the group and hurried to Maar's side. They knelt next to him, and he said, "Feel here."

They complied, feeling along the invisible wall as he had done, then they met his eyes and nodded understanding. "Ready?" Maar asked. They nodded. "Now!"

All four of them pushed. The invisible wall resisted for a moment, then they fell forward into the wall of mud.

Keirsh, Wana, and Aiol stood and stepped back. On his knees, Maar reached toward the mud. He fisted his hand and jerked it backward. The wall of mud exploded from the hole. Hosev jumped back, out of the way of flying chunks. Maar reached into the hole and pulled again. Another wave of mud flew from the tunnel.

Hosev scrambled further away as Maar made quick work of the murderers' hastily-filled entrance. Maar dropped to his hands and knees and crawled in, then more mud flew from the hole.

Round after round of chunks flew from the hole, until finally Maar's distant, muffled voice called out, "Clear!"

The Sovereign looked into the hole, leaned forward, and slipped into it. He made no movement to indicate crawling, but he disappeared.

Keirsh, Wana, and Aiol followed. Folia yelled instructions, the same as the Coordinator had given for efficient movement through the fortress gates, then she bent to enter the hole herself. Right behind Folia, Hosev crawled into the hole, and the rest of the army surged toward the spot.

49

Neilan mechanically pulled scrolls from a Treasury shelf and stuffed them into a bag. Keepers ran in all directions, doing the same with more urgency, but Elwyn stood a few paces away working as mechanically as he was.

Heat rose inside him. She'd been too busy for him ever since her parents came—or actually, ever since she heard they were alive. Then she'd all but given Solun a map to them, putting herself at risk yet again. Why did she keep doing that? She was infuriating.

But he'd failed her every time she'd been in danger. Maybe that's why she was too busy for him: she knew he was useless.

Her eyes kept flicking toward him, then away again, while the distance between them strained. He ached to be near her, but he'd tried. He didn't know if he could try again.

Elwyn moved closer, apparently on accident, but then her eyes flicked toward him again. Neilan hastily looked away, but his eyes drew back to her. She was hovering two steps from him.

Her closeness nearly overwhelmed him. He had to do something, anything, to keep her there with him. "You okay?" he asked, then he tensed. That was the worst question, of course she wasn't okay.

She glanced at him out of the corner of her eye and said, "Not really." Then she took a step closer, and Neilan's heartbeat sped up.

She opened her mouth, but then she closed it again without speaking. Neilan strained his brain for something to say, but the silence stretched.

Her posture slowly stiffened, and she shifted her weight to the leg further from him. She was going to leave again. How could he keep her with him?

A shrieking screech rent the air. Neilan's heart lurched, and Elwyn jumped. The alarm!

The Treasury exploded with commotion. Keepers all but flew through it, grabbing the full crates and sacks from the floor and running for the door. Neilan dropped his sack and bounded the two steps to Elwyn's side. He wrapped an arm around her and pushed her toward the door. She leaned into him for a blink, then she shook him off and ran.

C.K. Baeliti ran toward the pillar in the center of the room.

"Not yet!" C.K. Rusief screamed.

They stared at each other, locked in furious but silent battle for a moment, then Baeliti relented. "You better do it," she yelled.

"I will!"

Baeliti spared one last look at him, hefted a stack of crates, then bolted from the Treasury. Keepers streamed after her, arms laden with impossible loads, strength assisted with Magic.

Elwyn spun in a frantic circle. "Where are they?" she screamed.

Neilan herded her toward the steps. "They'll be fine! Go!"

She ducked under his arm and ran into the center of the room, searching wildly.

"Elwyn!" a voice came from the steps.

She spun toward it, and relief flooded her face. Theon and Cuinn were at the top of the steps, each carrying several sacks. Elwyn sprinted toward them, right past Neilan, and his chest tightened.

Then she turned and grabbed his wrist, pulling him along with her. He bounded into step next to her, and they bolted.

50

Hosev slumped to the floor of the cell he'd escaped from once before, while his fellow soldiers poured into it from the trapdoor above. The tide of bodies smashed him into the root-bars of the cell, making his knee throb and his temple ache.

Nearby, Folia's voice called out to Maar. "Subordinate, the tangle here must be the door. It appears to require Magic to open."

Maar squeezed through the packed cell toward the tangle of roots and closed his eyes, then he slowly brushed his hands across the tangle. Nothing happened, and Maar opened his eyes and frowned. "It's fortified against Power from the inside," he said gruffly.

The Sovereign appeared next to him, and Hosev could've sworn he wasn't there a second before. The Sovereign's mouth quirked, and he stepped forward, slipping right through the tangle of bars. Prickles rose on Hosev's neck and arms. It was as though the bars were nothing but smoke to the Sovereign—or maybe he was the smoke.

The Sovereign approached the windows with his eyebrows furrowed and his face set hard. Through the windows, a man with white-blonde hair stood frozen in shock, eyes so wide they were complete circles. It was the same man who'd pursued Hosev after he'd escaped this cell last time. A tiny bit of the pressure in Hosev's chest released—he hadn't killed the man. He wasn't as bad as they were.

The man's shock morphed into panic. He frantically pulled on a lever, and a distant ringing alarm changed tone. The Sovereign stalked toward him and the blonde man's mouth dropped open. He shook his head, eyes wild, and yelled, "Don't, please! I'll do anything."

The Sovereign's black orbs flashed, and his lips curled. "Anything?"

The man closed his eyes and nodded, and the Sovereign swept toward him. The man opened his eyes just in time and screamed. The Sovereign smacked into him, except they didn't collide. The Sovereign disappeared, slipping right into the man's body.

The man's scream cut off. His mouth closed and he looked down at his body, grinning without mirth. He stretched, rolled his wrists, and moved his fingers, staring at his own active limbs hungrily.

He spun and punched the root-lined wall, his fist cracking against the wood. His eyes gleamed. He strode into the cell room, hand bleeding and beginning to swell, and stared at the bars packed full of the Sovereign's soldiers. Hosev recoiled.

The blonde man closed his eyes for a moment, then his eyes shot open and flashed. He swept to the tangle of root-bars and gripped them. The root-bars unraveled themselves and opened into a wide hole, and the man's lips curled. He beckoned to the group inside the cell and said, "Come."

The soldiers jumped into action, pouring out of the cell. A shudder ran down Hosev's spine, but then heat rose within him. It was time to get his revenge. He joined the throng pouring from the cell room right behind Folia, and he was swept through two rooms and into a tunnel outside them. Under the glass floor, lucten trickled in ropes.

His mind kept flashing with the image of the Sovereign slipping into the man. Despite the order which had been so drilled into him by the Coordinator and Folia, he instinctively slowed, putting more distance and more bodies between himself and the Sovereign. Folia melted into the throng, but Hosev hung back until he was one of the very last in the procession.

He followed the group slowly, then he suddenly bumped into the slender man in front of him, who'd stopped. In fact, everyone had stopped. Hosev craned his neck to see over the sea of heads, but he couldn't make anything out. The front of the procession was too far ahead, around a turn.

The front half of the group surged into motion again, but the back half stayed put. As the front half pulled away, Maar barreled through the mass of soldiers toward the back, the red and yellow birds still perched on his shoulder.

"Back the other way!" Maar called out as he reached the very end of the procession. He took off, back up the tunnel. Everyone turned around to march after him, and Hosev found himself right at the front of the line. His insides knotted, and he began to sweat, but he set his jaw and marched immediately behind Maar, watching the yellow, red, yellow bob on his shoulder.

They rounded a bend, and a faint shuffling noise came from further up the tunnel. The sound grew as they marched, swelling to rapid movement, like when his siblings chased each other through the house.

They rounded the curve, and a door ahead was opening. Two people emerged carrying impossibly tall stacks of crates, and their eyes went wide. One fled back into the room, and the second dropped his crates and tried to push the door shut, but Maar was too quick for him. In a single movement, he reached him and wrenched the door open. The man was thrown sideways by the force of it.

Hosev caught up to Maar and held the door ajar. Inside, a group of people rushed through a massive room, a bit like the Capital Library in Merlum he'd visited once with Father. Shelves lined the walls on all sides, and a single, huge pillar stood in the middle. Archways branched in all directions, into what looked like similar rooms beyond.

The shelves looked forlorn—most of them were empty. People flitted about the room, stuffing what was left from the shelves into sacks and crates on the floor. Maar sprinted down the steps to the room's floor, the birds on his shoulder bizarre blurs of crimson and gold.

A man's eyes went wide, and he bolted toward the pillar with an arm outstretched. Before he reached it, Maar was on top of him, swinging his long, curved knife. Blood sprayed the floor, and someone screamed. The man dropped, and a gurgling sound issued from his throat.

The Sovereign's soldiers streamed through the door and down the steps into the room. Hosev was borne along with the current and found himself in the center of the room.

"Capture!" Maar boomed.

Limbs flailed in every direction, overwhelming the people scattered through the room. On all sides, people dropped to the glass floor, unconscious and bound. Hosev didn't know what to do— everything was happening so fast. The metallic tang of blood filled his nostrils, and his head spun. On the floor next to him laid the man Maar had killed.

Except he wasn't dead. He was soaked with thick, dark-red blood, sprawled on his stomach with his arms splayed out in front of him. His throat gurgled, and blood bubbled out of his mouth.

He pushed himself up on an elbow and pulled himself toward the pillar, then he collapsed flat onto his stomach again. Bumps rose on Hosev's arms, and his insides tightened.

The man's fingers clawed the floor, dragging himself another hand's breadth toward the pillar. One hand stretched up toward it, straining with all his might, then the hand dropped.

The man's chest rattled with thin breaths, but his eyes went vacant. Hosev's mind flashed with a memory from three years ago, another set of vacant eyes: Mother, laying flat on her back on the floor. Hosev had run to her, spoken to her, but her empty eyes remained unblinking, pointing straight up at the ceiling. Hosev had yelled to her, shaken her, but it had made no difference. Eventually, her eyes had closed, her chest rising and falling gently.

Hosev curled in on himself and squeezed his eyes shut, as though he could block out the image in his mind of Mother's empty eyes. His limbs felt cold. Movement and noise spun around him, but he crouched on the glass floor, arms wrapped around himself, unable to engage. Unable to move.

Sounds around him slowed. He opened his eyes, which fell immediately on the man sprawled on the floor. The man's chest no longer rose with breath, and his arm, still stretched on the floor toward the pillar, was limp. A smear of blood on the floor trailed his unmoving body, showing how far he managed to drag himself before he died.

Vomit rose into Hosev's throat. He swallowed it back and looked up, away, anywhere but at the body next to him. Maar bound an unconscious prisoner's wrists and ankles, then he heaved her up over his shoulders as one would a sheep with a broken leg. The birds launched from his shoulder in a flutter of crimson and gold, and they circled above Maar as he mounted the stairs.

He paused and turned to the rest of the soldiers. "Collect

everything."

Some soldiers hefted the rest of the prisoners over their shoulders and headed for the steps. The rest of the soldiers picked up the crates and sacks the people had been filling, and grabbed most of what was left from the shelves.

They filed up the steps and out the door after Maar. Hosev's head spun, dizzy from the tang of blood that hung around the man next to him. He put his sleeve over his nose and took a deep breath, then he shoved to his feet. He grabbed a leftover sack from the floor and followed the soldiers.

At the top of the steps, his eyes drew back over his shoulder. The body was splayed on the floor, alone in the now eerily empty room.

Hosev shivered. The man was one of the murderers, but Hosev's heart couldn't grow calluses that fast. He spun away from the body and hustled after his fellow soldiers.

51

Elwyn burst through the C.K. Wing archway into the Concourse where light from the luctenfall danced over a roiling mass of rushing people. Haveners streamed in from all directions, jostling one another in their haste to get to the Enex stairwell.

As she neared the mass, Elwyn had to slow nearly to a stop. Neilan and Theon squeezed in on either side of her, and she bounced on her toes, insides prickling. She pushed against the throng, but it made no difference. The mass continued to swell.

Theon pushed through the crowd toward the front, yelling commands over the heads around him, but the people ignored him. He reached the staircase and spoke to those in the front. A few moved the way he was pointing, and the front of the group began to flow quickly up the staircase. More and more people listened, and the swelling mass thinned, streaming up the staircase. Theon pushed against the current, back to Elwyn.

Something intangible swooped into her heart and up to her head. The din of voices all around her sharpened, each yelling or whispering something distinct, and the faces around Elwyn were no longer a jumbled mass of terror. Each expression now showed more complex, underlying emotions as well. It was as though her eyes and ears were opened for the first time. A woman ahead of her kept glancing over her shoulder, expecting Solun's army to appear at any second. The lines around her eyes and lips tightened with growing impatience and dread.

A man in front and to the left kept scanning the heads in the crowd in front of him, searching for a loved one. A child pulled against his mother's hand, wanting to go back for a toy he'd dropped. A woman ahead wrestled with the warring instincts of self-preservation and compassion, fighting to keep herself from plowing people over in order to escape.

Elwyn's head spun. She couldn't take it all in. Sounds jumbled into nonsense and the scene blurred to colors and indistinct shapes. She couldn't think. She was dazed, on the verge of falling over. The mass of bodies pushing in on her from all sides was the only thing that kept her upright. She closed her eyes hard and clapped her hands over her ears.

A hand pressed gently on her arm, and Theon's voice stood out from the din. "What's wrong?"

Through the dazing chaos, one thought was clear: Linguistic had come to her at last. But that meant—no. It couldn't be.

Elwyn opened her eyes a crack, and her head swam, so she clamped them shut again. She turned the direction Theon's voice had come from and asked, "Where's Cuinn?"

Theon's hand released her arm as he spun around. "No," he whispered under his breath.

He gripped her shoulder, and she braved opening her eyes to look into his face. His eyes were huge with terror and desperation. He turned to Neilan, his voice and eyes pleading, and said, "Get her out of here."

Neilan nodded, eyes wide but jaw set. He gripped both her

shoulders and turned her toward the Enex stairwell. Her head throbbed.

As Theon's back disappeared down the C.K. Wing tunnel, Elwyn's head pounded, and she squeezed her eyes closed again. Neilan's hands pushed on her shoulders, and Elwyn wove blindly through the tight space.

Voices and footsteps on all sides assaulted Elwyn's ears, and her head throbbed with each sound. She clamped her hands tighter on her ears, but it wasn't enough.

Her boot slammed into the bottom step, so she lifted her foot, eyes still tight shut, feeling for the top of the step. Neilan's hand caught hers, pulling it away from her ear.

Sounds slammed into her head like a mallet. Neilan's hand tightened around hers, and he pulled upward. She followed, trying to cover both ears with one arm. She pushed herself up, step by step.

Bodies streamed past her up the stairs while Elwyn's brain swam. Oblivion crept in at the edges of her mind, and her legs grew heavy, but she strained to lift her bodyweight up yet another step.

"Come on!" Neilan said in her ear.

She heaved herself up one more step, then another. Then her foot clipped the edge of a stair, and she collapsed onto the step.

Neilan's arms wrapped around her middle and heaved her to her feet. He pulled one of her arms over his shoulders and wrapped one of his around her waist. She leaned into him and dragged a leg up one more step, then she stumbled. Neilan's firm grip held her up. He adjusted his hold on her waist and took over completely, hoisting her up step after step. She barely registered the feel of wood under her slack feet as her head pounded.

Purplish light danced through her closed eyelids as she toppled out of the Enex hole. She blinked her eyes open. The hollow trunk of the entrance was gone, and splinters strewed the forest floor. Strong arms lifted her upright again, and hot tears burned in her eyes from the pain in her head.

She squeezed her eyes shut again and sagged in Neilan's grip. She yearned to collapse, to splay herself on the forest floor and give into oblivion. Neilan held her up and hauled her away from the Haven, foot by foot. She strained to pick up her feet, but they dragged.

Neilan bent and lifted her. He slung her up across his shoulders, then he pulled one of her legs and one of her arms to the front and wrapped his arms through her front elbow and knee, anchoring her to his shoulders.

Her vision blurred and her head lolled while he stumbled into a run.

52

Neilan's body trembled with adrenaline. He pulsed with so much of it that he almost couldn't feel the extra weight of Elwyn across his shoulders, but his mind was consumed by her. He wouldn't fail her this time—he would keep her safe. It was all on him.

Where had Theon gone? It didn't matter. Neilan would protect Elwyn, he had to. He ran through the trees, thirty paces from the Enex hole. Behind him, four C.K.s stopped and simultaneously pressed their hands to the ground, closing their eyes in concentration.

All the depressions from the fleeing Haveners' footsteps puffed back up until the forest floor was void of marks from their flight. As Neilan ran, he felt the ground press against his feet. Once a foot lifted, the ground filled the depression again instantly.

Elwyn groaned and pressed her forehead hard against his shoulder bone. What was wrong with her?

"Can I help?" a C.K. running next to Neilan asked.

Neilan shook his head. "No, I got her," he said, fighting to make his voice sound unstrained. The C.K. watched him for a moment longer, then turned away and focused on his own flight.

Neilan wouldn't let anyone else take her—no one else cared about her as much as he did. He had to protect her this time.

Neilan's legs dragged in the darkness as though he were slogging through mud, though the mountainside was hard and rocky. Elwyn's weight across his shoulders seemed to grow heavier every step he took. She'd been floating in and out of consciousness ever since they'd left the Haven yesterday.

They'd made it only halfway up the mountain so far, but he was so weary it felt like he'd already climbed three mountains.

The Darkday sky glittered with stars. The shadow shape of Fainor as it eclipsed the sun, rimmed by a spiderweb-thin thread of fire on one side, headed down toward the horizon. Evening was setting in, but the Haveners couldn't slow down. They'd traveled as hard as they could since yesterday evening, stopping only as briefly as possible for food and rest.

Neilan's neck and shoulders ached, and his body strained against the fatigue flooding his muscles. But he had to keep going. He had to get Elwyn to safety.

His foot slipped on a rock, and he dropped to a knee. Elwyn's weight tipped on his shoulders, and he tried to balance her, but his muscles didn't have enough energy left to respond. A set of arms caught her as she fell, stopping her from slamming onto the stony mountainside.

"Let me help," C.K. Oktoh's voice said.

"No, I'm fine," Neilan argued, trying to force his legs to respond to his brain, but his voice sounded feeble even to himself.

"Enough of that," Oktoh said, and he pulled the unconscious Elwyn from Neilan's grasp. His tone was commanding, in a kind way—he wasn't going to let Neilan exhaust himself completely. But

Neilan's chest ached. He was supposed to be the one to help Elwyn, to keep her safe.

When her weight lifted from his shoulders, he felt strangely light. Weariness still grated at his muscles, but the change gave him a burst of capacity. He pushed to his feet as Oktoh took off with Elwyn, sagging under her weight but moving quickly. Neilan hurried after him, a hand out toward Elwyn in case Oktoh lost his balance, but Oktoh was steady.

Neilan trailed him for another two hours, pushing his muscles harder than he'd thought they could go. They neared the top of a twin-peaked mountain, and they headed for the point between the peaks. Neilan was tempted to push Magic into his legs for the last stretch, but it wasn't worth complete shutdown. If he couldn't make it, someone would drag him, he hoped.

They reached the level space between the peaks. Twenty paces up one peak, the mountainside curved inward, and Neilan followed the rest of the Haveners up to the curve. Deep at the center of the inward curve, a crack opened into a cave, invisible except when standing right in front of it. Through the crack, firelight was faintly visible.

Haveners streamed through the crack, which was wide enough for two people to climb through side-by-side. Relief flooded Neilan's weary body as he was swept into the cave with the rest of the Haveners.

He dropped to his hands and knees, unable to stay upright anymore. A Medic-Keeper ran to him and poured silver liquid into his mouth. It was cool and fresh like spring water. As soon as the healing draft hit his throat, his weariness eased. He was still exhausted, but he was able to stand up.

Along the walls of the massive cave, much bigger than it appeared from the outside, people sat in small groups around tiny fires. Where had Oktoh taken Elwyn?

At the back, Medic-Keepers swarmed around people lying on blankets in rows. Neilan hustled to the line of blankets and scanned the faces. There! A mess of blonde hair shone in the firelight at the end of the second row. Neilan ran to her.

Elwyn was conscious again, groaning quietly and rolling her head from side to side. A medic reached her in the line and turned to Neilan. "What happened?"

"I don't know," Neilan said. "In the Concourse, she sorta shutdown, and she's been like this or unconscious ever since."

The medic frowned and knelt next to Elwyn. She examined her from head to foot. "No injuries. Doesn't seem like exhaustion, which most of these patients are suffering from. I'm not sure what it is, but I feel that she'll be okay in time."

Neilan clenched his teeth. He wanted to yell, *'Make her be okay, now!'* but he took a breath. "What can be done for her right now? She hasn't eaten since we left the Haven."

The medic nodded. "I'll give her a healing draft, and she'll need fed a few spoonfuls of broth every half hour. I have many to care for—can I entrust that task to you?"

Neilan nodded. He'd help her. He'd make her better.

The medic eyed him. "First, you need to eat. The Keepers who got here early to set up have hunted game and gathered wild root vegetables." She pointed to the scattered fires, where Haveners swarmed around blankets spread with piles of provisions. "Go. I'll bring her a draft while you eat."

Neilan frowned. He didn't want to leave her side.

The medic's lips quirked. "You can't help her if you starve."

She was right, though Neilan's heart still resisted. He reluctantly pushed his wobbly legs into action and obeyed.

Dawnday sunlight glowed at the cave mouth and seeped in. Neilan sat next to Elwyn, who still lay on a blanket lost to him. Her conscious times were longer, now, but she still didn't seem aware of what was going on around her.

Right now she lay still, squeezing her eyes shut while her arms were wrapped around her head, covering her ears. The medic had said she didn't have a fever or signs of illness, but if she wasn't sick, what was this?

Neilan scooped a spoonful of broth and poured it slowly into her mouth. She swallowed and squeezed her head tighter with her arms. People moved slowly through the cave, but Neilan felt disconnected, as though he was watching from a distance. Elwyn was near him, but he couldn't reach her. He was so alone.

She was there, though, which meant she was alive. He could still protect her—at least he had that. He wouldn't let anything more happen to her. She couldn't do anything for herself right now, so he had to do it all. It was all up to him.

Nearby, Astur and some C.K.s spoke in low tones, maps spread on the cave floor between them. Oktoh whispered angrily, his face almost as red as his hair. Neilan turned back to Elwyn. Whatever they were planning didn't matter, only Elwyn mattered. He poured another spoonful of broth into her mouth, and she groaned.

53

Hosev hovered near the door to the Sovereign's throne room, and the guards on either side of it eyed him. A distant scream sent a shiver down his back. What was he supposed to do now?

He'd done his part, so the murderers had been captured. Did he have to stay here?

Another scream rang through the stone hallway, and he shivered. Traveling back to the fortress with the prisoners had been too much. It gave the screams faces.

One face, though, he hadn't seen. They were all guilty of Father's murder, but the one who'd actually killed him hadn't been caught. Her face swam in his mind, and he clenched his jaw. He hadn't heard what had been done about the ones who'd escaped.

Another shattered scream rang in his ears. He had to get out of here—maybe he could go after the rest of them. Hosev took a step toward the doors to the throne room, then he stopped. His instinct for self-preservation screamed at him to leave, to flee, to go anywhere rather than approach the Sovereign.

But he had to. He couldn't go anywhere without the Sovereign's permission. If he wanted out of this fortress, away from those screams, to find the ones who'd escaped, he had to risk facing the Sovereign.

The guards raised their eyebrows at him. He dipped his head and said, "I'm here to receive my next orders," then he fisted his right hand across his chest.

One guard nodded and stepped aside, so Hosev pulled open one of the heavy doors enough to slip through. Across the throne room, Solun sat back on his throne, black orbs closed. He was entirely still.

Hosev scanned the empty room with his peripherals while his boots clomped toward the throne. He stopped twenty paces from the throne and knelt, bending his head, but the Sovereign remained still and silent. Hosev waited, his heart thundering, then he glanced up at the Sovereign.

"Well?" the Sovereign asked, eyes still closed.

"I, um, I'm," Hosev stammered. "I'd like permission to find the rogues who escaped."

The Sovereign's black orbs opened a slit. He stared down at Hosev, then he flicked a hand casually. "Not yet. Go enjoy the spoils of your victory with the others." A distant scream reverberated through the walls. "In the northern wing, you'll see what I've made of your friend."

Heat rose in Hosev's chest. Not yet? Why not? He wanted to ask, but the Sovereign wasn't one to question. The Sovereign closed his black orbs again and leaned back in his throne, his ears pricked toward the distant screaming.

Hosev bowed his head and stood. He waited, but the Sovereign stayed silent, so he turned and sped from the throne room. In the hall outside, he paused. Had *'Go enjoy the spoils'* been a command or a suggestion? The last thing he wanted was to watch the proceedings with the prisoners. Could he risk disobeying in the hope it was a suggestion, instead?

His chest tightened. The Sovereign didn't issue suggestions. He turned north and directed his steps toward the screams.

Torchlight flickered off the polished, black stone that made up the walls, ceiling, and floor. A pale silver carpet ran down the center of the hallway, accentuating the narrowness of the hall and the excessive height of the walls. It was like walking through a narrow ravine with sheer, stone sides. The place made him feel small, like the sea and like the chalk mural on the fortress wall, but in a yet different way. His insignificance crashed down on him like a boot coming down on a bug. He didn't matter, only the one who ruled the fortress mattered. The fortress told him so.

The hallway came to a T. The screams were louder from the right, so Hosev went that way. Ahead, bright sunlight streamed through a window—a long narrow fissure in the wall—and cut across the floor like a blade. As Hosev neared the window, the Brightday sunshine outside nearly blinded him in comparison with the low torchlight within. He squinted and hustled past, but the darkness within felt darker after seeing the light. Why were there windows at all? It was easier to live in the darkness when light never cut in.

The screams grew louder. Hosev's heart pounded and a chill ran down his spine. He picked up speed to keep his mind busy, to keep from imagining the face that could be making that sound.

He rounded a turn. Halfway down the hall, a door was cracked open, and the screams bled through it. He took a deep breath and squeezed through the door into a large room full of the Sovereign's soldiers. At the far end of the room, there was a ledge, and the soldiers looked down over it, engrossed.

The walls and ceiling flickered from a large fire down below. A wail reverberated through the room, and the metallic smell of blood wafted toward him. He cringed and pulled the neckline of his tunic up over his nose.

He slunk along the wall, around the side of the group to the ledge, and looked down on an expansive room with several long tables, on which bloodied bodies were tied by their wrists and ankles. He shoved his fist into his mouth to keep himself from crying out.

Soldiers hunched over the bodies, holding metal tools. The Sovereign's Communicator, his prematurely white hair set off by a shockingly green tunic, strode imperiously between the tables.

On one side of the room, there was a pile of sacks and crates, the ones Hosev and the rest of them had brought back from the underground lair. Soldiers rifled through them, sorting items into piles. The Coordinator, her long braids tied back out of her way, directed the soldiers as they unpacked and organized the information.

Maar leaned against the wall furthest from the tables, overseeing the process. The yellow and red birds were perched on his arm, eating seeds out of his massive hand. He stroked one bird's head while he watched the bloody bodies on the tables.

The Coordinator sent a soldier to the Communicator with a scroll. He took it and opened it, revealing a map of southwest Terralum scattered with unlabeled dots. The Communicator turned to a mangled, bloody body and said in a low voice, "What do the dots represent?"

The body didn't move. The Communicator gestured casually, and his gold rings flashed from every finger. The soldier hunching over the body swiped with her metal tool, and the body screamed—it was a live man. That shouldn't be possible, given the mangled state of him. Hosev's limbs went cold.

The Communicator said dismissively, "We'll just have to visit each place marked and find your rogue associates."

A soldier brought him a leatherbound book from a crate and said, "Record of unlawful trade, provisions conveyed through the region untaxed and without proper regulation."

The Communicator took the book and flipped through it while striding to another table. He bent and spoke to the woman stretched on the table, "Do the recipients of these provisions know they're illegal?"

"No!" the woman croaked.

The Communicator raised his eyebrows and studied the woman, considering her. "You're being honest," he said after a moment. "Those poor people—you rogues have implicated them without their knowledge. But ignorance is not innocence. We'll have to teach them to be more careful with whom they associate."

"No," the woman sobbed, her head rolling from side to side. "Please, no!"

A soldier brought over a pile of loose parchment. The Communicator flicked through the pages, pulled one out, then turned to the woman on the table. "These appear to be instructions in the use of Magic. Please describe a practical application of the Spacial Displacement Principle."

The Communicator waited a moment, but the woman was silent. "No?" He nodded to the solider hunching over the woman. The torturer was a young man with wiry limbs and blonde hair.

Hosev started. No, it couldn't be. The torturer glanced up at the crowd, and there was no way to deny it anymore—it was Tinol. Hosev's stomach turned.

Tinol whispered to the woman splayed beneath him, and the woman writhed and cried out. Tinol's metal tool flashed, and the woman screamed. Hosev wanted to look away, to flee from the glint in Tinol's eyes as he inflicted pain on another human being, but he couldn't. The horror splayed out below him pulled his eyes like a magnet.

Affirming grunts ran though the crowd. A smirk tugged at the corner of Tinol's mouth, glorying in the attention.

That couldn't be Tinol. It looked like him, but it couldn't be him. That was not the person Hosev had known all his life. Tinol had his issues, like anyone, but he couldn't be *that*.

The fire in the center of the room cast a massive, roiling shadow the shape of Tinol on the cavernous wall behind him. It made Hosev's skin crawl. It felt as though the darkness, which had fled from the fire's aggressive light, had found refuge hiding behind Tinol. It gathered there, awaiting its time to let loose once again.

The woman on the table in front of Tinol spasmed, then was still, and Hosev's chest burned. Tinol untied his victim's wrists and ankles, then he pulled the body off the table. He dragged it to a corner, where the deceased lay in a pile.

A desperate scream, different from the pained wails of the torture victims, emanated from the corner of the room. Hosev traced the sound. A barred cage, metal but similar to the one Hosev had been stuck in, stood at the far end of the room, packed with people.

A woman reached desperately through the bars and screamed bone-chillingly, "Pattri!"

Hosev followed her eyes to a soldier who carried a fresh victim to Tinol's table. It was a child.

Tinol tied the small body to his table and leaned over it. Hosev's stomach burned, and his chest shook. He couldn't watch.

The small boy stretched on the table was about the same size as Hosev's brother Refwah. With horrifying twistedness, Hosev's mind put Reffie's face onto the small body. Hosev's heart palpitated, and his stomach clenched.

The Communicator strode to the cage in the corner and spoke to the screaming woman, "Who leads the rogues? And where are the ones who escaped?"

She sobbed. "No, please! Pattri!" She threw her arms over her head and wailed, her body racking with sobs.

The Communicator watched her with an eyebrow raised. "It's up to you to save him. Tell me."

The woman folded in on herself, collapsing into a crouch, still wailing with her arms clutching her head. The Communicator gestured to Tinol. Tinol's tool flashed, and the child screamed. Hosev's whole body shook. His hands burned and balled into fists, and he squeezed his eyes shut, his head spinning.

Tinol was a lost kid, not a monster. What had happened to him? Against Hosev's will, his mind replayed the look on Tinol's face. Hosev cringed, hot tears leaking out of his closed eyes.

A child's wail tore Hosev's heart, and the woman in the corner screamed anew. Hosev's chest ached. He squeezed his fists tighter, and his nails dug into his palms.

A new fear descended into Hosev's heart: if the Sovereign could turn Tinol into that, what could he turn Hosev into?

The hairs on Hosev's neck stood on end, and bumps rose on his arms. He couldn't let himself be forged by the Sovereign. Mother needed him, and his siblings needed him. What would happen to them if he became what Tinol is now?

The child's screams shook Hosev's soul. He couldn't bear it. He couldn't be part of it—of any of this. Grunts reverberated around him, rattling his brain. He would not become like them.

He spun and pushed blindly through the crowd. Once he reached the edge of the crowd, he opened his eyes and bolted for the door.

54

Elwyn kept her eyes shut hard and squeezed her head with her arms. Her head was going to explode—the only thing keeping it together was the pressure of her arms. Every sound she heard and every light that penetrated her closed eyelids pounded through her head as though each one was a mallet hitting her.

Pain radiated down her neck and shoulders. It felt like every one of the muscles from her skull to the middle of her back was stuck in a permanent cramp. Tears squeezed out of her shut eyelids.

There was a nasty taste in her mouth, like something had gone bad in it. Her stomach was unpleasantly warm, with the unhealthy feel of food that had sat out in the sun for way too long.

She wished her head would throb, at least that would give her a momentary reprieve. Instead, it was constantly at the terrible peak of a throb without ebbing between heartbeats. She rolled her head back and forth along the cool, hard surface beneath her. The movement and the cold helped the tiniest bit.

A sudden correctness washed over her. The tension cramping her muscles eased, and pain began to fade from her head. Her brain felt ordered, as though something amiss was finally set right. She opened her eyes.

Neilan sat next to her, tense and wide-eyed. He watched her nervously, as though she might explode. Elwyn instinctively knew that he was terrified by her pain and desperately wanted to fix it, but he didn't know how.

She sat up. She was on the stony ground of a huge cave—thirty paces wide and fifty paces deep. Tiny fires flickered along the cave walls, and people sat around them in small, tight circles, eerily quiet. Even the children were silent and still.

Elwyn's brain interpreted: the smaller the group, the more nervous the people who made it up were. Those that allowed only a few into their circle glanced uncertainly around at the rest of the groupings. She understood that they didn't know how they'd gotten into this situation, so they didn't know who to trust. Solun's army was supposed to be contained in the cell, but they'd gotten out and done so much more damage than they were supposed to be able to do. The smallest groupings suspected betrayal.

Framed in the cave mouth, silhouetted by purple Twilitday morning light, Astur stood alone looking out. His stillness, stiffness, and hands clasped behind his back told Elwyn he was frustrated and afraid. He didn't want to do what he thought he must do.

Through the cave mouth, distant foothills were visible past another peak that met this one. Her brain estimated the distance from the cave mouth to the foothills as a half day's journey.

Instinctively, Elwyn squeezed her eyes shut, anticipating the same pain and mental shutdown as before. But it didn't come. She felt more aware than she'd been since they'd fled the Haven. Her headache was gone completely, now.

She blinked. Her head was clear, and her thoughts were ordered. Unlike when Linguistic had come to her, it now felt that the more information she processed, the more effectively her brain worked. It was in balance, now.

"You okay?" Neilan asked apprehensively.

Her brain took in his long legs, and estimated that he could reach the hills an hour faster than she would at normal walking speed.

Her chest prickled. This had to mean Logic had come to her. Apparently her brain was designed for Linguistic and Logic to work together. They fed one another and organized one another's information into more complete analyses.

But if Logic had come to her, Theon must be... No. He was alive, he had to be. But something was wrong. She had to find him, to save him from Solun. She had to save them all.

Her mind twinged. The last time—the last few times—she'd tried to handle things alone, she'd failed. She met Neilan's eyes, and he leaned toward her tentatively.

"Theon," Elwyn said.

Neilan started and frowned. "What?"

"He's in trouble—I just got Logic."

Neilan's eyes widened. Looking at him fully, Elwyn was accosted by the desire to touch him, to feel his warmth. She was unreasonably frustrated that he was even a couple of feet away.

The strain between them felt wispy, like it could dissipate if wind blew from the right direction. How could she make it happen? Her mind twinged. It wasn't a puzzle for her to solve, or a thing for her to fix. It was the space between humans, a space that could only be bridged by crossing herself, not by pulling him across.

Her chest warmed. She needed him, and it didn't feel scary anymore. She didn't need him to do or be something—she needed *him*. All of him.

She didn't just need him, she loved him. She didn't want to be without him. She wanted him with her, present in whatever she faced. She'd thought she was better off on her own, so she couldn't hurt anyone, but she had hurt people anyway. In fact, she'd hurt people *because* she'd tried to function alone. Looking into Neilan's eyes, it finally hit her: it wasn't good for a person to be alone. No matter who the person was.

Neilan's eyebrows drew together, and she understood she was making him uncomfortable by her silent intensity. That was okay—the wisps of strain between them were thinning. They were still there, though. He'd hurt her. And she'd hurt him.

The thought surprised her. She had, hadn't she? She'd been so focused on her goal, her guilt, and her own hurt that she hadn't taken the pain she'd caused him seriously.

"I'm sorry I treated you like you weren't important," she said. "I acted you like you'd always be there and you didn't have feelings. It isn't true—you *are* important."

Neilan sat entirely still, like last time she'd tried to share her heart with him, but she understood, now. Her Gift told her it wasn't from apathy or irritation, he was just overwhelmed. It was okay to be overwhelmed.

She went on. "I've been selfish. It feels like you're part of me, so I didn't see you as a separate person with needs of your own. But you are, and I've hurt you. I'm sorry."

Neilan looked down at his hands, which trembled. He pressed them together in his lap. "I'm sorry, too. I wasn't there for you," he whispered.

It felt like more was coming, so Elwyn waited.

"I was scared of you," he said in a voice so low she could barely hear it. "When you killed that man, you… changed. I couldn't get it out of my head."

Elwyn's insides burned. She remembered how he'd avoided her, how he'd pulled away when she'd needed him near her. It had hurt her, but it had been a reaction from his hurt, just like in the memories of Olin. She looked down at her hands. "It hurt. But I get it, now. I'm sorry."

Neilan whispered, "Me too."

Elwyn's heart stirred. She leaned forward and reached for Neilan's hands, still clenched in his lap, and she gently rested her hand on his.

He froze, and a shock ran up her arm.

Then his hand moved. He turned it over and laced his fingers into hers. He met her eyes, and his were wet. Elwyn's heart pounded, and her hand tingled in his.

She scooted closer to him. His eyes widened, and he stared into her face. Her insides tingled. She met his eyes and held them. "I love you."

A tear leaked out the corner of his eye, and he blinked. He reached up and brushed her hair back behind her ear, and his fingers lingered there. She leaned into his touch, and his fingers trembled. She leaned toward him and tilted her chin up to his face.

He tilted his face down, toward hers. His fingers ran through her hair until he held the back of her head. Her eyes closed, and his lips touched hers, gently. Her heart thundered, and her insides tingled.

She wrapped her hand around the back of his neck and drew him to herself, putting all the weight of her heart into her lips.

His strong shoulders rolled under her touch, flexing as he held her. She released his lips and laid her head on his shoulder. His arms wrapped around her and held her close. His heartbeat pounded against her chest, and her control broke. The weight of everything that had happened poured out of her in streaming tears. He held her tightly, one hand stroking her hair.

She let herself be held by him as she wept, her torso shaking with sobs. She buried her face in the curve of his neck, wetting his tunic with her tears.

He kept holding her, letting her lean on him. Letting her need him, letting her pour her heart out uncontrolled. He was her safe place.

As he held her, her heart lightened. It felt as though some of the weight of what had happened, of what she'd done, and of what she had to do now, which had before threatened to crush her, settled onto his strong shoulders. He helped her bear her burden.

She shook with relief and another wave of sobs, while he stroked her back. She wrapped her arms around him again and took in a deep, shaky breath. She squeezed him, then pulled back.

He kept an arm around her and looked into her face. He smiled, his dimples standing out, then he reached up and wiped her tears. He ran a trembling finger along her cheek to her jawline and tilted her chin up. She complied and stared into his deep, brown eyes. He leaned down, and pressed his lips to hers. She melted into his touch. Then he pulled back and whispered, "I love you."

She buried her face in his neck, and he wrapped her in his arms again. She slipped her arms around his waist and held him for one more second while her heartbeat slowed and her breathing evened. Her eyes were dry, now.

Neilan looked into her face and smiled. "My shoulder is soaked."

She laughed shakily. "Sorry."

He grinned, and she smiled in return, almost involuntarily. "What now?" he asked.

She sighed. "Figure out how to help Theon and everybody else."

He nodded. "When do we leave?"

She leaned into him. She wanted to say *'Now!'* but she paused and considered. There was more to it than that. They had to prepare, and they couldn't do it all on their own—she'd made that mistake too many times. They'd have to trust people: messy, broken people. Her chest tightened, but she knew it was true.

She needed to be conscientious, though, too. The Haveners' nerves were already heightened, so they were raw and vulnerable. If all of them, or even many of them, knew her plan, she'd send them into a panic. That wouldn't help anyone.

Her mind stirred. They needed Astur, no more and no less. She turned to Neilan and said, "First, we need food. And we'll need help."

She stood and strolled to the nearest fire, where some sort of wild bird was roasting. A pile of wild berries and foraged root vegetables Elwyn couldn't identify sat to the side. She knelt down next to a Keeper who was turning the roasting bird. "May I?" she asked.

He picked up a long stick and used it to tear off a chunk of the bird. She picked up a cloth from the ground and held it out to him, so he dropped the steaming meat onto it. She grabbed a few vegetables and berries from the pile and put them into the cloth, too. She wrapped it into a sack, then the Keeper handed her a waterskin.

"Thanks," she said. He nodded, and she hurried back to the corner where Neilan sat with his own small haul. They knelt and stuffed the food into their mouths. The meat burned Elwyn's tongue, but she was in too much of a hurry to wait for it to cool. She popped a few berries into her mouth.

She grabbed a dark red root vegetable and broke off a corner. It snapped so loud people in the nearest circle jumped. Elwyn turned away and crunched the hard vegetable between her teeth—it tasted like dirt. She washed it down with a swig from the waterskin, while Neilan scarfed his whole meal in what felt like seconds. He raised his eyebrows at her. "More for later?" he asked.

She nodded. They each set off to a different fire, choosing groups out of easy sight of the ones they'd already scavenged from.

At one fire, Vacca sat hugging her knees tight against her chest, staring into the flames. Her posture reminded Elwyn of Jevienna, from the memory of Olin. Her heart stirred. She aimed for Vacca's fire and crouched down across from her. "Hey, you okay?"

Vacca's eyes snapped to Elwyn. They were red and puffy, and tear streaks slashed through the dirt on her face. She shook her head and stared into the fire. "They got Jathdi," she said, and she started rocking back and forth. "He's all I have."

Elwyn glanced at Vacca's parents, a few paces away staring blankly into the next fire. "What do you mean?"

Vacca's eyes flicked at them too, then she laughed—a hard, bitter sound. "Jathdi's the only one who cares about me."

Elwyn's insides ached. She didn't know what the dynamic was between Vacca and her parents, but whatever it was, it was clear that Vacca was hurting. Elwyn caught Vacca's eyes and said, "I'm gonna find our people and help them. If he's there, I'll make sure he comes back safe."

Vacca's eyebrows came together. Elwyn gave her a small smile and turned to leave, then she paused. "Can you help me with something?"

Vacca raised her eyebrows.

"To get out of here without drawing too much attention, I'm gonna need everyone's attention focused somewhere else. Can you make that happen?"

Vacca's eyes glinted. "No problem."

Elwyn got up and hustled to the next fire for some food. She and Neilan returned to their corner, dropped off their loot, and went back to pillage for more. Neilan crept to the pile of sacks and crates near the cave wall. He pulled a sack from the pile, dumped it out, and brought it to Elwyn. She filled it with their rations, cinched the bag shut, and tied their waterskins to it. Then she slung it over her shoulder and asked, "Ready?"

Neilan nodded. Elwyn searched the crowd for Astur, whom she found locked in discussion with some Keepers. The conspicuous absence of Wuervik made Elwyn's arms go cold. Neilan's arm wrapped around her shoulders, and she leaned into him. His solidity grounded her.

She heaved the sack and strolled casually through the scattered groups of people, then she and Neilan stopped just inside the mouth of the cave. Cool air moved around her, and it hit her how stuffy the cave was. She breathed in deep, filling her lungs with the clear, cool air.

She looked back at Astur. As though feeling her eyes on him, he turned to her and they locked eyes. Ever so slightly, his shoulders drooped in defeat. He dropped his gaze, and her Gifts understood: he'd had a plan, and once again she was undoing it.

She kept her eyes on him until he met hers again. She held firm and raised her eyebrows in a silent invitation. He didn't move or even blink, but she was sure he understood.

Elwyn looked across the cave to Vacca and nodded. Vacca nodded back, then she picked up a large stone and stood. A rage that couldn't be anything but real took over her face. She screamed and threw the stone as hard as she could at the cave's back wall. It exploded against the stone wall and reverberated throughout the cave along with her ear-splitting scream.

Everyone in the cave jumped and stared at her. Elwyn and Neilan slipped out the mouth of the cave and hustled down the mountainside until they were out of sight of the cave mouth. Then Elwyn paused—she wasn't sure where to go. Would Solun have taken the prisoners to his fortress in Gravusfrig? Or somewhere else?

Neilan watched her, patiently. His back was straight, but his shoulders curved in the slightest bit. He didn't know what they were going to face any more than she did, but he was with her. She sucked in breath to warn him that she didn't actually know where to go, but before she could speak, he took a step down the mountainside and held a hand out to her.

It didn't feel like he thought she couldn't do it herself, but rather, it felt like an invitation. She took his hand, and her insides fluttered at his touch. She trusted him, and she knew he cared for her. No matter what they faced, that counted for a lot.

Her Gifts told her to take one step at a time. The first one was downward, so she took it.

A figure burst into view mere paces from them. Elwyn started, and Neilan jumped and pulled Elwyn behind him before their minds caught up with their eyes.

It was Astur, bearing down on them with blazing eyes. He looked torn between berating them and thanking them. Elwyn stepped from behind Neilan and tentatively approached Astur. "I have my Gifts, now," she said.

Astur's blazing eyes flashed, then his face fell. "I understand."

In her mind, she pictured the sticks Cuinn had leaned together. Adding a third would make them that much sturdier, but they all had to lean together fully.

"I have to help them," she said. "Will you join us?"

Astur's lips quirked in an ironic smile. "As usual, you have me off-kilter, Elwyn," he said, then he paused and considered. "Yes, I will."

55

In the faint starlight of Darkday morning, Elwyn reached the edge of a craggy ridge. A dark valley opened up below her, filled with a small but tightly-packed city. It was laden with a dense, heavy darkness, different than the lack of light from Darkday. No lucten flowed here, and even the lights from the city's windows seemed to be sucked back into the darkness.

"Gravusfrig," Astur said.

Neilan stepped up to the edge of the ridge next to Elwyn. She instinctively leaned toward him, keeping her eyes on the city. The lit windows of multistory buildings lined narrow roads. The buildings huddled together protectively, as the Haveners had done in the cave.

A dark mass rose from the center of the city: a high, rocky hill, topped by a forbidding stone fortress. It shot at angles from the rocky hill in juts of black stone, harsh and sharp against the star-strewn sky.

Long, narrow windows opened like cracks in the black stone, ablaze with light. Unlike the city lights, which were sucked up by darkness, these roared like bonfires, as though the heart of the stone was on fire. Darkness rolled off the fortress, dimming the immediate surroundings.

"Phaemin Fortress. They'll be there," Astur said, confirming Elwyn's fears. Nothing could reside in that center of darkness but Solun.

"It's fortified against Magic," Astur said.

"How do you know?" Neilan asked.

"Three centuries ago, two Keepers tried to break in by opening a hole in the wall, but the wall resisted them. Their mission was unsuccessful."

Elwyn squinted at the fortress. Just looking at it made a shudder run down her back.

Neilan's hand slipped into hers. "I'm with you," he said.

His nearness eased her fear. The gears of her mind began spinning furiously, considering and calculating. After a moment, it settled and she turned to Astur. "I have an idea."

She explained it to them concisely, and Neilan's eyes went wide but he nodded, then Astur dipped his head in acquiescence.

She stepped back behind the ridge and squinted in the darkness at one of the sparse trees that grew out of the rocks. She chose a thin bough and pulled it down, then she tore off the foliage, wove the twigs into a large triangle, and covered it with intertwined leaves. She handed it to Neilan and said, "Make it solid."

Neilan moved his hands over it, and the twigs and leaves melded together. She pulled on the tip of a twig to check that it was secure.

Astur stood with his back to them, looking over the ridge with his legs apart and his hands clasped behind his back. He was unreadable. It was unnerving—Elwyn had already gotten used to Linguistic's almost automatic understanding of body language. It was as though his emotions were so unsettled that his body language couldn't express them.

She tore off another bough and got to work. Her hands worked furiously: tearing, twisting, and tugging, until she held up another large triangle and handed it to Neilan. He melded it while she started on another one. Once she had four triangles complete and Magically secured, she stood.

She grabbed a fistful of twigs and leaves, tied them into a figure eight and filled in the circles, then she held it up to Neilan's face. It covered his eyes well. She made another eye covering and held it up to her own face. A little bit of light shone through the woven twigs, so she held both eye coverings out to Neilan. "These, too."

He waved his hand over them, then she held one to her eyes again. Better. She tore a few strips of cloth from the hem of her skirt and tied one eye covering onto Neilan's face, then she flipped it up so he could see. She tied the second to her own face and flipped it up as well.

"Okay, put your arms out to the sides," she told Neilan. He stood and stretched out his arms, then she tore a few more strips of cloth from the hem her dress and used them to tie one point of a triangle to Neilan's wrist and one to his ankle.

She did the same with another triangle to his opposite wrist and ankle. Then she wrapped the cloth around his chest and tied the remaining points level with his underarms.

She double and triple knotted the ties, then she pulled hard on them to make sure they were secure. Satisfied, she stood back. He looked like an overgrown bat, with sails stretching like wings from his arms to his legs.

"Perfect," she said, then she stretched her arms out to the sides. "Now do mine."

He looked at her and at the triangles on the ground. He tried to bend his arms, but the triangles tied to him held them stiff. He gestured with one hand, and the triangles on the ground rose into the air. They positioned themselves under Elwyn's outstretched arms, then a few strips of cloth tore from the hem of his tunic. They wrapped themselves around her wrists, ankles, and chest, securing the triangles. She waved her arms back and forth. The sails pulled on her ankles, and her wings beat the air. Perfect.

"Astur?" she whispered.

He nodded, still looking out over Gravusfrig. He slipped down the front of the ridge and disappeared into the valley. Elwyn and Neilan clambered to the edge of the ridge, careful of their hastily-made wings. They only had one chance, this had to work. They perched on the ridge, wings wide like bizarre birds. Below them, in the valley, she could see over the wall of Phaemin Fortress.

Neilan turned to her. "Ready?"

She nodded. He closed his eyes and rolled his wrists. A gust of wind hit them from behind, and they leapt from the ridge with arms outstretched and legs together, diving into the wind. Elwyn's stomach rolled over.

The wind buffeted them high and sped them toward the city. Elwyn carefully lined up her course toward the fortress, Neilan in line behind her. As soon as they flew over the outermost buildings of Gravusfrig, Elwyn shook the covering down over her eyes and squeezed her eyes shut tight.

Light burst into existence, flooding in from the edges of her eye covering, and seared her closed eyes. She squeezed them against the burn. Then the light disappeared. She used her shoulder to push the eye covering off, and opened her eyes. Darkness reigned once more, but her eyes still swam with the aftermath of the bright light.

That was nothing compared with the complete flash-blindness the fortress's guards would be suffering from right now, having taken the full brunt of the light. She squinted through the imprint of the flash and checked her course. They were pointed straight for the wall!

"Higher!" she whisper-yelled to Neilan. The wind she rode surged from below her and buffeted her up. The ground below sped by, rising to meet her as they soared over the rocky hill. Her arms ached, but she kept them straight out to her sides.

The wall loomed ahead of them. They were dropping toward it, too close. Her arm muscles strained. Just a few more seconds. The wind lifted her slightly, and the wall slipped beneath her, the edge of her skirt skimming the inside edge of the wall.

The inner courtyard seemed to come up to meet her as she sailed back to solid ground. Her feet touched down, and she collapsed onto the stone courtyard. Neilan collapsed next to her, then he waved a hand over their bindings and the ties broke apart.

Phaemin Fortress shot into the sky above them, its angles harsh against the starlight. Astur sped to them, his light cloaked once again by his human form. They shook off their wings and crept toward the dark towers.

56

Hosev's eyes burned from the flash of light that just burst through the windows of Phaemin Fortress. It was as though the sun had decided to turn on for a few seconds in the middle of the courtyard. His eyes were wide open, but he couldn't see anything. The light was still imprinted on his eyes as though burned into them.

A roar tore through the fortress. Hosev jumped, and all the hairs on his neck and arms prickled. He blinked hard and the bright spot began to fade. He focused to see through what remained of it, while people at the opposite end of the hall were rubbing their eyes and shaking their heads. One man tried to walk, but he smacked into a wall.

The lights finally faded from Hosev's vision, but the torchlit hallway seemed dark in comparison. A door stood open across the room, the direction the roar had come from. A few of the people at the opposite end of the hall wandered toward the open doorway, but the rest huddled against the walls.

Hosev hesitated. He'd lingered in this horrible place for two days, paralyzed by fear, but now his instincts told him this was his opportunity. He took a deep breath, stood up tall, and wound through the stragglers to the open doorway. A faraway voice boomed through the hallways.

The words were indistinguishable, but the tone was unmistakable: the Sovereign was in a fury. Even so, Hosev was drawn toward the voice. A few more people slunk in the same direction, so Hosev slowed to blend in. He went as quickly as he could without drawing attention to himself. The voice stopped abruptly, leaving behind a ringing silence.

As Hosev neared the throne room, thick, cold terror emanated from within it. The people he'd been walking with turned at the main doors of the throne room and heaved them open, but Hosev stayed outside. The throne faced the doors—he wasn't about to put himself in the Sovereign's direct line of sight after that rage.

The heavy doors closed, and Hosev continued down the hallway. He turned down a side hall toward the maids' entrance to the throne room, which he'd found as he'd wandered the halls yesterday. He crept up to the door, turned the latch as quietly as he could, and cracked it open.

He peeked into the cavernous throne room. On its platform, the throne towered over him, but it faced away. The Sovereign was looking straight ahead, at those who'd come through the main doors. Hosev slipped just inside the maids' entrance door and flattened himself against the wall, blending into the shadows.

The room was full of people, but the whole crowd put together felt smaller than the single figure presiding over it from the platform. The Sovereign sat forward on his throne and glared down at the people cowering below him, anger radiating from him in waves.

The main doors creaked open, and half-a-dozen armed soldiers walked slowly into the room with their heads down in submission. Their shoulders were tense.

The Sovereign's voice boomed over the crowd. "What happened?"

Two of them pushed the rest forward. The four soldiers, with bows strung over their backs in addition to their sheathed swords, shifted their weight and pressed their lips closed, staring at the floor. The temperature in the room dropped as the Sovereign's anger built again.

"I asked you a question," the Sovereign said dangerously. "Explain."

The men kept silent. The Sovereign's anger grew, becoming nearly tangible in its intensity. Hosev retreated closer to the maids' entrance door.

The men looked at one another furtively out of the corners of their eyes, then one of them stepped forward and lifted his head. He didn't meet the Sovereign's gaze but stared somewhere near the Sovereign's feet. "It was all dark," the man said. "Then there was a bright light inside the wall. Then it went dark again. We couldn't see anything for a while. Then… then we were brought here."

"Inside the wall?" the Sovereign's asked. His voice was low—terrifyingly low. The man's face lost all color.

The Sovereign slowly and deliberately stood up from the throne and descended the steps of its platform. In a panic, the man looked straight into the Sovereign's face, eyes wide with terror.

The Sovereign crossed the room, rage building within his calculated movements. His voice was barely a whisper, but it carried easily through the tense, silent room. "Inside the wall?" he repeated. "How did he get inside the wall?"

The man's face was so pale he might soon be transparent. He stared with horror into the Sovereign's face. "He?" the man asked shaking his head. "I… I… don't…," he stammered.

His words were drowned in an ear-splitting, blood-curdling roar of rage which reverberated off the walls. An accompanying scream of terror issued from the man's mouth as the Sovereign tipped forward and melted into the man.

Hosev shuddered. In the corner of his vision, Maena, Maar, and Raenin slipped out the main doors.

The man's body shook, and his head twisted way too far. Crack! Hosev's stomach dropped, and the body fell to the floor. The Sovereign slipped out of it, and the roar of rage again filled the room. He tipped toward another of the men who'd been guarding the wall.

The place exploded into a frenzy. Pounding footsteps echoed through the room as everyone bolted for the exit. Hosev slipped backward out the maids' entrance and slid down the hallway a few paces, then he flattened himself against the wall, listening. Screams of terror reverberated through the open doorway, along with bone-chilling cracks and heavy thumps.

Hosev didn't dare look into the room again, but he listened hard while more and more bodies thumped to the floor. His stomach lurched. His heart pounded so hard someone might've heard it, but nothing could be audible over the Sovereign's screams of rage. After a few horrifying minutes, the Sovereign's screams abated, and he left behind a terrible, pulsing silence.

For several minutes, Hosev stood, his back pressed to the wall, listening to the silence. He barely dared to breathe. Then the main doors creaked and hesitant footsteps crossed the floor. A terrified voice spoke into the silence, "Sovereign?"

"Find him."

"Sovereign?" the first voice said again. "Who?"

"Find him," the Sovereign repeated, terrifyingly steady.

The soldier seemed to think better of asking again, so soft footsteps retreated toward the doors.

"Wait," the Sovereign's voice came again. "Secure the prisoners."

"Yes, my Sovereign," the first voice said, muffled as though he was bending in a low bow. The doors creaked again and the footsteps disappeared.

'Him?' Hosev's mind spun. On instinct, he took off down the hallway toward the main doors. As he rounded the turn, retreating footsteps faded down the next hallway, and Hosev followed them.

57

Elwyn crept across the starlit, stone courtyard, her ears ringing from the screams that had just poured from the building. The main entrance was straight ahead, but she instinctively turned to the north and rounded the massive, black towers.

At the northmost tip, the ground floor was lined with narrow, dark windows. Elwyn crept under them, and Neilan crouched down next to her while Astur flattened himself against the wall. She stood up to peek through a window and dropped back down, then she replayed the image in her mind and studied it. The black stone room was unlit and empty. She turned to Neilan and said, "Melt the glass."

He started. "But the fortress is fortified against Magic."

"Not all of it."

He frowned. "How do you know?"

"It can't be," she whispered—it all clicked so well in her mind, "since that level of Magic is costly. It'd drain the Magic users, so building it would take forever, and it'd make upkeep difficult, to have to keep undoing the fortification, fixing the problem, then refortifying it. They'd probably only put that much effort into the outer wall." Elwyn looked up at Astur. "Right?"

He dipped his head and said, "You are most likely correct." His tone made the back of her neck prickle.

"What?" she whispered.

He raised his eyebrows at her, but she stared at him steadily, waiting. "I'm beginning to understand why Solun fears the Gifted lines joining."

She shrugged and turned back to Neilan, who reached toward the glass window. It melted, and the molten glass trickled down the stone wall then hardened in drips on the stonework.

"Give me a lift," she whispered, and he reached toward her. "No, not with Magic. We need to conserve your energy when we can."

He knelt, and she stepped on his knee. She pushed herself up through the open window frame and dropped to the stone floor, then Neilan jumped up after her. He got his torso into the frame and pulled himself through, then Astur appeared inside the room. The three of them crept to the door, and Elwyn leaned her ear against it, but there was no sound on the opposite side.

She opened it, and torchlight spilled into the dark room. She peeked into the bright, black-stone hallway and checked both directions. It was empty, so she took a few tentative steps into the hall, her faint footsteps echoing eerily on the stone floor. Instinct told her to go right, so she hustled that way, Neilan and Astur in her wake.

The hallway ended in a fork: two more torchlit hallways. Left, this time. They crept down this hallway, still meeting no one. Elwyn's skin prickled, unnerved by the torchlight—it was much easier to sneak in the dark, and the roiling flicker of flame put her on edge.

At the end of this hallway, a hall branched to the left and a multistory staircase to the right. She sensed a flow in the hallways and the turns, a beauty in the movement which pointed where she needed to go. A sort of spirit flowed through the fortress, bringing the design to life. It must have been designed by an Heir of Logic.

She climbed the stairs, but as she reached the first landing, a noise from higher up the staircase smashed her heightened nerves. Her limbs went cold, and she bolted into the hall that branched from the landing, herding Neilan and Astur into an open doorway.

They piled against the wall in an unlit room crammed with spare furniture. Elwyn pushed the door almost closed and stared through the tiny crack she left.

Footsteps and voices grew louder, and Elwyn held her breath. She pressed her head flat against the wall just inside the door, keeping an eye focused on the thin sliver of hallway she could see through the crack. Voices rose on the opposite side of the wall, then figures passed her doorway in a clump—at least half a dozen people. Their footsteps continued and faded around the next turn.

Elwyn let out a long breath, but then another noise caught her. Soft, careful footsteps inched past her doorway. She leaned forward to squint through the crack, as someone crept down the hall after the group. It was a teenage boy with short, straight, black hair: Hosev.

She shrank back while heat rose up her neck. He'd brought Solun to them. She wanted to scream at him, to make him undo it, but she shook herself and refocused: there was something off, here. He was sneaking, as she had. Her chest tingled as her mind began to spin. She beckoned to Neilan and Astur, then she opened the door and crept into the hallway after Hosev.

At the end of the hallway, Hosev disappeared around a corner, so she hurried after him as silently as possible. At the corner, she paused. She peeked around it and pulled back instantly, then she replayed the image in her mind. The next hall turned again in less than ten paces, and Hosev was standing on this side of the far corner, watching whatever was happening in the next hall. A door stood open just behind him, and her mind piqued. That was it.

She whispered her idea to Neilan and Astur. Neilan's eyes went wide, but he tensed as though ready to take action. Astur just stared at her, apparently unable to conclude what he thought about it. She held Astur's gaze, giving him a moment to decide if he'd participate. He nodded, and she hustled around the corner.

As they neared him, Hosev sensed them. He started to turn around just as Elwyn slipped into the open door behind him. A step behind Elwyn, Neilan grabbed Hosev around the middle and pulled him through the open door with a hand over his mouth.

Hosev bit his hand.

Neilan stifled a shout and Elwyn closed the door silently. Cutting through the darkness, tiny lights glowed silver—Astur's irises. Blue-black shadows shrunk from his light, hiding behind an upturned table and lurking in the corners of the room.

Elwyn turned to Hosev, who was struggling against Neilan's hold. As soon as Hosev looked at her fully, he froze. His eyebrows came together, and his eyes shadowed. "You again."

She raised an eyebrow. "*You* again."

Her insides burned, and heat rose up her neck. An instinct to punch him ran through her, but she held it back. In the faint light from Astur's irises, Hosev's eyes were sunken with dark circles around them, and his whole body was tense, poised to spring. He reminded her of Olin in the first memory she'd watched of him. The rising heat drained out of her, and her heart stirred.

She took a step toward him, but he jerked back and balled his hands into fists. She stepped back again, considering. She was the one who'd done this to him. How could she expect him to do anything but bring Solun to them, after what she'd done? She'd been the first aggressor, the one who'd started all of this. Her heart constricted.

She looked into his face until he met her eyes. She willed him to see her heart, to understand. "I'm sorry," she said. "I'm sorry I killed your father."

His eyebrows came together, and Elwyn persevered. "I'm sorry I hurt your family. I wish I could change what I did. And I'm sorry for how angry I've been with you for bringing Solun to us. I forgive you."

Hosev's eyes narrowed, and he glowered at her. She held his eye contact with an open countenance, relaxing her face, and she willed him to understand that she truly meant it. Hosev's glare eased the tiniest bit, but his eyes still told her how much he hated her. Her eyes burned, and tears welled at the corners. She blinked, and a tear ran down her cheek.

58

Hosev watched a tear roll down Elwyn's face. His insides, which had been knotted since his first glimpse of Tinol's face, clenched even more. That openness in her face, that vulnerability, would be scorned by his allies, but it made his heart stir.

He stared into her face, and she held his gaze. Her eyes reminded him of Manell's when he'd returned from visiting Father. Raw, honest pain. He tried to close off his heart, but he couldn't block her. She was too—human. She wasn't posturing, or putting up a wall for him to beat at. She was just her broken self.

No attack, no show of power could hit him like this. Her vulnerability, her weakness itself, was a force to shatter him. He clamped his mind down on the tide that began to well up within him and tried to wall it off in a deep corner of his mind. His throat constricted, but he willed his mind to push down the emotion, to shut it out. To shut *her* out.

It didn't work. Tears welled in his eyes and poured out of them. He squeezed them shut and swiped away the tears, but even as he did so, more leaked out.

Everything crashed down on him. The images from the torture

room assailed him, flashing through his mind again and again. He sank to the floor and pressed his face into his knees. A hand touched his shoulder, and he jolted.

Elwyn sprang back, startled. Her eyes were wide open windows, showing deep into her soul. He read in them concern and the willingness to be in it with him, whatever 'it' ended up being. The only other eyes he'd seen like that were Manell's.

He pressed his face into his knees again, and Tinol's face flashed across his mind. The only reason Elwyn would be here was to free the prisoners. Deep in his gut, he knew he couldn't live with himself if he neglected to help when he had the chance.

What would happen afterward? He knew what—his family would be targeted. He paused, his mind warring with itself. He knew what he was going to do, even though prudence screamed at him not to.

He looked up at Elwyn and said, "I'll help you." The strain in Elwyn's eyes softened, but another tear fell down her cheek.

Hosev trembled. He was about to do the most foolish thing he'd ever done, but it felt right. He let out a long breath and pushed himself to his feet. "There are six soldiers guarding the door to the prisoners' cell," he said. "It was open when they got there, but they closed it and did something with a Power to lock it. It's the only way in or out that I can find. Inside the room, there's another room overlooking this one, but the only way down from there is to jump, and it's ten paces down."

Elwyn's face tensed, determinedly. The boy drew closer to her and set his jaw. The man with them, with the eerie glowing eyes, was as still as stone.

Hosev considered, his mind whirring. "We can't fight them. I'll draw away the guards, and you'll have to figure out how to open the door."

Elwyn's eyes went wide. "What if they figure it out? What'll they do to you?"

Hosev shrugged. "I'll deal with that when it happens."

The man with the glowing eyes shifted and said in a low voice, "I'll do what I can."

A shiver ran down Hosev's spine. He had no idea who the man was, but somehow he knew he had power. Not Powers, but power.

The boy with Elwyn tensed for action and asked, "Ready?"

Hosev nodded and pressed an ear to the door. No noise issued from the opposite side, so he opened it and peeked out into the empty hallway. He crept out, closed the door behind himself, then stood up tall and confident.

He strode around the corner, to the hall with the wide, metal door closing in the end, which was guarded by six soldiers. He paced toward them with long, confident steps, and called out in a nonchalant tone, "The Sovereign wants you."

The soldiers frowned and shifted. The one closest to him called back, "What d'you mean, boy?"

Hosev shrugged, though his heartbeat was speeding up. "He sent me to get you."

The soldiers looked at one another and mumbled, making no move to follow him. Hosev's arms prickled. This had to work. He called out in an indifferent tone, "Whatever you want. I'll let him know you said no." He turned and lazily walked back the way he'd come.

"Wait!" a voice rang out. "What's he need us for?"

Hosev paused and turned halfway toward the voice. "Reinforcements, I think. Dunno what for."

"We're supposed to secure the prisoners," another soldier said.

Hosev shrugged. "Guess he changed his mind."

"Says you," said a soldier.

"Fine," Hosev said, trying to sound as though it didn't matter to him either way. "I'll tell him you wouldn't come."

The soldiers grumbled to themselves, but there was a tense edge to them now. Hosev turned away and took a few more slow, easy steps away from them. Their grumbling grew louder and shuffling footsteps approached behind him.

Without turning to check on them, he strode down the hall to the corner. As he turned it, he peeked at them with his peripherals: all six had followed. Relief flooded his chest. He rounded the corner and strode past the door where Elwyn was hiding, and he made an effort not to look at it. As he turned the next corner, it hit him: now what?

He'd said the Sovereign wanted them, so he'd have to take them to the throne room. But what then? As soon as they showed themselves, the Sovereign would know what Hosev had done. What then?

His own words played again in his mind: *'I'll deal with that when it happens.'* That's all he could do.

59

Elwyn's ear throbbed from how hard she pressed it against the door. Footsteps and grumbling voices passed her doorway and continued down the hall. They turned, then faded. She waited a moment longer, just to be sure, then she pulled the door open a crack. The hallway was blessedly empty. She pulled it all the way open, burst out into the hall, and ran around the corner the soldiers had come from.

The hall ended at a wide, metal door set in the stone wall. She hustled to it then stopped a pace from the door. There wasn't a handle or a hinge, it was just a blank expanse of dark metal.

She reached out to touch it, but fingers closed around her wrist before she made contact. "Don't!" Neilan managed between heaving breaths.

"Wh—"

"It's been manipulated with Magic," he panted. "I can feel it."

Of course it was, how had she been so careless? Astur came up behind Neilan and studied the door. He stood entirely still for a long moment, eyes unfocused.

"Astur?" she whispered.

His eyes refocused. "I'll go through, find the captives, and let them know you're coming. Elwyn, study the door. Find the place. Neilan, when I signal, apply Magic where Elwyn indicates."

Elwyn's mind raced. "What?"

But without another word, Astur disappeared through the door.

Okay, study the door? Elwyn closed her eyes, took a deep breath to refocus her mind, then opened them. The door was the same, an impenetrable expanse of metal set in stone. There wasn't even a seam where the door met the stonework frame—it looked like the metal was fused right to it. How could it swing open?

Her mind stirred, and the stone around the door frame caught her eyes. She studied the polished, black stones and the barely visible lines of mortar between them. She mentally scoured them, running her eyes along them as though she were using her fingers.

Some of the seams were slightly wider than the rest. The wider seams ran in a line winding up the wall and into a wide arc around the metal expanse. There was a tiny groove in a stone to the right of the metal expanse, at least eight feet from the floor. At first, it looked like a natural crack, but something about it felt artificial. She squinted at it.

An arm burst through the metal expanse. Elwyn jumped back then realized it was Astur's. Before she could second-guess herself, she pointed at the groove and said to Neilan, "There!"

His eyes widened, but he looked up at the groove. He closed his eyes and reached with Magic toward the spot. Around the groove, the stone melted away. A complex, metal locking mechanism appeared, shining in the torchlight.

Neilan tilted his head, eyes still closed. His fingers moved in the air, and he twirled his hand. A click rang out from the lock above. His eyebrows came together, his eyes still closed. The mechanism twisted, then there was a heavy thunk from the opposite edge of the door frame.

Neilan's eyes popped open, and he jumped backward. Elwyn instinctively did the same, just as a huge section of the wall swung toward them. The expanse of metal and the surrounding stonework separated from the rest of the wall along the jagged line of wider mortar seams.

The stone, metal, and all swung open to reveal a stone archway with a tunnel disappearing into darkness behind it. Astur stood just inside the arch, looking up at the massive hunk of metal and stone. "Good."

He met their eyes and continued, "The prisoners are at the opposite end of the tunnel, ready for you. None of Solun's soldiers or servants are within: Wuervik said they'd been suddenly called away a few minutes ago. This is a precious and fleeting opportunity—the High King's blessing continues to be on you. Use this moment well." He paused, then he said, "I'll do what I must to give you time."

Elwyn's chest prickled, but Neilan caught her eye and nodded. She gave him a quick smile, then she plunged through the archway into darkness. Neilan followed right behind her, as she knew he would. The tunnel turned, and all light disappeared, so Elwyn put a hand on the wall to guide her. For a bizarre second, she felt like she was back in the hidden tunnel in the Haven, sneaking along with Neilan a step behind her.

Around another turn, a faint light glowed. It grew, then she passed through the opposite end of the tunnel into a vast room. A few paces ahead stood a massive cage packed with Haveners.

A ragged Wuervik stood at the front of the group. His cheeks were sunken, and his eyes were bloodshot and rimmed with dark circles. Many of the Haveners around him had the same haunted expression in their eyes. Elwyn scanned the crowd of faces, but neither Cuinn nor Theon were visible. Her insides twisted, but she took a breath.

One thing at a time.

She hurried to the door, and Wuervik said quickly, "It's fortified from the inside. We can't do anything." His voice had a desperate hollowness to it.

Neilan reached toward the locking mechanism and waved a hand over it, but nothing happened. Elwyn bent forward and studied it. It was made up of a series of metal disks, each with marks etched into it. As she stared at it, her brain took the disjointed etchings and ordered them into a complicated, geometric design.

Understanding bloomed. If she turned the second one a bit, it would line up with the first. She grabbed onto it, but it wouldn't budge. It was solidly in place, as though the disks were all one piece of metal.

She considered. The building was planned by Heirs of Logic and fortified by Heirs of Magic, and the outer door required Logic and Magic to work together. "Neilan, turn this one until I say stop." He grabbed onto it. "No, with Magic."

He hovered a hand over the disk and turned his hand clockwise. The disk turned along with his hand, and Elwyn watched closely. "Stop!"

With a tiny, metallic "click," the etchings lined up to form the beginning of the geometric design she'd imagined. "Now the next one."

Neilan did the same with the next one, then the next, until the final disk. The last etchings lined up, and the cage door swung wide open. Wuervik and those in front spilled out onto the ground from the pressure of the Haveners behind them. They scrambled to their feet.

"Come on!" Elwyn yelled and pointed to the tunnel. "Through there!"

They ran headlong into the tunnel's darkness. While Haveners streamed from the cage into the tunnel, Elwyn scanned the faces that flashed by. Where were her parents?

When the cage was nearly cleared, the back of Cuinn's head came into view. Elwyn pushed through the last few Haveners to her. Cuinn's back was to the exit, pushing on the bars at the opposite side of the cage.

"What're you doing?" Elwyn screamed. "This way!"

"He's there," Cuinn sobbed. "He's there! I can't get through!"

Elwyn followed Cuinn's gaze. At the opposite end of the vast room lay a pile of lifeless bodies with familiar faces. Elwyn's insides clenched, and she shut her eyes. She willed herself to forget the sight, but it forced itself into her mind. But then there was a spark of hope: Theon's face wasn't in that pile.

Elwyn's eyes flew open, and she scanned the room. On a table just this side of the pile of bodies lay a bloodied body with Theon's face. "Come on!" Elwyn yelled at her mother. Cuinn still clawed at the bars of the cage, lost to the rest of the world in her panic.

Elwyn wrapped her arms around Cuinn's middle and pulled, but Cuinn clung to the bars as though Theon's life depended on it. "This way!" Elwyn yelled.

Another set of arms also circled around Cuinn's middle. Elwyn heaved, and Neilan's and her combined strength was enough to overpower Cuinn. They dragged her toward the open cage door.

"No!" Cuinn screamed, writhing and scratching at them.

"Cuinn!" Elwyn yelled back at her. "Come on!"

Cuinn refused to give in. Her whole mind was lost in terror for Theon. Elwyn and Neilan managed to drag her through the cage door, then they turned at the door and rounded the cage, still pulling Cuinn with them.

Cuinn finally understood, and she stopped resisting, though she still hadn't looked at either of them. It was clear she didn't know, or care, who they were—she only had thought enough for Theon. Cuinn caught her balance, then she wrenched herself from their grip and ran to Theon. She flung herself onto his unmoving, blood-soaked body and yanked at the bindings holding his wrists and ankles.

"Out of the way," Neilan said urgently. Cuinn refused to move, so Neilan pushed her with his shoulder to get within reach of the bindings. He passed his hand over them, and they broke open. Theon stirred.

"Theon!" Cuinn screamed.

Neilan leaned over to lift Theon, but Cuinn clutched at him. Elwyn tried to hold Cuinn back while Neilan hefted Theon across his shoulders and locked his arms through Theon's elbow and knee. Cuinn pulled at Theon, nearly yanking him off Neilan's shoulders.

Elwyn grabbed Cuinn and roughly turned her toward herself. "Look at me!" Elwyn yelled into Cuinn's bewildered face, and she gave Cuinn a tiny shake. Cuinn blinked, then comprehension bloomed behind her eyes.

"Elwyn!" Cuinn burst, as though she'd only just seen her.

"Yes!" Elwyn said, relieved. "Come on!" She pulled on Cuinn's arm, and Cuinn finally responded. Neilan was already heading into the tunnel with Theon.

"Tell the Sovereign!" a voice shouted from up above.

Elwyn squinted up at the ledge that overlooked the room. A familiar-looking man with sandy-blonde hair stared down at her, then his ice-blue eyes widened and he shouted, "Wait, it's the girl from Regsenfrag!"

A shiver ran down Elwyn's spine as she and Cuinn bolted into the tunnel after Neilan and Theon.

60

Hosev approached the doors to the throne room, the six soldiers still trailing him. His mind spun, but he only had a moment left to decide what to do. One of the guards at the doors opened his mouth, but before he could speak, Hosev burst out, "Here to report to the Sovereign."

The guard shifted. "This isn't a good time, you may want to wait."

"He's expecting them," Hosev said, careful not to include himself.

The guard raised an eyebrow, but he didn't object again. "May his favor fall on you," he said apprehensively as he slowly opened one of the doors.

The soldiers filed in, but Hosev held back. As soon as the last soldier entered, Hosev saluted the guard with his semastud and hustled down the hall. He wanted to flee, to run straight out of the fortress, but he had put those soldiers in the Sovereign's way. He couldn't just abandon them.

With his chest tight and his will fighting him every step, he turned a corner toward the maids' entrance. Once he was out of sight of the guards, he ran. He rounded the second corner and paused at the door of the maids' entrance to the throne room. No sound came from within—had the Sovereign already killed them?

Hosev's heart raced as he silently opened the door. Inside the room, the Sovereign stood on the edge of his platform staring down at a figure: the man with the glowing eyes. The six soldiers cowered against the back wall, but the Sovereign only had eyes for the man facing him. He didn't seem to know or care that anyone else was in the room.

"Hello, old friend," the man with the glowing eyes said. His voice was low but it radiated through the room as though he'd shouted. Prickles ran down Hosev's neck and arms.

The Sovereign hissed. Darkness leeched from behind him, creeping hungrily toward the man. The room grew cold and dark, the shadow stretching around the Sovereign and sapping the room of warmth and light.

In the growing darkness, the man's eyes glowed brighter, and a harsh brightness bloomed around him. Hosev's eyes burned, seared by the light.

The Sovereign screamed, and the darkness poured out of him at the man, as though to consume him. The light around the man swelled, becoming so bright Hosev thought he'd go blind, but he somehow couldn't look away. The light collided with the darkness, pressing it backward.

The darkness surged in response, roiling at the light. The light pierced the tendrils of darkness, battling as though the two were tangible. Heat and cold shot through the room as the darkness and light swelled and smashed into one another, again and again. The Sovereign screamed, and the darkness rose, pushing the light back toward the man.

The light rebounded in response, and the man yelled in a straining voice, "You can't stop it!"

"You dare use it against me! It belongs to *me!*" the Sovereign screeched.

"It once was yours," the man said, his voice tinged with regret. "You gave it up."

"He betrayed me!" The Sovereign screamed. His voice had become so shrill it was almost inaudible. "I did it!" he screamed. "*I* controlled the chaos! *I* ended war, *I* conquered them! I alone accomplished it all, and he forsook me! He took it from me!"

The whine in the Sovereign's voice, his prideful posturing, sent shivers down Hosev's spine. He'd never seen the Sovereign show insecurity like this, as though he felt inferior to another.

"It was a warning," the man said in a low but booming voice, "which you did not heed. Conquering was never our assignment."

The Sovereign shrieked, and the darkness slammed against the light. The soldiers against the far wall abandoned caution and bolted out of the room. Their movement unfroze Hosev, relief flooding him. He backed toward the maid's entrance and fled, while the Sovereign's shrieks reverberated through the hallway around him.

61

Elwyn dragged Cuinn out of the tunnel, and they fell through the stone archway into the hall, which was packed with Haveners. Two rushed forward to help Cuinn and Elwyn up.

Elwyn scrambled to her feet and waved them away, but Cuinn didn't seem to have any strength left. A Keeper lifted her to her feet, and she swayed where she stood. The Keeper put Cuinn's arm around her shoulders and supported her weight.

Neilan's voice boomed from somewhere up ahead, "Then out the window. Got it? Come on!"

The group surged forward, and Elwyn bolted after them. They rounded the first turn then the second. Ahead, she caught sight of Neilan struggling under Theon's weight. Haveners flooded past him, toward the staircase she and Neilan had come up. She tried not to look at the dark red stain that was growing on Neilan's tunic under Theon's limp body.

She followed the stream of Haveners down the stairs and to the left down the hall. Just as they reached the next turn, a tumult rang from behind: a mass of Solun's servants sprinted toward them.

"Hurry!" Elwyn screamed. The Haveners surged around the

corner, but they were slowing. Their limited energy was depleting. The clanging and footsteps behind them were getting closer.

Neilan lagged. She couldn't help—she wouldn't be able to hold Theon's weight. They were going to be caught and there was nothing she could do.

Three Keepers broke away from the group in front of her, then they stopped and turned backward. Elwyn started to yell at them, but they waved her forward. The second Elwyn and Neilan, the last of the group, had passed them, they waved their arms in a synchronized, violent motion.

A crash resounded as though the whole world were caving in. The ceiling and walls collapsed, blocking the hallway behind them. Dust swirled in the air, and the stone walls on all sides creaked. Elwyn coughed and watched in horror as the cracks expanded. Logic told her the integrity of the structure was compromised.

Screams of rage resounded behind the wall of rubble. Her mind showed her how the tower would crumble, the people behind the rubble trapped inside. Her chest constricting, Elwyn sprinted away from the screams. Tears burned in her eyes.

Ahead of her, Neilan stumbled. He couldn't hold Theon's weight any longer. Elwyn reached for him, but he collapsed to the floor. Theon's body rolled from Neilan's shoulders like a sack of vegetables. Elwyn shuddered. Theon's entire front was soaked with blood, and innumerable slashes in his skin showed through his torn tunic.

The Keepers who'd collapsed the ceiling caught up to the them, and two of them lifted Theon's body. A grunt escaped from Theon and Elwyn's heart leapt, but the sight of his wounds as the Keepers lifted him brought her spirit back down.

Pebbles and dislodged stones started falling around them. The Keepers hefted Theon onto one of their shoulders and took off.

Elwyn took Neilan's hand and pulled him back to his feet, dragging him into a run.

The floor creaked ominously under them as they caught up to the rest of the group, who were cowering with their arms over their heads just outside the door to the room through which she'd come into the fortress. Rocks and debris from the ceiling showered them.

"Why's everybody stopped?" Elwyn yelled.

Haveners cried out and jostled each other, lost to reason. A child sobbed. The walls groaned, cracks widening. A long way away came the thunderous pounding of many running feet. More of Solun's servants were coming for them. They weren't in sight yet, but it was only a matter of time.

Elwyn's brain worked out a plan. She pushed through the sea of people to Wuervik, who was staring wide-eyed at the cracks in the walls and trembling. "Wuervik, we need you," she said.

His haunted eyes drooped, hopelessly. Panic spun in his eyes and those of every Havener who'd been in that cage. Elwyn felt it rising in the group like a bubble, almost ready to burst.

She put a steady hand on Wuervik's shoulder and looked straight into his eyes. In the calmest tone she could muster, she said, "We need to get through this room. We need you to wrap everyone in a shield, to protect us from the falling rock."

Wuervik's whole body trembled, but he nodded.

"Listen," she called to the group, in the same calm tone. "We're going through this room and out the window. It's the ground floor, so the fall is minimal. Wuervik is going to shield us from the stones, but he'll need support. Every Magic user who has some strength left, help him." She paused, staring into the terrified faces all around her. "Move as fast as you can."

She turned back to Wuervik. He took a deep breath, and reached over the mass of Haveners. A shimmering, translucently green bubble rose over them and expanded.

Scattered through the mass, arms reached up toward the bubble and Magic flowed from them, strengthening the protection. A translucent rainbow of color swirled and mingled, like oil on water. It stretched over the whole group and descended around them. The stones fell faster, but they bounced off harmlessly.

Elwyn threw open the door. Half the ceiling had caved in, and the floor was trembling. She ran into the room, and the Magical shield surged with her. Haveners poured into the room behind her.

Elwyn sprinted for the open window frame. Stones pounded the shield, sinking deeper into it before bouncing off, now. She launched herself through the open window and landed hard on the stone courtyard.

She scrambled out of the way as a swarm of people flew out the open window after her and collapsed onto the stones. She scanned the faces: no Neilan, Cuinn, or Theon, yet. Her heart pounded. More and more Haveners streamed from the window. There! A Keeper pushed a barely conscious Cuinn through the window, and Cuinn dropped to the ground.

Elwyn ran to Cuinn and dragged her out of the way of the people pouring from the window. The flow from the window thinned, and Elwyn's chest trembled. She held her breath. Neilan burst through the window. As soon as his feet hit stone, he spun back to the window and reached through.

He reappeared holding Theon's legs. More of Theon's body appeared, then came Jathdi, holding Theon's upper half. Elwyn breathed again.

A few more Haveners jumped out the window. Then finally Wuervik, the last of the group. As soon as he touched the ground, the Magical shield burst.

Massive chunks of stone broke off from the walls and cascaded to the courtyard. Screams rang throughout the scattered mass of Haveners. The Haveners dispersed, sprinting in a frenzy. Elwyn dragged Cuinn further away from the wall, while screams emanated from within the fortress. Elwyn's chest constricted.

Out of the way of the falling stone, Wuervik stared wide-eyed at the chaos of Haveners screaming and running in every direction. "Wait!" he yelled, but it came out as a croak.

Elwyn hustled to his side. "Stop!" she yelled. "Come here!"

People slowed and turned to her. She calmed her tone but kept her voice loud. "Come back, we need to work together."

People ran toward her calming presence. She beckoned. "All the way."

There was movement above the sea of heads: archers were turning toward them. "Put up a shield! Now!" she yelled.

Wuervik reached out. A translucently green wall of shimmering Magic exploded into being between them and the archers.

"Help him!" Elwyn said.

Magic users reached toward it, and power flowed from them into the shield. Jathdi's arm was one of the first to rise, one of the first to send power to Wuervik's aid. A shiver ran down Elwyn's spine. He'd inherited his Gift, too.

Arrows bounced off the Magical shield. Elwyn ran to Cuinn and hefted her to her feet, but Cuinn swayed. "Come on!" Elwyn said in her ear.

Cuinn blinked at her, took a vague step, then stopped. A Keeper moved past her, holding Theon's body over his shoulders. When Cuinn's eyes found Theon, she lurched after him. Finally!

"Run for the gate!" Elwyn called out. Together, the group surged toward the iron gate, carrying children and the wounded or exhausted. Elwyn ran with them, eyes on the back of Cuinn's head.

A figure burst from the front doors of the fortress. Hosev! Relief flooded Elwyn's body. His eyes were wide, and he joined the fleeing throng without a word. Elwyn's mind whirled as they approached the solid, iron gates, then she yelled, "Melt the hinges!"

Some of the Heirs of Magic let the rest handle the shield and reached toward the gate's hinges. The Magically-fortified gate resisted them, creaking under the strain.

"They need more!" Elwyn yelled.

Most of the Magic users released the shield and turned toward the gates. Wuervik alone held it up, leaving it solid green again. He lifted both arms above his head and stretched toward it. His muscles strained, and a vein pulsed visibly in his neck and forehead.

The hinges shook. Magic slowly ate away the fortified metal, flake by flake. The archers pounded the shield with wave after wave of arrows. Wuervik's whole body trembled, then the shield dropped.

An arrow released. Elwyn's mind mapped its course: directly for Jathdi, a few paces ahead of her. "No! Jathdi!" she screamed and sprinted at him, her mind calculating in a heartbeat how fast she needed to go to generate enough force to move him out of the way.

He barely turned toward her scream before she slammed into him, shoving him out of the arrow's trajectory. The arrow whooshed past her shoulder and clattered onto the stone courtyard. Jathdi caught his balance, then spun toward Elwyn with wide eyes.

Arrows rained down from the wall. Before Elwyn could scream a warning, several Magic users reached up, and a translucent, shimmering wall expanded over the group's heads. The arrows bounced off harmlessly, and Elwyn let out a breath she hadn't realized she'd been holding.

Astur burst from the fortress, sweeping toward the front of the group of Haveners. At the same moment, the combined power of the Magic users finally won out: the hinges disintegrated, and the gate teetered. Haveners pushed it with both Magical and physical force.

The gate fell outward and crashed onto the craggy hilltop, making the ground shake. Haveners poured through the space, trampling the gate and following Astur down the hill.

Elwyn dared a glance back. Solun's servants streamed from the fortress. A deafening crash rang out, and the middle of the fortress crumbled in on itself.

Screams issued from within—all the people still stuck inside. Elwyn's heart hammered, and her chest constricted. She paused, torn, looking back and forth from the building to the Haveners streaming out the fallen gate.

A hand closed around her wrist and pulled. "There's nothing you can do for them!" Neilan yelled.

Her eyes burned and welled up, but she gave into Neilan's pull on her wrist and staggered into a run.

62

Neilan sprinted through the opening in the wall where the gates used to be, in the middle of the stream of Haveners. Wuervik, at the back of the group, crossed the opening and threw back a burst of Magic, which expanded into a shield across the space.

It wouldn't hold for long, but it was something. Wuervik's body shook. He staggered and swayed, then started to fall. A Keeper ran to him and grabbed his arm, balancing him. He put Wuervik's arm over his shoulder and hurried off, supporting him.

Partway down the hill, the Keeper who carried Theon staggered under his weight. He slowed down, and Cuinn hovered next to him. Neilan and Elwyn gained on him. The Keeper's legs shook, then he collapsed. Neilan caught up and the Keeper turned to him with wide, helpless eyes. "I can't—"

"Go!" Elwyn yelled. The Keeper glanced down at Theon once more, then sprinted away. Cuinn collapsed onto her knees beside Theon, who was soaked in blood. His shredded tunic revealed a mutilated torso. Neilan's head spun, and his stomach clenched.

Haveners streamed past, and Elwyn yelled, "Help us!"

Several people ran on without a glance, but one woman slowed as she neared them. Medic Pena dropped to her knees next to Theon and bent over his torso. Neilan stepped back, out of her way, and Elwyn leaned into him. She was shaking. Neilan's neck and shoulders were tense, his throat tight.

Med. Pena passed her hands over Theon's torso. In their wake, Theon's muscles, skin, and everything else knitted back together.

"Is he okay?" Elwyn's voice barely made any sound.

"He's lost a lot of blood. I've done what I can for now, but he'll need more extensive care to survive." Med. Pena's eyes were wide, and her jaw was set hard. She stared past them into the crowd that ran by them.

"Go," Elwyn said in a shaky voice. "Thank you." Med. Pena hesitated, then jumped up and ran.

Theon twitched, and Neilan's heart thumped. He twitched again, then he stirred. His head rolled, and his eyes fluttered. Cuinn cried out, and Elwyn burst into tears.

Theon managed to open his eyes. He tried to lift his head, but it dropped back to the ground. Neilan touched Elwyn's shoulder. "We have to get moving."

"I know," she said, but she stayed where she was.

Neilan bent and wrapped his arms around Theon's middle. Elwyn helped him heave Theon over his shoulders, then they stumbled down the steep road that led from the fortress gate. Neilan's legs wobbled.

Cuinn hurried alongside them, her eyes constantly on Theon's face. Far ahead, the teenager who'd helped them in the fortress peeled away from the rest of the group and ran off to the right.

"Hosev!" Elwyn called out after him. "Where are you going?"

He yelled over his shoulder, "He knows I helped you—I need to get my family!"

Elwyn yelled, "Wait!"

Neilan groaned. She couldn't just keep going, could she? She had to save everybody. Elwyn opened her mouth to yell, but Neilan yelled out first, "Hold on, we're coming!"

Elwyn turned to him with eyebrows raised. He shrugged. "You're gonna help him, so I guess I am, too."

She beamed, and Hosev slowed down, tense.

Elwyn stopped the nearest Keeper and pulled Theon down from Neilan's shoulders. "Take him!" she yelled.

The Keeper hesitated, but then he lugged Theon over his shoulders. He staggered, then he caught himself and headed off again. Cuinn ran alongside Theon's weak form, eyes ever on his face.

Elwyn and Neilan sprinted toward Hosev. Hosev's face was drawn tight, and he bounced on the balls of his feet. They'd barely reached him before he took off running again, and they hustled to keep up.

Part of Neilan's mind followed the Haveners streaming toward the west, away from this forsaken city. Elwyn had been making apparently impulse decisions since they'd gotten to the fortress. He wanted to grab her, to drag her to safety. To tell her that she was important, she needed to stay alive.

But he held his tongue. He'd told her he was with her, and he'd meant it. He'd known then that it wouldn't be easy—Elwyn rarely made things easy.

She trusted what her Gifts were telling her, but Neilan had had his Gift for a long time, and he knew they were fallible. They couldn't fix everything, and the person who used them was still mortal. Elwyn continued on incautiously. Her confidence and decisiveness were part of what he adored about her, but they also drove him crazy.

Right now, they led her to run recklessly into danger. And as always, Neilan was right there with her. A tiny part of him wanted to leave her to do what she wanted and protect himself, but that was only the tiniest part. He'd never leave her.

He belonged *with* her. He couldn't fence her in—she was too strong to be controlled like that. Plus, the world needed her. So he'd go with her, protect her by being there rather than trying to hold her back. Whatever she got herself into, he'd be mixed up in it, too. And then he'd help her get out.

Neilan's legs shook, but he kept following her. The road ascended a small hill, with a dense line of trees around the top. Neilan and Elwyn hustled up the hill in Hosev's wake. Rounding the trees, they followed Hosev to the door of a little cottage. Hosev threw open the door, and the three of them ran into the house.

They panted in the doorway of a small room, stuffed to the brim with people. A woman sat on a worn rocking chair, and a pack of children were piled on the floor. Elwyn spun around and slammed the door shut behind them.

Hosev stood in front of the rocking chair and pulled on the woman's arm. "We have to go, Mother," he said, his voice tinged with panic.

His mother stared up at him with vacant eyes. Bumps rose on Neilan's arms.

"Come on!" Hosev yelled. "The Sovereign'll be here soon! You have to come with me!"

The woman sat stonily in her chair, staring into Hosev's wild face. He turned to the mass of children on the floor. "Manell?"

A girl around Elwyn's age met his eyes and nodded. She detangled herself from the pile of children and stood. She handed the baby she held to a girl around eleven and sped to Hosev's side. She grabbed her mother's opposite arm, and they heaved her up out of the chair.

Manell grabbed her mother's face and looked into her eyes. "Mother," she said in a calm, firm voice, as though speaking to a child. "Let's go."

A tall figure burst through the wall. Neilan jumped, and the children on the floor screamed.

63

Elwyn jolted as a figure flew through the wall. She tripped over a spare boot that lay on the floor and fell to the ground. The figure towered above, surveying the small, packed room. His hair was ashen, like soot. His skin was dingy, like dirty cloth. His features were twisted with malice, but the facial structure was the same she'd seen in Astur's memory. Solun's eyes no longer had any whites at all, they were just black spheres lodged into his eye sockets.

Hosev pulled his mother behind him and pushed Manell back into to the pile of children. His mother dropped into her rocking chair, and Hosev threw himself forward, into the space between Solun and his family.

Solun's black spheres narrowed. "You've disappointed me, boy," he said and stepped toward Hosev. "But you won't pay the price." He smirked. "They will."

Chills ran through Elwyn's whole body. Hosev's eyes widened, and he stretched out his arms, blocking his family from Solun.

Solun sneered. "That won't make a difference, boy." He took a step closer. "*You* are going to kill them."

Hosev's eyes went so wide that the whites were visible all the way around. Elwyn's heart hammered, and her mind spun. Solun was like Astur, he couldn't touch the physical world, right? She second guessed herself as her brain reeled. What was he going to do? And how could she stop him?

Solun approached until he was inches from Hosev. His twisted smirk grew, then he tipped toward Hosev. Hosev kept his arms out wide, but he closed his eyes. What could Elwyn do? Her brain circled but didn't give her any solutions.

Solun disappeared into Hosev's body. Hosev shuddered, and Elwyn's limbs went cold. A child screamed.

Hosev's whole body shook. His eyes grew maniacal. Then they returned to his normal expression, then grew maniacal again. One of Hosev's hands reached toward the long knife at his hip. His arm shook violently, his fingers stretching toward it.

His fist closed and stopped moving, then it stretched toward the knife again.

A tingly tug in Elwyn's middle pulled her toward Hosev. She stood up and ran to him. She grabbed his shoulders and stared into his face. "Hosev, you're still in there."

Hosev's shoulders trembled in Elwyn's grip. His eyes met hers and grew fiendish as a scream erupted from him.

Neilan pushed himself between Elwyn and Hosev, but Elwyn yelled, "No!" and nudged him out of the way. He stepped to the side, but he stayed right next to her, alert. Hosev's hands inched up toward Elwyn.

"I'm here with you, Hosev," she said. "Fight him!"

Hosev's eyes cleared, and his body shook violently. Solun's torso appeared, as though it was being pushed from the inside. Elwyn sprang back as the rest of Solun followed. His head appeared last, and the room erupted in an ear-splitting scream of rage. He flew at Elwyn.

Neilan dove at him, but he fell right through Solun and crashed to the floor. A rush of cold ran through Elwyn, then Solun appeared behind her. She shuddered.

Solun spun to face his would-be vessels. His black spheres were wide, darting from person to person, and his twisted mouth gaped open. He screamed in rage again, then he tipped forward and flew at Hosev's mother.

"No!" Hosev screamed and ran at Solun, but Solun slid around him.

Hosev's mother's eyes barely flickered as Solun slipped right into her—she didn't so much as shiver. Solun's sneer overwhelmed her expressionless face, and Elwyn's chest went cold. Hosev stared at his mother open-mouthed. She, or rather Solun, smirked at him. Elwyn shuddered, and a child on the floor burst into sobs.

Hosev's mother turned to Elwyn. She leapt out of her chair with alarming speed, stretched her arms out, and ran at Elwyn.

Elwyn backed away, and her back slammed into the door. She fumbled for the latch, but hands closed around her throat, and Hosev's mother leaned in hungrily. Elwyn's throat ached, and pressure rose in her lungs.

She grabbed the hands that pressed on her airway and pulled. It made no difference—she was powerless against Solun's strength. Her lungs screamed, and her head spun. Solun's viciousness gleamed out from the woman's eyes, hovering inches from her own.

In her peripheral vision, Neilan grabbed a frying pan from across the room and ran at Hosev's mother.

Hosev tackled him. They crashed onto the rocking chair, which splintered beneath them as a child's voice screamed. Hosev and Neilan rolled off the ruined chair, still struggling. Lights popped at the edges of Elwyn's vision, and her mind started to go fuzzy. She waved her hands wildly behind Hosev's mother's back.

Neilan threw Hosev off, jumped up, and ran at Hosev's mother. He grabbed her around the middle and pulled, fruitlessly.

He let go and went for her arms instead. He yanked as hard as he could and the pressure on Elwyn's throat released a tiny bit, then re-engaged with force.

Blackness blurred the edges of Elwyn's vision. Hosev appeared, and he pulled back his mother's middle fingers. The grip on Elwyn's throat slackened.

Magic flowed through Neilan's arms, strengthening him, and he yanked hard on the hands around her throat. The grip slipped, and Elwyn dropped to the ground.

Neilan and Hosev dragged Hosev's mother a few paces away. Elwyn coughed and spluttered, her throat aching. She felt she could never swallow enough air to make up for that last minute. Her mind cleared, and her vision returned to normal.

Across the room, Hosev's mother's hands flew toward her own throat. Hosev and Neilan grabbed onto her arms and pulled, but the hands kept getting closer. Elwyn ran to them and joined, putting her whole weight into pulling on the woman's arms. They managed to keep her hands an inch from her throat, but Elwyn's muscles shook. Her strength was slipping.

Hosev's mother's eyes glinted. Solun was playing with them.

Magic flowed through Neilan's arms again, and they got her hands another inch from her throat. Solun's smirk grew in the woman's face, and she said derisively, "How long do you think you can hold me off?"

Neilan's Magic flowed weakly—he couldn't keep it up forever. Solun was going to overpower them.

There had to be another way. Elwyn let go, and Hosev's mother's hands closed around her own throat. Her eyes bulged.

"No!" Hosev screamed, and several children burst into sobs.

Elwyn grabbed the vicious face and stared straight into the fiendish eyes. "I'm with you," she said to the woman who still existed somewhere within. "You're not alone."

A flash of cognition flared in her eyes, gone as quickly as it came. Solun overwhelmed the eyes again.

Elwyn's heartbeat sped. She stared firmly into the eyes again and willed the woman to hear her. "You are not alone. You are *loved*."

Deep in Hosev's mother's eyes, as though surfacing from within a deep, dark pool, a light grew. Her body shuddered, then her hands let go of her throat, but they hovered barely a finger's breadth from it. Her shuddering grew to whole-body shaking. Her eyes flashed, and her hands strained.

Elwyn held her face. "You are not alone. You are loved."

Manell stood and put a hand on her mother's shoulder. The rest of the children gathered around, hugging her legs and touching her back. Her body convulsed violently, and she collapsed.

She writhed and convulsed on the floor. Hosev dropped to his knees and held her head, keeping it from slamming onto the ground.

He met Elwyn's eyes, and his soul was bared through those small, round windows. He was helpless to save his mother. Just as she'd been helpless to save herself what felt like a million years ago, facing wolfskin-shrouded men. When Hosev, a stranger, had come to her aid.

She put a gentle hand on his arm, while his mother screamed Solun's scream. Her head rolled from side to side. Elwyn bent over her and repeated the truth to her again and again, over her ear-splitting wails. She was not alone. She was loved. Her children held onto her, and Hosev caressed her face.

Solun's torso was squeezed from her body, then he sunk back into her. She shook uncontrollably and still screamed that terrible scream.

Solun's entire being burst from her as though thrown. As he

surfaced, he shrieked at such a decibel that Elwyn had to cover her ears. Through her hands, her ears still rang with the scream.

Solun's face twisted, his black spheres wide and mouth gaping. Elwyn's insides clenched. He quaked like a cornered cat, and he spun from person to person with wild, maniacal eyes.

Instinctively, Elwyn stood and took a step toward him. He backed away from her, black spheres twitching. She reached a hand out to him.

Solun took one last look at her and disappeared through the wall. His shriek echoed into the night as he sped away from the hilltop.

A weight on Elwyn's heart lifted. She turned to the woman who lay on the floor and knelt down at her side. Hosev's mother's chest heaved with deep, hard-fought breaths. Her limbs laid limp on the floor, and her head hung exhausted in Hosev's lap.

Her face was nearly as expressionless as it had been before, except for her eyes. The light that Elwyn had seen awaken glowed gently in the previously glassy eyes. Hosev cradled his mother's head and stared into her face. A teardrop fell from his cheek and landed on hers.

He looked up at Elwyn through wet lashes, his eyes gleaming with fresh tears. His mouth moved soundlessly. He cleared his throat, looked back into his mother's face, and whispered, "Thank you."

Elwyn's chest warmed. Her eyes burned, and tears welled in the corners. She blinked them back and dipped her head.

Neilan knelt down next to Elwyn. He put a gentle hand on her shoulder and said hesitantly, "We still need to evacuate." He looked down at Hosev's mother. "He'll send someone."

Elwyn nodded. Hosev kept his eyes on his mother, but he nodded, too.

His mother's hand came up and touched his cheek. She wiped

away his tear and blinked up at him. Hosev smiled—a tiny smile, but it held more joy than Elwyn had yet seen on his face.

Elwyn pushed up from the floor and turned to Manell, but Manell was already in action. She stood, and the trembling children followed her. She huddled them around her and took the baby back from her sister's arms. Hosev gently pushed his mother up to sit, then he pulled her to her feet. With and arm around her shoulders, he walked her gently but urgently toward the back of the house.

Manell herded the children ahead of her, to follow their mother and brother. Two of the youngest turned around and tried to fight the wave of siblings to get back to Manell.

Manell pointed to the back door. "Follow Hosev." She pushed a little at the back of the group. The older ones of the group hurried through the door, with a few nervous glances back, but the youngest ones turned in circles.

Elwyn bent down and picked up a girl, maybe two years old. The girl squirmed to get out of her arms and looked wide-eyed into Elwyn's face. Elwyn smiled calmly at her, and the girl stopped squirming, but she perched uneasily in Elwyn's arms.

Neilan picked up a boy about four years old, and the boy froze. Neilan tickled him along his collar bone and smiled, and the boy relaxed in his grip.

Manell, Neilan, and Elwyn herded the rest of the children after Hosev, and they spilled out the back door into the night.

Hosev led his mother down the back side of the hill, and the rest of the children followed, directed by Manell. They descended to the bank of a narrow, gently flowing stream. Far away, the tinkle of metal and clomp of galloping hooves rang in the night. Hunting dogs barked and howled.

Elwyn's heart dropped, and Hosev met her eyes, fear bursting to life behind them.

64

Elwyn held the little girl tighter and rubbed her back, as much to comfort the little girl as herself. Hosev dragged his mother into the stream, wading up to his thighs. Manell cried out, and Hosev looked at her with a hard expression in the faint starlight. "Come on."

Manell recoiled, but she nodded. She arranged the baby in one arm, then gently pushed the rest of the children forward. They waded into the stream, and a few cried out at the cold, but Manell urged them on. One small boy was submerged to his chest.

Elwyn waded in to her hips, and the cold hit her like ice. She sucked in a breath and held the girl in her arms out of the water. Neilan splashed in behind her, holding his charge and grunting at the cold. A few of the children cried softly.

The galloping hooves pounded up the hill toward the cottage, and sounds crashed through the door. Elwyn's heart pounded, and the girl in her arms sobbed.

"Shh," Elwyn whispered and rubbed the girl's back. Hosev led the way down the middle of the stream, and they hurried after him. The stream bent to the right, through a thick knot of trees and bushes. Elwyn ducked to keep the branches from catching her hair.

Running footsteps and barking dogs burst into the night from the hilltop. The group in the stream picked up their pace, but they moved carefully to limit their noise. They followed the stream around another hill.

The barking behind them grew urgent, and Elwyn held her breath. Even the children had stopped crying, sensing the danger.

The barking moved all the way to the bank of the stream, then it halted. The dogs still barked, but they seemed to have stopped moving. Voices cursed into the night. One voice yelled in frustration, and the sound of it chilled Elwyn's blood. She shivered.

Her heart pounded as she hurried downstream with the rest of the group, and the yelling and barking grew fainter. The dogs were moving again, on the opposite bank of the stream.

Elwyn and the rest hiked and hiked through the water. At every step, her boots stuck to the muddy bottom of the stream, and the cold crept up her body. She had no idea where this stream led, or how long Hosev intended to remain in the water. In the faint light, the small boy who was submerged to his chest was shivering.

"Manell," she whispered. Manell turned back to her, and Elwyn pointed to the boy.

Manell nodded. She handed the baby to the next-oldest child, a boy of about thirteen, then she reached into the water and pulled out the soaked, shivering boy. Manell held him close to her body and rubbed his back rapidly. The boy laid his head on her shoulder and clung to her. After some time, his shivering slowed.

Elwyn breathed in relief and adjusted the little girl higher in her arms. The dogs' barks still rang distantly, but the voices were inaudible, now. Elwyn's pounding heart eased.

Elwyn's legs ached, and her head swam with exhaustion. They'd long since left the stream, and the dogs' barks had faded into the distance miles ago. The little girl Elwyn had held now walked next to Manell, holding tight to Manell's skirt.

The adrenaline that had coursed through Elwyn for so many hours was gone now, and her whole body trembled in its absence. She wanted to curl up on the hard ground and fall asleep, wet and cold as she was. Even if she retained the mental strength to keep going, her body might collapse of its own accord.

The long darkness of Twilitnight, Darkday, and Darknight faded. The base of the mountain range rose into the sky in front of them, glowing purple as the sky slowly lightened. The light grew until the whole sky was a dazzling pink.

Elwyn kept her feet moving. One step. Another step.

The sun burst above the horizon behind her and shone on the mountains ahead. The rays warmed her back, and she took a deep, clear breath of Dawnday's glorious, golden morning. Hope rose in her chest with the rising of the sun.

A small voice in her mind asked, *'Now what?'* It wasn't the end. Solun would recover from the shock and come after them. But she ignored that small voice—for now, they were wonderfully, miraculously alive.

The ground became rocky and uneven. She scanned the peaks in front of them, but none were familiar. Her stomach dropped. She'd been so consumed by everything else that she hadn't thought about how to get back to the cave. She paused to focus her mind, closing her eyes and visualizing the map of southwest Terralum she'd studied so many times.

She imagined the long trek she'd taken with Neilan and Astur through the mountain range to Solun's fortress, and she laid it over the map in her mind. Then she imagined the course from the fortress to the stream, and from the stream to the base of the mountain range.

She plotted the course onto the map, then she followed it in her mind until she found their current position in relation to their starting point.

Her mind began to get fuzzy. The picture in her head came in and out of focus. She was approaching the boundary of the Gifts, which meant mental shutdown. She didn't have long, but she focused on the map in her head and memorized the way to the cave. She opened her eyes and turned to Neilan, then she hurriedly described where they needed to go.

He nodded, but his head drooped. His eyes were hard and exhausted. He looked like he might collapse at any moment, too.

She shook her head in frustration and called to Hosev, who turned back to her. Exhaustion etched his face, too, but there was a little more life behind his eyes, a little more focus. Elwyn racked her brain for the map, though her mind was fading to blackness. She blurted out as much as she could manage, but the words came out in a tumbled mess.

Hosev stared at her blankly for a moment, but his mind worked behind his eyes. He sorted through the mess of words she'd tossed into the air and made sense of them. His eyes came back to the present, and he nodded, then he turned in the direction Elwyn had wanted him to lead.

Elwyn breathed in the incredible, welcome release of burden. They'd get where they needed to go. She grew light, as though all that had weighed her down over the last days was gone. She wasn't needed. She wasn't in charge. She no longer had to strive, to fight, or to exert willpower.

Black oblivion overcame her mind, and she welcomed it. Somewhere far away were shrieks and hurrying footsteps, then even that faded in her blissful relief.

65

Neilan caught Elwyn's head before it hit the ground, but he nearly fell over, too. Her chest rose and fell with serene breathing, and her face, which had been taut with anxiety for weeks, was peaceful. Warmth permeated Neilan's chest.

He leaned down and tried to pull her up over his shoulder, but he wobbled. Hosev's sister rushed over and helped lift Elwyn up. They balanced Elwyn across his shoulders, and he linked his arms through Elwyn's knee and elbow.

He pushed himself to his feet, but he staggered. Manell caught his arm and helped him find his balance. Elwyn was lighter than Theon, but Neilan still swayed. His legs shook, and he willed himself to steady. Strength returned to his tired body, and he hustled onward.

Within minutes, he was draining fast. It hit him that he'd been unconsciously using Magic. In his already exhausted state, using it was dangerous. He tried to hold his Magic back, but his body didn't want to let it go. With a huge effort, he managed to stop the flow of Magic. He staggered a few steps, and his knees threatened to buckle.

He took one step, then another. Manell hovered next to him, hands at the ready. Neilan focused on one step, then the next. Then the next. He kept his mind on one second at a time.

What felt like years later, but the sun hadn't moved very far across the sky, Neilan took step after step up a mountainside in Hosev's wake. His legs wobbled.

Voices called out, and people came running down from above. Neilan squinted up, but the Dawnday sunlight blinded him. His knees buckled, and he collapsed. He just managed to stop Elwyn's head from slamming onto stone before blackness overwhelmed him.

66

The warmth of sunlight on Hosev's head disappeared as he led Mother through the cave mouth. Voices murmured all around him, and his heartbeat sped. His eyes slowly adjusted to the low light, and he found himself in a cave packed with people. Somewhere in the back of his mind, he wondered how many people had been in that underground lair, if there were still this many survivors. Hundreds, at least.

One face drew his attention—a boy, around Seralie's age. His face looked strangely familiar. He reminded Hosev of someone. A second later, a face popped into his memory: the dying man dragging himself toward the pillar in the lair's giant library. Hosev's gut twisted.

He'd led the Sovereign to their lair. What would these people do to him?

What had he been thinking, following Elwyn's directions? He put an arm around Mother's shoulders and held her protectively. She leaned into him.

The man from the fortress with the glowing eyes approached. In the corners of Hosev's vision, people stopped talking and watched them warily. Hosev pulled Mother behind him and blocked her from the man.

The man stopped, facing him. "There's no need for that."

Hosev glared at him.

"Hmm," the man said, his mouth in a hard line. "I'm Astur—Protector of these people who used to live in the Haven." Hosev kept staring at him, waiting. The man was leading to something. "I would like to offer you and your family sanctuary among us."

Hosev raised an eyebrow at him.

"I'm offering you forgiveness," the man said, "and asking yours in return. I'm sorry for treating you as the enemy."

Hosev's gut burned. But his instincts drew him toward this strange man, just as they had toward Elwyn in the fortress. Astur watched him for a long moment. "You've spent time around Elwyn, so you'll know what I mean when I say she has turned my world on its head."

So Hosev wasn't the only one.

"I'm not sure how it is going to work out, or *if* it is going to work out, but I'm trying openness for the first time in many years. We're capable of providing you shelter, nourishment, and protection. In return, we ask you to integrate into our community, to care for these people to the best of your ability, and to be willing to be cared for *by* them. Will you and your family join us?"

Hosev's chest trembled, and a shiver ran down his arms. His habitual self-reliance was slipping. He grasped at it, reaching for suspicion like a lifeline. He raised a practiced, dubious eyebrow. "Do we have a choice?"

"Yes," Astur said. "You do."

Hosev forced suspicion into his tone and tried to smash it into his heart. All his training opposed this thing, this trust, that was growing inside him. "What'll you do if I say no?"

"I'll provide you with sufficient provisions to get wherever you intend to go, send an escort with you through the mountain range, and ask the High King to protect you on your way."

Hosev stared at Astur. Even his trained wariness couldn't find a syllable of falsity in this man's statement. But it couldn't be true. Hosev's intuition, which he'd never had reason to question before, seemed to be failing him. Every inch of his soul believed this man.

Only his mind held out, refusing to accept it. It went against everything he'd been taught directly or indirectly, against what he'd seen in everyone he'd ever observed. His mind piped up: everyone except Elwyn. Even his mind betrayed him, now.

He closed his eyes while his understanding of how the world worked crumbled. His hands trembled, and he took a deep breath. "Yes, we'll join you."

Astur nodded gravely. "I know what that decision has cost you. Thank you." Hosev hung his head.

An elderly woman stood and walked hesitatingly toward Hosev. Her eyes were puffy and red, and her cheeks were streaked with tears. She held something in her gnarled fist, and Hosev's heartbeat quickened. The woman reached him and lifted her fist toward Hosev. He tensed, then she opened it, revealing the roasted leg of a wild bird. She held it out to him.

Automatically, Hosev reached out and accepted it. She gave him a small, sad smile and patted his hand, then she nodded and turned away. As though it woke them all from a trance, the people who'd been watching him since Astur approached settled back into conversation with those around them.

A teenage girl approached seven-year-old Jaeveh with a handful of berries. He eagerly grabbed them and stuffed them into his mouth. She gestured to the nearest fire, where her family sat. "Want to sit with us?" Jaeveh glanced up at Hosev. Hosev nodded and tried to smile, his heart still pounding.

Jaeveh bounced over to the girl and sat next to her, and the rest of Hosev's siblings followed. Hosev led Mother to the opposite side of the small fire and sat down. He watched the shadows that the people around the fire cast on the cave wall, small though the fire was. The shadows were faint, partially lit by the rest of the fires that lined the wall around it. The shadows pinged his memory, bringing forward Tinol's massive, roiling shadow in Phaemin Fortress.

Tinol's horrifying smirk flashed across Hosev mind, then his metal tool glinting over a small body. Hosev's limbs went cold. His chest ached, and he squeezed his eyes shut, but the images assaulted his memory. His heart pounded, and he balled his fists. He couldn't reconcile the person Tinol had been to the monster he became.

The back of his neck prickled. He'd thought of Tinol in the past tense. Tinol had probably met his end in the collapsing fortress—so many had. But he may have survived. Some did.

Hosev didn't know which he hoped for. It didn't feel like that should be the end of Tinol's story. It wasn't an accurate endpoint to the trajectory of Tinol's life as a whole. It shouldn't be the culminating moment of his life.

If that was the end, Tinol had no chance for redemption. But if he had survived, as horrifying as he became, he could still get worse. He could inflict more pain, cause more suffering.

Hosev's insides knotted, and his chest ached. He couldn't process it all. His eyes burned, and he squeezed them shut. Sobs rose in his throat. He tried to hold them at bay, but one came out despite him. He laid back, half-sitting half-laying on the uneven stone, and stared up at the ceiling.

Mother reached for his hand. She pulled it onto her lap and clasped it with both hands. The corners of his eyes burned, and he leaned his head against Mother's arm. She squeezed his hand in one of hers and rubbed his forearm gently with the other. His arm tingled, and his chest burned, then his body shook.

His eyes welled up, and all at once, tears streamed down his face. He gave in. With that release, all his warring emotions bubbled out of him. Fear, relief, anxiety, grief, anger, guilt, repulsion, love, and gratitude all exploded out of him into racking sobs.

He cried for a long time. Finally, his body ceased shaking, and his breathing slowed. Mother reached across and stroked his hair. It sent comforting tingles from his scalp all the way down his body. He couldn't remember the last time she'd done that—probably not since Seralie was born and Mother had never really recovered.

His chest constricted, and tears leaked out the corners of his eyes again. If this was possible, could come of only a brief alliance with Elwyn, what else could happen?

He had to be part of her community, to work alongside her and learn how to extend Mother's healing. And to do for more people what she'd done for him.

The small voice in the back of his mind told him that to do so, to truly work with Elwyn, he'd have to forgive her. His heart clenched. Even now, part of him wanted to hold onto his anger—the part of him that still believed he could undo it, that if he held on hard enough he could will Father back into life.

It felt like if he let go of his anger, he'd have to let go of Father. To accept that he wasn't coming back.

But Father *wasn't* coming back. No matter how hard Hosev held onto the anger, reality was the same: Father was gone. Hosev closed his eyes and leaned into Mother's arm. He breathed in and drew strength from her. He found the anger that seethed in a tight, walled-off corner of his heart, then he tore down the walls and released it.

It flowed through his heart and tried to take hold. Heat rose in his chest, and his hands balled into fists. But Hosev pushed it onward until it finally flowed right out of his body and dissipated.

He breathed out, and with it, the tension that had held him for a month—or really, for years—finally left, too. He opened his eyes. Colors seemed somehow brighter.

In front of him, the fire danced. He felt more of the light and warmth it produced than the shadows it cast on the walls.

Manell, her face turned away from him, held her palms toward the fire, warming them. Faell sat in her lap, curled into Manell's chest with her eyes closed. Manell dropped a hand to Faell's head and absently stroked her hair. Hosev's heart warmed and the corners of his mouth pulled up.

As though she felt his eyes on her, Manell turned toward him. Their eyes met, and Manell's simultaneously widened and softened, then her shoulders relaxed. She smiled, and the corners of her eyes crinkled. Tears welled again in Hosev's eyes, joyful and cathartic. His heart swelled, and he smiled back.

67

Elwyn sat on a boulder in the center of the cave, Neilan at her side. She ate slowly, her arms heavy as she lifted a roasted leg to her mouth. People swirled around them in all directions.

Her parents sat, staring into space, on the opposite side of the fire in front of her. Theon was recovering, thank the King. Once the escaped prisoners had made it to the cave, he'd been one of the first to receive extensive medical care. But his eyes still had dark circles around them, and his face was sunken and gray. His repaired tunic hung loose around his emaciated chest. Cuinn's skin wasn't as gray as his, but her eyes had the same dark circles around them.

Behind them, at the next fire, Oktoh sat on the ground hugging his knees, with a splotchy, red face and puffy, empty eyes. He slowly rocked back and forth.

Both his wife and son had died. After hearing how it happened, Oktoh had said he was glad Chel didn't have to live long after what they'd done to Pattri.

Elwyn's chest constricted, and her eyes burned. It was her fault. She was the one who'd left the Haven and brought its existence to Solun's attention in the first place. Then she'd let Hosev out and gave

Solun the way right to them. Tears leaked out the corners of her eyes and fell hot onto her cheeks.

Cuinn got up and put an arm around Elwyn's shoulders. "I'm sorry," Cuinn said.

Elwyn started. "For what?"

Cuinn looked down. "For failing you. I wasn't a help when you needed me—I was a burden."

Elwyn's insides burned. "You wouldn'tve been there if it wasn't for me. All of it was my fault." Against her will, her eyes drew back toward Oktoh.

Cuinn followed her gaze, and Theon's voice came from across the fire. "You didn't kill those people."

"But I—"

"You didn't kill them," he said firmly. "You made several poor choices, choosing self-interest over prudence and refusing to consider the consequences. But I want you to remember: you did not kill those people."

Elwyn tensed. "But it wouldn't have happened if it wasn't for me."

"That's most likely true—you gave people an opportunity to make choices, with the high likelihood that they would choose the terrible option. But either way, the people themselves were given the opportunity to choose whether to murder or to protect, to hurt or to show mercy. Their actions are on their hands. You made rash, imprudent decisions, and I hope you will not do so in the future. But I repeat again, you did not kill those people."

Elwyn's chest constricted. She met Theon's eyes and nodded. Then she took a deep breath and considered another thing weighing on her. "I'm sorry I took your Gifts."

"Oh, Elwyn," Cuinn said. "You didn't take our Gifts. They're yours."

Elwyn drew her brows together.

"Mine left when Solun's soldiers knocked me out in the C.K. Wing," Cuinn said. "It was time, I guess."

"And I sent mine to you when we were in the fortress and had tried every means of escape we could think of," Theon said. "We had no more hope." He paused. "That was the hardest thing I've ever done, knowing it meant you'd come for us. But we needed you, all of us did." He smiled sadly.

Elwyn's eyes welled up. Theon looked at Cuinn and said, "It's time to see Med. Pena for my next dose."

Cuinn nodded and stood. She lifted Theon to his feet and pulled his arm across her shoulders, then she reached down to Elwyn's shoulder and gave it a quick squeeze. Elwyn tried to smile.

Cuinn and Theon hobbled away toward the back of the cave, where the surviving Medic-Keepers had set up a makeshift Medical Ward. A curtain separated it from the rest of the cave.

Astur emerged from behind the curtain. He scanned the cave and spotted Elwyn, then he wove through the scattered Haveners toward her, nodding to Cuinn and Theon as he passed them. When he was nearly to Elwyn, Wuervik intercepted him. "The protective barriers are in place, Magical and otherwise."

"Good," Astur said. "Did your Keepers remove the signs of the Haveners' tracks here, both from the Haven and from Gravusfrig?"

"Yes, and I had them lay a few false trails."

"Well done. Let's speak in private," Astur's said, then his eyes shifted uneasily. Resolve settled on him, and he spoke his mind right there. "The harshness of this environment will make these people's recovery take longer. I don't want to remain here long."

Elwyn's arms tingled. She sensed he was on the edge of something important.

"Where else can we go?" Neilan asked, inserting himself into the conversation.

Astur's eyebrows drew together, and his jaw tensed. He looked at Neilan, but he didn't reprimand him.

Elwyn decided to push him further. "Is there another one?"

Astur started, and his eyes shot to hers. She shrugged apologetically. "You can't start a thing like that without Logic and Linguistic finishing it."

Astur glared at her, but his eyes twinkled. "Correct."

Wuervik straightened. "There are more?"

Astur clasped his hands in front of him. "There are several Havens, each run by a Protector. They're kept secret from one another—that way if any one is infiltrated, they aren't all compromised. In this case, that has worked well for us. As soon as everyone here is settled, I'll go to the Heads of Havens. I'll inform them what has happened, and we'll prepare for the war that is coming. Now that Solun is aware of us, he'll hunt us ceaselessly. All of the Havens must prepare.

"The Heads and I will decide which of the remaining Havens would best be able to support bringing in this many people. Then I'll return and we'll begin to migrate. It cannot be done all at once, for that would draw undue attention."

Elwyn's heart pounded. "Can I say something?"

Astur and Wuervik turned to her, eyebrows raised.

Elwyn looked at her lap. "I brought this on all of us. I know you said you accepted my actions, Astur. But I'm the one who brought the Haven to Solun's attention, then let Hosev out to bring him directly to us. Everything that happened to everyone here is my fault. I'm sorry."

Gentle pressure settled onto her shoulder. She reached up, expecting Neilan's hand, but the shape she felt there was unfamiliar. She looked up into Wuervik's face. He gave her a sad smile and squeezed her shoulder.

"Solun finding us was inevitable," Astur said. "We weren't going to last forever."

Elwyn looked up at him.

"Solun was already moving against your parents. I believe this was the moment we were going to unravel whether or not you acted as you did. But even if it hadn't been, even if this generation had escaped this pain, another generation would have suffered it. And the longer we let Solun reign, the more suffering he causes in the world. We can no longer accept our safety and comfort as a sufficient trade-off for the suffering of the entire world."

A shiver ran down Elwyn's spine.

"We must act. Especially because now, for the first time, we have a place to start." His lucten-silver eyes sparkled, despite the sadness that etched his face. "Thanks to you."

Elwyn's eyes drew to Hosev's mother across the cave. She sat on the floor with Manell's head in her lap, stroking Manell's hair.

Solun's terrified face swam into Elwyn's mind, and the way he'd quaked just before he'd fled from her. Maybe what she'd started *could* make a difference. But was it enough?

"Before anything else," Astur said, "I'll check on our Haven and make sure the Treasury's collapse and destruction went as it should have."

Hosev, who was meandering past, paused. "That place was supposed to collapse?"

Astur looked at him, and his eyebrows drew together. "Yes."

"I don't think it did," he said nervously. "I was one of the last inside. I mean," he looked down. "One of the last alive."

Astur's eyes tipped down at the sides. "I'll go with some Keepers to bury our dead with dignity." He considered. "But we will leave the Haven intact. It's collapse wasn't triggered at the moment we needed it, so the information is already compromised. The Haven may yet prove useful."

Elwyn's mind twinged, but she sensed that this was a subject she shouldn't press him on.

Astur turned to Wuervik. "Let's see which Keepers are healthy enough to travel with me."

Wuervik nodded, then paused. He turned to Elwyn and Neilan and said, "Thank you for coming to free us."

Elwyn gave him a small smile and nodded. Neilan dipped his head, then Astur and Wuervik walked away.

Neilan turned to Hosev and gestured to his family across the cave. "How're they holding up?"

Hosev shrugged. "Well enough. As well as could be expected, I think." He turned to walk back to them, then he paused and turned to Elwyn. "I've been wanting to say something to you."

"Yeah?"

"I forgive you."

A chill ran down Elwyn's arms.

"For my father," Hosev continued, then he looked down. "I was so angry with you. But I'm not angry anymore. I forgive you."

Elwyn's eyes burned and tears spilled over. Hosev shifted his weight uncomfortably. Elwyn wiped her eyes and squeaked out, "Thank you."

Hosev nodded. He glanced at Neilan and gave him an uneasy half-smile, so Neilan smiled back reassuringly. Hosev turned and headed back to his family.

Neilan put an arm around Elwyn's shoulders and pulled her close. She leaned in, feeling cocooned by him. Her heart lifted, then she gently unwound his arm and reached for her waterskin.

Jathdi and Vacca, his arm around her shoulders, met Elwyn's eyes from across the cave, and they walked tentatively toward her. Neilan took Elwyn's hand, caught her eye, and raised an eyebrow.

When they got close, Vacca leaned into Jathdi and whispered, "Thank you. For saving him."

"Of course," Elwyn said.

Vacca shook her head. "No, not of course. We've always been terrible to you, and you saved him. He told me about the arrow."

Elwyn shrugged. "I wasn't going to just let him get hit."

Vacca looked down. "I know. But most people would have."

"No they wouldn't."

Vacca met Elwyn's eyes. "If I'd been you, I would have."

A shiver ran down Elwyn's spine and bumps rose on her arms. She looked into their faces and held in her heart the raw gift Hosev had just given her. "I forgive you."

They stared.

"For everything. For all those years. I forgive you both." She smiled.

Tears welled in the corners of Vacca's eyes. Elwyn reached out and squeezed her arm gently. Vacca looked down, and Elwyn patted her arm then released her. Jathdi gave Elwyn a small smile and gently led Vacca away. Elwyn took a deep breath and released it slowly, then she turned to Neilan.

"Wow," he said. "Never thought I'd see those two act like normal people."

Elwyn shrugged. "They've always acted like normal people: reacting to their own pain by inflicting more pain on more people. We've done the same thing." She clasped her hands in her lap and stared at them. "But we don't have to keep doing that. We can take responsibility for our own actions and, instead of hurting people because we've been hurt, we can stop the cycle of pain from continuing beyond us. Then we can help people heal instead—build a community that cares for instead of hurts one another."

Neilan put a hand on her shoulder and looked at her seriously. "I'm proud of you."

Her insides tingled.

He smirked. "Solun was right—you *are* dangerous." She glared at him, but she couldn't keep the smile from the edges of her lips.

Haveners swirled around them in every direction. A hand patted her shoulder as someone passed by, and Elwyn glanced up. The woman nodded over her shoulder as she continued on her way across the cave. Elwyn's chest warmed.

Another person squeezed her upper arm, while her companion said, "Thank you." Elwyn smiled at them as they kept on their way.

Elwyn's heart rose, and the weights that had borne down on her as long as she could remember lightened. This was what she'd always imagined freedom would feel like.

68

Neilan stuffed food into his mouth. He didn't think he'd ever be able to eat enough to make up for his energy depletion from the last few days. Elwyn sat next to him, watching the Haveners move through the crowded cave. Her eyes had dark circles around them, and she sagged where she sat. As though she felt his eyes on her, she turned to him.

He started to turn away but she caught his eye. She smiled, a sad, tired smile and said, "I love you."

Just like that.

His chest tingled. The turn they'd taken still had him off-balance. Well, it wasn't a turn, really—they'd loved one another their whole lives. But it was as though they'd been swimming in the shallows until now, then suddenly they'd dived deep underwater. The fear in him didn't want to trust it, but the real him, the him that knew Elwyn's soul, leaned into the joy. He smiled at her and reached for her hand, giving it a little squeeze. She squeezed back.

He leaned back and stared into the crowd. A few paces away, a group of young kids squatted in a circle, playing some game they'd invented. Each had a stick, and there was a pile of rocks in the center of the circle. One of them gestured with his stick and a rock lifted unsupported into the air. Neilan's heart slammed into his ribs.

It hadn't occurred to him before: every kid who had a parent die in the Haven or the fortress now had the Gift.

His heart hammered, and adrenaline pumped through his body. He remembered the exhilaration of Magic as a kid, the ecstasy. But with it came the danger, the unrestrained power.

Another kid picked up a rock and moved it along the circle. The first kid, the Magic-user, picked up another rock and skipped over the second kid's rock.

"Hey, you can't do that!" The second kid yelled and pushed the Magic-user.

The Magic-user fell backward and landed hard on his elbow. His eyes flashed at the kid who'd pushed him, and power gathered in his body as emotion surged.

Neilan dove for him and screamed, "No!" He threw out a Magical shield between the kids, just as the kid's raw, emotional Magic burst into being, so strong it manifested visibly as light.

It slammed into Neilan's shield, which absorbed the light, but the power ricochetted off of the barrier and knocked over everyone in a ten-pace radius, including the kid it came from. People screamed as they were slammed to the ground.

Flattened by his own power, the kid curled into a ball, shaking. Neilan crawled over to him and put a hand on his shoulder. "Hey, man." The kid trembled under Neilan's hand. "Hey, you didn't mean to." He rubbed the kid's back. "It's a lot to deal with."

The kid's mother ran over, eyes wide and mouth open.

Neilan tried to give her a reassuring smile. "Being a Magic user at this age is tough. Help him calm down."

She bent down and picked up her son. Big as he was, he wrapped his arms and legs around her and laid his head on her shoulder. She stroked his back and walked toward the back of the cave, away from the stunned eyes boring into them from all around.

Neilan turned to the would-be victim of the Magical burst, who sat on the cave floor wide-eyed, hugging his knees. Neilan walked over to the kid, bent down next to him, and put a hand on his shoulder. "You okay?"

The kid nodded.

"I know that was scary. When a kid has Magic, sometimes it can burst out of him when he's feeling big emotions."

The kid nodded, still staring at the spot where the Magical burst and Magical shield had met.

"I'll help your friend learn how to control his Magic," Neilan said. "I'll teach him how to use it for good things."

A teenage girl hurried over, the kid's sister. She put her arm around the kid, and he leaned into her. Neilan patted the kid on the back and stood. His stomach rumbled. Even that one burst of Magic took a lot out of him. He still had far to go for full recovery. He turned around, back toward Elwyn, but Wuervik was running toward him, mouth hanging open.

"I... I..." Wuervik stared at the kid with his sister and at the spot where Magic had exploded out of a seemingly harmless child.

"I was watching!" he burst out, his eyes wide. "But I didn't see it coming!"

"Yeah," Neilan said and shrugged. "I had Magic as a kid so I know what could happen. At that age, it's easy to accidentally go overboard and hurt yourself or someone else. An emotionally-charged situation like that could get out of hand fast."

Wuervik paled and shook his head, eyes wide. "Thank you for intervening." Then his voice grew contemplative. "How did you survive?"

Neilan looked down and forced a laugh.

"Truly, I'm asking," Wuervik said. "You're a miracle."

Neilan's chest constricted. Still staring at the floor, he shrugged.

"We have many young Magic users, now, and you're the only one who knows what they're facing. Will you take charge of training these Gifted children?"

Neilan's eyes snapped up to Wuervik's face. Was he serious?

Wuervik smiled. "You're the only one here who understands them. They need you. We all do."

Neilan's mind spun with ideas, games he could play with the kids to help them practice. His chest swelled. "Yeah, I'll do it."

"Thank you." Wuervik smiled. "Let me know if there's anything you need."

Neilan nodded, and Wuervik dipped his head and walked away. Dazed, Neilan made his way back to Elwyn. Her eyes were wide, and she asked, "You okay?"

He sat down next to her, in front of the half-full plate he'd abandoned a few minutes ago. "Yeah." He picked up a wild berry. "I got a job."

She raised an eyebrow. "Oh yeah?"

"I'm gonna train the kids who have Magic now, 'cause no one else knows what it's like."

Her face lit up. "That's brilliant!"

He shrugged, but his chest warmed. "Yeah, I think it'll be fun." He popped the berry into his mouth.

"You've always been great with kids."

"Yeah, I guess."

Her eyes sparkled.

"What?" he asked, swallowing the berry and reaching for his waterskin.

"I'm glad you're good with kids."

"Why?" He took a swig of water.

She smirked. "'Cause I want to have lots."

He choked and sprayed water all over her. She shrieked and wiped her face with her sleeve. Once her face was dry, she looked at him. Her blue eyes were shining, and she raised a questioning eyebrow.

His chest tingled and he met her eyes. "Deal."

ABOUT THE AUTHOR

Christine Sharp earned a bachelor's degree in English from Biola University, and she has spent the past ten years raising her children while writing and rewriting *Elwyn*. She relies heavily on stories, as they are her best escape from the pain of chronic migraines. She lives in Southern California with her husband and their two children. *Elwyn* is her debut novel.

www.christinesharpbooks.com